Copyright © 2014 Heather Robinson

The right of Heather Robinson to be identified as the Author of the Work has been asserted by her in accordance with the Copyright, Designs and Patents Act 1988.

All characters in this publication – other than the obvious historical characters – are fictitious and any resemblance to real persons, living or dead, is purely coincidental.

ISBN 978-1500464776

Wall of Stone

by

Heather Robinson

Chapter One

AD121 A tear rolled slowly down his cheek as Marcus knelt in solitary prayer. The timber pillars of the tiny temple closed in around him giving some comfort in their solid familiarity. How Marcus longed for the warmth of his mother's arms hugging him, holding him close, soaking up his grief and misery.

"I will miss you Flavinus, my friend, my comrade. You saved my life by giving your own. It should not have been." Marcus whispered the words as he knelt before the stone plinth, holding a simple effigy of Jupiter carved from animal bone tightly in his hands. It had belonged to his father and been presented to him when he left Rome as a proud member of the Legions. Warm, sunny, safe Italia. He squeezed shut his eyes and with furrowed brow tried to recall its beauty, momentarily succeeding, taking respite in a rustling olive grove. The moment too brief before an agonising vision of Flavinus invaded. The axe in his bloodied head, wielded with such angry strength that it pierced through the metal helmet splitting the skull beneath. The sweating horse snorting wild, frightened breath still running with its rider slumped and sliding unnaturally down the animal's flank.

"The axe was meant for me." Marcus spoke in a whisper still, audible only to the gods from whom he was seeking answers. "Why did you take Flavinus instead? It was I who provoked the Briton. I am worse than *Geryon*." A rage born from confused grief and hatred of his own deed tore through him, every bit as painful as a searing sword through flesh. "*Brittunculi!*" he yelled. "Mars, I do not want to fight these savages any longer. They do not use swords nor do they take up fixed positions in order to throw their weapons. Take me from this wretched frontier. There is no hope here. I cannot do this any more. Are you listening Mars? I have failed Flavinus." Marcus slumped against the wooden pillar to the right of the altar and gave in to the wracking sobs that strangled him now.

When the numbing tears subsided, Marcus saw that the dumpsy light of evening had become moonlit darkness. He felt cold. A bold moon shone high in the sky to the northeast. Stars abounded and the air smelt clear and dry. With the weariness of a guilty heart, he started back to his barracks in the fort. Noticing the bone effigy of Jupiter still in his clutched hand, he sent up a silent prayer to this king of gods, sky god, god of rain who uses the thunderbolt as his weapon. As he continued up the grassy slope towards the East Gate, drawing near to the bathhouse, a mist appeared in front of the moon veiling the sky above him with a smudgy greyness. Oddly, the stars continued to shimmer through it with scintillating splendour. The surprise of rain on his skin broke through his introspection. The shower was short but sharp and stopped after only a minute. Almost without delay, the moon was shining boldly again. Had it not been for the glistening moisture on his face and beneath his footsteps, Marcus would not have believed it had rained at all. The air was again dry and clear. Feeling some slight lifting of his burden as though Jupiter had noticed him, he straightened his shoulders and spoke aloud.

"I have been weak of flesh, Flavinus. From this moment, it will be Roman women only, as you wanted. That is my vow to you. Goodbye my kind friend, my brave comrade. You were wise beyond your years. I will make you proud to have saved me." Marcus spoke these words as an oath, taking strength from their very utterance. So cruel was the anguish in his heart, in his soul, in his being, that to survive he'd spoken a simple vow by which he would live. He could not have known the pain it would bring him and others yet unknown.

…………

"An account of the raid given by yourselves has been scribed to the Legion's records." Lucius stood next to Marcus, both in full military regalia and standing to attention, as they listened to the legate to whom they'd been summoned.

"The death of Standard Bearer Flavinus Gretianus is deeply regretted, but I am aware of the difficulties posed by these raids from the barbarians. They are a huge irritation to us with their chance attacks and irregular fighting tactics." Scanning the account on the writing tablet in front of him, he continued.

"I see you were attacked by a single Brigante who died in the skirmish." He looked at the two young legionaries with wisdom in his eyes gained from many years of service for the Roman Empire. He paused and looked at each in turn, nodding his head very slightly, almost imperceptibly. Marcus had been staring at the wall above the legate's head, but the pause in the speech caused him to look towards the man who seemed to fill the room with his presence. This was the response the legate wanted. Having caught Marcus's gaze, he held it with his own. Blue glacial waters staring into conker-brown pools.

"The death of your comrade is therefore avenged." Another short silence. Marcus stared at his patch of wall again taking relief in its blandness. The intensity with which his officer had looked at him had been unnerving. His blue, blue eyes seemed to bore into his mind, reading facts Marcus would prefer him not to know. Guilty facts that he'd kept to himself. A secret Flavinus had known and lost his life because of. A secret known to the Brigante who lay silent in death with the other. A secret he hoped a dark haired, fair skinned young Brigante woman, barely even a woman, would never tell another. Marcus wanted to keep this secret locked firmly away in the dark recesses of oblivion and smother his guilt there too. It was his *Geryon*, his monster and to bury it was easier than facing it. The legate continued.

"As a unit we have experienced many such raids with some losses to both sides. We have sometimes provoked these attacks in our attempt to extend The Empire. Other times we have been victims of plunder by the Brigantes. Defence of territory or the need to regain something we have taken from these people seem to be causes for their raids. Unlike the Picts and Celts who seem weaned to flail grapnel and relish the consequences, if we do not invade the lands or disturb the livelihoods of the Brigantes, our presence is usually tolerated. A loose ally to Rome that the Imperial Palace would be wise to repress. I do not like accepting that these Brigantes do not wish to conform to the Might of the Valiant Roman Empire, but I can as a fighting man at least understand their reasoning if not their combat tactics." He paused again and Marcus could feel his penetrating gaze upon him once more. "There does not appear to be a clear motive for this attack which unsettles me, and by a single Brigante? It is unusual and I cannot understand it." The legate stopped speaking once more and the silence echoed at Marcus louder than a thousand thundering hooves on cobblestones. To be summoned directly to the legate and briefed in such a manner was not customary and disturbing.

He must know...but he can't...keep your composure...watch the wall...don't look at him...he doesn't know...he's guessing...watch the wall. Marcus's mind was a jumble of urgent messages bouncing around. If the legate caught his eye again he felt he would crumble. Army discipline took charge and he remained steadfast in staring at the wall. The legate made his decision.

"The Legion's records will show this raid as a chance attack on three legionaries of the Third Century of the Fourth Cohort of the Twentieth Legion, on reconnaissance for the unit in preparation of territory gain. A copy of the report will be sent to your centurion. You are dismissed."

....

As the door closed behind the two soldiers, Legate Peterna Maxinius sat in the sturdy oak chair at his desk. Pensive, he watched through his window that looked out along the paved street that led directly to the main North Gate of the fort and listened to the sounds of the garrison going about its daily activities. He could hear the thudding of beater against hide coming from the tannery, and the high-pitched chink of hammer on metal as the farriers made horseshoes. He couldn't hear any noise from the bakehouse as the ovens were situated to the far western side of the fort to minimise the risk of fire spreading to the other buildings of the camp. He could, however, see wisps of smoke and steam rising from that area so he knew the ovens were alight.

There wasn't much his Legion couldn't achieve with their mixture of skills. The chair he was sitting on was a fine example of garrison craftsmanship. It was made from pieces of oak sawn locally and sanded patiently into smooth planks. Jointed with dovetails it would outlast his lifetime he knew. The tanners had provided the leather, probably from an ox or deer, which covered the seat, arms and backrest. Sheep's wool, goat's hair or a mixture of the two would form the wadding that padded out the stretched leather. The civilian settlement that seemed to spring up around any fort, lured by the prospect of troops with money to spend, provided any additional goods and services not available on the fort.

The untidy scatter of these settlements irritated his orderly Roman nature, but he knew they must be tolerated. Not just for the trade, but for the housing they supplied for the strictly illegal wives and families of some of the soldiers. A blind eye was turned to these shenanigans as long as they didn't interfere with their serving duties. He felt aloof to any that dwelt there feeling they owed a debt to Rome for showing them a better, more opulent way of life.

Peterna breathed in deeply pursing his lips into a straight line causing his chin to cockle. Born in Rome to an Italian father, but of Swedish lineage on his mother's side, he'd served the Roman Empire within the political administration as an army strategist for a decade plus three years, before being posted to Britannia as legate. Although employed as a civilian, he'd been attached to different legions for his specialist knowledge and fought through skirmishes with the ranks. He'd received political honours from Emperor Trajan himself following the successful campaign conducted in Dacia in AD105 – AD106. It had been a mighty battle in that ancient region of the eastern Roman Empire and throughout the long year of fighting, Peterna had shown strong strategic qualities and exceptional loyalty to The Empire. His desire to prove he was as Roman in spirit as those born of complete Italian blood was voracious.

Quintus Pompeius Falco came to mind. Peterna narrowed his eyes as he thought about his recent visit, confused rather than perturbed. Appointed Governor of Britannia by Hadrian three years ago, the man was amiable enough and Peterna had not felt uncomfortable by his presence. In fact, he had welcomed the opportunity to discuss his concerns of a local uprising. Falco had experience of the same, his promotion to Governor coming after his successful suppression of the Southern Caledonia uprising three years earlier, a massed and bloody affair that had reduced the numbers of the Ninth Legion quite badly despite the victory. Falco had listened with patience, neither agreeing nor disagreeing. A typical diplomat, Peterna realised, allowing him to air his views without offering assistance in concluding or resolving them. The vague puzzlement of Falco's visit drifted from Peterna as he contemplated his own position.

"Legate…a fine achievement," he muttered, "for a blue-eyed half-Roman!" He'd been taunted by these words throughout his youth. How he'd cursed the colour of his eyes. Blazing blue for all to see, a constant public display of his Scandinavian bloodline. Years of teasing during his youth had left him feeling inferior to his brown-eyed Roman peers. Brown eyes, conker-brown eyes, like those he had been staring into a few minutes earlier.

Peterna had sensed the uneasiness of Marcus when he'd held his gaze. He couldn't quite determine what was wrong. It was true the boy had just lost a friend and comrade and killed a man in return, but it hadn't been his first experience of close battle. Peterna had called for the scribe to check the Legion's records. All battles, skirmishes and other military engagements were dedicatedly recorded on writing tablets, and an annal relating to Marcus Guintoli of the Third Century of the Fourth Cohort of the Twentieth Legion had been found. No such entry was recorded against the name of Lucius Seniarus who'd also stood in his office before him. Of the two, he would have expected any uneasiness to have come from the latter, this being his first recorded attack. No, something else was troubling Marcus Guintoli.

Legate Peterna Maxinius made his second important decision of the morning. Guintoli's unease was becoming an excuse for his own restlessness. Those brown eyes had sparked his desire to prove his worth once again. The march of the Valiant Roman Empire would not be ceased. The Brigantes, along with the Celts and Picts from the north, would be defeated and the lands of Britannia ruled wholly by Rome. He wanted this glory, for himself and for the birth land he so cherished. Dipping his pen nib in black ink he wrote neatly and concisely on the scroll in front of him.

"Let us see what you are made of Hadrian," he muttered sealing the note with a wax insignia of the Twentieth Legion. "Let us see if you are a worthy successor to Trajan as Emperor. I have seen nothing but decline to The Empire since your induction. Give me the troops I need and let us march on." He left his office and walked to the far end of the headquarters building. The small, square room adjacent to the pillared area of the courtyard, doubled as the scribe's office and the dispatch station. Leaving orders indicating the importance of the letter, he walked with purpose from the building. Feeling buoyant and slightly aroused he crossed the wide street, the *Via Principia*, and headed directly for the Commandant's house where he hoped to find his wife in a willing mood. It had been a while since he'd felt like making love this early in the day. He hoped she wouldn't question his desire. He wouldn't tell her about the letter yet. No need to concern her at this time, better to await a reply before incurring her disapproval. Oddly for a legate's wife, she strongly disapproved of territory gain through force and did not hold back in telling him so.

Chapter Two

The mosaic-topped table was strewn with dried flowers and various seed pods. Julita loved flowers and plants and was skilled at producing arrangements to decorate all areas of her home. The autumnal range of seed pods available in this chilly but fertile land had charmed her.

"Look at these Cloelia. *Lunaria annua* - translucent silvery mirrors with seeds like splinters showing through. See them?" Julita passed a sprig to her daughter who didn't share her mother's passion for flowers but tried to appear interested. After all, it was her mother's birthday party they were preparing for. Cloelia was not looking forward to it and feeling guilty at her lack of enthusiasm. The senatorial tribune in charge of the fort at Vindomora, ten miles to the southeast of them, was coming to dinner with his wife and twin sons. Sons still full of snot, unfortunately, pre-pubescent. No doubt they would grow into fine young men one day, she mused, but it would not be in time for her. At fifteen seasons she was more interested in the young legionaries under her father's command. It was not by mistake that her evening stroll took a circuit that passed the bathhouse on her way down to the river. No mistake either that the circuit looped back passing the barracks. No, this dinner party was not her idea of an ideal celebration, but she would try to be positive about it for her mother's sake.

The food would be extravagant which was not something they were used to in the army. The citizens of Rome, yes, but the more mobile existence of the troops led to a less lavish diet. Paradise in Rome was where the pigs ran around already roasted. Paradise on the frontiers was finding a pig to roast! She knew her father had put out a lot of orders for this meal though. He wanted a feast 'fit for Caesar' as he kept quoting. She was enjoying keeping the secret of the dormice from her mother. Twenty had been captured and were being fattened on nuts in earthenware jars, stored in the scribe's office of all places. They hadn't eaten dormouse since crossing the sea from Gaul as they'd always been on the march. This fort was the most settled they'd been and Cloelia silently thanked the Brigante tribes for slowing their progress. Just thinking of eating the dormice was making her mouth water. Rich, red wine would be served too, undiluted, as it was a special occasion. They normally mixed wine with water, but undiluted it would help the conversation to flow. There were some positive sides to this party she decided. Perhaps the musicians would be young and handsome, and there was the bonus of two guards from Vindomora joining them to make up the required nine guests needed to honour the nine muses. She found a lot of these traditions rather tiresome and somewhat ludicrous, but her father defended them vociferously. It was easier to fall in line and put up with them than argue. That lesson had been learnt quite quickly. Feeling less dispirited about the event, she said,

"The rose hips are gorgeous Mama. They're like big, crimson pearls." Cloelia held one to her ear.

"They would look nice made into a garland and worn in your hair," replied Julita. "The red suits your fair colouring. I will make you one. I hope you will enjoy the evening. You are caught a bit between the ages are you not?" Julita didn't wait for a reply. It was a question said just to show her daughter that she understood she would rather be elsewhere with friends. She knew about the 'bathhouse circuit', she and Peterna would giggle privately over their daughter's clumsy attempts to disguise her reasons for the evening walk.

Catching sight of her husband leaving the Headquarters building, something about his demeanour made her curious. His gait was jauntier than she'd seen in a while and it was an unusual time of day for him to be heading to the house. Mother and daughter shared a direct look. The elder composed and knowing, serene yet with a warm flutter growing below her breastbone. The younger, naïve yet learning, not fully understanding but sensing, becoming flustered and embarrassed without properly knowing why.

"I will walk to the settlement, Mama, see if I can find some ribbon for the garland in the warehouses." With a kiss to the cheek and a flourish she was gone leaving Julita amongst the dried flora to greet Peterna with a sensual smile, quickening heartbeat and curious mind. He was a competent lover, thoughtful of her pleasure that more than compensated for his galling loyalty to The Empire's cause.

....

Cloelia hoped Brutus would be guarding the South Gate that opened on to the road leading into the civilian settlement. She liked Brutus with his easy smile and long, rambling stories. He was the best raconteur in the legion. She'd got to know him in the hospital where he'd rested for a month recovering from a fever followed by a severe rash of angry pustules that covered his body leaving cratered scars in places. It had been a strange incident with no diagnosis made. They'd feared it could spread throughout the fort and so kept him in isolation until the fever passed. The cleaning regime in the hospital was strict and they succeeded in containing the disease, whatever the disease was. Brutus himself told such imaginative stories as to its origin and how he'd contracted it that no one knew quite what to believe, Cloelia least of all.

Once the fever had passed and the fear of infection was over, she'd visited him just as she would visit any patient during their recuperation. She cared about people who were down on their luck. The time spent listening to Brutus had been very entertaining, and although she was pleased that his recovery was complete, she had been sorry when he rejoined the legion for duties. There were fewer opportunities for chatting outside of the hospital, which is why she hoped he'd be on guard duty at the gate. Considering she lived on the fort amongst the unit, it was surprising how few of the men she knew, especially by name. Being the Commanding Officer's daughter put her at a disadvantage on that score. They all knew her name and who she was but conversation was kept to a polite minimum. No one wanted to be put on extra latrine duties for being too personal with the legate's daughter! She knew her parents had ideas of marrying her into wealth, probably a member of the senate, dripping with jewels but wobbling with excess tallow beneath their togas no doubt. Cloelia shivered at the image. It was not for her, she was quite determined to marry for love.

Approaching the gate, she could indeed see Brutus. He seemed to be supervising two other soldiers who looked as if they were undertaking repairs to the flat slabs that lay by the stop-block at the entrance. Stripped to sleeveless tunics with leather moccasins laced to the knees, they were sweating with their labouring whilst Brutus leaned languidly against the masonry with a verdant cape of cloth across his shoulders. He clearly had not been labouring. Judging by the caterwaul she could hear, followed by a guffaw from one of the other two, Brutus was entertaining in his usual rumbustious manner.

"Hello Brutus" she said with an easy smile. "How are you?"

"Fine, I am fine. As fine as a balmy breeze from Italia blowing warm grains of white sand over bare feet. Fine, fine" he rambled. One word would never do for Brutus. "And how fare you kind maiden with locks of golden silk and almond eyes, the beauty of which this land has never seen before?" All said in an expansive voice with gestures to match. It could have been construed as mocking except for his smile. As wide as a plump slice of melon it dimpled his cheeks and filled his eyes with a mischievous sparkle. It made a person relax.

"I am well, thank you. Off to roam the warehouses for some ribbon. Mama is having a birthday party next week with guests from Vindomora."

"Ah, yes" he nodded his head thoughtfully a few times, "that will be why we are making these gate repairs" he said to the two sweating men. "Cannot have the Vindomora tribune tripping over a flagstone as he enters."

"His wife and children are coming too," said Cloelia. "They will need to get a cart through."

"By the time my colleagues, with skills equal to the master stone masons of Rome, with minds equal to, if not greater than, the sagacious architects who design the colossal colonnades of that fine city," Brutus's voice rose in rich resonance as he over-acted once again, "and with fighting bodies of pure, honed, rippling muscles to match any champion gladiator," he paused for effect, then stated quite flatly, "of course they will get a cart through."

"Do not tease me Brutus," she laughed. "Who are your highly skilled colleagues? I do not think we have met."

"Let me introduce Lucius Seniarus, master craftsman, horseman, gentleman and musician. No finer husband material could you find if you scoured the whole of the blessed Known World." He made an extravagant bow towards Lucius who'd stopped working to acknowledge the greeting. Still kneeling on his left knee with his right elbow resting on the other leg bent at ninety degrees, he threw his head backward in a loud, amiable laugh.

"You are the genius, Brutus. A genius at jesting" replied Lucius. "A master…"

"…raconteur" he and Cloelia spoke the word together and laughed in friendly agreement.

"A master idiot!" grunted the other soldier who didn't break from his work but continued rather rudely. Cloelia's smile ebbed and she felt a little quashed by his behaviour. A little confused too. Or was it embarrassment, she wasn't sure. Something about him disconcerted her in an indefinable way. Her heart thumped wrongly as she studied him. Brutus came to the rescue.

"Take no heed of my saturnine friend fair maiden. Marcus Guintoli is his name. Renowned and crowned throughout the lands as the most eligible bachelor of the Twentieth Legion, with poems of passion, the softest songs and a touch to surpass both, all perfected on many a clement evening. He is a little off kilter today due to reasons of a personal nature that I will not bore you with. You should forgive his ignorance and enjoy your sortie to the warehouses." Cloelia recovered her smile but left the group with a vague feeling that she had seen Marcus Guintoli somewhere before but couldn't place where.

....

Julita looked anxiously out on to the darkening courtyard. The rain was pelting down like spears from a hundred legions at once. Jupiter was in angry mood. As the rain hit the flagstones it ricocheted like black sparks a foot in length, blurring the area into a murky lake. Her guests should have arrived some time ago. Something was wrong.

"I presume the weather has put them off," she said to Peterna and Cloelia. "I cannot blame them for that, but you would think they would send word via a runner. The daylight is nearly gone and I was expecting them midway between sun height and sun down. There has been time for a runner to reach us. Perhaps you should send someone to check, Peterna."

"I will not send a man out in this," he grumbled. "A beast itself does not deserve that, let alone a man."

"But what if they have met with a mishap? What if their cart has overturned?" Julita's voice was getting higher as her mind began to race. "Oh, no! Peterna, you do not think they have been attacked do you?" She grabbed his arm in alarm.

"Do not be foolish woman," he snapped, "raids do not occur south of here and Jupiter is lashing even Mars into submission today." His voice was strident. "No man would venture to fight in this. Besides, it is just as well they are not here as the wretched entertainers have let me down. They will be publicly flogged as an example if I find them." He was feeling aggrieved that the day was spoilt, for himself, and for Julita. He'd been looking forward to a celebration. Much effort had gone in to the organising and the local civilian settlement was wealthier at his expense. And quite some expense it was. His ill-tempered tone belied such feelings of disappointment however and Julita misinterpreted his thoughts. Wounded by his anger she turned her head from him, stiffening slightly as unwanted tears welled threatening to spill. Her throat constricted at the same time, rendering her unsafe to speak in anything other than a tight squeak. Experience had taught her to remain silent at moments like these. Cloelia stepped in to diffuse the brewing explosion.

"Perhaps you should send someone, Papa. Just to check. It would ease Mama's mind. Then maybe we could carry on with our own celebration. We cannot let the meal go to waste. I peeked into the kitchen earlier, what a feast they have prepared." Before anyone else was able to speak, two figures could be seen running towards the buildings from the South Gate. Cloelia joined her parents at the window and they strained to identify the running pair in the gloom.

"They have sent news. Thank the gods!" breathed Julita. "Go! Peterna, go and find out what has happened."

....

Trouble had indeed struck the party from Vindomora en route. It was not an attack as Julita had irrationally feared, but problems with the cart as suggested. Although the cart didn't overturn, it did encounter difficulties. The road between the two forts had not yet been metalled like the Fosse Way further south. There was talk that it would be done as soon as enough troops mustered in the area to warrant the expense. Indeed, Falco had spoken of its need during his visit. Men from local tribes would be used for the heavy work under guard by the army. But as it was, the road was more of a wide track. It was easily passable by horse or on foot and, due to its natural stony content, normally adequate to pull a cart along. But Jupiter had spat with such disgust that day that the track had developed intermittent patches of bog.

The journey was slower than usual due to these obnoxious conditions, but the party made steady progress to begin with. The tribune's wife and two sons were enjoying the bumpy cart ride. Huddled together beneath a large, leather cape, they were keeping reasonably dry and treating the whole experience as an adventure. Their spirits were high until they became stuck in a particularly glutinous patch of oozing clay that had not been spotted by the tribune who was riding the horse pulling the cart. The cart stopped so abruptly that its passengers were flung forwards. The result was a very inelegant heap of bodies covered completely by the leather cape. The younger of the two boys landed at the bottom of the pile thus cushioning the fall of the other two who came out of the accident unscathed. Once recovered from the shock and slight winding, it seemed his only wound was a bruise to the right side of his forehead just below the hairline. It quickly swelled to the size of a large haw, turning the same vibrant red.

The tribune's horse had reared as it was jolted backwards by the cart's sudden halt. He'd almost held on but ended up sitting in the quagmire next to the cart, unhurt but filthy. The guards became just as dirty, coating themselves in mud as they manhandled the cart from the sticky mess. As they were more than half way to their destination, the decision was made to continue, albeit more cautiously. The mood in the cart was less blithe than earlier, with the battered boy taking umbrage at his mother's attempts to cheer him. The bump to his head was taking on a damson hue matching his growing annoyance at his brother's teasing grin.

The guards had checked the cart after the accident and thought it secure, until a mile or so further along a pin fell out unhitching the cart from the horse. Temporary repairs were made that held for a while before the pin worked loose again. And so they continued in this rather staccato pattern of travel not encountering another living soul until they reached the fort gate, ragged, filthy and weary.

....

Peterna threw his arms in the air at ninety degrees to his shoulders with his palms facing upwards.

"Well, we now have guests and we have food but we have no entertainment. Now what shall we do? A feast cannot be a feast without entertainment. We need a poet, musicians, songs." Up went his arms above his head in exasperated defeat.

"Leave it to me Papa," said Cloelia. "You have always said there is nothing this legion cannot achieve. By the time our guests are washed and changed, we will have entertainment." She hitched up her dress with her hands and shot off in an excited rustle, leaving him no time to object. This party is turning out to be more interesting than expected, she thought as she ran to the kitchen.

She called to a servant boy.

"I need you to find Brutus Antonini. He will be in the barracks or the bathhouse. Try the barracks first. It's urgent. Bring him straight to the house, and be as quick as you can. I will wait by the front door."

"Brutus Antonini" the boy repeated.

"Yes, go! Tell him Cloelia needs him," she urged, pressing a coin into the boy's hand.

Brutus appeared in no time wearing a sleeveless tunic of soft, golden tanned leather, not gathered by a belt, but falling loosely to mid thigh, and barefoot. Quite inappropriate dress for the weather Cloelia thought. Had she taken this line of thinking a little further she may have concluded he'd dressed in a hurry. Had she been a little older and wiser, she may also have noticed his anxious look and protective deportment as he came to her side not knowing why she'd called for him. But she didn't. Instead she told him quickly of how the hired entertainers for their dinner party had let them down.

"We just need a poet or a storyteller, some music and songs, Brutus. I thought of you immediately" she enthused. "Your stories are always so amusing. And I remembered you said the soldiers working on the gate with you last week were musicians and singers. Would they do it Brutus? You will all be paid well and I will make sure some dormice are saved for you. We have been fattening them for weeks and I know they are your favourite dish. You told me once in the hospital."   Brutus stood dumb for a moment. A rainbow of emotions had twisted into a tangled rope that was throttling his speech. This girl standing before him, so innocent and vulnerable, so kind and uncomplicated, so young, so beautiful, so fresh, so unaware of his feelings for her, had just hired him as the party's entertainment! When the servant boy had found him in his barracks preparing to visit the bathhouse, with a message that Cloelia needed him at the house immediately, he'd thought…what had he thought? He didn't know, it wasn't clear, he hadn't thought, he'd just gone to her side without hesitation. He scratched the back of his head with his right hand and managed a half-cocked smile. Stalling for time to think clearly, he began to ramble as only Brutus could.

"With a hostess as beautiful as you, whose golden hair is set on fire by the garland of rose hips upon purple ribbon, ribbon as smooth and velvety as a crocus of the same rich hue, a party has no need of further entertainment."

"There is not time for you to tease me now, Brutus" she interrupted. "The guests will be ready soon. Will you do it?" Cloelia was standing like a cat waiting to spring, slightly curled shoulders with both hands clasped into fists beneath her chin, and forearms tensed together in front of her developing bosom that was threatening to spill from the scooped neckline of her gown. She didn't think he'd say no, but wasn't sure. She held her breath waiting for his answer. Brutus continued to speak. The words came without effort, freeing his mind to decide on an answer to her unexpected question. It was a most unorthodox question – legionaries, entertaining at their own legate's dinner party? He'd enlisted to fight for the Empire and bask in its glory not to read poetry to his commanding officer. Telling stories in the barracks was different. But standing there, at that moment, how could he say no? He didn't have it in him to refuse her. Love her, cherish her, protect her, yes. Hoping always that her heart would see what her eyes failed to. Waiting, as he knew he must, for her to feel his desire and return it. The wait was painful, especially at that moment as his eyes were being drawn to the jewel that hung around her neck and sparkled teasingly a fraction above her cleavage. Until she offered herself though, he would wait. To advance before she was ready would crush the friendship leaving scars beyond repair like those on his skin he so abhorred. Shaking his head slightly and raising his eyebrows, Brutus broke into his melon-slice grin.

"Cloelia…for dormice…we will make it happen." She released her arms and shoulders from their tensed state, jumping with a squeal of delight as she raised her hands to the gods.

"Papa will be so pleased," she laughed. "You have a third of the sundial Brutus. See you in the triclinium and thank you, thank you." He wasn't as certain that 'Papa' would be as pleased as she thought, but it was all soldiers to the shield now. No turning back. Marcus and Lucius would bleed him dry for this.

"Cupid, you got me into this predicament," he muttered to the god of love, "but I will need the favour of Fortuna, great goddess of luck to get me through it."

....

The dinner party was a resounding success for most involved. Cloelia had not given her father the opportunity to object to men of his legion entertaining them. She'd cleverly manipulated the arrivals so that the guests were settled on the large couches, with the serving of the first course merely minutes away, before the three legionaries-cum-entertainers were presented. Relying on her mother's punctilious nature and her father's desperate desire to salvage the day, she'd been rewarded when a single withering look from Julita immediately silenced Peterna when he saw his men entering dressed in party garb. One was carrying a lyre, another a cithera, and the third was empty handed. A scene would not be made in front of the guests just as Cloelia had thought. A questioning look mixed with a brief frown was all she had to deal with then. She smiled radiantly in response. Any scolding would come later, by when flowing wine and a satiated appetite would have softened the sharp edges of it.

The couches were arranged around three sides of a square, with a low, rectangular table in the centre. The fourth side was left open for serving. There were three people per couch, each propping themselves on their left forearms. They would use their right hands to stretch for the food and drink that was now arriving and being placed on the central table. Decorated red Samian ware dishes overflowed with asparagus, peas, beans and carrots, lettuce, endive, radishes and cucumber. An egg dish was served surrounded by oysters and mussels. The party could only marvel at how it had all been acquired.

Chickens drowned in red wine appeared, followed by a platter loaded with slices of ham and piled high with the plump dormice, the tails of which were entwined around the neck of the roasted swan that rose majestically from the centre of the dish with its white feathers and broad, flat bill still in tact. Its eyes had been removed and replaced with shallots. A further platter of small pigeons plucked, handsomely baked and glistening with drizzled honey was served on a bed of hot nuts. Swan instead of peacock was the only indication from the feast upon the table that they were not eating this in the grand Basilica within the walls of Rome itself.

Rinsing her fingers in the provided bowl of rose scented water, enriched with velvet orange petals of the same flower, Cloelia was glowing with happiness. It didn't matter that she was sharing her couch with the two pre-pubescent boys who had little to say once the story of the bruised forehead had been told. She didn't bother to force the conversation. Brutus was entertaining with his poetry and she smiled gratefully at him. But only the once before she became transfixed by Marcus.

    The feeling of knowing Marcus from somewhere would not leave Cloelia. She studied him furtively to begin with, then more boldly as the wine flowed and the meal progressed. He was certainly handsome. Strong with chiselled features. His dark hair was cut short all over and she rather liked the vague shadow of stubble that covered his chin and shaded his jaw line. Watching his fingers as he delicately plucked the strings of the lyre, the realisation came with an inward gush that caught her breath. She'd seen those hands holding a carving of Jupiter. The night of the raid that had killed the standard bearer, the raid her father had been so perturbed by. She'd passed this man on her evening stroll back from the river. He hadn't seen her and she hadn't spoken. An aura of pain mixed with anguish, defiance and confusion had shrouded him as he went by and she remembered feeling a little scared by the emotion he exuded. Scared and rude, as though she was witness to the vulnerability a man wouldn't want a woman to see.

    Marcus sensed her staring and returned her gaze. Any hope of controlling her raw feelings dissolved as her heart sparked when their eyes locked. She felt she could see beyond the exterior deep into his inner sanctum. To the very private sacred spot not often revealed. A secret hollow of tender ferns amongst toughened brambles. She'd glimpsed it before during their brief encounter but not understood it. Marcus didn't smile but let his eyes drift down to the jewel hanging around her neck. It was sparkling as her cleavage rose and fell with each breath. Pert nipples erect beneath the velvet dress that scooped to reveal the young, creamy flesh of her breasts. Liking what he saw, his eyes lingered there and Cloelia felt the path to the hollow closing. Her insides were alive from her breastbone down to her pelvis and she so desperately wanted to be taken back to this man's inner sanctum, for him to allow her there, her and nobody else.

    Brutus was the only one to see the exchange. He watched and silently grieved at what he saw.

Chapter Three

Jolinda knew the argument would not be resolved. Her mother's views would not change. She was simply strangled by a gripping fog of grief over the matter.

"But we must trade with the Romans," Jolinda implored. She was speaking in her native Bryothonic tongue, a Celtic language evolved from the Welsh. This was the only language her mother knew, although Jolinda could also converse in the Roman tongue. Her father had arranged for a *menthor* to tutor her – with great foresight, she realised. "We need their Roman coins to purchase grain and fodder from the southern people who've turned to their ways. We can't grow enough on our northern hills to survive. We've always traded with our southern neighbours, the only difference is now we must use their new trading methods, coins not barter. And to get the coins we must first trade with the Romans. It's just an extra step that's all. Ma, can't ya see we don't have a choice? The animals will starve, we'll starve. We must trade with them."

"I won't let ya father's memory be tarnished. I will not. He's been in his grave one moon is all and ya want to forsake him. No, Jolinda, no, he died by their hand." Her voice rose with exasperation as she spoke the words. How could her daughter even consider the idea? "We're the fourth generation of Teviots to live freely off this land and we'll not be forced to succumb to anyone. D'ya hear me? I would rather rot slowly with a foetid wound of maggots than trade with the Roma…" the word died in a trembling choke of misery. Jolinda felt the burden like a hundredweight sack across her shoulders. She went to her mother's side and gently rubbed her back. Giving comfort to the older woman who was failing in her attempt to stop the tears, brushing them away with the back of her hand as she continued to pound the grain in the large wooden bowl, polished smooth over the years from grinding. Jolinda spoke softly.

"It'll be all right Ma, I'll make it all right. Tamsin can take over some of my chores to help ya run the housestead. I'll farm the land like Da used to. I've heard of a new piece of equipment that can be dragged along by oxen to turn the soil. If we can get one maybe we could sow more wheat and barley. The boys can help me. Kye's pretty good at wielding a sickle these days and young Aaron's old enough to sow and harvest. It'll be all right." Even as she was speaking, Jolinda knew the task was too great. As strong and independent as her father had been, he'd always bartered with the southern folk for extra fodder and grain. It had been easier before the south had romanized.

Sometimes he'd exchange goods for meat over the winter months when the hunting was poor. The winters were harsh in these northern crags. Her father had often laughingly said the piercing wind alone was enough to send even a woolly mammoth to find a burrow. A lazy wind he'd called it – goes through ya 'stead of round ya!

Her heart lifted a little as she remembered his rugged smile and gruff words. A solid exterior had covered a melting heart. Providing for and protecting his family had been his life. He'd found the challenges of the wild countryside fulfilling and the love of his woman satisfying. Energy exuded from every pore, creating an aura of optimism that breathed through the family. Jolinda, his eldest, had a similar trait. A smaller sheaf of energy but her presence always pervaded a room as she entered. She knew clearly, more clearly than she'd known anything before, that she would have to defy her mother's wishes and trade with the Romans for their coins. With or without her family's understanding she would do so, or they simply would not survive.

"I don't know what happened that day Da," she silently whispered. "But I hope ya understand why I must do this."

....

"I am going to the warehouses, Mama" Cloelia called out as she found her cape. "I want to find something warm to wear. The wind is biting." Julita came to the hallway smiling and rearranged her daughter's hair that had become partly tucked inside her cape.

"You look lovely" she said and kissed her forehead. Holding her gently by the shoulders at arm's length she asked, "Is there someone special in your life I do not know about? You have such a radiance about you."

"That is the radiance of youth, Mama!"

"Hmm, youth may be radiant, but youth is also unwise. Remember the saying of Publilius Syrus: even a god finds it hard to love and be wise at the same time." Julita laughed as she spoke. "As your mother, have I taught you enough I am wondering? I trust you would ask me if you wished to know anything." The latter was said more seriously. Cloelia dodged the issue becoming eager to get away.

"There is a new stall at the warehouses that sells shawls. They are beautifully crafted in chunky yarn and the colours are gorgeous. I saw some last week with a gold thread woven through. I should have bought one, but there was such a bustle of people at the time. I hope the stall is there again." Julita got the impression her daughter was wittering to hide her embarrassment.

"Have you enough coin for two? Buy a second if you have no objection to your mother wearing the same as yourself." she replied with a smile as her daughter skipped away, all eager energy and bounce. Closing the door against the chilly wind that was swirling leaves along the courtyard gutters, she shook her head and breathed deeply in puzzlement. Was that girl up to something? Intuition told her yes, but it was just a vague feeling with no substance. Julita wasn't even sure why she felt puzzled at all.

The sound of a horse's hooves on flagstones interrupted her reverie and she looked to see a dispatch rider bring his mount into the courtyard. That's a fine looking animal she thought as she watched the rider tether it to a wooden rail, patting the strong horse's neck as it snorted out hot puffs of breath in the cold air. The ride had clearly been hard. Julita could see the rider talking to his mount when Peterna appeared from the headquarters building. Julita watched them exchange a small package and saw Peterna slap the rider twice between the shoulder blades in a grateful gesture, as he led him into the building.

"Get this soldier wine and food," ordered Peterna, "and then show him the bathhouse and a space in the barracks. He will be resting with us for the night." Turning to the dispatch rider he said, "That was a lot of country you covered today. Did you encounter any problems, any skirmishes?"

"No skirmishes, sir, but the road network is less advanced here than in the south. The Fosse Way from Lindum right through to Aquae Sulis is an excellent road. Lindum north to Ebracum is not too bad, but after that the riding is tougher." The legate listened with interest.

"I have heard of Aquae Sulis. Is that where they are building a temple around the hot springs?"

"Yes, sir. The goddess Sulis Minerva swirls her healing powers through the water and it steams straight from the ground. It is said to heal no end of ailments, sir. There are plans for a huge complex of hot houses combined with temples."

"The Roman goddess of springs is Minerva, why do you call her Sulis Minerva?" Peterna had not heard this name used before.

"Sulis is the Celtic name for our goddess, I believe sir. This place was sacred to the natives, I think Sulis Minerva is a compromise." The dispatch rider became a little uncomfortable as he passed on this information. He sensed the Roman legate bristle at the explanation. Peterna certainly didn't like it, but he checked himself as he began to frown, jutting his chin out slightly and pursing his lips. Insolent barbarians he thought, but shifted his mind on to more immediate matters without saying more. He was suddenly eager to read the letter the rider had brought.

"Report to me here at daylight tomorrow," he said, dismissing the dispatch rider and moving to his desk.

The package was a flat rectangular shape, measuring ten inches by six, and one inch thick. Peterna studied it for a moment. It was well wrapped but innocuous in its appearance, giving no indication of its origin or destination, finding its way to him through explicit oral instructions, passed from messenger to messenger at each outpost along the network linking Rome to its entire Empire.

He knew it was instructions from the senate, but wondered if Hadrian had written it himself. He hoped so more than he wanted to admit, but Hadrian was known to travel a lot and Peterna was not privy to his current whereabouts. When he'd put pen to scroll a full moon cycle plus a half ago, Falco had mentioned that Hadrian was passing through Gaul heading for Rome to check on the progress of the construction of the Pantheon in the great city. It was reported that the huge circular hall was ready to be topped by an arch dome one hundred and thirty-eight feet in diameter and Hadrian wanted to see the impressive arches begin to take shape.

Peterna hoped his request for troops had been opened directly by the Emperor and not relayed to him via the senate. Somehow he was testing Hadrian. Was he a worthy successor to Trajan? Peterna needed to know. He wanted the troops and the orders to march so they could overrun the Brigantes and quash the northern tribes of Caledonia too, thus claiming the lands totally for Rome. Then he could retire a content man, return to the great city and see this extraordinary Pantheon as well. Cloelia deserved to be married to a wealthy Roman citizen and he may be able to find a senate member agreeable to the idea if they returned. She was of the right age now, so time was pressing.

His thoughts were drifting, so Peterna made a mental note to speak to Julita about his plans for Cloelia and returned his attention to opening the package. He used his knife to cut through the two narrow strips of soft leather that had been carefully bound around all four sides, interlocking as they crossed and neatly knotted. Care had certainly been taken in the wrapping. Anticipation was growing in Peterna as he opened out first one layer of leather, then a layer of sacking cloth, followed by a third layer of soft, pristine white cotton, the same that was used in making robes for the senate. His breathing was quickening as he unwrapped the cotton to reveal a scroll wrapped around a small, flat piece of wood. He looked straight to the bottom of the specially prepared animal skin and saw it was signed and waxed by Hadrian. Excellent! He read the message:

> *Extra troops denied at present.*
> *Do not advance. Consolidate your line.*
> *Deployment to Africa essential.*
> *Io Saturnalia. Rome celebrates with you!*

Peterna Maxinius read the message again, suddenly breaking the silence with a thump of his fist to the desk.

"*Pleb!*" he yelled. Throwing the scroll on the floor he stormed for the door, his face puce with rage. "Nobody is to enter my office until I return," he boomed to the guard as he left. Standing ramrod still, the guard saluted, holding his breath, not daring to exhale. The dispatch had clearly not brought good news! Not his place to worry, and definitely not his place to comment or look at the message. His throat constricted at the very thought of disobeying the legate's orders – he'd lose his head for it.

The clerks looked up as Peterna made his way out of the building, across the courtyard and down towards the South Gate. Peterna didn't care, he didn't even notice. His anger filled his whole world and was suffocating him. It was driving him to walk with long, strident, pounding paces. He was on a mission but he didn't know to where. Anywhere! Anywhere away from the scroll.

"Io Saturnalia…Rome celebrates," he mumbled. "Ha!" he yelled, stomping on. Mumbling again, "idiot, fool, half-wit, simpleton". Yelling once more, "imbecile!" He rumbled along like a moving flameless bonfire of wet leaves billowing thick, choking smoke. With angry thoughts continuing to bang the inside of his head as he left the fort walls and entered the civilian settlement.

Chapter Four

Trade on her stall had been swift that morning and Jolinda was feeling relieved. She examined the Roman coins with interest. "Survival!" she muttered with a slight shake of her head and a tiny, wry smile. It was ludicrous really, having to sell something for a coin, so you could buy something else with the coin. Much easier to do a direct swap and barter. But then again, there was a limit to what you could swap. You had to have something the other person wanted. If you didn't, it made trading difficult and you could end up on the bad end of a deal. She remembered the time her father had cussed all evening over a bad trade.

"Use every morsel of that there brace of duck and grind them tiny bones for thick'ning tomorrow's soup, woman," he'd grumbled. "I was done good 'n' proper on that trade. A right lousy barter I made. Four bundles of good hay I gave for them...four...can ya believe it? Us can't eat hay though and we needed meat more than I can hunt down in this weather." Jolinda smiled at the recollection.

She'd been surprised at the number of people who passed through the warehouses. She didn't enjoy the crowded town area, preferring instead the wild openness of the hills where her homestead dwelt, an undulating two-mile hike to the northwest. The bustle of the streets was quite stifling. People, noise and smells hitting the senses from every recess and gully. Aromatic smells from herbal stores mixed with baking aromas from the taverns and eateries couldn't quite mask the putrid waft of rancid meat and rotting vegetables that always inhabited the alleyways. Unsold stock left uncaringly by lazy traders. The same lazy traders no doubt who were inclined to relieve themselves in the same alleyways, marking their territory like dogs, leaving the acrid stench of urine that seems to bite at the back of the throat.

The warehouses were sited at the top end of the main stone-paved street. A single timber barn, a hundred feet by thirty feet, with one arched open end, was divided into a series of individual pens by slatted partitions that rose from the dirt floor to just above the height of an average adult male. Each stall was thus afforded some privacy from its neighbour. Twenty-two pens were housed in the barn - ten down one long side, and ten down the other, with two along the short side at the far end from the street. Jolinda's stall was the second on the left as you entered through the high and wide arched opening. Weekly rent was paid to the owner, a surly looking Celt, bearish in build and similar in speech. Not a man you'd want to owe money to. From behind the wooden trestle positioned near the front of her pen, Jolinda could see down the main street as far as the tavern that housed the brothel. Beyond the haphazard arrangement of buildings behind the street that made up the civilian settlement, she could see the walls of the Roman fort. Like it or not, it was an awesome sight amidst the countryside. It rose as a silent statement of Roman power and resolve. She resented its symbolic arrogance, yet was drawn by its bravado at the same time. She'd never had need to go within its walls, and thus it held a certain fascination.

Jolinda returned her attention to her stall. The five shawls she'd crafted had sold very quickly and some of the soldiers had been interested in the chunky woollen hand warmers. Said they'd never known a land so cold. The hand warmers were easy to make. She could whip them up in no time using oddments of yarn. The shawls took longer and she had only a small amount of the gold thread left. Perhaps Tamsin could get her some more, she wondered. Jolinda pondered again where her sister had acquired it. She'd not said, just smiled and said it didn't cost her anything. A flicker of worry pressed at her temples as she wondered about her sister's flirtatious manner. "Nothing you can do, Jolinda," she muttered.

Little interest was being shown in the goods left on the stall – woven matting, scraped hides and unworked fleeces, so Jolinda decided to give it just a while longer before packing up. There was still a full day's work waiting for her at the homestead and she didn't want to be missed. Her plan was to get enough done today, so that she could make some more hand warmers tomorrow for sale next week. She was pleased with her efforts and relieved she could now buy some grain and winter fodder for the animals. If there was enough left over, she could begin to stock the larder a little too. If her mother saw food on the table, she would have to see that it was right to trade with the Romans. Trade or starve was how Jolinda saw it. They didn't have a choice.

Wrapped up in her thoughts, she didn't notice Cloelia at her stall until she spoke.

"Hello. I am pleased you are here again. The warehouses are bustling again, are your goods selling well?"

"Oh…hello…yes, sorry…I was with me thoughts." An audible breath and a smile came from Jolinda as she tucked the silver coins into the leather pouch tied to the waistband of her skirt and gave full attention to her customer. "Yes, trade's been swift this morning." Cloelia noticed the girl's accent but said nothing.

"I was admiring the shawls with the gold thread in them last week. Do you have any?"

"All five I had've been traded this morning."

"Oh, I should have got here earlier." Seeing Cloelia's sunny smile fade to grey disappointment made Jolinda feel awkward.

"I could make another for ya and have it ready for next week." The words tumbled out even as Jolinda wondered how she'd find the time to make a shawl on top of everything else.

"Could you? That would be kind. You make them yourself do you? I actually wanted two, is that possible by next week? The second is for my mother." Cloelia felt compelled to add the last comment, as she didn't want to appear greedy. The girl in front of her was beautiful with her milky skin and fresh salmon-pink cheeks glowing, devoid of beauty powders. Strong, dark eyebrows arched above thick lashes that protected brown-flecked blue eyes. Glossy black hair with a silver shimmer was held at the nape of her neck by a simple, wooden clasp and hung down her back like a horse's tail. Cloelia envied the straight mane. It couldn't have been more different from her golden locks that tumbled to their will. She saw beauty in the face, but sensed a proud impecuniousness. No jewellery, no adornment to the clothing. Simple cotton and sensible woollen materials for the clothes. Her father would say she was a caste adrift, yet Cloelia felt such warmth towards her. She exuded a calm self-assurance and poise, aplomb, seeming content with her simplistic appearance. Cloelia was intrigued.

"Two might be difficult in a week, but I'll see what I can do for ya."

"I will pay double for them if you can."

"Oh, two coins for each shawl?" Jolinda was taken aback. This trading was all so new to her. "Thank ya!"

"Can I have one in purple and the other in that beautiful sunset orange I saw before? Both with the gold woven through? My name is Cloelia." Her sunshine smile was back as she extended a hand, palm up, revealing two gold coins. "Two coins now, the other two when I get the shawls. Is that fair?"

"Jolinda Teviot. Pleased to do trade with ya. A fair exchange is no robbery my Da always said."

"That is not a Roman saying," laughed Cloelia. "Papa is more likely to say 'fortune favours the valiant' or something equally heroic."

"Are ya from the fort?"

"Yes, Papa is the Commander. I will count seven sunrises and see you here."

Jolinda agreed and watched as the golden tumble of curls weaved out through the crowds to the street. She could see Cloelia enter a metalware store. The Romans like their frippery she thought. Not enough to do in their lives. She was still gazing that way when she saw Cloelia emerge from the same store walking very closely with a legionary, obviously happy in his company. Although dressed in off duty garments, Jolinda knew immediately that he was from the fort. You could pick them from a group as easily as a jackdaw amongst sparrows. Many Romanized local people chose to match the soldiers' casual wear and clean shaven appearance to show their allegiance to Rome, but they didn't have the same imperious quality. That pride of Italian blood mixed with the protection of army discipline and physical training. It spawned supremacy. It couldn't be purchased. Jolinda didn't much care for it, yet without knowing, she possessed a similar trait, although with much softer edges.

She cleared away her belongings, wondering what the shouts she could hear rising above the warehouse humdrum were about. They seemed to be coming from the area of the tavern.

....

      The pendant had cost him fifteen denarii, a sizeable sum for a gift thought Marcus. It had delighted Cloelia though, so he hoped for sweet rewards from his investment. Fifteen denarii wouldn't even get you sucked in the whorehouse he mused. Earlier, he'd tossed two silver sestertii into the fountain as he walked up the street. One for Cupid and one for Fortuna. With the good grace of both, he could be blessed with copulatory exhaustion by sundown, and all for a fraction of what Lucius had paid to his strumpet. This was good Roman class too. The legate's daughter, she would surely marry a Senator or noble of Rome. It excited him that he would take her before the nobility got a chance, he could hardly believe how Fortuna was smiling on him. Flavinus must be sitting at her right bosom. The thought of his slain friend and the vow he'd made brought approval to this liaison. He ignored the niggling fear of being caught by the legate. Youth felt dominant in lust, they wouldn't be discovered. Cloelia had been adamant that her father never came to the settlement.

      "He is not interested in the peasant life" she'd insisted. "I can read him like a Greek philosopher reads the stars. He is dogmatic in his ways. Running the fort keeps him busy. And Mama" she added with a teasing twinkle. Thus the tryst had been arranged.

      With meticulous planning, typical of a Roman, Marcus had scouted a haymow and stashed a goatskin in a corner. It was the nature of this race of peoples not to leave anything to chance. Coition to complete satisfaction was his goal and he didn't plan to shiver or shrivel. This northern land didn't lend itself to naked exposure to the elements. With the wind slicing icicles, it would dull even the hottest Italian passion, yet the haymow would provide shelter enough. Marcus felt himself grow hard with his thoughts. He could sense that Cloelia was ready to yield to him and the anticipation was both demanding and thrilling. He wanted to savour the feeling and fire the iron a while longer that day before forging it. But the dice of Fortuna was still rolling.

....

      A crowd had quickly gathered and was spilling backwards into a semi-circle from the tavern door out on to the street. It formed an instant arena for the scrapping women, giving space for their flailing limbs. Jeering cheers came from the onlookers, as they seemed to revel in the combatant's public discord. Black hair intermingled with fiery red hair in a grapple as bestial as attacking wolves. Snarling like angry dogs the two women scratched and kicked in demented frenzy. A whirlpool of frothing wrath.

      The crowd was now five or six people deep and swelling. Curiosity over the commotion was spreading along the street like a droplet ripples across a pond. Marcus and Cloelia were drawn to the ruction.

"Can you see?" Cloelia asked Marcus, frustrated that she wasn't able to.

"I think it is two women fighting, but I cannot see properly." Marcus was judging by the cat-like screams rising from the centre. You could hear them above the taunting gibes still droning from the crowd.

"Push closer," she urged.

Marcus forced his way through reaching the front with Cloelia at his tail.

"Do something Marcus! Stop them!" implored Cloelia as she saw the melee.

Unsure if he wanted to get involved, Marcus was summing up the situation just as a second ruckus spilled from the tavern. A hirsute giant ox of a Celt, six feet tall and half as broad, was brandishing a cudgel at Brutus. With a sickening thud it landed across the young Roman's forearm raised to protect his head from the killing blow, before it impacted across the side of his head. Brutus fell to the dust groaning, unconscious but alive. A smashed arm protruding splintered bone at the elbow, the current price for his life.

Shocked by this sudden new drama the crowd fell silent, which in turn defused the anger in the squabbling women who stilled their fighting. The air hung turbid with suspense. For Marcus the world spun in retrograde motion as the abyss of oblivion he'd visited before opened up. To his left, untangling herself from her red haired opponent, was a dark haired, fair skinned – skin now marked with fresh scratches lucent with blood – Brigante girl. To his right, scything a swath through the crowd like he was on the battlefield, was his legate. At his feet was Brutus, friend and comrade, beaten and battered. At the door of the tavern he saw Lucius appear. To his rear was Cloelia, beseeching him with her wide eyes and reaching out to steady herself against him, afraid she would faint. A vision of the comely body of Fortuna sprouting the three heads of the hideous *Geryon* he'd tried to bury rushed towards him. The Celt came as well. With strength borne of primeval anger, Marcus let out a guttural growl as he charged at the oncoming assailant of his prone comrade. Yelling his Legion's name and motto, *Twentieth Legion of the Eagles, proud to fight for Rome and comrade*, he rammed his right shoulder in low to the Celt's torso and tackled him to the ground. The surprise attack gave the smaller Roman an advantage and Marcus made full use of it. His dagger slashed across the Celt's left cheek opening a wound that spurted blood along the glinting blade onto the hand of Marcus. He held the dripping steel at the throat of the bearded man as he knelt on his burly chest, pinning his head to the dirt with his other arm. The vision of the *Geryon* faded and Fortuna reappeared whole. Marcus sagged weakly and tasted bile, and then Lucius was beside him, lending his weight to holding the wounded but still struggling ox-man down. Cloelia broke from the crowd and went to tend Brutus. Legate Peterna Maxinius could not believe the scene laid out before him. His soldiers, his daughter, this melee. What was happening?

With the Celt now restrained and the action apparently over, the crowd began to disperse as it lost interest. The appearance of the legate in the town was causing some to whisper as they left the spectacle. By sundown Peterna knew this story would have been re-told many times with several versions, some would be accurate but most would be exaggerated.

Recovering his wits, Marcus looked round for the Brigante girl. She was gone. Running towards him was the red haired half of the fight. Flinging herself at the feet of the legate she wailed in a tongue Marcus could not understand. Still simmering over the orders from Hadrian, Peterna wasn't in the mood for histrionics. This waif was obviously pleading for the life of the Celt – her father he presumed. To him, they were peasants not worthy of his time. On any other day he would have had their heads placed on poles as an example, but today was not normal. The blazing winds from Acheron were even blowing cold. The presence of Cloelia injected a softer edge to his decision.

"Get that soldier back to the fort hospital," he rasped at Marcus and Lucius, pointing at Brutus. With his sword drawn he strode to the prone Celt and sliced off his right ear with a single slash. Turning his back, he left the red haired girl sobbing as she tore strips from her skirt and began wrapping them around the bleeding man's head. He started back to the fort without another utterance.

Chapter Five

Legate Peterna Maxinius dipped his pen nib in black ink and wrote to Emperor Hadrian for a second time. Peterna knew his men were becoming idle. *Use makes men ready* was a phrase his father had often spoken. And to quote Vegetius, *if you want peace, prepare for war*, then you had his reasoning for arguing with the highest ranked man in the Known World. He was baiting himself to the African tigers with this disrespect for orders. Never before had he disputed even a single order, but he felt so strongly that advance was the only possible solution to their fragile safety in the area, and therefore to the safety of the structure of the Valiant Empire, that he was prepared to speak out and be judged.

> *As a loyal Imperialist, I must advise you reconsider.*
> *Advancement is imperative or Rome will begin its fall.*
> *Signs of a barbarian rising from within are evident.*
> *Troop morale is low.*
> *If you want peace prepare for war.*

He wax sealed the scroll and packaged it round the piece of wood as Hadrian had done with his, re-using the cotton, sacking cloth and leather wrappings he'd undone earlier. The package would leave tomorrow once the Dispatch rider was rested.

With the letter written, he felt much calmer. Still seated and with his fingers resting lightly on the desk, Peterna closed his eyes. He breathed deeply pushing his stomach out to ensure his lungs were filled to capacity, then exhaled to a slow count of ten, pulling in his abdominal muscles to squeeze the lungs empty. He exercised this controlled breathing four times before re-opening his eyes. The incident in the town was to be addressed.

The Legion had a system in place for dealing with such events. The soldiers involved would be questioned by their Centurion and reprimanded with a condign punishment awarded if necessary. A detailed report would be scribed to the annals, and a summary copied to the legate. Peterna would have no need for involvement unless he so desired. Those brown eyes of Marcus Guintoli came to him. What was it about that boy that disconcerted him? Peterna had seen him charge the Celt and had been quietly impressed by his courage and loyalty to his comrade. His judgement was to leave this one to the Centurion, but why was Cloelia at the scene? Her presence there certainly complicated the situation. Leaning his elbows on to the desk, he clasped his hands with interlocking fingers and rested his chin on them in a quiet pose of thought. Soldiers, men and the army he always understood. His wife, women and politics he sometimes understood. But his daughter…she was an enigma!

"Not enough to do," he thought aloud, speaking the words softly through his still clasped fingers. He continued with his thoughts in silence. The men I can employ. Extra marches, extra weaponry drills. We will prepare for war more earnestly. But what to do with Cloelia? He sighed and made another mental note to speak to Julita about their daughter. It would be a long moon cycle waiting for Hadrian's reply.

······················

Skipping in to the hospital, Cloelia caught her breath as her heart contracted at the sight of Marcus and Lucius laughing with Brutus. They were sharing a conspiratorial story. It was so good to see Brutus laughing and sitting up in bed. His sword arm, the one that had taken the full impact of the bludgeoning, was bandaged securely to a splint and supported by firm pillows so that it struck an angle of ninety degrees from his shoulder pointing towards his toes. His head was also bandaged around the crown. A smile came easily to her face as she approached the trio.

"Brutus, you are looking so much better today. Six sunrises ago I feared you would lose your arm if not your life. Now look at you, sitting up and laughing with the gaiety of a newborn lamb."

Marcus noticed Cloelia was wearing the pendant he'd bought for her and felt a confusing mixture of embarrassment, shame and pleasure. He knew why he'd bought it and so did the gods. Was Flavinus trying to guide him still? Was that why the Brigante girl had been flashed before him, as a sharp reminder of his erroneous ways? But Cloelia was of Roman blood, so he wasn't breaking his vow. Searching for answers to his questions, Marcus had sloped off daily since the fight to visit the tiny temple situated at the bottom of the grassy slope below the bathhouse. He only went there in times of personal strife. Its secluded site not far from the banks of the Tinae Fluvius, at a point where the river was deep and flowing swiftly but silently, purveyed a gentle calm. He'd learned enough to know that his goatskin stashed in the haymow would be better left idle for the present. Cloelia was of a better class than him, and deserved better too. He had no promises for her other than sexual pleasures. Avoiding eye contact, he struggled out a flat-lipped smile at her. Rising from his stool, he indicated to Lucius with a flick of his head towards the door that he was ready to leave.

"Centurion has us down to clear the outside trench of thistle," Lucius told Cloelia in way of an explanation for their departure. "We are being kept busy to keep us from straying into further trouble. Extra duties, extra drills and a big march and training exercise coming up. I think we are being primed for a surge to the north." It wasn't a question, but Lucius was casting his opinion hoping Cloelia may know what the legate's plans were and let a secret slip. He was to be disappointed.

"Papa does not discuss military plans in the house. He definitely thinks we are all idle though. I am to be tutored in music and needlework as soon as a suitable tutor can be found. There will be little leisure time for any of us."

"Seems that you are in the best place Brutus," said Marcus. "May your recovery be complete but slow! Rest easy my friend." With a fleeting glance at Cloelia, he and Lucius left.

"Come and be seated beside me," Brutus said in a bright voice to Cloelia. He could see the sadness flickering through her eyes like tendrils of dark smoke drifting in front of the sunlight. He aimed to restore full shine. "This is like old times, Cloelia." His cheeks dimpled as he smiled and the teasing twinkle that appeared in his eye foretold the beginning of a long, rambling story better than if he'd spoken its commencement. Cloelia couldn't help but smile as she shook her head in exasperation, knowing that Brutus would have her sides aching with extensive laughter by the end of her visit.

....

"Oh, ya poor lass! Look at them scratches." Tamsin yelped with pain as her mother applied a thick poultice of witch hazel to the lacerations. The fire crackled in the charred circle of dirt at the centre of the hut as it devoured the fresh logs Kye had added to it. The round hut was warm with a musty smell of drying earth, except where the chilly outside air was channelling in via the entrance opening, assisting the smoke to swirl away through the roof hole. A heavy blanket was secured across the gap during darkness, but was draped to one side during the day to allow light in. Kye returned to the yard to supervise Aaron who was enjoying splitting logs.

"Hold still child! We have to keep the skin moist as it heals or ya'll be scarred like an old fighting cock-bird. Ya to stay away from that settlement, and ya too Jolinda. I've said it before and I'll say it again, them Romans and all does associate with them, is evil."

Jolinda let her mother say her piece without interrupting. She was ruminating over Tamsin's telling of the fight and events leading up to it. Something didn't seem right. Tamsin had said she was attacked because the Celtic girl's drunken boyfriend had been paying attention to her as she took a drink of water from the fountain. She hadn't encouraged him she'd said, but the girlfriend's temper had flared as suddenly as tinder put to the spill. Came at her like a wildcat possessed of demons. She'd had no choice but to defend herself by fighting back. It was a plausible story but Jolinda sensed her sister was lying.

"Ya weren't in the tavern I hope."

"No, Ma! I told ya…I was drinking from the fountain. It weren't my fault Ma. Ow!"

"Oh, ya poor lamb, nearly done."

Jolinda was not as sympathetic as her mother and locked eyes with Tamsin in a hard gaze. It was Tamsin who looked away first.

The rest of the family was asleep when Jolinda put down her wool knotting and made ready for bed. She was close to completing the first shawl she'd promised to the Roman girl, but the deadline for two would be difficult to meet. Tamsin had at least produced another skein of the gold thread, so she had the materials, just not enough time. As to how Tamsin had acquired the thread, Jolinda didn't know and was too exhausted to spare energy for caring. She turned back the furs and gently climbed in beside her resting sister, careful not to disturb her. The girls had first shared a cot before sharing a bed, and seeing Tamsin in innocent slumber caused an unexpected surge of soft love in Jolinda. Kin has birth roots you can't ignore, she thought as she stroked a ruffled tress away from one of the poultice-lacquered scratches. Kith you choose, but kin you are bound to…like or dislike, agree with or disagree with, you cannot deny that bind. She fell asleep caring and despairing about her sister in equal measures.

....

It was difficult rising before the sun awoke the somnolent land, but the whole Teviot household was about their chores well before light was infused in to the sky behind the crags to the east. Tamsin was adding kindling to the sluggish embers, poking and coaxing the fire to re-ignite to its previous prestige of flames. Jolinda was preparing a pot of root vegetables that would be slowly stewed in a rabbit stock saved from an earlier meal. The big iron pot, smoked black underneath and up its sides, would sit nestled in the very centre of the burning logs. Aaron, the youngest son who stood as tall as his mother's bosom, was helping her scrub and rinse dirty clothes at the sturdy bench table at the far end of the room. They had a system of two wooden vats. One filled with warm water with a root of soapwort resting at the bottom of it. The second filled with clear, cold water. Ma Teviot scrubbed the clothes vigorously in the warm water, stopping periodically to rub soapwort over a garment before going at it again. The saponin in the soapwort created a soft lather, and when she felt the suds begin to dissipate into a film on the water's surface, she'd pass the washing to Aaron. He would gently knead them in his vat of clear water. The clothes would later be draped over a rack fixed to the inside roofing of the laundry hut, a separate, much smaller structure where they could drip without troubling anyone, before being transferred to a similar rack situated in their living hut where the clothes would air in the warmth from the fire.

Kye was in the outhouse across the yard tending to the animals. The wooden building measured seven by five long strides and was home to two nanny goats and sixteen chickens. Constructed from whole trunks of birch saplings lain atop each other and bound by leather strapping, it didn't have a straight line anywhere. The nature of the building materials meant the air circulation was constant, yet it kept warm in winter and cool in summer due to its landscaped position. Using the terrain to its maximum potential, the building snuggled cosily into the corner of a small scarp. Protection from the elements was thus provided on two sides. The roof was made of more lashed saplings, supported by five flat crossbeams with turf lain on top. Over the years, the turf had matted densely and grown to a depth the length of a grown man's forearm and provided wonderful insulation. The roof sloped so that the back of the outhouse where it joined the scarp was higher than the front. This took care of the drainage, although it did cause a muddy area prone to puddling at the entrance. Today was no exception.

Having scattered fresh corn for the chickens and added clean drinking water to the troughs, Kye secured a netted bag of green hay to the other side of the outhouse for the goats to eat. The straw bedding didn't need changing so he stroked and petted the goats, talking soothingly as he adeptly checked them for abnormalities.

"Jolinda'll milk ya later gels. I've got to round them sheep and move them down the slopes. They ain't got ya sense. Needs us folks to lead them ." Satisfied with the condition of the animals he checked the coop whilst the chickens were pecking at the scattered corn. He found two eggs, the first in a while.

"The longer the day, the more chucks lay," he hummed the adage. "Doesn't like the dark hours does ya gels? There'll be catkins on the trees and celandine opening in the fields soon, then ya'll be laying a basketful."

Kye opened the door just wide enough to let himself out and keep the chickens in. As he did so, a fox slinked in like a silent shadow. Kye felt it weave past his legs but didn't have time to react before the sinewy creature had its jaws clasped fatally round a chicken. Realisation of the intruder's presence pervaded and bedlam broke out. Chickens half flew and half ran on extended legs, squawking, flapping and crashing to the sides of the outhouse in their panic. One goat was so startled it sprang vertically with all four hooves leaving the ground simultaneously, then landed on a fleeing chicken creating a cascade of fawny-brown feathers. Skipping a frenzied dance, both goats bleated in urgent despair. But the fox, with its quarry firmly in its mouth, was interested only in retreating to safety, to an undisturbed place where its kill could be eaten. The wild animal's appearance was indication that this was its first meal in a while.

The snatch happened with such speed that the fox was passing Kye at the door, heading for freedom before the boy had even moved. Kye instinctively let his right foot fly in a sweeping kick trying to strike the fox. His leg arced through fresh air, missing its target completely and causing Kye to overbalance, landing on his back with a sickening thud in the puddle, twisting his left knee below him.

Having heard the clamour, Jolinda was already crossing the yard. The fox escaped but she was able to shut the outhouse door to prevent the birds and goats from following. Kye cried in pain as he tried to stand.

"It's me knee. I twisted it."

"Come on, lean on me. We need to get ya inside."

Jolinda looped her brother's left arm round her shoulders and helped him rise. Tamsin arrived and did the same with his right arm. Together they supported him as he hobbled to the house, Aaron meeting them halfway.

"Ma says to sit him by the fire and put his leg up. She's getting a cold compress ready."

"'He's lathered in mud," replied Jolinda. "Find a blanket will ya Aaron. Be quick."

By sundown, Jolinda knew with certainty that she would be unable to finish wool knotting the second shawl by her promised deadline. With Kye out of action, the task of herding the sheep would fall to her. A full two days of work that couldn't wait. It was doubtful she'd even make it to the warehouses. Her resolve was to complete the order as soon as possible and deliver it to the fort. She would have to lie to her mother again.

"Sorry, Ma," she whispered to herself. Jolinda wasn't comfortable lying, but these were desperate times. Breathing deeply and exhaling noisily through her nostrils, the eldest Teviot child drew on inner reserves of strength and stood proud. "Da always did what he had to for the family, and so will I."

Chapter Six

Three sunrises past the deadline, Jolinda was approaching the fort from the north. The air was colder today, yet the wind was absent so it felt warmer. She was thankful the sheep were now close to the homestead as she sensed snow was coming. The sky behind her was laden with pewter coloured clouds that seemed to bulge with heavy pregnancy.

This was the closest she had ever been to the fort and her midriff was fluttering with a mixture of nerves and curiosity. Even from a distance it was an impressive sight, but she'd not gauged its size until now. A massive sloping rampart made of turf loomed eleven or twelve feet high and was surmounted by a five foot wooden parapet. Earthen blocks a foot and a half long, by a foot wide and half a foot thick were stacked one upon the other, overlapping side by side so as to interlock.

In front of the rampart, a pair of ditches surrounded the fort. The first ditch was fifty feet from the wall, V-shaped and nine or ten feet deep. The second ditch was twelve feet closer to the wall and cut differently. It was a distorted V-shape, with the slope nearest to the fort being shallow, whilst the outer slope was nearly vertical. Jolinda couldn't think why, but noted it was cut this way consistently, so concluded it was for a reason.

She scrambled across the ditches feeling very self-conscious. Some soldiers were working further along the inner ditch to her right and she sensed them watching her. Readjusting the package of shawls she was carrying under her left arm, Jolinda advanced towards the gateway along the levelled pathway that abutted the ditch, looking unfinished as though a bridge across was still to be constructed. The gateway consisted of a dual portalled entrance flanked by small guardrooms, with a pair of wooden lookout towers rising above the oaken gates. It was heavily manned.

Feeling unsure, she straightened her back and raised her chin slightly to give herself height and confidence. In her best Latin that was stilted in places, she explained to the nearest guard why she was there.

"I need to deliver this to the Commander's daughter." She extended the package and unravelled it for the guard to inspect. The sentry invited her into the guardroom. He had a pleasant manner but authoritative and orderly. Satisfying himself that neither the parcel nor the visitor concealed any weapons, he took Jolinda's name and scribed it neatly on to a scroll bound to others containing similar entries, adding the reason for her visit alongside and completing the entry with his name, rank and legion. The details were repeated to a smaller independent scroll that he gave to Jolinda.

"Keep this with you and show it to the guards at the Commandant's House. You will need to get it signed here again when you leave the fort. Do you know your way to the house?"

"No, I've not been here before."

"Have you been to any Roman fort?" Jolinda shook her head and must have looked puzzled by the question, as the guard explained.

"Every fort across the whole of the Empire has the same internal layout." He seemed proud of this fact. "It eases navigation and gives any vagrant legionary the immediate comfort of familiarity." Jolinda could see the logic and followed the guard as he moved back outside. Pointing straight ahead, he gave directions to the Commandant's House. "This is the main street, the *Via Praetoria*. It will take you to the *Principia*, that is the administration headquarters." Jolinda was thankful for his patient explanations. "Here the *Via Praetoria* intersects with the *Via Principalis*. Turn left towards the East Gate and the Commandant's House will be on your right. Remember to show your pass to a guard there."

Low wooden barrack buildings, with plastered and whitewashed exteriors, lined both sides of the *Via Praetoria*. The roofs were made of wooden shingles angled off, all to a uniform length. Jolinda was stunned by the contrast to the rusticated civilian settlement, and indeed her own homestead. These buildings were gay and without a ruffle in view. Orderliness was prevalent.

Soldiers came and went in considerable numbers here and Jolinda felt conspicuous in this male dominated realm. She hoped Cloelia would be at home and greet her with friendship. The young Brigante girl was in desperate need of an ally in this unfamiliar world she'd entered. It was like wading through waist deep, cold waters with an unsure footing.

Reaching the road intersection brought fresh astonishment. Jolinda stood and stared across the broad *Via Principalis*. *The Principia* was a vision she could not have imagined. It was made of uniformly cut blocks of buff coloured stone, not timber. A hundred feet wide, it stood a full storey higher than the barracks. A long portico with ten or more stone columns graced the lower storey at the front and flanked an arched gateway in the centre. The angled roof of the portico matched the higher angled roof of the building, both were fitted with contrasting terracotta tiles. It was beautiful and so unexpected.

The guards too were beautiful in their regalia, standing in pairs, one facing the other, at every entrance. Wearing full armour, each was holding a long spear at an angle of forty-five degrees from their feet, so the glinting tips met in the centre. Each guard also held a shield at his side. Bright blue and decorated with a painted design of white eagle wings and yellow thunderbolts, it contrasted with their cherry red capes creating a living tableau of mosaic colour.

Turning left, Jolinda could see a second stone building as equally elaborate in its style but smaller. This too was heavily guarded and she knew it must be the Commandant's House. She felt the eyes of the land staring at her as she showed her pass to a guard.

"Wait here," the guard ordered, then disappeared into the house leaving her with the second guard. The first snowflakes began to fall as Jolinda waited nervously, all conversation eluding her as she again felt the eyes of the land focusing on her, none more so than those of the soldier beside her. Cloelia's greeting could not have been more welcoming, and Jolinda could not have been more relieved. A special bond between the girls was formed in that single moment.

....

"I will walk to the fort gate with you," Cloelia said. "Which gate did you come in through?"

"The North Gate," replied Jolinda.

"Let me wear my shawl. Orange or purple, Mama, which do you think?" Cloelia held the shawls to her face in turn for her mother to choose. She was so pleased Jolinda had come to the fort. She'd feared never to see her again when she'd not been at the warehouses as arranged, and had felt so let down. Unreasonably let down, and a doleful cloud had engulfed her that she'd been struggling to disperse since. Jolinda's visit had dissipated the cloud instantly, replacing it with a surge of joy.

"The purple shawl, I think," Julita decided in answer to her daughter's question. She smiled and raised her eyebrows at Jolinda, silently inviting her opinion. Jolinda responded with her own smile. The apprehension she had felt whilst waiting for entry into the Commandant's house earlier, had been extinguished by the warmth and respect with which she'd been treated within. Flickers of the same apprehension had flared during awkward moments of conversation, but were always snuffed immediately by the genuine kindness towards her and easy flowing laughter of the two Roman women. Jolinda had spoken more than she intended, lulled by the gentle non-probing conversation. Julita had learnt a lot about her daughter's new Brigante friend.

She learned of a sister and two brothers, all younger and all helping their widowed mother to maintain a homestead a few miles to the north of the fort. She learned the father died just over two moon cycles ago, but she didn't know the cause of death. The topic was obviously still wretched for the girl. Yet she sensed a warm eagerness for life amidst adversity, and an open integrity in this handsome girl who dressed with no adornment, yet seemed completely at ease without it.

The only concern this unexpected visitor had brought was that she was at the fort without her mother's knowledge. She'd been honest enough to admit that her mother would not approve, but had been reluctant to convey why, saying only that her mother had good reason that Jolinda respected but was unable to comply with. Julita chose not to press the issue. She would mention it to Peterna though, as she felt he should be aware of the feelings of the local tribes-people. Any animosity towards Rome was a danger to their position.

"Yes, the purple shawl," agreed Jolinda. "Like the ling that smothers the hills, turning them beautiful hues of purple 'n' mauve at sun-season's end."

"Or the swathes of lavendula that decorate the edges of the olive groves along the coast of Italia. Their perfume pervades on the warm breezes. Look, I have nurtured a sample from seed brought with me." Julita crossed to the large, stone sill beneath the window returning with a potted cluster of lavendula. "Try it in your homestead. It clearly likes the local soil and I believe it will cope with the chill of winter." Jolinda received the gift with a warm smile. "Let the flower spikes dry to seed on the stems before harvesting."

"Oh, Mama, enough about the flowers," groaned Cloelia rolling her eyes, "Jolinda wishes to get home in daylight! Please save the harvesting lecture for her next visit. You will be my craft tutor then Jolinda, oh I cannot wait!" Cloelia let out a mouse-like squeal of delight as she excitedly pulled Jolinda to her feet, swung her round in a full circle before skipping her out towards the front door. They heard Julita call after them.

"Your father must agree to it first."

"Oh, Papa will agree. He said I was to be tutored in craftwork."

"Needlework was his wish."

"Wool knotting is a type of needlework, Mama. It will do and I will get my way with Papa, do not doubt it." With that Cloelia and Jolinda were gone, leaving Julita to giggle at how she indeed did not doubt that Cloelia would quite easily win her father over. Why else does a daughter have eyelashes?

....

The snow had stopped falling and with the lifting of the clouds the temperature had dropped to below freezing. The finger-deep layer of snow was already crusted with ice crystals. As Jolinda left the fort via the North Gate, her mind was consumed with all that had happened inside. If she was to visit the fort regularly, she would have to tell Ma, but how was she to explain it? Perhaps Ma wouldn't be against her tutoring a Roman, perhaps it was just trading with the Romans she didn't like. Giving a service for money was really the same as trading, Jolinda knew this, but she needed to think of an effective argument to win her mother over and this line of thought seemed her best chance. Teaching the Romans a Brigante craft was after all a start, albeit a small one, in preserving their customs and even spreading them. A Brigante tutoring a Roman…would this persuade Ma?

Still deep in thought and trying to decide the best opening phrase for broaching the subject at home, Jolinda reached the inner ditch surrounding the fort and dropped down its shallow side. She was about to learn why it was cut in the distorted V-shape she noticed earlier, and it was to be a lesson she would always remember.

Standing at the bottom of the ditch, she was taken aback at the sheerness of the outer slope. Scrambling down it from the other direction had been relatively easy. Climbing up was not so easy. The small layer of iced-topped snow made the task even more difficult. Three times Jolinda got part way up, just to slide gracefully back to her starting point. The more she compressed the snow, the more slippery it became. She moved to a patch of virgin snow to try afresh, succeeded in gaining a little more height, but ended up back in the ditch. This could be fun under different circumstances she mused. Kye and Aaron would love it, and she wouldn't mind if she was in their company, had time to spare and felt she wasn't trapped. Instead frustration was mingling with embarrassment, as she was sure the guards on the lookout towers were laughing at her. Refusing to look round, she concentrated on climbing the sharp grade again.

"It is a steep climb, is it not?"

Jolinda was startled by the deep voice, lost her momentum and slid down the scarp in another thwarted attempt, arriving spread-eagled at the bottom, looking up at the feet of the soldier standing at the top of the ditch. Her clothes were now sodden and her hair was clinging in wet straggles across her face and shoulders.

"Ya made me jump! I lost me grip! I would've made it that time!"

"I agree that was your best effort so far, but you will not get to the top without help, not in these slippery conditions. We cut the ditch this shape to dupe would-be attackers by inviting them forward with the shallow slope, then trapping them on the nearly vertical unseen outer slope. As they flee, it is simple target practise for our javelins. A legionary's craft."

Jolinda didn't like the image it conjured but could see it was a simple yet effective defence. She stood up smoothing her skirt and found a sharpness still in her voice.

"Are all Roman crafts laced with violence?" she challenged.

"A crafted army hastens peace. That surely is a worthwhile craft or would you have us all talented in needlework only?"

His words were curt and direct, yet his voice did not sound mocking. Jolinda looked at him to determine whether he was being scornful or not. He wasn't. Her gaze fell upon a face full of warm strength. Short, dark hair framed skin the colour and smoothness of a ripened acorn. A long, straight nose pinched in slightly along the ridge causing a faceted appearance that was matched by his angular jaw that tapered to a square-cut chin. Eyebrows arched boldly above eyes that captivated Jolinda by their deepness. She allowed herself a moment to swim in the conker-brown pools.

"We had peace before ya army came. Now ya chase peace via conquest. Why don't ya leave us our lands and let us be? We only defend our Brigante existence."

Jolinda was surprised to see a flicker of pain ripple through his eyes. She hadn't meant to be so bigoted and blushed.

"You are Brigante then? I thought you were with Rome, you speak Latin and your name…your name, it sounds Roman. I thought…no matter," his mood had changed from jaunty to melancholy.

"How do ya know my name?" Jolinda challenged again. The conversation was becoming disconcerting. This man was confusing her on every level of consciousness and beyond. He remained silent for a moment before answering, distracted by a memory Jolinda could see was deeply painful. He was filling her with many questions.

"Uh...Cloelia..." he automatically glanced back to the fort as he spoke her name. "I was in the guardroom opposite when you left. The snow storm gave us a reason to retreat from our thistle-pulling task." Jolinda recalled seeing two soldiers working in the ditch when she arrived. He tried to inject a little humour into the conversation by adding, "A tactical manoeuvre as the thistles had us flanked and outnumbered." He gave a wry smile that disappeared quickly as Jolinda didn't respond to it. Her tone was still aggressive.

"What else did Cloelia tell ya about me?"

"She was very excited that you were to be her needlework tutor. She said..."

"Wool knotting...not needlework!" snapped Jolinda.

"Yes...indeed...wool knotting...sorry..."

Suddenly Jolinda smiled widely and laughed, holding her palms upward at waist height and gently shaking her head. The soldier's expression was one of such complete complexity as to the workings of a woman's mind, that it traversed the racial divide more swiftly than any words were able. He stood indecisive as a rabbit in danger. Jolinda couldn't help but laugh harder as she realised the absurdity of the scene fully. There she was standing in a snowy ditch, there he was standing inert at the edge. One wet and bedraggled in dull woollen garb, the other sharp and bright in Roman uniform, verging on an argument that had begun in politics and ended in wool knotting.

Her merriment was infectious. When both drew breath from laughing, Jolinda willingly sank into the deep, dark pools as their eyes met again.

"Jolinda Teviot."

"Marcus Guintoli, at your service. My mother's favourite herb," he said, nodding at the lavendula plant.

"Come on," laughed Jolinda hitching her skirt and running at the scarp, "race ya to the top!"

"You will not make it," was his reply, running at the slope too.

"Just ya watch me."

....

"You are still beautiful, my wife. The years have increased your curves."

"And that is to your liking?"

"It is," Peterna's answer was muffled as his tongue sought her nipple.

"It is the softening hue from the oil lamp that is my ally," Julita smiled. She parted her legs with a gentle gasp as her husband's hand slid purposefully across her stomach to her groin and she willingly let his fingers open the delicate folds of skin that lay hidden to the sexually inexperienced.

He gave a soft groan of his own as his fingers explored her. He would bring her to an orgasm with his hands before entering her for his release, having learned from his young, hurried days that her complete arousal would heighten his own pleasure.

He moved his mouth from her nipple to her ear breathing warm air into it as he nibbled the lobe. Julita concentrated on the sensations rising within. They were quite without parallel. A soft cry preceded short gasps as her anticipation grew. Arching her back slightly she reached for her breasts moving her body with the rhythm of his strokes. Peterna's erection throbbed as she panted out her climax and he adjusted his position to keep his own orgasm at bay.

As Julita quieted she rose and turned onto her knees. Oblivious of the cold night she discarded the furs and straddled her husband, eager for him to enter her now, aware that a greater sexual acme was still to come. Slowly his member filled her. Peterna's hands were around Julita's hips and they moved in rhythm. Peterna gave a guttural grunt, fuelling the intensity. As his involuntary groans became louder and the moment of ejaculation burst through him, he held her firmly down pushing hard with his pelvis to penetrate deeply. She screamed out a second surge of pleasure.

Lying closely beside each other in the mellow aftermath of their lovemaking, Peterna was the first to speak.

"I saw Cloelia walking towards the North Gate with another girl today, with long, dark hair. Who is she?"

"A charming girl from a local Brigante family."

"And what business did a Brigante girl have on the fort with Cloelia?" Julita noted the dubious tone in her husband's voice and choosing her words carefully, said:

"It seems she was fulfilling a promise made to our daughter by bringing garments Cloelia had purchased. Beautiful shawls, fine craftsmanship." Julita was highlighting qualities that she knew Peterna would admire. "It must have taken quite some pluck for her to have come alone. She spoke Latin quite well too, once you accustom yourself to her accent."

"You are leading up to something woman, what is it?"

Julita laughed softly.

"Have we been married so long that you know my thoughts?"

"A friend is another self," he quoted. "And a wife of two decades must be an enduring friend."

He was speaking earnestly and Julita pressed herself a little closer, thankful for his love and protection, thankful for his being. It had not been easy watching him leave for battle over the years, praying to every god available for his safety. Perhaps it was the battles that had kept their love fresh by emphasising the fragility of life.

"The girl's name is Jolinda and she will make an excellent tutor in needlework for Cloelia. I have hired her services at two sestertii per session. She plans to come to the fort one morning in every seven. Cloelia walked to the North Gate with her to arrange a regular entry pass. I am quite sure it is a good deal, having seen the girl's wool knotting."

"What is wool knotting?" queried Peterna.

"It's a Brigante craft, a type of needlework that involves winding sheep's wool round long, blunt needles made from wood or bone. I think Jolinda said you could use goat's hair too, it sounds fascinating." Julita was genuinely interested. "It is a start towards the tutoring you spoke of following that unhappy incident in the settlement."

Peterna had not spoken in detail to Julita about the fight he and Cloelia had witnessed, nor had she gleaned much information of it from her daughter, other than that one of the legionaries who had entertained them at her dinner party was recovering in the hospital, having sustained a broken arm and head wounds. Julita sensed the topic wasn't finished with yet, and was probing gently as a nurse would tend a healing sore. She let her fingers move in soothing circles ruffling the grey flecked dark hairs on his chest as she asked the next question.

"Are you worried about an uprising from the local tribes?" Julita was wondering when she should mention the animosity towards Rome held by the Brigante girl's mother. Peterna was silent for longer than seemed right causing Julita to still her fingers and raise her head to look at her husband. His expression was one of indecision. Studying his face for a moment she spoke again.

"Yes, I believe you do. Before the settlement incident I saw you receive a package from a Dispatch rider. Now you wish to keep Cloelia closer to home by occupying her time. I have noticed the increase in drills and hear rumours on the fort that a big march and training exercise are planned. Marriage of longevity does indeed allow some words unspoken to be heard my husband, but not all. Tell me, are you preparing to defend our position or is an attack for territory gain in your mind?"

His ice-blue eyes, so untypical of a Roman, reflected the low lamplight as a tarn throws back the light of the moon. His next words stabbed alarm in Julita's heart.

"I wish you to begin making arrangements for yourself and Cloelia to go to Rome and remain there until I can join you."

"Peterna, no! I will not."

She was sitting now and he mirrored her position, resting a hand on either shoulder with arms outstretched so he could look at her properly. His gaze was intense but she met and held it with her own, fired by defiance.

"What talk is this?"

"You must do it for Cloelia. She is at an impressionable age and this isolated frontier is unfair to her. She needs Rome with its Italian culture and finery. Great things are happening there. Have you heard that the arched dome is in progress for the Pantheon? Cloelia should see this and be a part of its birth, be a part of the great city that pulsates as the heart for which we fight. She cannot go alone."

Julita was absorbing his speech. Breaking his eyes from hers by looking down, he continued in a more subdued tone.

"It has taken longer than I expected to conquer Britannia, Julita. I am sorry. I had expected to sweep the north as Augusta did the south and already be idling my last few years to retirement as a content man in Rome, sharing daily roast dinners and theatre visits with you and marrying our daughter to a wealthy member of senate. I had not accounted for Hadrian's ineptitude. Perhaps…" he faltered, "perhaps my loyalty has been misguided."

The majority of what her husband had said was not a surprise to Julita. She knew of his desire for an opulent retirement in Rome, with an arranged marriage for Cloelia. It had been this dream that had lifted him through difficult times. This dream and his insatiable need to continually prove his complete allegiance to The Empire that had kept them on the move from forests to shores as a political army strategist. She adored his Scandinavian blue eyes, but cursed all those who had taunted him for them. She had tried many, many times to persuade him that his duty to Rome's Emperor and citizens was more than fulfilled and he was overdue a less hostile posting. Let the senate negotiate fresh borders with diplomacy, she would argue. Rome is strong enough to do that now thanks to the scars you bear. Then he was chosen to add impetus to the stalled conquest of northern Britannia and she knew they would go. For the love of a man she was travelling to the end of the World, for the love of an Empire and all it stood for he was leading her there. So to hear him speak so lowly of Hadrian was a shock.

Peterna was wrestling with how much detail he should give to his wife. In the norm they did not discuss military issues, but in the norm neither did he ask her to leave for Rome with their daughter.

"Hadrian has refused my request for more troops. I have advised him to reconsider. Troop morale is low and there are signs of an uprising. Without reinforcements we will be delayed on this frontier and time is not on our side with Cloelia. This spring the bathhouse circuit will not be of innocent amusement to me." He was referring to the walk Cloelia had made when the evenings were lighter. The route took her down to the river passing the bathhouse when it was at its busiest, then looped back via the barracks. She was showing too much interest in the legionaries, it was not part of his dream.

"You have never asked me to leave you before."

"Cloelia has never been of this age before. Neither has it been this dangerous. Julita, it is unstable politically and it seems I must fight my own with reason as sharp as the sword that slays my enemy. My focus must be without distraction. The sooner it is done, the sooner I will join you. Write to your cousin in Rome and I will send it with my next Dispatch rider. It will take time to organise your arrangements, meanwhile I agree to the Brigante wool knotting tutor. We may build an ally in that camp and I do want Cloelia occupied on the fort other than by the legionaries."

…………………

A fresh snowfall was making it easy for Kye to track Jolinda's footsteps. He was curious to know where she was going. It was unusual for his sister to be secretive, yet she had lied to Ma, he was sure of it. He knew Ma was gullible.

Without Da around to frighten the truth from him, he had deceived her himself. Deceived them all in fact. The secret was to keep your habits varied. He always chose a different time and venue for his meetings with the Picts.

A small tribe of them had come down from the Caledonian Mountains last summer and he had first met the two brothers whilst on a hunting foray with Da. Da had thought them troublemakers and ordered Kye to stay away, but a lasting impression of wild tattoo-brandished roughnecks was now too intriguing to ignore. They displayed a savagery above that of the farming Brigantes and Kye, seeking a little adventure, had recently made contact with them. Yes, he was fast becoming a master of deception and knew a lie when he heard one, so what was Jolinda up to?

He could feel excitement mingling with apprehension as he tracked his sister closer and closer to the formidable Roman fort. The crags in the countryside afforded him some concealment until the landscape flattened four or five hundred feet before the first defensive ditch. Kye chose to remain hidden behind the last rocky outcrop. He didn't want to be seen by the Roman guards. How would he explain what he was doing? From where he was, it looked as though his sister's tracks went all the way to the gate of the fort. Kye was astonished. Was Jolinda inside the fort? Ma would take the meat cleaver to her if she knew. No wonder she'd lied. But why was she there, what was her business? He would wait and catch her by surprise as she returned. The Picts were always telling him that surprise was a great strategy.

....

The regulation pace of twenty-five miles in five hours was not being met in the snowy conditions the Fourth Cohort found itself marching in. It was to be expected, but Legate Maxinius had put out orders for this to be achieved. He wanted the men to be pushed to fatigue. The exercise would not harm them, and neither would the discipline. If Rome was to gain its glory, these men were facing some harsh battles. The *Brittunculi* were savages and would fight as savages, making them as reckless and dangerously unpredictable as a rat trapped in a corner. Having fought alongside legionaries under the command of Trajan in Dacia, he knew the advantage of having discipline, order and fitness. They were weapons in addition to swords and shields, and he would send no man into battle without them.

The march was unnaturally quiet. The snow was muting the usual rhythmic beat of iron studs upon road that so often inspired the marching songs of the soldiers. The five columns of ninety men each tramped in silence, save the rhythmic chink of scabbards against metal lorica. All units now favoured this new armoured tunic over the older style chain mail, as it allowed more freedom of movement. Full battle gear of lorica, helmet, groin guard, greaves, sword, dagger, shield and javelin were always carried during training exercises. No allowances made.

As Maxinius was riding his horse back along the length of the columns, he could hear the brutal comments of encouragement from the centurions and their second-in-command optios, urging more speed from their weary men. Most centurions and optios were well chosen and respected individuals who led by example, but some appointments were badly made, and poor leadership by a centurion could prove disastrous in battle. Maxinius was using the training marches as an opportunity to assess how his officers were interacting with the legionaries. Each of the ten cohorts on the fort was being assessed in turn. He was comfortable with what he was seeing in the Fourth Cohort. Morale was lower than he wished, but this was a general problem throughout the legion and one he hoped he was beginning to resolve. The army had been static for too long. They needed to strike a decisive blow to the Britons to reassert their dominance. Hadrian must be made to see this. These were good fighting men, loyal, and they deserved better than to be left to rot as discarded compost with the local tribes picking at them like birds on a worm pile.

The chance attack by the lone Brigante that caused the death of the Standard Bearer still preyed on his mind. It had been a strange incident, involving the Fourth Cohort he recalled. Glancing through the ranks as his mare trotted by he looked for the two legionaries whom he had questioned over the incident. Their names escaped him but their faces would not, especially the taller of the two, whom he had last seen astride a beaten Celt.

Marcus and Lucius were keeping their heads low. The last thing they wanted was to be spotted by the legate. Following the fight, they had been very relieved not to be hauled in front of him, much preferring to endure the interrogation of their Centurion. Marcus could still feel the legate's intense icy stare piercing his conscience during the inquest over Flavinus. As for the dinner entertaining, Brutus was still paying for involving them in that! They really needed a spell of anonymity and Marcus knew he would have to stay away from Cloelia. He did not relish explaining to her but knew he must. She was a sweet girl offering an attractive package but he could not take the risk of further jeopardising his career - he could end up in the gladiator's ring. Anyhow, his mind was full of a more serious problem that he was struggling with. A memory of laughter and beauty sliding in the snow was bewitching his dreams, yet he remembered his vow to Flavinus.

....

Brutus was restless for the Fourth Cohort to return from its march. His broken arm was causing him pain and he was tetchy. It wasn't mending well. The camp physician was talking of manipulating and re-setting it, a process akin to torture, which did not fill him with cheer. Better that than a useless arm though. If he were unable to throw a javelin the army would deport him to Rome on a pro rata pension, a pittance, not enough to survive on. His prospects would be gloomy. He was cheered even less when he thought of his chances with Cloelia. He let slip a curse of Cupid, then quickly corrected it with a double prayer. He would need the god of love to help him couple in marriage with her. His reliance on Cloelia adopting the modern idea of marrying for love and not prospects was even greater now. Although legionaries were not supposed to marry, many resolved the problem by illegal ceremonies, using their salaries to rent homes in the local settlements, sneaking to their wives whenever chance allowed. Would this suffice for a legate's daughter though? It was unlikely. Nay, it was impossible! He slapped his thigh crossly to be rid of the dream. Damn, he needed a session in the bathhouse! Where was the Fourth?

Heading along the *Via Praetoria* past the granary, towards the South Gate, to await the arrival of his unit, it took three shouts by Cloelia to attract his attention. Turning, he saw her smiling and waving from a window at the back of the Commandant's house. She was saying something but he was too far away to hear properly, so using his good arm, he cupped his hand round his ear to indicate the problem. Cloelia shouted the words louder, but it was still no good. Brutus shook his head and repeated the action of cupping his hand round his ear. Understanding, Cloelia held both arms in front of her, palms down with fingers spread, signalling him to wait where he was. Brutus showed his agreement by a nod of his head and a wave of his hand. When Cloelia reached him, he was sitting on a sack of corn, the first in a row of six that were all leaning against the stone column bases of the granary, waiting to be transported to the bakery. The granary itself was made of timber and always a busy building, although the bustling activity did not extend to the side Brutus was sitting. Jolinda was with Cloelia.

"Thank you for waiting Brutus. Where are you going? Am I keeping you from something important? It is good to see you out of the hospital. How is your arm today? Oh, it is hurting you, I can see you are in pain. You should not be out, I will speak to the duty surgeon, why ever do they force you on to your feet so soon?"

For the first time since the early darkness of that day when sleep had been overpowered by pain, Brutus found a reason to smile and it felt good. His wide grin dimpled his cheeks and crinkled the skin around his eyes.

"Cloelia, you are a tonic more powerful than any salve, potion or opiate available to our medical staff and I thank you for it. Are you aware that you are rambling in the manner for which I am reputed? Our conversation could last until the day folds to nightfall. A thought that delights me I would add. The hours hold no pain with you beside me."

The concerns Brutus was having with regard to deportment were adding urgency to his courtship of Cloelia. Before his accident, patience had been his plan, trusting in Cupid to guide her to him in time without his pressing her. The threat of deportment was truncating this time and his plan needed rethinking. Although still trusting in Cupid, he was choosing to add some mortal assistance. He fervently hoped the gods would not take offence at his meddling with fate, but the stakes were high and worth gambling on. Not seeming to notice his compliment and laughing at his reference to her rambling, Cloelia asked again where he was going. Jolinda was standing quietly a little behind and to her friend's right. Brutus glanced at her and Cloelia, apologising for her lack of decorum, introduced them.

"Miss Teviot, Jolinda, has been tutoring me all morning with little to show for her diligence. I have much wool knotting practise to do between now and next week." Cloelia smiled at her friend.

"Ya did well. Ya can't expect to master it in a day, it does take practise. I've been knotting since a pip." Seeing their confused expressions at the phrase, she added, "It means since I was young."

"We were just checking on the weather and preparing to leave when we saw you passing. Jolinda has to leave via the North Gate and I thought you may like to walk that way with us if you are not busy."

"It will do my credibility in the barracks no harm at all to escort two beautiful ladies through our fine fort." He wanted to add more to let Cloelia know his deep feelings but the presence of Jolinda was making it difficult. He would wait until they were alone on the return walk then seize this unexpected opportunity. It became suddenly important to get going.

Brutus was to decide later that the next turn of events was a direct slap from Cupid, a rebuke, to remind him who controlled the fortunes and fate. Rising from his seat of corn he caught his boot on the tufted corner of the sack and fell sprawling to the ground. He fell onto his uninjured side into soft snow, but the jolt as he landed sent an excruciating rod of pain searing through his damaged arm. He cried out an expletive that Cloelia and Jolinda ignored as they went to his aid. He lay still a moment, his eyes tightly shut with lips pulled back baring clenched teeth, consumed wholly by the agony until Cloelia's voice came drifting through his senses. Then a trumpet sounded and he could hear the shouts of the centurions, the Fourth was returning. He heard Jolinda's accented Latin telling him it was all right to take his time before moving, but it wasn't all right. He wanted to scream that it wasn't all right. He was missing his chance to be alone with Cloelia and tell her of his feelings. The returning cohort would be marching past them soon, and in it's midst was Marcus Guintoli, long time friend, comrade, confidante – except in the subject of Cloelia.

He winced at the memory of the dinner party and how he had introduced them. It wasn't odium he felt towards Marcus, but inordinate annoyance. Having spilt blood together in battle, sharing the adrenalin euphoria with the repugnance of war and its intimacy with death, having shared barracks, and the daily rituals of eating together, sleeping, washing, working, socialising, constantly being together - he, Brutus, Marcus, Lucius, and Flavinus too before the gods claimed him for their world, had acquired an unspoken bond of kinship. With it came a love and greater understanding of the other man, than of one's own self. Brutus knew that the union of Marcus with Cloelia was a mismatch of personalities, yet he held no malice, such was his love and understanding of Marcus. He knew it was without intention that her sweetness would be slowly ground like corn milled to flour. It was all as clear as spring water to him and painful waiting for Cloelia to see with clarity too. The charm Marcus unwittingly exuded was blinding her.

Damn his arm and the cursed Celt who'd smashed it. Damnation to the heart of *Acheron* that he was visiting the whorehouse the one day Lucius wasn't satisfied with one whore, deciding to take a second without paying the first. The Celt had mistakenly thought it was he. Who would believe he was innocent in the resulting fight? An unfortunate series of events that may now end his army career and force him from the people he wanted to be with. Yet there was still time to speak alone with Cloelia before Marcus marched by with the unit to distract her.

With a renewed urgency, Brutus rose to his feet. A debilitating wave of nausea immediately blackened his vision, causing him to sink to his knees to avoid fainting.

"Brutus, you are not fit to walk anywhere," stated Cloelia. "Jolinda will wait here with you, I will fetch an orderly." She was gone.

Chapter Seven

Sitting with his back leaning against the sack of corn that had tripped him, pain fogging his mind, Brutus listened to the troop of men marching closer. He found the familiar shouts and bellowed orders comforting. Becoming drowsy he welcomed the respite of sleep as his eyes rolled behind closing eyelids and his head lolled towards his chest as the muscles in his neck loosened their support. Concerned he was losing consciousness, Jolinda began asking questions, the first thoughts that sprung to mind.

"Where's ya family home, Brutus? Are you from Rome? Do ya have any brothers or sisters? I'm the eldest of four, with a sister 'n' two brothers for me sins." Receiving little response other than a weak mumble, she changed her tack. "Wake up Brutus! Brutus! Listen, do ya hear the trumpets?" Her sharper tone brought him round and Jolinda smiled with relief.

"It is the Fourth," he told her.

"Is that your unit?"

"Yes, Brutus Antonini, Third Century of the Fourth Cohort of the Twentieth Legion, at your service. In pain with a buggered arm and decimated dreams, ill favoured by Cupid and Fortuna together it seems, destined to be mute of his love to Cloelia Maxinius, thus it goes unnoticed, with the sweetest taste of honey teasing his palate yet he is not offered to swallow the golden nectar. Fearful of being cast adrift without purpose and torn from men he cherishes more than a brother of blood, men of the Fourth, Marcus Guintoli and Lucius Seniarus, barrack and soul companions. Dour, resigned to failure and feeling very sorry for himself, wondering if joining Flavinus in death may be less grievous, Brutus Antonini at your service."

Jolinda raised her eyebrows as she absorbed the tirade. A reflex flutter of warmth was jostling the inside of her chest at the mention of Marcus's name.

"Cold as well," he added.

"That was quite a speech."

Brutus did not reply. He was staring blankly, looking at her but not seeing her, sullen in his thoughts, not caring that he'd spoken so openly to a stranger. Wanting to keep him focusing and awake, Jolinda persisted with the conversation, conscious that the noise of the marching unit was getting louder as it neared the fort.

"Don't ya talk some slaver!" Her sharp rebuke caught his attention. "And there's me thinking ya Romans is full of fighting pride, when all ya full of is sop 'n' gush. We all have problems. A dose of Brigante spirit is what ya need. Talk to Cloelia. Never say die!" Realising it was an unfortunate phrase to say to a soldier, Jolinda flushed and a short silence pursued.

"I'm sorry," she said. "Ya in pain. How did it get broken?" She smiled softly as she added, "that's ya arm I mean, not ya heart."

Brutus grimaced expelling an audible breath as he readjusted his sitting position.

"A brawl with a Celt in the civilian settlement, nearly a moon cycle ago now. A misunderstanding at the tavern over two whores." He was beyond wondering what this girl may think of him, he'd said so much already and it was healing to talk his problems aloud. The aura of optimism Jolinda emitted was gently lifting his mood. "You probably heard about the fight, it caused quite a stir. The legate is rarely seen in the settlement and he arrived just as Marcus flew at the Celt. The Celt's attack on me stopped the two whores in their fight Marcus tells me. The red-headed trollop was the Celt's daughter apparently. Do not know about the other – a dark haired beauty Lucius was happy to employ at the time."

Snakes of ice slithered into knots in Jolinda's stomach as she listened. She didn't want to believe what she knew. The shards of information now recovered in whole slotted into an ugly mosaic. Tamsin, her sister, was a whore to the Romans. Her face burned with shame. Brutus mistook her blush as a continuation of her previous embarrassment.

"Thank you Jolinda, Brigante friend of Cloelia Maxinius, now also, instiller of optimism and firm ally of Brutus Antonini in his quest of happiness." He extended his good arm for Jolinda to shake and the pair shared an earnest gaze as the first ranks of the marching column came into view through the South Gate and Cloelia with two orderlies carrying a stretcher appeared trotting towards them from the north.

....

Cloelia and the orderlies arrived first.

"The pain is easier now," lied Brutus. "The stretcher is not necessary, I can walk to the hospital." Seeing the orderlies exchange an irritated frown at being called on a fool's errand, he added "sorry lads, I confess to a little overacting on behalf of the ladies here." Although as a legionary Brutus outranked the orderlies in status, he chose not to rankle them. Instead, he winked and displayed a discrete hand gesture, hoping the men would think he'd been playing the sympathy ruse. No way was he lying on a stretcher for all his officers to see as the unit marched past. Advertising his slow recovery would not assist his cause in staying on the fort, neither would a stretcher report on his hospital notes. Jolinda had given him renewed hope and determination. He was no longer feeling utter despair at his situation, but ready to grapple with the gods to stay with the Twentieth Legion if he must.

Rising slowly and keeping his head low to avoid a repeat of the earlier faintness, Brutus summoned reserves of will power to keep the rising vomit that threatened to spew from surfacing. Recalling words he had once memorised from a comic play written by Plautus, he spoke with dramatic intent in an attempt to disguise his true sorry physical state.

"Be gone fellow idlers, make haste to your work, whilst I away to mine. My legion needs me. You are dismissed with a kick of a mule, sirs."

An orderly snorted a chortle at Brutus's acting, and Cloelia laughed with relief at his apparent recovery.

"Brutus, really!" she admonished him with a smile. "If I were not so relieved to see you well enough to tease, I would be hurt by your earlier prank. Please do not attempt to trick me again or how will I know what to believe?" She apologised to the orderlies for wasting their time. Only Jolinda saw through his antics, yet she remained silent. Consumed with shame for her sister, wanting to leave the fort immediately, to run and hide from her newly found Roman friends. It was all too confusing.

The First Century of the Fourth Cohort was passing the small group now. Judging by the exhausted state of some of the men, the orderlies decided their assistance might well be needed at the hospital so they left at a jog. Being so close to a marching cohort in full battle dress was a new experience for Jolinda. During the previous summer she had sighted them snaking across the hills at a distance, looking like a glinting reptile described in the legends of ancient monsters, but never had she been so close. The uniformity was numbing. The definable individual melded to an indomitable whole. No group of native warriors with their discordant garments and assortment of weapons could look as insuperable. A desperate desire to return to the familiarity of home swooped through her.

"Cloelia, I must be going to me home." Jolinda almost implored her friend.

"Oh, Jolinda, no, stay and watch them all pass by. Tell her to stay, Brutus." Cloelia felt pride mingle with girlish excitement whenever she saw the army march. Brutus, struggling to maintain his act of good health, knew he must disband the threesome as soon as possible. At that moment he would welcome a dark, solitary pit just to moan alone in.

"The legate will not be pleased to see us idle," he said.

Cloelia's face contorted into a grimace. She knew Brutus was speaking sense in this matter. Papa's mood had been quite taut of late and she'd noticed a tense atmosphere between her parents that was unusual.

"Is he with this march?"

"I can see his horse coming through the gate." Brutus indicated the direction with a nod of his head. "We would be well advised to disappear like dormice in daylight."

"I was hoping to see Marcus, but you are right. Thank you for your prudence, Brutus." Kissing him lightly on the cheek, she collected Jolinda's hand in her own, "come on, we had better hurry."

For a moment Brutus watched them skip off before turning away from his unit and making his way between two rows of columns supporting the granary buildings. Once out of sight, he gave in to his body and sinking to his knees stained the snow with vomit.

....

Capable of accommodating fifty men at a time, the bathhouse was always noisy with flushing water and the raucous laughter of off duty soldiers. It was a place where the discipline and rigour of life in the legion could be forgotten and the swapping of lies and embellished stories were expected. Two small groups were gambling in games of knuckleball and dice, sitting on the flagstone floor in two circles near to the statue of Fortuna. The end of one game was announced with loud cheers from the winners and curses from the losers.

Entering the big rectangular changing rooms, Lucius and Marcus could see Brutus sitting on the stone bench that lined the long side of the room containing the seven wall niches that housed the series of seven statues representing the days of the week. The names of each statue were clearly inscribed below each bust – Sol, Luna, Mars, Mercury, Jupiter, Venus and Saturn. Brutus was waiting by Sol, the furthest from the entrance, the closest to the hot rooms.

"Hail comrades," he greeted them with the formal words of welcome the Roman army used when meeting soldiers of different legions.

"Why the formality?" questioned Lucius as he sat next to Brutus on the bench, "and do not drown me with too much 'Brutus spiel'. I am not ready for that yet. Mars, what a march! Let me into the baths." Removing his boots revealed raw skin just below his right ankle, and he saw a large water filled blister protruding on the ball of the same foot as he looked underneath. "Damn these army boots, they never fit both feet the same. Look, the left is fine." He stretched out both legs to display both feet, unintentionally kicking Marcus in the process.

"Ouch…shit…cramp!" Marcus hobbled about grasping his lower leg, flexing his foot in an attempt to cease the painful spasm.

Brutus grinned, "Crack the flail did he, the legate."

"Ahh…bugger…you might well laugh my friend," gasped Marcus. "That was the worst bloody march I have ever been on. I swear on the name of the goddess Minerva that with all her healing powers it will take a moon cycle to lift the soreness." Then remembering Brutus's plight, still bent over holding his leg and grimacing, he nodded towards the broken arm, "sorry, forgot, what is the progress?"

"We would be lucky to make one healthy man out of the three of us," replied Brutus shaking his head and grinning still. "Rome's finest reduced to tatters even before the anticipated battle with the native savages our fine leader wishes us to engage in." It didn't take a scribe to decipher the legate's plans. Rumours of a surge to the north had spread through the camp like tendrils of ivy, pieces of information rooting here and others there, until the whole area was covered.

"When will you be fit to do something other than chat with the women then?" Lucius asked Brutus. "We saw you with Cloelia. Rehearsing for a play at the Circus Maximus it looked like. Luckily for you, the legate was on the other side of the column. Do not give him a further excuse to ship your rump and carcass back to Rome." They were all aware of the plight facing Brutus should his arm remain useless. Lucius was harbouring great guilt about it all. "Even Marcus is listening to his brain and not his penis where the legate's daughter is concerned and that is not easy for our very own Italian stud." Lucius slapped Marcus on the back in a gesture showing he was proud of him, resulting in a wince from Marcus.

"Passion is on hold, I am far too sore." He rolled his shoulders gently to loosen the knotted muscles.

"To answer your question," said Brutus, "I am scheduled for a session with the physician tomorrow. Brutus Antonini will be back to strength, and stronger, in the time it takes a larva to pupate. I will be your Centurion yet. Never doubt it."

"It is good to see you so positive," Lucius raised an eyebrow questioningly.

"Just a little Brigante spirit, donated by a dark beauty named Jolinda Teviot," replied Brutus staring pensively into space as he thought of his earlier conversation with Jolinda.

Marcus's pulse quickened on reflex at hearing her name. So Jolinda had been in the group of five gathered by the granary. A short jab of adrenalin caused a momentary surge through his chest. He hadn't realised it was her. Too enervated from the gruelling march at the time, he'd had no interest in identifying those with Brutus and Cloelia. The idle stretcher had indicated the non-urgent presence of orderlies and his exhaustive state had settled with that. Demanding impulses darted through his body as he found his mind invaded by images of their encounter in the snowy ditch. So vivid was her face before his eyes and the warmth of her laughter in his head, that all else was eclipsed.

He was brought back to reality by another slap on the back from Lucius.

"Is that not right Marcus?"

"Aah! Whatever you say, yes that is right…just stop slapping me will you!" The sudden soreness blackened the images of Jolinda, but only dulled the impulses leaving them to smoulder unawares.

....

All three men were now undressed with their clothes folded neatly on a rack below the seating. There was no concern of theft as in public baths. The penalty within the army was too severe to contemplate such an act. Cradling his right arm with his left, Brutus crossed the changing rooms to the latrine on the eastern side of the building. Marcus and Lucius limped across behind him, exchanging banter with the group playing knuckleball as they passed.

A quarter of the size of the changing rooms, the latrine had large stone benches with holes lining three walls. There were two small windows positioned high up but no other doorway. Conversation was limited by the constant flush of vigorously flowing water delivered by the aqueduct system. Deep channels ran under the benches collecting sewerage, herding it immediately out of the building and guiding it to the river bank where its journey away from the fort was continued by nature.

A pair of narrow channels was also cut into the floor in front of the benches, giving constant fresh water for cleaning the personal sponge attached to a stick that rested in a small hole within reach of each seat. Although a communal room, the noise of running water combined with the act of opening ones bowels or bladder led to quiet contemplation and private thoughts.

The trio regrouped in the changing rooms.

"Wish they would heat that bloody latrine in this obnoxious weather," complained Lucius. "Still, let us get the cold plunge done, then we can relish the warmth and dream of balmy Italian summers. Lead me to the *frigidarium*!" His fatigue was lifting just at the thought of the cleansing rituals.

Following the quick cold plunge in the *frigidarium* was the pleasant warmth of the *tepidarium*. Flues beneath the floor and within the walls carried in heated air from perpetually stoked furnaces. Brutus had slipped two sestertii to the slaves tending the furnaces to ensure the fires were kept roaring. The second *tepidarium* was heated with steam, not dry air and the gentle process of light sweating began in preparation of the visit to the steaming bakehouse heat of the *caldarium*. A neat row of sandals covered a shelf along one wall of the lobby to the *caldarium*, which the soldiers slipped their feet into before entering. The stone floors were at their highest temperature here due to the close proximity of the charcoal furnaces. Without sandals, the skin on the soles of the feet would blister and melt like tallow on hot metal.

The *caldarium* was bigger than the *tepidarium* and four wooden tables were arranged in a square in the right half of the room, each draped by a white cotton sheet covering a thin padded cushion. Slaves of eastern origin melded with the tiled walls decorated with blue and white mosaics of river scenes, standing quite still and mute until their services were requested. Lucius led the way into the D-shaped hot bath that nestled into the bottom of the left half of the room. Grunts borne of purgatorial pleasure were released as each man entered the steaming water. Pores opened and expanded in luscious agony forcing to the surface the grime and impurities that lurked unseen.

Marcus was first to leave the hot bath, dripping across the room to the nearest of the wooden tables. Laying on his front with his face turned to one side, he let both arms dangle towards the floor, allowing gravity to gently stretch the heat-stimulated muscles in his limbs and across his shoulders and back. Sublime relaxation washed over his body like a wave smoothing a ragged pile of sand on the beach. A slave came forward and without preamble began massaging Marcus's torso and limbs using tiny drops of lavender scented oil taken from a small, highly ornate bottle that was dangling at his hip. A deep groan escaped from Marcus's lips as he succumbed to the carnal pleasure of aching muscles becoming invigorated with fresh blood. Lucius underwent the same treatment on the table opposite. Brutus, indicating his broken arm, waved the slave away, choosing to forego the massage and lay quietly instead.

As soon as the whole length of the body was rubbed, buttocks included, the slaves scraped away the oil, sweat and dirt with their narrow strigils leaving a cleansing tingle all over. Lucius was particularly impressed when his slave delicately treated his blisters with a cooling cream, a duty above and beyond the norm. He made a mental note to reward the slave with a coin before he left the baths. Before returning to the changing rooms to dress, the three took a final, very short cold plunge to relieve themselves of the built-up heat and to close their pores to the elements. Refreshment was total.

....

Leaving the bathhouse the three young legionaries were ambling up the snow covered grassy slope towards the fort proper, in a lighter mood than earlier and keenly anticipating their midday meal, when their attention was drawn to a commotion on the riverbank below and to the right of them. A rider was urging his sweating mount along the footpath heading for the bridge that traversed the *Tinea*. The legion's engineers had erected the bridge soon after the fort became established beyond a marching camp. Ease of access across the river was imperative due to the regular shipment of supplies from the depot that was sited on the coast due east at the town of *Arbeia*. It brought a lifeline of food and equipment to the men of this northern outpost, replenished by the navy of Rome as it sailed from Gaul to the shores of Briton and back.

"What is he in such a hurry for?" muttered Marcus, scanning the surrounding countryside for pursuers.

"It looks like he is alone." Lucius instinctively increased his pace wanting to reach the top of the slope so he could see the visitor's arrival at the East Gate more clearly. Brutus and Marcus did the same.

Having crossed the bridge the rider reined his horse in bringing the agitated animal under control as best as he could whilst shouting out a request to speak to the legate in charge. Snorts of white mist puffed from the creature's nose as it scampered on the spot, flattening the snow beneath it, unable to be still so soon after such a hard ride.

Shouts could be heard coming from the guards as they challenged the rider and hurried to alert their superiors. Lucius could see the red-crested helmet of the watch's centurion hurrying to the gate. He recognised him as Centurion Bendiaco, from the Fifth Cohort. A scarred veteran not renowned for his patience with subordination but respected by his troops for his willingness to lead by example in battle. A trait most centurions possessed, but the ribboned decorations on Bendiaco's breastplate indicated his exceptional skills of survival.

"State your rank, soldier," Bendiaco ordered.

"Auxiliary attached to the Ninth Legion in charge of the supply depot at *Arbeia*, sir!" The horseman struggled out a salute as his horse continued skipping and stamping uneasily, withdrawing his arm rapidly to save from being unseated. The brevity of the salute irritated Bendiaco and the struggle to withhold a reprimand added a strained edge to his already harsh voice.

"And what is your business with the legate?"

"*Arbeia* is under attack, Sir! The depot is on fire. I am to request immediate assistance, Sir!" The soldier held up a wax tablet that was slung across his body, to show he had written orders.

By now, Marcus, Brutus and Lucius were within earshot and exchanged concerned glances. *Arbeia* was a crucial supply depot. Brutus nodded to the eastern horizon where a faint glow was becoming visible against the already smoke-grey clouds, like a breaking dawn creeps up from the ground.

"It is the truth unless dawn has come before night. You two had better get prepared in case the Fourth is mustered."

"Do you think we will be?" asked Lucius.

"The legate will not send less than four cohorts if what the rider says holds up under scrutiny of the orders," replied Brutus. The Fifth is on watch duties and the Sixth to Tenth Cohorts are still out marching. From when I saw them march out, I judge the closest group will be well out of trumpet range. He will not risk a delay in sending troops. My guess is you will be mustered."

"Brutus is right Lucius. Crass! We had better make haste." They broke into a jog towards the barracks, all soreness numbed by adrenalin at the thought of active service. Slapping his thigh with frustration, Brutus called out after them.

"Remember lads, three inches of point beats six inches…"

"…of side!" They completed the drilling instruction with a thumbs-up sign as they ran. The instruction of how to handle a short legionary sword in battle had been adopted in the group as a good luck ritual, they'd heard it said so often during training.

The two-tone assembly signal sounded from the trumpets as the two girls were reaching the North Gate. The eerie wailing of the instruments carried through the still winter air with clarity. Cloelia stopped in mid stride clasping a hand around Jolinda's upper arm to stop her too. Making a slight gasp, she drew in her breath and held it, staring straight-ahead listening intently.

"What is it? What's the signal for?" asked Jolinda. Cloelia didn't reply and Jolinda remained quiet as she could see her friend was concentrating. She found herself holding her breath too, waiting for something to happen. The notes died away but the sound seemed to linger in the air.

"Oh Jolinda! They have mustered the first four cohorts. I counted the signal. Something terrible must have happened. I must return to Mama immediately and you had better get out quickly before they seal the fort. I do not know what the problem is, but it must be serious for four cohorts to be mustered. The fort has been so relaxed of late, I have grown unaccustomed to the feelings of uncertainty of battle."

"Of battle…what do ya mean? Is me family in danger?" Jolinda looked anxiously at her friend.

"Oh no, I am sure they are not…but…no of course they are not." Cloelia was trying to be reassuring but her concern could not be hidden. "It is most likely an attack on the marching columns."

"I thought they were back in the fort."

"The Sixth to Tenth are still out. They went out later than the others. Oh Jolinda, I do not know what the problem is, but you must go." Her thoughts turned to Marcus. "Oh, poor Marcus, and Lucius. They looked exhausted after their march, and now this. They have not been back long." Her mind now full of caring and worry for the soldiers, she kissed Jolinda lightly on the cheek before hurrying away towards the busying centre of the fort. Jolinda stared after her for a moment. It was as if the fort were suddenly alive with ants. She could see men running to and from the barracks, all with speed and purpose. Shouts could be heard but not distinguished. Even in chaos there seemed organisation, and columns of fully armoured men quickly began to form. Not for the first time she found herself a little in awe of how these individuals melded so efficiently into a seemingly insuperable one, that was the Roman army.

Recalling her own plight drew her from the entrancing spectacle. Cloelia had said she must get out quickly before they sealed the fort. Tension knotted her stomach. She must get home. Running towards the gate she held her leaving pass tightly, ready to show it to the guard. She was innocent, yet felt guilty and flustered, flushing scarlet and stumbling over her answers to the guard's questions. He scrutinised the wax tablet and double-checked his records before allowing her to exit.

"Oh no, the ditches," she breathed aloud. The sentry heard her. Remembering the difficulties of traversing them previously, she bravely forced a weak smile and asked the sentry for assistance. Amidst extreme caution, six soldiers came through the gate with swords unsheathed, surrounding two others carrying a plank. More legionaries could be seen at the top of the gate towers, javelins at the ready. As soon as Jolinda was across, the eight men marched in disciplined formation back to the fort. The contrast to the casual assistance given by Marcus seven sunrises ago added to Jolinda's unease.

Apart from her tracks made earlier in the snow, there was no disturbance to the overnight fall on the ground ahead or to either side. The vista was a sparkling serenity of fluffy white, broken only by the looming crags that rose in ragged disharmony due north. These crags were the beginning of a series of rocky crests that hung like frozen waves across the land, presenting their sheer faces northwards. A geological ripple that started in the Caledonian Mountains and decreased in intensity as it headed south, ending in rolling, smooth-topped hills.

Distracted by her worries, with thoughts of danger for her family jostling for attention with thoughts of Marcus and battles, Tamsin and prostitution, Brutus and Cloelia, along with her own disloyalty to Ma's hatred of all things Roman, it was no surprise that she failed to notice her solitary tracks had merged with another line of footprints.

Kye let her pass by and walk on several paces before he fell in step behind his sister. This was easy, he mused. With a smile flickering at the corners of his mouth he continued stalking Jolinda for a few minutes, enjoying the build up of excited tension throughout his body. With quiet and steady movements he scooped up a handful of snow. Planting his feet still and square he took aim and threw the snowball, simultaneously yelling 'attack!' using the Caledonian version of the word learnt from the Picts. Jolinda's head whirled round and Kye just had time to see her wild look of panic before the missile obliterated her face in a soft explosion. A small gasp left her lips as she fell backwards landing heavily on her bottom. The snowball had not been thrown hard but had caught her unexpectedly. It was the shock that caused the tumble.

With an enormous grin of boyish satisfaction, Kye whooped with delight as he loped over to his fallen victim holding an imaginary spear with his arm drawn back aimed ready to finish his kill.

"Surrender or die!" He was having a great time.

With the shock subsiding and the realisation that the danger wasn't real, Jolinda began to notice a burning pain in her left wrist. Grimacing she cradled it to her stomach and held it with her right hand, hunching her shoulders as she remained sitting on the ground. The pain eased with the warmth and she let it free, gently shaking out the knots. Gathering her wits she straightened her back and glared up at her brother.

"Ya ignominious ass! Ya terrified me, what ya playing at?"

Still enjoying himself, Kye continued the charade of victor demanding surrender or death. Jolinda's sense of humour failed her at that moment and rising to her feet she turned her back on her brother and began striding towards home. Kye ran to catch her up.

"Hey, escape ain't part of the deal!" His buoyancy was lowering.

"Kye, I ain't in the mood for ya childish games. I really ain't. We need to get home. Something bad is happening at the fort and it ain't a game."

"Is that why the trumpets sounded? What does the two-tone signal mean?" Excitement was rising in him again. Jolinda didn't answer. Kye repeated his question and became nettled when it was met with further silence.

"Been cosying up to the legionaries have ya?" His words spilled out in a sulky pout. It was a vivid reminder of Tamsin's dealings at the tavern and Jolinda's stomach churned. She couldn't tell Kye it was their sister who was a Roman prostitute, not herself. She remained quiet.

"Ma will draw and quarter ya when she discovers ya've been in the fort. Don't think I won't tell her if ya don't confide in me." Kye was hitting where he thought it would hurt, looking for a lever to prise information from his sister. Resentment that she had been inside the formidable structure that he had been too afraid to approach was insipidly taking a hold on him. He was a boy verging on being a man, driven by impulses searching for thrills. The Picts would treat him as a hero if he could reveal inside information about the trumpet signals to them.

Within sight of their homestead now, Jolinda stopped abruptly and Kye copied anticipating an explanation of why she had been visiting the fort. He thought he had her trapped, but Jolinda dismissed his threat with a reproachful 'tut' and a 'shush' as if he were a child playing petty games. She was intending to tell Ma of her tutoring anyway so his threat was idle. She'd stopped because the trumpets were sounding again, much fainter now but still clear. They seemed to be heading away from them which filled her with relief and she found herself counting the blasts wondering if they were orders for the Fourth or not.

Piqued by her scorn, Kye spoke indignantly, "I can hold me own in a fight and them Romans ain't so tough. I saw it took eight of them to escort ya over the ditch. Eight, huh! If I'd been armed I could've axed the lot of them."

Jolinda was amused, "Kye, ya ain't no soldier. Heck, ya ain't no man yet! It wasn't so long ago a fox grounded ya. Outwitted and upended good 'n' proper. Soldiering ain't for boys." A vision of Marcus in uniform came to her, strong and proud, and she was rocked by the glow of protection it gave her. She couldn't put her brother in the same frame. He just didn't fit. Kye was brooding.

"The Picts..." he was about to say the Picts didn't treat him as a boy, but checked himself quickly, glancing anxiously at Jolinda to see if she'd noticed. She hadn't. Dismissing the idea of Kye as a warrior as absurd, her thoughts were already turning to the problems waiting at home. Clamping his jaw shut, Kye chided himself for almost divulging his secret meetings to his sister. They walked the final distance in silence.

....

The confrontation with Ma was terrible. Time had not done much to soften the older woman's opinion of the Romans, although a flicker of pride had weaved through her face when Jolinda explained she was tutoring the Romans in Brigante crafts. It hadn't been enough to placate her but Jolinda was grasping at this tiny seed of hope as she lay with her back towards her sleeping sister.

The dark room was very still and the night outside was quiet. Jolinda was laying on the edge of the bed, cold and uncomfortable but reluctant to move closer to Tamsin's warmth. The words of Brutus were echoing in her head, whore and trollop, whore and trollop, over and over. Longing for the respite of slumber, she closed her eyes and focused on seeing the darkness. She fell asleep wondering what was happening on the fort. Where was the Fourth?

Chapter Eight

A cavalry squadron of thirty men and horses, led by its decurion Gius Autemius, a close and trusted personal friend of the legate's, had galloped ahead of the marching column with instructions to scout the area, gain information and report back to the legate. Under no circumstances were they to take unnecessary risks to engage the enemy, Peterna needed reliable details on what was happening at *Arbeia*. How was the supply depot under attack? The glow on the horizon that was creeping ever higher and gaining in intensity as the cohorts marched closer, was proof of the fire, and although the messenger had brought details of the raid, Peterna wanted no surprises.

If the account on the wax tablet was accurate, and by the gods it had better be or he would have the head of the tribune in command, then there was no mass of barbarian warriors to fight, just a raging fire. Started by an arson raid from both within and outside the fort simultaneously. Planning and pre-meditated co-ordination would have been needed to pull off such a plot, which indicated foul play by either trusted members of the local workforce who were permitted in the depot or corruption through bribery among the Roman ranks. Peterna slapped his thigh in frustration. It was a bad business either way, and one more example of the political instability of the region. A full enquiry would be required, with those responsible punished by crucifixion, Roman or barbarian, no exceptions.

Digging his heels into his mare's flanks, Legate Peterna Maxinius rode to the head of the column barking orders to the centurions.

"Double speed, alternate miles!"

As the lead century broke into a unified jog, the increase in pace rippled along the whole column until all four cohorts were moving at double speed. Marcus's lungs were burning as they neared the end of the first mile. Although mentally recovered from the earlier training march, physically he was not. Tired muscles forced to run in armour carrying full battle gear of shield, sword and javelin were demanding more oxygen than he could supply. Just when he thought his chest would explode, the order to slow to regulation pace was given.

Managing a glance at Lucius beside him, Marcus was relieved to see that his friend was blowing hard too. As the gasping abated, Lucius let out a curse of his ill-fitting boots that were now rubbing his fresh blisters raw.

"Third Century, double speed!" The order floated across the cold air as the column reached their third mile. Iron discipline came to the fore and the men were jogging again. White plumes of hot breath shrouded the cohorts and a symphony of jingling metal mingling with the men's panting and rhythmic crunching of snow under boots was worthy of a paying audience. They kept to the Stanegate, the Roman road that linked *Arbeia* to the forts. It favoured low-lying terrain, roughly tracing the north bank of the *Tinae* but straightening out its meanders, so that the symphony took on a chorus of chuckling water over pebbles at varying times.

A legionary peeled away to the side of the column a few rows in front of Marcus, doubling over straining for breath. The optio's immediate kicking of the fallen man, who suddenly found enough vigour to rejoin the group, obliterated any thoughts Marcus had of doing the same. Riding back down the column, Peterna noted the visible exhaustion of the Fourth Cohort. The timing of this assault had been particularly bad for them having the least chance to recover from the training march, yet he could not let them delay the arrival of the column, not with the depot burning. Swiftness was imperative, and to split the cohorts with possible raiding parties in the area was foolhardy. He wouldn't risk his men like that. Making a mental note to give the Fourth Cohort the least demanding role on arrival, if such an opportunity occurred, Peterna continued riding up and down the lines as a visible reminder of discipline.

....

The scouting squadron returned with information that verified the original report given by the tribune on the wax tablet. No sign of any barbarian warriors, but the fire was severe and encircled the depot. Now within five miles of *Arbeia*, Peterna could see a mass of swirling, pewter grey smoke rising above the orange coloured flames. The fire had clearly taken a firm hold on the timbers.
"What equipment do they have?" he demanded of the decurion.

"Ballistae, pumping engines and reed mats, Sir! There is a plentiful supply of sand and water from the nearby beach. Buckets, ceiling hooks, grappling hooks and mattocks are available, Sir!"

"Decurion Autemius, take your men and return to *Arbeia*. Assist where you can until we arrive but keep your horses well away from the area and get them rested. We may need to send for more cohorts should this fire prove difficult to quash."

"Yes Sir!" The decurion saluted before wheeling his mount round and riding back to his cavalry, handling the animal as if it was an extension of his self. The man would never baulk at an order, but Peterna knew Gius was wondering why he wasn't sending for extra men immediately. Peterna was following an instinct that this arson attack was not going to be an isolated incident, but the start of a series of raids. He had no proof, just a feeling of ill boding in his gut that experience had taught him not to ignore. Leaving the fort unprotected was not his first choice under the circumstances, and he hoped the Sixth to Tenth Cohorts were already back from their route marches giving back-up to the Fifth, left there on watch duties. His resolve to send his wife and daughter away to Rome strengthened as he turned his mind to concentrate on the immediate task.

Despite the pain in his hands, his hunger, filth and cold, Marcus slept for ten dreamless hours. For over two days the fire had burned, and for over two days the legate had kept his men on their feet. At first, it had seemed the ballistae had succeeded in creating a firebreak around the centre of the depot. The crews had loaded the huge catapults with boulders and water bombs again and again, relentlessly pounding a pathway through the wooden buildings, continuing their quest long after the sun had left the horizon.

By the end of the first night the flames were contained to the perimeter of the depot. Two human chains stretched from the beach to the outer turf ramparts, which offered relief from the searing heat. Empty buckets were transferred down one chain and returned via the other, full of either water or sand. Reed mats were continuously dampened and used to smother flaming beams. Under the protection of a cool jet of water shot from the copper nozzle of a pumping engine, a team of legionaries now stripped of their armour would run from behind the turf rampart, thankfully impervious to the torch, hold down their freshly doused mats for a count of five, then return to cool safety, passing a second team on the way. It was ordered and disciplined.

Marcus and Lucius had found themselves passing buckets near the beach end of the chain. Monotonous work but less demanding physically than loading the ballistae or running the mats. Marcus's mind had drifted as he watched the surf roll in and break on the shore. Would Jolinda like the water as he did? Would she know of the joy of riding the waves, the exhilarating freedom of surging in on a breaking crest? He'd felt a stirring in his loins despite his weariness and a powerful longing in his chest. A slosh of cold water down his thigh broke his reverie and cursing he returned his attention to the buckets.

Encouragement came to the tired men before dawn and a ragged cheer went up when the announcement was given to down buckets and form ranks. They knew sleep would not be theirs until the debris was raked and tended, but it seemed the first stage of the fight was won and a good deal of the depot had been saved.

Peterna ordered all hands to be deployed in immediate clearing of the burnt area. Ceiling hooks, grappling hooks and mattocks were issued. The legate was relieved to have gained control of the fire so swiftly, and without the need to draw on further troops from the fort. He could push these men a little further and deny the embers any chance of re-igniting before he allowed them food and rest. Once the ashes were dead he could hand command of an official enquiry and re-building project to the senior tribune and return to the fort with his cohorts. Already he was thinking about his written report and the political weight this incident could add to his request to advance with more troops. These raids were dangerously demoralising.

With an increase in daylight came a strengthening breeze. Marcus and Lucius raked through the smouldering beams of what had been a barrack. Timbers were separated and smothered with sand or rolled in the quagmire of blackened soil turned muddy by melted snow now trampled and glutinous underfoot. All around them, soot-flecked and mud-splattered men were doing the same. Peterna looked over the scene with pride and respect for his army, his eyes scratchy through lack of sleep. He knew every man was weary yet still they toiled. These men deserved recognition for their loyalty and he would get them glory or ruin his own prospects trying, by the gods he would!

....

An unstable beam crashed to the ground behind Marcus startling him. Sparks splintered up and were immediately caught on the breeze and like crazed insects starved of nourishment they crossed the firebreak crackling into instant flames as they drew energy from the unburned but heated timbers. Peterna saw the incident. Recognising the potential disaster unfolding, Marcus was the quickest to react. If the fire took hold this side of the firebreak, they would lose the rest of the depot and the thought of spending another day battling with the intense heat, choking on the acrid smoke, spurred him into combat. Grabbing a discarded reed mat and shouting at Lucius to do the same, he scrambled over the rubble giving orders for sand and a pumping engine as he went. The legionaries followed his lead without hesitation. Marcus threw his mat over the flaming wood denying the blaze oxygen, suffocating it in its infancy.

"Get those buckets over here now! Douse these timbers!" The mat became uncomfortably hot and Marcus cried out in frustration at the scolding pain in his hands, refusing to let go until the water arrived. Blinking away smoke induced tears from his stinging eyes, he heard the legate championing the pumping engine crews, then saw he was dismounted and moving the equipment with them.

"Centurion! Form all units up on this side of the depot. We need to concentrate all our manpower here. Get this area dead of sparks before the wind carries them." Peterna cursed the strengthening breeze as he threw his shoulder against the pumping engine, straining to keep it moving over the rubble.

The crew was successful, allowing Marcus and Lucius to fall back from the area away from immediate danger. Marcus's body began to shake. Small blisters were swelling on his palms, which were throbbing with excruciating pain. Warning cries of a second breach of the firebreak went up to their left. Despite his sorry state, Marcus responded quickly, scrabbling in the direction of the cries. Would this enemy never die?

The battle was finally won as the moon waned under the light of the third dawn rising since the Legion's arrival. The air was still and crisp and the last spark died in the raked ashes. The men of the Twentieth Legion had fought continuously against each new fire outbreak, believing every hour that it was over only to be denied by a vagrant whipped up ember. The situation had never allowed the legate to send for fresh troops.

Withdrawing his men to the temporary camp on the outskirts of *Arbeia*, cautious still in posting a watch, Legate Peterna Maxinius hunched himself wearily over a desk in his tent. He would write his report before he slept. Slowly rubbing his fingers along his strongly arching eyebrows and massaging around the eye sockets, he breathed deeply to focus his mind. Conker-brown eyes came to the fore. Guintoli...that was the lad's name. Marcus Guintoli. Picking up the stylus, he began to scribe.

....

"We need to keep the infection out of those blisters. Keep your hands clean and smear this salve on morning and evening sparingly. See me in seven sunrises, earlier if the blisters begin to ooze." The camp physician nodded curtly as he passed a phial of foul smelling cream to Marcus before turning his attention to the next wounded in the queue. Marcus turned left on leaving the room, away from the hospital exit. The corridor became quieter as he made his way to the end. Approaching the room Brutus had adopted again, he heard Cloelia giggle and he checked his stride for a moment in indecision. He was feeling guilty for not having spoken to Cloelia in several days. In truth, he was feeling guilty for not having thought of Cloelia in several days. It was always Jolinda who occupied his mind. At times he wasn't able to form a vision of her face, on other occasions her image would flash vividly, if only briefly, before him. It was confusing and distracting, and making him very restless.

Taking a steadying breath, he continued forwards. He could not ignore Cloelia forever and he needed to see how Brutus was getting on. The physician had spent some time manipulating and re-setting the damaged arm whilst the unit had been fighting the depot fire. Brutus's career was riding on the outcome. Standing in the doorway he remained initially unnoticed. Cloelia was sitting with her back to the entrance, her position blocking the line of sight to Brutus, who, as usual, was causing hilarity with an anecdote about something. Marcus couldn't help but smile, and shaking his head slightly he tapped lightly on the door as he entered.

"Do not believe a word he is telling you, Cloelia."

"Marcus! Oh..." There was a moment of awkwardness before Cloelia dissolved into giggles again. "Bring that chair over Marcus, join us. Brutus is really on form today. I am aching with laughter."

Sitting with his arm splintered in front of him as before, with a treacherous glint of merriment in his eyes, Brutus echoed her words. The happy atmosphere that shrouded the couple was tangible and in that moment Marcus felt absolved of his guilt towards Cloelia and with absolution came a joyous release of tension. Flashing a wide, knowing grin at Brutus he used his forearms to lift the spare chair over to the bed.

"Oh! Marcus, your hands, they must be painful." Cloelia jumped up to assist him. "Was it really awful at *Arbeia*? I have heard of your heroics."

Eager not to destroy the happy atmosphere, Marcus dismissed the question a little brutally.

"Do not fuss! I would rather be told which story our master raconteur is delivering today."

Not waiting for a second prompt, Brutus continued with his narration, back-tracking on some important details so Marcus could follow the plot. Cloelia soon recovered from the rebuff and was laughing long into the morning.

....

Jolinda was not laughing. Life in the Teviot homestead was far from harmonious. Four days on from confessing to her Roman connections, Ma was still as frosty as the rime on the hawthorn. Tamsin seemed smug that Jolinda was suffering this treatment, so often directed at her. Kye was distant and sulky, growling at his younger brother for simply breathing. At nine years, Aaron was old enough to notice the tetchy mood of his family but not to understand it. He dealt with the obfuscation by melding into the background as quietly as possible, but still Kye would snarl at him.

Trying to ease the dark tension, Jolinda asked Kye if he'd seen the fox hanging round the chickens lately. It was meant as small talk to initiate a conversation, but her choice of subject was not well thought. Kye took umbrage, and like a simmering pot with added heat, his temper bubbled over. Kicking a wooden vat that puffed up dust as it scraped along the dirt floor, he flounced out of the room.

"Don't ya wait up for me!" he yelled, grabbing his coat and a hunk of bread left on the worktop as he crashed out of the hut with as much drama as he could.

"Where ya goin'?" cried Ma, her hands still plunged in the laundry tub. There was no reply, and no chance to stop him. A chilly silence hung like a melting icicle forming a drip, before Ma turned on her elder daughter, coursing a spray of grey water across the room as she flailed her hands, venting her concerned fury in a tirade. The words stung like hailstones on bare skin in a blizzard wind. Hot tears of humiliation prickled at Jolinda's eyes. Never had she experienced such spite from her mother, never had she missed Da more. Without speaking a word, she too left the house, wrapping a fur quickly over her head and round her shoulders. Running across the yard, stumbling slightly but not looking back. Hearing the door slam behind her she gave in to the tears, letting their salty flow stain her cheeks as she kept running. She had to get away!

....

Snow still covered the hills although it was no longer fresh. Its fluffy layers had been partly thawed and refrozen giving it an icy crunch under Jolinda's footsteps. The sky was a uniform pale grey and didn't threaten a further storm. Grateful that the wind wasn't howling its common winter tune, she slowed from her sobbing run to a sniffing walk. The open countryside was calming after the oppressive tension in the little kitchen. Where had Kye gone? The shepherding shack maybe? Yet a shadow of a query was niggling at her conscience. Something Kye had said when they'd been returning from the fort together the day the trumpets had mustered the Roman troops. She couldn't quite recall his words, and soon other memories of that morning on the fort were submerging the niggling thought.

Already more than half way to the fort, Jolinda knew she was heading for its sanctuary. She felt its pull of protection like a strong tidal current. A channel to warmth and caring that had been missing from her family for a while. Cloelia would not turn her away, neither would Brutus, and Marcus...how she desired to know he was safe.

....

Security on the fort had been increased due to the arson attack on *Arbeia* and Jolinda was made to wait in the guardroom whilst the sentry organised a clerk to take a message to Cloelia. Her weekly pass was no longer valid without verification. Fixing her gaze towards the floor, Jolinda stayed silent as she waited. Her forehead was throbbing with the pressure of tear-wracked sinuses and she was conscious of her red, swollen eyelids. The sentry sensed her reluctance for conversation, so busied himself with checking a list. Jolinda was grateful for his thoughtfulness.

She was even more grateful for Cloelia's kindness. On entering the guardroom the young Roman girl gauged that Jolinda needed immediate privacy, so dismissed the sentry and the clerk from the small, square room, requesting politely that they remain close by to act should they be required. Taking her friend in a hug without a question, she gently stroked her glossy, black hair as fresh sobs shook through her.

"You are safe," she soothed.

"I'm a right mess, ain't I?"

"It does a plain Roman girl good to see you look as terrible as she does when you cry."

"Ya ain't plain, Cloelia!"

"And ya ain't plain either, Jolinda!" she said mimicking her Brigante accent perfectly. "Come on, let us get home and restore your beauty. Here, wrap my shawl over your head. It will cover your face enough that you need not fear strange looks from the legionaries. Men cope badly with female tears."

Together, the girls made their way down the wide *Via Praetoria*, turning left at the stone built *Principia*.

"Papa's office is behind the second column of the portico to the left of the central gateway," said Cloelia, pointing as they passed. "He is working there now. Mama is feeling unwell and resting in her private quarters, so we will not be subjected to any immediate questioning."

Jolinda gave a wan smile.

"Ya read me mind like a spirit."

"Only some of it. The rest you must tell me. No secrets Jolinda. True friends have no secrets." Reaching the Commandant's house, Cloelia clasped

Jolinda's hand and giggled flirtatiously at the guards. "Let us go and swap secrets," she whispered to her friend.

....

"Then you must stay here Jolinda, for as long as you need to. Mama and Papa will agree, I will see to it." The girls were sitting alone on Cloelia's bed in her private room, facing each other with their legs curled out to one side in a mirror image. Jolinda was absently smoothing the silky-soft sheen of the velvet fabric that covered the bed in voluptuous folds of deep sea green. Braided tassels of the same colour fringed its edge and rippled like sea grass along the polished wooden floor with the movement. They matched the braided tassels that decorated the bottom of the double drapes held open across the window by contrasting satin sashes of crimson. The same satin crimson that bordered the embroidered hunting tableau that hung on the opposite wall.

"I'm grateful to ya. I hope Kye finds shelter."

"Oh steel swords to Kye! He will be fine Jolinda. Men do not appreciate comfort anyhow. Indeed, the gods seem to help them flourish when faced with rudimentary surroundings."

"Ma will fret."

"Oh steel swords to Ma too! She should show you more consideration. She has Tamsin...the trollop!" Cloelia's face darkened into a pout and the left corner of her mouth twitched as she frowned. Jolinda, now calmer after outpouring her burdens, was feeling a little guilty for revealing so many family secrets. It had seemed natural at the time to tell her friend why Ma hated her race. She'd explained that their hand killed Da although she knew not the details. The niggling doubt she had of Kye and how his temperament had changed without Da's controlling wisdom came tumbling out, along with the pressures she shouldered as the eldest child. The responsibility of earning coin to trade with weighed heavily on her shoulders, and the responsibility of providing enough food for the family to survive the winter months. All this Cloelia had absorbed without a changing emotion, until Jolinda told the shame of her sister.

"Brutus doesn't know it were Tamsin at the whorehouse. But I know it were, I saw the scratches on her. I'm so ashamed. Ya won't tell anyone, will ya? What will they think of me?" Jolinda's heart was thumping in panic. Cloelia became very serious.

"It is a secret we must keep. People *will* tarnish you with her ways if they find out." Cloelia was looking earnestly into Jolinda's eyes and taking hold of her friend's hands in her own, she swore an oath of silence to Juno, wife and sister of Jupiter, goddess of women. "You have shared your secrets, now it is my turn. We will then be an equal partnership again." Releasing Jolinda's hands and shifting her position slightly, Cloelia relaxed the atmosphere by breathing in deeply through her nose and exhaling audibly. "I will marry for love or not at all! There, it is said...you have my biggest secret."

Jolinda's eyebrows arched highly in surprise.

"Mama and Papa have intentions of uniting me with a senate member, wealthy yes, but wrinkled with age, with a sagging stomach, drooping excitement and pompous ideas of men in power! That is not for me Jolinda. Love is the greatest of riches and I will not marry without it. If I bring shame to the house of Maxinius by staying true to my heart then so be it." Cloelia folded her arms and straightened her back in a pose of determination.

"Ain't that what ya parents did, marry for love?"

"Mama and Papa were lucky. Their marriage was seen to be arranged, but Papa is of Swedish descent and his mother was forgiving with the rules and manipulated the situation, so Mama tells me. I do not know the full story and neither does Papa I believe."

"Then surely ya ma will understand that ya want to choose for ya'self." Jolinda wasn't able to see the problem. Brigante culture didn't revolve around wealth at all costs.

Sighing as she deflated from her pose of determination into a hunch of weary sadness, Cloelia fidgeted with her pendant.

"Papa does not have his mother's Swedish lenience on this subject. His ideals are more Roman than Caesar." Jolinda remained silent waiting for her friend to continue. "Marcus gave me this pendant. I felt love then and realised its power. I thought..." her voice caught in hesitation, "...I thought he felt it too but now I am not so sure. Maybe it is different for men or maybe I am not his intended. I am not sure, yet I feel my search is within the legion. Oh, Jolinda, am I talking foolish nonsense? I do not think so. Papa has said I am to go to Rome with Mama and my heart crumples at the thought of leaving the legion."

Jolinda's eyebrows shot up again, this time in panic.

"Ya never said ya were leaving!"

"I will not leave!" Her pose of determination returned.

"Then what ya going to do?"

Cloelia held her breath for a moment, thinking as the room became silent. Her gaze was directed towards the hunting tableau on the wall but her vision was focusing on her dream. Suddenly breaking the silence with a mid-pitched growl, and simultaneously jumping from the bed, she performed a series of quick-footed stamping steps, shaking her head and hammering the air with her fists like a frenzied tribal dancer, her blonde curls vibrating with the movement. The frustration out, she became still and serene once more.

"I do not know what I will do Jolinda, but I do feel better for that! Let us go to the kitchens and eat. After, I would like us to visit Brutus in the hospital. We are both in need of his entertaining skills and a very good laugh. He can always be relied upon to make me smile and my problems become suspended when I am in his company."

Remembering Brutus's outpouring of emotion at their last meeting, Jolinda wondered whether he had spoken of his feelings to Cloelia since. She guessed not as Cloelia had not mentioned it.

"Is Brutus's arm mending now? When he fell that time, he was fretting 'bout the army deporting him to Rome. Would the army do that?"

"Yes, without rancour! What use is a legionary that cannot fight?" It appeared obvious to Cloelia. "The camp surgeon is a wonder. He has manipulated Brutus's arm and I have no doubt it will heal superbly. The legion will never lose Brutus, it is unthinkable that the gods would even contemplate such an act."

"Why?" Jolinda was bemused by Cloelia's attitude.

"Because laughter surrounds him, so the gods must be smiling on him too."

"Brutus doesn't think so. Ill favoured by Cupid and Fortuna he told me. Destined to be mute of his love, or something like that." Jolinda was studying Cloelia's face carefully. Cloelia was giggling.

"Brutus talks a lot of nonsense. Actually, Brutus talks a lot, end of sentence." Catching Jolinda's earnest gaze, her giggle faded. "What? What is it?"

"Dear Cloelia...ya listen but ya don't hear. Ya see but ya don't notice."

"Do not speak in riddles Jolinda. What have I not heard or seen? Tell me! Oh..." her hand shot to cover her mouth, "...mute of his love...mute of his love for whom? Whom does Brutus love? He has never spoken of anyone to me." It was Cloelia's turn to feel the flutters of anxiety undulate between her ribs.

"Ya still ain't made it to the end of the furrow." Jolinda was gently amused. "This god Cupid of yours, is waiting for ya there. Work it out Cloelia, I ain't telling ya, but it's a real possibility that Brutus's arm won't mend strongly. How would ya feel if he weren't here?"

....

The hospital corridors were not busy and echoed in empty cleanliness as Jolinda doubled back to the small room near the entrance that served to house the cleaning equipment. She found she was praying to the Roman god of love on behalf of Cloelia and Brutus and smiled to herself. Please aid them in communication, not just speech, she muttered. Jolinda had said enough to open Cloelia's mind. Once the young Roman woman had digested that it was a real possibility Brutus may be deported, she realised the depth of her feelings for him. All thought of eating evaporated and haste was made to the hospital.

"I'll be fine waiting Cloelia. Go! Talk to Brutus. Come and get me when ya ready. Ya say there's a couch in the cleaning room? I'll rest there."

Recognising Jolinda's profile as she disappeared through the doorway, a bolt of heat rushed through his chest. It was an easy decision to follow her in. Two rows of buckets with mops standing to attention were leaning against the wall to the right, below a high window that was throwing shafts of light across to the leather couch opposite. Piles of white linen cloths were uniformly stacked on a wooden bench that stood a little off-centre along the other wall of the square room. Jolinda looked up sharply and a short gasp escaped her lips, replaced quickly by the most beautiful smile Marcus had ever seen. The ability to speak eluded him as he returned her smile. The small amount of light that shafted in was adding silver shimmers to her dark tresses cascading like a black waterfall across her shoulders and back.

Moving closer, hard with simple desire, Marcus slowly enfolded her with his arms, allowing Jolinda time to withdraw should she wish to. There was no preamble. No words were spoken as she accepted his lips to her own in a gentle kiss that became more demanding as she moved her hands to caress the clipped hair on his nape. The vow Marcus had made after the gods took Flavinus was wavering vaguely in his memory, but the surging senses of the mortal moment suppressed it. Drawing out of the kiss but still embracing and breathing hard, emotions heady and swimming in each other's gaze, neither one spoke. Their mouths joined again. As they separated for the second time, Marcus found his voice.

"It is good to see you Jolinda Teviot." Standing a head taller than her he stooped to rest his forehead against hers, moving his hands up to touch her hair, stopping at the last moment. "Damned hands!" he cursed smiling. "You picked a poor time to come to me. How is a man supposed to cope with such beauty in front of him when he is unable to touch it? Never again will I take the use of my hands for granted."

"Good with words 'n' arrogant too," replied Jolinda, eyes twinkling with happy spirit. "What makes ya think I'd let ya touch?"

"Because I know how I feel and one soul cannot feel this much alone. From the very first moment I felt it."

"Felt what?"

"It...a connection...something...something special." Marcus was stumbling over his words. He wasn't used to doing that, expressing himself easily to women until this moment.

"Show me ya hands." Jolinda scrunched her nose up as she examined the healing blisters, holding each hand softly underneath.

Chapter Nine

Having spent the night after storming out of the homestead alone in a shepherd's hut, kept from sleeping by the unfamiliar groans and creaks of the rickety structure, despite it holding happy memories of family visits at lambing time, Kye was resolved to make it to the arranged meeting with the Picts. They were looking to him for information about the Roman trumpet signals. All he knew was that the number of the two-tone blasts given in a single series related to rallying the different cohorts. It wasn't much, he'd hoped to impress them with much more, but at least it was something.

Being unable to sleep during the night had enabled him to keep the small fire burning in the hearth, it had taken several attempts with his flint striker to get the damp kindling to flame when he'd arrived, so he was relieved not to have to start again. He'd been lucky there was oil still in the lamp to put a taper to. The shepherding huts were not stocked for winter survival and he'd left home with very little. His hollow stomach was complaining audibly as he devoured the remaining bread hunk, swilling it down with melted snow brought to the boil. The drink left an unpleasant metallic taste on his tongue but at least it was warming in his guts.

Using more snow-melt from the pot hanging above the fire, Kye rinsed his face rubbing his hands vigorously over his cheeks allowing the tingling sensation it created to invigorate him. He couldn't afford to be sluggish at the meeting. Drawing his fingers and thumb of one hand across his chin revealed a slight growth of soft down that extended to the area above his top lip. He still had a way to go to match the hirsute Picts but his dark colouring made even a fine covering of facial hair noticeable. It was far better than the shaven nakedness of the Romans.

Kye was surprised to see so many at the meeting. There must have been three score, all with ragged beards and unkempt hair, filling the area of the barn not occupied by the restless sheep that were constantly bleating and bumping each other. At least the building was warm from the animal's heat although sloppy under foot.

He shuffled along in the wake of the two brothers he'd met at the arranged site a mile down the track. Kye was uneasy and nervous sweat secreted from his armpits and palms. The brothers had received his details of the Roman trumpet signals with initial eagerness that had turned to disappointment at the dearth information. Although disappointed, they'd clapped him on the back saying it was a helpful start, before herding him silently and swiftly to the barn.

Moving through the crowd was difficult and Kye mumbled an apology as he knocked the arm of a burly man as he passed by. Hearing him swear in Celtic made Kye look up into a face he recognised from the tavern in the settlement. Kye's eyes were drawn to the side of the man's head where a mangled, scabby lump protruded instead of an ear.

Like a deer scenting trouble on the breeze, Kye quickly scanned the throng looking for other faces he may know. His connection with the Picts was supposed to be a secret. Tension caused his throat to constrict.

"Hadn't realised so many of ya Picts were gathered in this area," Kye said to the younger brother, annoyed at the nervous shrill that edged his voice. The three of them had stopped pushing their way through the throng, finding space next to the haymow away from the barn door. Clearing his throat to loosen its tightness Kye continued to probe, "are there more of ya heading here to over-winter in our warmer climes like them sheep? I've heard ya get it bad in them mountains of ya's!" His attempt at humour was feeble, and fortunately unnoticed by his companions, both of whom were alternately rubbing their hands together furiously and cupping them to mouths for a blast of warm breath. Although cold from waiting in bushes for Kye, their demeanour was buoyant.

"The Caledonian War Council is never short of members keen to rise against the Romans," replied the younger brother. "This is just a tiny few. We're the outriders you might say. Come down in discrete groups so we didn't attract attention. The Elders of the Council want us to be like the mickle of midges that invade our Scottish lochs in the summer, irritatingly persistent but quick to disperse. The lessons of history are being heeded and this time we will succeed in ridding our lands of foreign scum. We're not planning a direct attack in great numbers as tried in the past, but a slow pummelling until we grind the dreams of them Roman bastards into demoralised dust until they scamper back to their homeland burrows. We will not succumb to their invasion like the southerners. Weaklings without pride!"

The elder brother nodded in agreement and Kye's heart thudded nervously at the fanaticism he saw gleaming in their eyes. Cold sweat prickled across his back. He didn't want to Romanize but neither did he share this venomous Pict lust for independence. He'd just been searching for some fun. Something to alleviate the daily drudgery of working the homestead and the Pict brothers had made him feel alive with importance during those first meetings. Dubiety at his choice was gripping him, but he was committed for now.

The murmurings in the barn dissipated to a hush broken only by the sounds of the animals. The crowd organised itself into a semi-circle around a stocky man with skin creased and weathered, standing on a wooden crate holding his arms aloft waiting for silence.

"The Council thank you for coming. Be seated Brethren." The voice was harsh with a brutal northern accent stronger than that of the brothers. The stocky man stood down from the crate as the crowd settled their positions. The slop on the ground didn't seem to bother them Kye noticed, amused with a certain respect for their lack of decorum, yet grateful that he was able to use the edge of the haymow as a cleaner place to squat.

"This meeting will be brief, Brethren, as we risk revealing ourselves in such numbers. We are not here to discuss or dispute any matters. The Elders of the Council have already undertaken this at length. The purpose of our gathering is to update you on the success of the raid on the Roman supply fort..." a ripple of cheering was quickly suppressed by the speaker holding his hands aloft again, "...the time for celebration is not yet, Brethren. Mounted Roman scouts have been more frequent since the raid and I doubt you need reminding that the Council's plans rely entirely on stealth. We *must* remain unobtrusive in numbers so let me impart the necessary information quickly so we may scatter again."

Kye was finding the speech difficult to follow.

"What's he saying?" he whispered to the younger brother sitting beside him. "Shut up and listen! You might be called to stand."

Knuckles of fear punched inside Kye's chest.

"Me...to st...stand," he stammered. "What for?"

"What d' ya mean?"

"You got a head full of sawdust or what?" The Pict brother looked at Kye with irritation at his lack of comprehension. "Bribery, we're talking bribery. It didn't take much to persuade a handful of the so-called 'Roman-trusted' locals to help us set the fires inside *Arbeia*. 'Trusted', ha! It wasn't even difficult to bribe some of the fort-based auxiliaries to turn a blind eye, venal bastards." He hawked a ball of phlegm spitting it with derision into the haymow. "It's tougher to corrupt the legionaries though, they have the scruples of the birth blood of Rome, but their blood doesn't run a deeper red than ours when we fight for independence. We will break them. Uncertainty breeds corruption and our tactics will make them uncertain. Once we have the collaboration of a few, that's all we need, just a few, we can worm our way into their forts and destroy their bravado from within. Shadows of distrust will lurk inside their own barracks like a spreading plague."

Kye was still confused. "So why do ya need my input so badly? How does knowing the trumpet signals help with corrupting legionaries?"

"Horse shit! You are dim ain't you? It helps to know when their numbers are split, it helps to know when the fort is most vulnerable, it helps to know how many cohorts they have mustered. We get inside their heads by listening at a discrete distance, then we nibble at them until the irritation is unbearable. Soldiers understand battle, but with no mass of enemy to accost, no confrontation to vent revenge, the loyalty of some will waver and then the Roman invasion begins to crumble into bribery and mutiny."

"Sshh!" his brother rasped at him. "He's calling for standers. Be ready."

Kye was relieved as the meeting began to disperse. He'd been called to stand, but only to acknowledge the thanks of the Council. The elder brother had imparted Kye's knowledge of the trumpet signals to the crowd, cleverly disguising their brevity and Kye knew he was indebted to him.

"Uh, thanks." Kye shuffled nervously, not confident enough to look the Pict in the eye. He was right to be nervous. His stomach churned as his upper gut seemed to plunge in a violent gush right down to his bowels as he realised the two Pict brothers were waiting for the rapidly emptying barn to become clear. The elder Pict brother was seething with quiet menace. As the last man from the gathering left the barn, he indicated to his brother with a slight nod of his head. The younger Pict grabbed Kye from behind, pinning his arms tightly into his back, stretching the left shoulder to screaming point, whilst holding his head in an arm lock around the throat. Kye instinctively struggled only to have a searing pain shoot through his shoulder that momentarily took his breath from him. Immobility eased the burning spasm and he stood helpless as a fly in a spider's web, breathing in short gasps, his eyes wide with fear.

"This is for letting me down." The elder Pict thumped Kye in the midriff, causing a soft explosion of air from Kye. "You owe me for making your pathetic piece of information look good today." Another punch. "You've a reprieve Brigante Boy. Lucky."

"Lucky because the Council are playing this so slowly. You have time to get us better information before we begin our raid on the fort near your homestead. That's our next big target. Two full moons from now. Fail us this time and it'll be your last mistake. And if you're thinking of going to ground, then keep this as a reminder that we will hunt you down." A knee was rammed into Kye's crotch, sweeping nausea through him. "There is no thicket that will hide you, no burrow deep enough, no cavern that won't become your grave. The next full moon we'll be at Swine Lake. You know it?" Kye managed a mumbled yes. "Be there with the information!" The younger Pict let him go and Kye fell into a heap and retched, a final kick to his face splitting his lips and leaving him laying unconscious in his own rancid spew.

....

The puke on the ground was still warm when his wits returned. Cautiously raising himself onto all fours, he laboured for breath as his chest and stomach recoiled in pain at the exertion. A broken rib or two, he deduced. Tasting fresh blood on his lips, mixed with the acrid aftertaste of vomit, brought a wave of repulsion at his own filthy state giving him encouragement to move again. He crawled across to the water trough.

Wincing in pain but at least clean and feeling a little more human, Kye propped himself against the end of the trough. He needed to think. What a fool he'd been to trust the Pict brothers. Whatever had made him think they thought highly of him? They were no different to the Romans when it came down to it. Arrogant and domineering with violence, all of them. For the first time in his life, he could understand the simple pleasures his father had found in farming the wild hills for the love of his family.

Damn! Ma would be worried, but he couldn't go home yet. Pushing pride aside, he wasn't physically capable. No, he would have to rest a few days before trekking back. At least he had water, shelter and food available. He didn't relish slaughtering a sheep and spilling its innards, but he had the knife and skill to do so. Da had taught him two summers ago. The thought of eating raw offal churned his guts, but it would have to happen if he was to gain enough strength to get home. Unless...no...he wouldn't trust anyone, not any more.

The thought had occurred to him that no shepherd left his flock for more than two days, so assistance could be sought when they came to the barn to tend the sheep. It was an appealing option but his recent beating had given him a hard edge of mistrust that formed a protective crust on his decisions. He would survive this ordeal alone.

Feeling fatigue sweep his body, Kye knew he must sleep. Wary now of being found, he scanned the barn for a hideout. The rear of the haymow as it abutted the side of the barn away from the entrance was ideal. Crawling round the edge of the pile of fodder, Kye was delighted to see a break in the rough planking of the barn's structure, big enough for him to see part of the path he'd walked earlier with the Pict brothers. The view was limited but gave him a link with the outside world. Burrowing into the haymow, ensuring he was completely covered, he drifted into pain-induced sleep with the sweet smell of dried summer in his nostrils.

Chapter Ten

The rebuilding project at *Arbeia* was moving far more quickly than the enquiry. This was not a surprise to Peterna. As legate he was well aware of the two sides of the Roman Army. The capability of the legions in achieving swift engineering results was as awesome as the slow grinding cogs of bureaucratic paperwork was irritating. He was still awaiting a response from Hadrian to his last letter. With good fortune his report on the arson attack would filter through the system before the Emperor replied. It certainly added strength to his argument of an uprising, and he was in need of support if he was to avoid ruin. The precariousness of his decision to question Hadrian's orders was gnawing at his thoughts.

Shaking his head, he thumped the desk in frustration. Life was much simpler when there was an enemy army to confront. A battlefield victory was glory for all to see. He knew the *Brittunculi* were out there, somewhere, teasing and toying with his men, but it seems they wouldn't mass and fight like warriors as they had two years ago.

Sitting back in his chair, looking out over the camp towards the North Gate, Peterna drew on his experiences as legate. Calmness soothed through him as he reached a decision, trusting his instincts. Unrest was in the air and it was not right to ignore it. It was as clear to him as mountain spring water that the *Brittunculi* would be planning more covert raids like the one at *Arbeia*. It wouldn't be the local Brigante farmers. He'd learnt enough to know they weren't the type of people to instigate fighting. They fought only when provoked to protect what was theirs. No, there must be other tribes infiltrating the area inciting trouble. The Picts from the north most likely, and Celts as well no doubt. These barbarians seemed to breathe war and sup blood as wine.

If his instincts were right, then a large army was not amassing, but there must be an increase of warriors in the area. There had to be. Some sign of them would be found if he searched. Hadrian was yet to supply him enough troops to make a successful advancement to end this campaign, that was the true way forward, but he didn't have to wait for the natives to show their hand. Play fire with fire. It was time to assert Roman superiority.

"Clerk! Have the tribunes and centurions gather in the Cross Hall at first darkness." With that decision made, Peterna strode away from the Headquarters building to find his wife. Ordering Julita to leave for Rome would be a far harder task than ordering the burning of all villages and homesteads that would not allow access to his Legion for thorough searching. So far he'd failed to persuade his wife it was necessary, using all lines of argument, especially Cloelia's age and passage of marriage that was fast looming. He'd sensed Julita weaken a little where this was concerned, yet she had not consented to go.

Cloelia's reaction had been far from favourable too. That child could liquefy granite with those eyelashes and bouncing curls he thought. He would have to drill a core of Spanish steel through his resolve to keep it firm.

…...................

Marcus had made the problems of home seem distant to Jolinda. Not forgotten, more as if they were floating in a parallel existence shrouded in fog. They'd shared five days of laughter and warmth. Days of simple pleasures, walking along the muddy banks of the *Tinae* sharing conversation infused with lingering kisses that left her breathless and flushed despite the chilly wind.

This morning the air was still and a strengthening sun was warming their faces as they were sitting on small boulders by an oxbow turn in the river. The stones were worn smooth through travelling with the river before being deposited as the *Tinae* meandered, losing its power to transport them further. The potential of spring could be felt ready to burst through the land.

"Listen Marcus! I can hear a squirrel. Do ya hear it?" The noise came again from the nearby cluster of alder trees that flourished beside the river.

"There! A sort of vibrating rumble."

"I hear it."

Jolinda shifted her position so she could lay her head against Marcus's shoulder with her face angled up towards the sun. Closing her eyes she sighed with contentment, soaking in the ambience. Marcus could smell the freshness of her hair and was enjoying the gentle pressure of her body on him. His eyes were open and lingering over the soft curves outlined by her clothes. With his blistered hands recovered enough for a return to duty, he was puzzling over how best to tell Jolinda about the forthcoming campaign that would take him away for a spell.

A mossy hollow would be welcomed, he yearned to consummate their relationship. A dart of guilt dashed his thoughts as he remembered a certain goatskin stashed in a barn and why it was there. It passed through quickly and without damage and was replaced by a simper that twitched his lips slightly. As if linking in to his thoughts, Jolinda spoke warmly without moving her position and still with her eyes closed.

"I'm so pleased Cloelia 'n' Brutus have talked properly to each other. I was thinking she was going to be blind to his love forever. Not all her fault I guess, Brutus was as bad. He told me his feelings, but didn't tell her! It's lovely seeing them so happy together."

A silence pursued. Her sweet odour was addling his senses and he found himself again in the unaccustomed situation of struggling for the right words. How many times in Italia had he enraptured the girls with poetry that came so easily? Where were the lines now?

"At least Brutus can be in the hospital for a while yet, perhaps Fortuna is smiling on him more than he thinks," was all he could say.

Jolinda gave him a quizzical look, sitting up and twisting to face him.

"And being in the hospital is lucky?"

"No...yes...damn!" He stood up stumbling a little on the round stones. Jolinda rose too.

"Talk to me Marcus Guintoli," she said softly. "Don't be dumb like Brutus. Say what ya need to say. What's troublin' ya?"

Her gaze was one of sincerity, giving an air of honesty and vulnerability that seized him. He stooped to kiss her, cupping a hand around her nape, drawing her inwards. Groaning with the pleasure she aroused in him, he wanted to burst. The words came in a gush.

"Our time is running out. I am back on duty tomorrow and the legate has a campaign planned that will take me away from the fort. I do not know for how long, nor when our next opportunity to be together will be."

The shift of his kisses to her throat and shoulder spoke his intentions more clearly than words. The onset of a creeping fear coursed through Jolinda obliterating her own arousal but she didn't pull away. Her mind was racing over his words. Marcus's mind was consumed with desire as he moved his hand under her garment. He hadn't noticed her concern and with a throat dry with anticipation he spoke huskily.

"Let us find a mossy hollow, woman."

"What is the campaign?"

"Uh...we are heading north, flushing out barbarians. They burnt *Arbeia*, we will burn them. No more talk of 'attack'." He spat the word 'attack' with scorn in the Pict tongue.

"Burn them, what do ya mean?" She pulled away.

This time Marcus didn't miss her concern, and already regretting his loose words, tried to smooth over the dents. How could he have forgotten she was not Roman? He'd used the word barbarians to her as if they were a hated irritant to be stamped out, swatted in passing like a bothersome fly. He was shocked to realise that this was no longer true on a personal level. He had felt like that about them all, but not now. His vow to Flavinus charged him with a force that constricted his chest. *Jolinda was not Roman.* The phrase refused to be silenced as if all the gods were manifesting the point. He wanted it not to matter but how could a vow be retracted? If she came over to Rome, if she would renounce her family and Brigante roots, the gods would allow it he felt sure. Had there not been harmony with them together these past few days when she'd appeared Romanized? The gods would not have teased them with that if it displeased them completely.

"Marcus, what do ya mean, burn them? Is me family in danger?" Repeating her question delivered him his voice and he began speaking with fervour, intent on persuading her to stay.

"Jolinda you must remain on the fort, pledge alliance to Rome, you..."

"If me family's in danger, ya must tell me," she interrupted.

"No-one is in danger if they co-operate but you must stay with Cloelia, for me..." he was about to say 'for us, for our future, but she broke in again.

"Co-operate with what? How? What's ya army planning?"

The relevance of it being 'his' army did not go unnoticed. Knowing it was hopeless to attempt an explanation without giving more information, a short sigh of frustration escaped from him. Standing a pace apart he gently held her shoulders.

"Have you ever witnessed a crucifixion Jolinda Teviot?" His gaze was direct. "You must swear an oath that you will not repeat what I tell you next to any soul outside this fort. My life depends on it. I would die an agonising death nailed to a cross if the legate discovers I revealed orders of a campaign to a barbarian."

She winced at his use of the word barbarian again, but his conker brown eyes bore the severity of the truth in their unwavering gaze. Feeling the warm strength their deepness emitted, just as she had when they first met in the snowy ditch, she understood he'd used the word deliberately this time to show how it would look to his superiors.

"I swear on me Da's grave, I'll not tell. If me family's in no danger, I'll stay here with Cloelia."

He relaxed a little at these words.

"No Brigante is in danger if they co-operate. We are to begin searching all villages and homesteads to the north and take prisoner any warrior rebels that have come down from the northern mountains." He emphasized 'warrior rebels'. "Picts and Celts. The legate does not believe the Brigante tribes are behind the arson attack, but some must be sheltering the warriors. They may not have a choice. We are to rout them out, that is all. We have to take the initiative and push forward or this will never end. Your family will be safe."

"What did ya mean about burning them?"

"We are to fire all homesteads and villages that resist our searches." It seemed fair to a soldier who was trained in warfare but spasms of consternated fear unsteadied Jolinda.

"Oh, Marcus! Then I *must* go home. Ma will resist. She's innocent but she'll resist. I know she will. Ya don't know her like I do. She hates ya Romans, she has reason to. Da was killed by the Roman sword."

Marcus could feel Jolinda trembling and her eyes were imploring his understanding but raw emotion was scrambling his thoughts. A blush of anger at the gods was heating his jaw line and creeping up his cheeks. It should be easy, he'd found a woman to be happy with, a deep and satisfying happiness, returned tenfold he knew, yet the gods were mocking them.

"I must go home Marcus, I must," she whispered the words seeing anger wring in him. A sudden scrabble of branches from the alder trees captured their attention. A squirrel was racing with delight. Seeing the freedom of its movements as it stolidly tracked along branches seemingly too thin to withhold its weight, deftly leaping, flying almost, over gaps five times its own length, broke their own inertia. Jolinda's confidence of the goodness in life returned. Reaching up to Marcus, she brushed his left cheek with hers.

"Let's be together now my Roman."

They stumbled across the pebbles and made love with great urgency standing beneath the alders, using a trunk for support. The release was swift, his voice cracking as he called out in his moment of desire. She felt her body beginning to spin with the intensity, surprised by the strength and suddenness of the sensations now that the twinge of pain from first entry was over. She gasped for him to stay inside, inhibitions gone with her virginity.

"Now that is barbaric Jolinda Teviot! You are proving your race is not civilised." Marcus was shuddering just watching her.
"It's beautiful, it's cleansing. Join me."
"I am not getting in that river with you, it is freezing. I will wait for the civilisation of the bathhouse thank you. Does it ever get warm in this land? Does the wind ever feel gentle?" These were not the questions he should be asking, but he didn't want to crush the air of mellowness their lovemaking had created. The question of how her father had died by a Roman sword would keep a little longer. As he quietly marvelled at how she unfalteringly waded waist deep into the chilling waters, dipping straight under and rising with her dark tresses shining in silver sleekness, he wondered how long it would be before she left the fort. Would it be immediate or would she wait until he left on campaign? She was smiling as she swam ashore and he wrapped her in the discarded woollen shawl as she reached him. Shivering, she quickly wrung her hair and dressed. She too was rapt in the moment, her mind free and easy.

It was this absorption into nothing that doubtless allowed the thought to come to the fore. Something Kye had said, the word he had used when he'd been pretending to attack her that day in the snow when the trumpets had been sounding. A thought had niggled at her but not shown itself fully. Marcus had used the same word earlier. The Pict word for 'attack', he'd spoken it with derision. Disquiet came to her again and Marcus saw fear freckle her expression.

"Kye is involved with the Picts," she whispered. "That must be where he ran away to. Oh, Marcus, he ain't a man yet, he thinks he is, but he ain't."

There was no point in further words. The euphoria was gone. In its place slipped an oppressive preponderance of parting. Holding her close, he asked simply,

"How will I know it is Kye?"

"He looks like me, my Roman. You will know him when you meet if you keep my vision clear in your mind. Keep it clear for me Marcus and you will know him. Please spare him."

There was not a doubt between them that the two would meet during this campaign. It was as if the gods via the ripples of the river behind them were speaking it.

....

Ma's welcome was stiff for only a moment before relief at seeing her eldest child return safely took over. Wiping away a tear threatening to spill, she hugged Jolinda.

"Hello Ma, where's Aaron and Tamsin?"

"They've gone to the settlement for supplies." Ma turned away to continue peeling the skirret.

"Kye?"

"No news."

A short pause made the silence loud. Ma filled it with a thrumming harangue that she didn't mean but acted as a vent for her pent up anguish.

"I should put ya across me knee 'n' tan ya backside young lady for what ya put me through. Ya know I should, 'n' don't think ya too grown up for me to do it either. Runnin' off 'n' leaving ya chores. What were ya thinking child? I'm surprised me tresses didn't fall out with the worry of it all. Help me peel these skirret."

Jolinda chuckled at her mother's tone.

"I ain't missed ya nagging Ma." Jolinda was trying to contain her smirking but gave up as her mother bristled further. Finally, Jolinda's infectious giggle touched them both and the pair laughed until they were breathless. Jolinda sobered quickly.

"I've something to tell ya Ma. It's important but ya ain't gonna like it or understand it or want to hear it even, but ya must heed me."

Ma Teviot began to object but Jolinda interrupted her.

"Ya must heed me Ma. Times ain't as they were, not for any of us." Choosing her words carefully, and giving no mention of Marcus, Jolinda explained of the arson attack on *Arbeia*, stressing how the Picts and Celts were inciting trouble in the area and causing reprisals by the Romans.

"Why won't them all just let us be Jolinda?"

"I don't know why Ma."

"I doesn't favour them northern warriors any more than I favour ya Romans." Jolinda let the reference to it being 'her' Romans pass without comment. "Ya father told me last summer he had a run in with a couple of Pict brothers. I remember him saying they were full of trouble. 'Rebel rousers intent on silting our rivers with blood' were his exact words." Ma began chewing at her fingernails as she became silent with her memories.

"Why did Da attack the Roman soldiers the day he was killed Ma?" Jolinda spoke softly yet the question seemed to fill the room, clinging to the air like river mist. Ma's chin lifted and her shoulders straightened in response.

"He were a fair man your Da. Not easily riled." A happy memory drew a small smile from Ma and Jolinda waited for her to continue without prompting. "I first saw him really mad when ya was just a pip in the cradle. Some rover we gave a bed to one night, took a handful too much of me bottom as he were leavin'. Got a bit familiar with me he did. That made ya Da mad, having our hospitality repaid like that." The smile was gone now, replaced by a wistful sadness. "Nothing meant more to him than his family. He were protecting ya sister that day Jolinda, and ya'self." Jolinda's expression was showing her confusion so Ma continued.

"He were protecting the Teviot name. Ya sister had been abased...physically like...by one of them legionaries. Another stood by watching, holding his horse 'n' laughing whilst he did what he wanted. Filthy scum forced her." Ma's face was pinched white with anger and disgust. "Ya Da never uttered a word when Tamsin told us, just took off with his axe."

A frown puckered Jolinda's forehead.

"Tamsin didn't tell me any of that, Ma."

"She were suffering trauma over it, poor lamb. Too dirtied by their actions. It were some weeks before she told us, 'n' that were only 'cause she couldn't hide the bleeding. I give thanks she miscarried, it were the seed of evil inside her."

"A miscarriage!" I remember blood on the bedding, but I didn't know it was a miscarriage."

Mother and daughter became quiet with their own thoughts, the chopping of vegetables the only sound. Doubt at Tamsin's innocence preyed on Jolinda's mind, but what good would it do to tell Ma that her sister had been whoring for the Romans? The words stuck in her throat.

"So, what will these reprisals from the Romans be?" Ma asked, her heart weighing heavily. "I fret for Kye but there's nought I can do. I don't know where he is."

"I don't know," Jolinda lied, remembering Marcus's warning of crucifixion that ushered a brief vision of his face to her.

"Don't know, or won't say?"

"Can't say."

"Ya brother's life may be riding on it."

"His, and others. I'm doing right, Ma. Da is my judge." Gentle acceptance came from her mother with a sigh.

"These are bleak days, but ya a good person Daughter. I know you'll do right. Ya share a common spirit with ya Da, and I'll trust in it."

....

Bursting through the door, bringing with him a rush of cold air, Aaron was breathless, his boyish features burnished with news.

"There's a squadron of Romans riding this way." He drew up short seeing Jolinda, the surprise momentarily silencing him. Exhaling a cheerful whoop, he rushed to hug her, quickly resuming his animated narration.

"I could see the squadron from the ridge. Left the fort by the North Gate, them don't usually do that. I counted thirty men 'n' horses, all heading this way. They'm wearing helmets 'n' got shields and swords, all of them. Do ya think they're going on a raid?"

"Where's Tamsin?" Ma asked, concern adding a sharp edge to her voice. "Why ain't she with ya? I told ya to stay together."

"She sent me on ahead, Ma. The warehouses were hectic 'n' she still had stuff to get." Aaron's timbre had become defensive as he cowered a little from his mother's rebuke. "She don't like leaving ya alone too long Ma. We didn't know Jolinda were back. I ran all the way, so we ain't been apart for long."

Ma sighed and softened her tone.

"I just want everyone safe Aaron, that's all." Hugging her youngest child, she drew on his innocent strength.

"Were there any foot soldiers Aaron?" asked Jolinda.

"No, just horsemen."

"It's a scouting party then, not a raiding party." Jolinda said.

"Scouting for what?" It was Aaron who asked the question, but both mother and brother were looking to her for the answer. Her reply was measured.

"Checking the lay of the land. Mapping where the buildings are, that sort of thing. They won't be looking to fight without the legionaries."

"Why do they need to know where the buildings are?" He was a boy trying to understand, but his questioning was pushing Jolinda into a corner.

"Aaron, ya questions must stop. There's trouble brewing but I can't tell ya. Ya must heed Ma 'n' me and stay close to the homestead. How long will our supplies last without getting more, Ma?"

"If Tamsin brings what she should, we'll have enough t' stretch a month maybe."

"Then we'll look to ourselves for a while. Should any northerners come looking for lodgings, then send them away. Any stranger come to that. We look to ourselves only. If we do that, then we have nothing to fear from the Romans when they come. I want to know the minute ya see the legionaries marching. Don't no-one ask me anything more, there's chores t' be done."

Chapter Eleven

    Stooping slightly to enter the low wooden barrack, Brutus felt as bleak as the damp morning. It was two hours past dawn yet the drear mist refused to allow the day to lighten. The room was empty of people yet their presence lingered in the stale aroma of sleeping bodies and fading smells of cooking, and it went part way to easing his restlessness. The fort was unnaturally quiet.
    Sitting on his bedroll that had been empty for too long, he rested the elbow of his good arm on his knee, cupping his palm under his chin. His body was leaden with melancholy, the ache in his damaged arm a constant reminder of his plight. His recovery was too slow. The unit couldn't afford to be undermanned indefinitely, and his chances of regaining combat fitness were receding and he knew it. The legate would have no choice but to deport him and if they lost men in numbers during this campaign, it would surely speed the process.
    Seeing his javelin hanging alone on the racking, he wondered how the cohorts were faring. The legate's plan was to spread the cohorts at ten-mile intervals and sweep northwards in a long, thin line. It was a large area to cover and unusual tactics, indeed foolhardy tactics for attacking a massed army, but their instructions had been to rout warrior rebels in hiding and to burn villages and homesteads harbouring them. The orders indicated the scouts had not found an armed horde, and he prayed to Mars and Jupiter that their intelligence was accurate or it could be a massacre. Swiftness of the campaign was imperative, surprise being a major element, which was why such an extensive area was being covered, stretching the depth of the army to a dangerously narrow battle line. As legionaries, doubts of their superior's commands may be thought but would not be spoken, such insubordination was to seal your own death.
    A sharp gust of wind whistled under the door, causing the sackcloth covering his shield to flutter, drawing his attention. Tired of his lugubrious mood, he rose and moved over to the shield. Removing the sackcloth, he smiled despite himself at the workmanship. Caressing its gilded edges, he hefted it on to his arm. The weight of it was reassuring, familiar and he hunkered down behind it for a moment. Putting the shield aside, he picked up his sword. It felt awkward in his left hand.
    "Three inches of point, beats six inches of side," he muttered as he feinted towards his bedroll, trying to master control of the weapon that seemed to move at its own will. Practise is all I need, he thought. Practise! Perhaps my weak arm will then be good enough to carry the shield. He spent the next ten minutes making circles and lunging movements in the air, cussing at his own inadequacy.

……………

The Fourth Cohort was marching at double pace, forty-eight rows of ten legionaries traversing the landscape like a fervid caterpillar, turning the ground to mud now that the snow had thawed. They were soon upon their first homestead. Reaching the crude outer ditch of the small dwelling, the cohort was deployed into centuries, encircling the encampment. Looking up at a grassy mound, topped by a protective palisade, smoke could be seen rising from the largest hut within. The Third Century was positioned in front of the entrance gates, anticipation was embracing the dank. Marcus was edgy.

"Chance, not wisdom, governs human life," muttered Lucius. Marcus knew his barrack-comrade was feeling his strain too. They had spoken little of the campaign, but Lucius was aware that Jolinda dwelt close to the fort. Neither knew if this was her home or not. He whispered a prayer.

"Vulcan, god of fire, direct our flames on the deserving only this day." Nervous sweat prickled Marcus's back despite the cold.

"Third Century! Shields high and low!" commanded the centurion.

The row closest to the palisade shuffled into position, with alternate men dropping to one knee. Those crouching were holding their shields bottom edge to the earth. The men standing were holding their shields high, interlocking with their comrade's, forming a solid, protective barrier.

"Archers prepare!"

Kneeling behind the shield-barrier, the archers readied their weapons. Beside each bowman was a second legionary holding a burning spill.

The sound of rasping steel filled the air, as the remaining rows of legionaries unsheathed their swords. Marcus and Lucius were at the front of this group, out of arrow range but with a clear view of proceedings.

The centurion called forward the negotiator. Marcus felt his guts braiding with tension. *Open the gates...do not resist...let us search! Open the gates...do not resist...do not resist!* Over and over, the same words formed in his head, as if by focusing his thoughts, he could influence the actions of those behind the palisade.

The bleat of a goat was the only response to the negotiator's first hail to search. This, and the rising smoke dissipating into the grey murk, was the only signs of habitation. The stillness was strident. The negotiator called out again, and a third time. Nothing.

"Swordsmen, to me!" commanded the centurion.

"Mars, guide our hands this day," muttered Lucius in prayer.

Marcus fell silently in line beside his comrade, and, with five-dozen others, sprinted up the grassy mound. The palisade was only effective as an obstacle if defended. Within minutes the first wave of legionaries, led by their centurion, was dropping out of sight of their comrades, as they clambered over. Marcus and Lucius remained on the outside with the main group, pressing their backs close against the fencing, with their shields held high for protection. Flushed with adrenalin, they awaited further orders.

"Somebody is at home," hissed Marcus. Tension searing his voice with grit. "Why do they not show themselves?"

Lucius spoke no words. The deep look into his friend's eyes, saying far more. They'd been in fighting situations before, but never against a foe that may be a soul mate. This was unique.

"No resistance met! Gates open!"

Marcus exhaled a breath in relief at these words from his centurion. Running through the gates into the compound, he and Lucius fanned out under direction.

"Form up! Make squares!" Practised drill-work took over, and Marcus found himself standing in formation in front of a small, circular mud-hut drowned by a straw roof that spread almost to the ground. The largest hut with the rising smoke was to his left, and a second small hut, was nestling behind that.

Search parties were sent in to the dwellings. Marcus and Lucius remained in formation, watching. The lowing of a cow and a repeat of the goat-bleat were coming from the hut furthest away. The hut nearest was quiet. A commotion was occurring in the large hut. *Do not resist...do not resist.* Marcus was focusing on his silent words again, helpless to do anything else. A cry of alarm came from within the large hut. Emerging from under the straw roofing came a legionary dragging a young girl by unkempt locks. Pain was keeping her silent, wide eyes revealing her fear. Some blood was smeared across one cheek, a bite mark on the legionary's hand revealing its source.

"Sir!" The legionary was unable to salute, with the urchin in one hand and his sword in the other, but stood to attention before his officer.

"Make your report."

"Sir! Two barbarians in the large hut, hiding under animal skins. *This...*" he spat the word with derision, pulling harder on the girls' hair as he did so, "...and a woman with a fever. She is under guard, Sir."

"No men? No weapons?" snapped the centurion.

"Nothing, Sir."

Representatives from the other search parties made their reports. A store of furs and worked hides, probably for trading, livestock and supplies, but no signs of warriors and no cache of weapons.

"Negotiator, ask the girl where the rest of her family is."

"Yes, Centurion."

The girl was mute with fear, and it seemed to Marcus that the day was hanging in aberrancy with her silence. The negotiator tried a softer approach. Dropping to one knee and gently holding the girl's shoulders, he persuaded the legionary to let go of her hair. It was a mistake. As soon as this restraint was gone, she sank her teeth into the negotiator's forearm, taking him quite by surprise.

"Wretch!" he cried, splitting the silence. Marcus flinched, his nerves stretched taut.

Scuttling towards the large hut, the girl was caught by the legionary, only to wriggle free again after clawing successfully at an eye. The centurion grabbed her next, and with one strong arm around her slight torso, hoisted her on to his hip, where flailing limbs hit armour and not flesh. She quieted under his hold. Ducking into the large hut, he emerged minutes later without the urchin, followed by the guards.

"Our orders are to rout rebel warriors. There are none here. Stand the archers down, Optio, and form the men up. We move on." The second in command saluted and shouted his orders.

"This day will be long," breathed Marcus, as he and Lucius marched from the homestead.

"Fourth Cohort, double pace!" The order rippled down the columns and soon the Third Century was jogging towards its next target.

....

"They're coming! The Romans is coming!" Aaron didn't know whether to be frightened or excited. Jolinda, Ma and Tamsin were sitting around an animal fur they'd been scraping. "It ain't a scouting party this time Jolinda." Aaron was remembering her words. "The legionaries are coming, hundreds of them." His eyes were wide and iridescent, reflecting the flames from the hearth. "The gels heard them first. I was trying to milk them, but them were skittish. I found out why when I went outside and saw the Romans coming."

Jolinda's heart was thumping hard, then she calmed. A contrast of stillness following Aaron's burst of activity into the hut. As Jolinda met the gaze of her family, she experienced a quiet warmth. A warmth of trust in Marcus.

"The Romans is looking for warriors. We let them search. They'll find none here 'n' be on their way. We let them search. We don't resist." Jolinda's gaze rested on Ma's. "We don't resist."

Ma gave an exiguous nod. Tamsin concurred with a larger nod. Breaking the moment of stillness, Jolinda raised her arms out to Aaron.

"Pull me up, Brother. Let's get the animals in here with us, so we knows them is secure, then we'll open the fences."

It was a relief to Jolinda that the Roman campaign was beginning. The waiting was over, and with a beginning, there could follow an end.

....

"Prepare and pray again," murmured Lucius, as the Cohort encircled the encampment as before. The Third Century was again positioned at the bottom of the mound, in front of the entrance gates.

"Third Century! Shields high and low!" commanded their centurion. "Archers prepare! Arm swords!"

"She lives here. This is her place." Marcus was looking up the grassy bank, his face set with concentration. Lucius took a furtive glance at his friend.

"How do you know?" he hissed.

"I just do. This is the Teviot homestead. This is her place."

Lucius took a more incredulous look at Marcus.

"Is that the best persuasion you have for me? Where is Brutus when I need him? His instincts I trust."

"And mine you do not?"

"And yours I do not. Not since a child in Italia." The reference was to the many boyhood scrapes that had landed them in trouble. It had long been a joke between them. "Brutus has the intuition, you have the charm, I have the looks and Flavinus, the brains. Remember?"

The mention of Flavinus reminded Marcus of his vow, and of what he was trying to achieve. He had to keep Jolinda safe. Just as importantly, he needed to win her over to Rome. The legate's decision to rout the rebels was the right one, Marcus agreed, no doubt about it, the uprising had to be thwarted. But, if he was to have any chance of a future with Jolinda, the campaign must run smoothly, with as little disruption to the local tribes as possible.

A reprimand from their Optio brought them to silence. The negotiator hailed a request to search. A woman's voice replied in accented Latin. *It is her...she is not resisting...she is not resisting!*

"Swordsmen to me," commanded the centurion.

With joy-tinged nervousness, Marcus fell in to line. This time, there was no sprint up the grassy mound. Instead, the legionaries marched a controlled pace up and through the fences, fanning out under direction to form squares inside the compound. It was orderly.

He saw Jolinda immediately, standing aside the doorway of the central hut. The construction of the dwellings was identical to the previous homestead, but with a slightly different layout. The largest hut was to the left of the two smaller huts, rather than centred between them. Jolinda had a comforting arm around the shoulders of a boy that reached to her bosom in height.

Aaron, thought Marcus. *That must be Aaron, but where is your mother...is Kye back...do not do anything foolish...where is your sister...do not resist Jolinda!* Silent words were his only route of communication, and again, they scrambled through his mind with intensity.

Seeing so many legionaries surrounding their huts was unnerving to Jolinda. The spectacle was threatening, even though she was aware of their intentions. Drawing on her Brigante pride, she stood tall, with her chin held high, displaying a calm she didn't feel within. Her eyes darted along the rows of soldiers, desperate to know if Marcus was amongst them. Identifying one amidst so many in uniform was difficult, but she succeeded. Her heart bolted as they shared a glance. It was enough to settle her nerves, and his too. Feeling easier, Marcus risked whispering a smug quip to Lucius, as the centurion striding towards her claimed Jolinda's attention.

"It seems I have charm *and* intuition this day."

"The charm was never in doubt."

"And the intuition? Can you deny that, now you see she lives here? I am beginning to feel good about this whole campaign."

"I reluctantly concede you were correct on this occasion, but it is still the instincts of Brutus Antonini I trust. It will take much more than one lucky guess to convince me of yours! Now shut up will you, or the Optio will put us on remand. I preferred it when you were edgy." Lucius was not sharing in his friend's new-found optimism.

Marcus suppressed a smile. He was indeed starting to believe that the outcome he desired was attainable.

…...................

Jolinda had no need of the negotiator, preferring instead to converse directly with the centurion. Marcus was unable to hear the words between them, but a sweep of her arm, palm open towards the skies, was indication enough that she was giving permission for the huts to be searched. She was doing everything right. Satisfied that full co-operation was being received, the centurion shouted the command to sheath swords. The search would be conducted in a non-threatening manner, a further reason for Marcus to relax.

Seeing Jolinda raise a thumb and forefinger before pointing to the large hut, he deduced she was telling the centurion that two more people were inside. Her mother and sister, Marcus presumed. Kye was still missing then. *Show me so I can be sure, Jolinda...bring the two outside...let me see who is with you...bring them forth.*

The centurion must have requested the same, and Marcus watched as Jolinda called to those inside. Curiosity was filling him. Now that his nervousness had dissipated, he was eager to see what Ma looked like? It was well documented in Italian culture, that a wise man should study the matriarch before wedlock. This brought a wry grin. How would Jolinda fare with age? Would Ma carry any of the same beauty as Jolinda, or would the years have smothered it? With impish interest, he found himself keen to eye her sister too, and the rogue in him conjured thoughts of a threesome.

"You are a lucky bastard, Marcus Guintoli." Lucius was guessing at his thoughts, as he studied Jolinda. He too was beginning to relax as Jolinda's co-operation was making this search much calmer than the last.

"Let us see how her sister compares, shall we?"

"One each? Or were you thinking of an orgy?"

Marcus raised an eyebrow and grinned.

"You are a *greedy*, lucky bastard, Marcus Guintoli," Lucius chuckled. "But I have heard the local people prefer monogamy. You are advised to stick to one at a time." He was ruefully referring to his taking two whores together at the tavern, and the resulting brawl that shattered Brutus's arm.

Watching with intrigue, they saw Ma emerge. Following closely behind her was Tamsin. Marcus observed, a mother, two daughters, one son.

All individuals, but bearing a striking resemblance. *He looks like me, my Roman.* The words Jolinda had spoken about Kye came back to him. *Looks like me!* How had he not made the family connection before? A dark haired, fair skinned Brigante girl. His *Geryon!* The world fell black and silent around him. The abyss was open once more. Disorientated, staggering, he was moving along it in rushing wind. He could focus on nothing but Tamsin. Tamsin was his *Geryon.*

....

Closing the gates behind the departing legionaries, Jolinda felt an empty relief. Leaning against the wooden stakes for a moment, she tried to gather herself. Her family and homestead were safe, but why had Marcus passed her over as they left? She'd sought to catch his eye for reassurance, as on arrival, but there had been nothing. His look was vacant. Was he angry with her? She must have done something dreadfully wrong, but what? Turning the events over in her head didn't provide an answer.

Chiding herself for such immature insecurities, she muttered her way back to the large hut. Everything had gone well, except for that one strange look. She told herself there would be a rational explanation. There was plenty to keep her busy and she vowed to remain positive until this campaign was over. He would send word to her when he could. *Look out for Kye, my Roman...may the good spirits watch over you both.*

....

A further two homesteads were searched by the Fourth Cohort before Lucius ventured to speak to Marcus.

"It seems there are no rebels hiding close to the fort, at least. We march on a settlement next. Perhaps the legate's fears will be uncovered there."

Marcus did not reply. Lucius spoke again.

"We are making swift progress. That is good for the campaign."

Still, there was no answer from Marcus and Lucius drew silent with him, shaking his head, not knowing how to break through his friend's sudden moroseness.

As the morning's patchy drizzle thickened to heavier rain, the column was called to a halt. The legate's brief had been to move swiftly and silently, so no trumpets blared. Instead, the centurions communicated to their optios with hand signals and soft shouts. A moving column of armoured men could never be devoid of noise, but nothing carried on the air as a trumpet's blast did, and the mood was one of muffled quiet.

"The sting is always in the tail of the scorpion." Marcus's tone was sullen.

Lucius, relieved his friend was speaking, looked at him intently, waiting for his next words.

"Did you see the girl with Jolinda?"

"I saw her," replied Lucius. "How could I forget that face? Brutus is paying a high price for her services to me that day. The moment is one to regret, but the remorse is mine to deal with."

"That was Tamsin, Jolinda's sister."

"So, Jolinda has a whore for a sister. All is not lost for you because of it. I do not understand."

Marcus felt wretched. How much should he tell Lucius? Flavinus had witnessed his guilty act with Tamsin in the hills that day and was later killed for knowing his secret. Was it fair to burden Lucius too by confessing his guilt? His answer came as a lone swan beat noisy wings as it tracked southwards above them. The Augurs would interpret this as a sign of solitude. Marcus must bear his guilt alone. To elucidate the connection between Jolinda and Flavinus's death would be explanation for his misery. He would withhold telling Lucius of his rape of Tamsin.

The sentence echoed amidst the rain. Speaking the words seemed to tumefy the reality and Marcus needed a moment before continuing.

"I revenged the death of Flavinus. Jolinda's father died by my sword."

"The man was enraged. He was *Brittunculi*. You had no choice or he would have slain you both." Lucius clasped a rough hand to the side of Marcus's neck above the shoulder armour. "You had no choice."

"I cannot undo what I have done. Lucius, I made a vow to the gods. Flavinus wanted it...Roman women. Only the basest dolt would believe he could overthrow a vow. I must put Jolinda behind me. We fight for the Empire. Let us get recognition before the legate and move on from these lands." There was steel in his eyes.

Chapter Twelve

Watching through the broken planking, Kye tracked the shepherd as he walked along the path away from the barn. He resolved to give proper thanks for his concealment at the first opportunity upon returning home. He would visit the bridestone and make an offering. He didn't visit the site often, but the good spirits deserved his gratitude for shrouding him these past weeks. That he'd remained unnoticed in the haymow, especially when the fever had gripped him in the first few days, was due to more than simple luck. The debt must be repaid.

Rubbing his arms to ward off the chill, he once again thought through his plan for getting home. He would leave the barn two hours after nightfall, tonight. Conscious of his shabby appearance, he had no wish to meet anyone, not Pict or Roman, neither Celt nor Brigante. Confident of his way over the hills, he would shun the main paths in favour of the animal tracks. He hoped to reach the homestead before dawn but his fitness was untested and if daylight came first, he would hide in a thicket or badger's burrow till darkness returned. He shivered a little at the thought.

Shifting to a more comfortable position, he gathered his resolve. Staying longer was not an option. The next full moon was due soon, and two Pict brothers were expecting him at Swine Lake. What to do about that problem, he didn't know, but the answer would not be found in the barn. Settling down to wait, Kye estimated it was two hours until dusk. A tension seemed to scutter on the breeze.

....

Four hundred and eighty armoured soldiers marched into the settlement without warning to the inhabitants. Although a smaller unit than usually deployed, they filled the narrow street with an impressive display of uniformity and discipline, made greater by its unexpectedness. Men and women stopped their working to look, as a hush rippled through the community, broken by crying infants and snorting horses. The ringing of hammer to hot iron carried across the growing silence, the blacksmith unaware in his forge of the army's arrival. Some doors were hurriedly closed. A boy ran shouting towards the river to alert a group of women who were washing garments. Closer by, a mother clutching three youngsters to her side, was backing slowly away, unsure if she should flee or not.

The negotiator was summoned to the front rank. Before he began speaking, a shout went up from the rear of the column. A squadron of horses, including the legate, was approaching at a canter.

"Stand by! Let the legate through!" The lead centurion motioned to the negotiator to wait. Legionaries shuffled aside, opening a channel in their ranks, and sealing it by shuffling back into formation, as soon as the horses had passed along. Legate Maxinius dismounted quickly, acknowledging the officer's salutes with a curt nod.

"What is the situation here, Centurion?"

"Sir! The negotiator is about to request a search of the settlement, Sir."

"Have you met with any resistance?"

"None as yet, Sir. We have searched four remote homesteads without sign of weaponry stores or rebel warriors. This is our first group settlement, Sir."

The legate pursed his lips in thought.

"We have received intelligence detailing a possible rebel meeting site to the east of this settlement. Can you continue here with four hundred men plus the mounted squadron, Centurion?"

"Yes, Sir!"

"Then I will take the Third Century and investigate this site. I am reluctant to diverge from the plan, as the success of our campaign rests on swift scrutiny of the area to the north, but acting on what I have heard, I feel this site must be investigated immediately. Continue with your orders, Centurion. Use flame readily against resisting parties, but only against resisting parties. We need to display dominance, but not unnecessary provocation. I will return the Third Century to you with haste for the remainder of the campaign".

"Understood, Sir!"

Legate Maxinius took a moment to study the saluting officer's face. It was impassive, his expression giving away nothing of his thoughts. Much depended on these men following his orders to the feather tip. They had proven themselves in battle, but would they hold steady in these unusual circumstances? Centurions were not chosen for their diplomatic restraint, and Maxinius wondered if they would remain loyal to his leadership. To add weight to the importance of the situation, he added,

"If flame is used, I will expect rebel prisoners or a cache of weapons as justification. Failure to provide justification will be seen as a direct breach of orders. This is punishable by flogging and deportation." With a grunt and not needing a reply, he snapped an order to rally the Third Century.

Peterna Maxinius was enjoying a clear mind, as he led the legionaries across the tussock-pitted hillside. Although an accomplished horseman, the rhythm of a march, especially at double pace, suited him better. He noticed the inclines a little more than he used to, but was pleased by his stamina. This seemed to have increased with the years, compensating for age ravages elsewhere. He found the rhythm of a marching body soothing, allowing clarity of thought without effort.

The day's campaign was going well. Scouts had been keeping him informed of the progress of each cohort. Throughout the morning they'd encountered remote homesteads, and the reports had been similar: little resistance to searching, no signs of rebel warriors. This was the pattern across the area, and it had not been unexpected. The rebel warriors, and he stood steadfast in his belief that they were grouping in small numbers, were far more likely to be flushed from the larger settlements. Indeed, the success of the Sixth Cohort was proof.

The Sixth Cohort was the first to reach a tight cluster of homesteads. Instead of perching atop a mound protected by palisades, as was the case with the individual homes, the village formed a nucleus beside a stretch of river that flowed strongly. This offered a natural barrier along one side, but no protection was in place elsewhere. Initially, it was thought they must simply feel secure in numbers and arrogance, until the discovery was made of two well concealed caves with escape routes channelling through the bedrock in opposite directions. Flight was their preferred defence and a thorough search of the caves and tunnels had revealed recent use plus a small cache of hunting knives. The senior centurion of the Sixth Cohort was convinced that two people had used the tunnels to escape as the Roman's arrived. The tracks were fresh.

Questions put to the inhabitants had produced the intelligence he was now acting on, and it had been given without the need to burn the village. As he had hoped, it seemed the Brigante tribes were not fervent supporters of the northern rebel rousers. His theory that these strongly independent people regarded the Picts and Scots as much invaders in their lands as the Romans, was proving right, and becoming a useful tool. Aware that the information may be false, and he could be risking a trap, he was arrogantly confident that he was hearing the truth. All pieces were fitting together.

He knew of the barn they were heading to and it was positioned well as a control point for hitting at *Arbeia* and his fort. Knowing that word of their searches was spreading as the day was lengthening into shadows, increased his urgency for results. This in turn, was providing a welcome burst of energy to his fatiguing body and he urged his command a little faster across the countryside.

....

Hissing a curse, Kye burrowed a little deeper into the haymow and listened, hardly daring to breathe. The Pict brothers burst into the barn, agitating the sheep in to a cacophony of bleating and scrabbling.

"Shut up, you lousy creatures!" rasped the younger brother, his voice sibilant through a lack of breath, kicking out at a nearby ewe. "These sheep'll give us away, we'd be safer hiding in that badger sett we passed. Why didn't you stop when I shouted?"

"Think, you cretin!" spat the older brother. "We've no time to hide our tracks, and a sett only has one way in and one way out for us. If we are being tracked, we'd be fish to the spear caught in a sett. We'd have done better to keep going, but for your wheezing."

"That's if they're chasing us at all. We don't know they are." There was a faithless question of hope in the younger Pict's tone. After escaping via the caves, they'd avoided another settlement riddled with Romans, and from a distance had spotted the lone century snaking across the hills. Watching from their vantage point, it was clear the legionaries were on a mission and heading their way. Indeed, it appeared they were following the very same route, and were it not for their swift pace, the older Pict would be convinced they were tracking them. Either way, they decided to run, being forced to take refuge in the barn, when the younger brother's chest grew tight in complaint, severely restricting his breathing.

"Well, they're looking for someone, and they mean business. You saw the prepared arrows with lighting spills they were carrying. How could they know about The Council's plans? They must have an informant." The older brother's face formed a sneer and his fists curled into ball.

"Could be that Brigante stripling we did over here. Ain't seen him about since then," offered the younger brother, rubbing his chest to ease the tightness still there. "Damn, this winter sickness," he complained.

Beads of sweat broke out on Kye's forehead as he listened, laying rigid, taut with fear.

The older Pict considered his brother's suggestion for a moment, before dismissing it with a derisive snort.

"Fear of us will keep that runt quiet. He ain't got the guile for it."

Kye flushed with anger and bit hard on his lip to contain it. At that moment, he couldn't have hated any person more than the Picts so close to him. Rage flamed in his gut, but he knew revenge would not be achieved now.

"Can you run on now you've rested?" the older brother asked.

"I can lope but I can't outrun those bastards this day." The older Pict heard the remorse, and cursing their ill luck, slapped his sibling on the shoulder in a gesture of commiseration.

Hearing running footsteps on the track outside, Kye risked a look. Already regretting not leaving the barn earlier, he bared his teeth in a silent grimace as he recognised the Celt with the mangled ear. The burly man splintered the door as he entered and was greeted by a crouching Pict caught by surprise. Bearing a hunting knife and ready to pounce, his eyes were glazed by blood lust. The Celt stilled, eyeing the steel blade for a moment, before speaking.

"The Brothers sent me. The barn is marked. They want it burned."

A spasm of ice shot through Kye.

The Celt remained inert, wary of any movement startling the Pict in to further action. He'd seen the same wild look in a cornered beast. As surprise of the Celt's entrance settled, focus replaced the glaze in the Pict's eyes.

"Roman butchers!" growled the Celt, sneering with antipathy at the memory.

"You say The Brothers want the barn destroyed because it's marked?"

"Yes, and soon. The scum are heading this way." Nervous impatience was starting to agitate the big man. He hadn't anticipated this delay.

"What do you think, Little Brother?" asked the older Pict, still brandishing the knife, "is our mutilated friend here speaking the truth, or could he be our informant come to meet the Romans? Convince me which it is, Big Man, tell me what ya know." The Pict began to circle his quarry slowly, menacingly. The Celt followed him with his eyes.

As big as he was, the Celt knew it would be difficult to take down both the Picts together, and with time pressing he felt ambushed in to speaking.

"You've seen the Roman show of force. It seems some Brigante tribes have loose tongues when threatened with fire. The Romans have been told of our meetings here. They are looking for warriors, The Brothers want to give them ashes."

"Why burn it?" asked the younger Pict. "We've left no evidence."

"The Brigantes will think the Romans destroyed it, and they won't thank them for slaughtering the livestock." Snorting with approval, he continued to explain. "It will increase our number and add strength to the uprising, but we have to act now so it looks like their hand caused the fire." The Celt was relieved to see the Pict nod his understanding and relax his fighting stance.

"Do you have a horse close by?" asked the younger Pict, still concerned about his chest. "My running is hindered by the winter sickness."

"I have no horse," was the gruff reply.

The haymow crackled and smoked, then ignited with a lick of flame, sizzling the loose strands to powder in an instant, as it probed greedily for a more substantial target to feed its hunger. The bleating increased as the sheep stammered out their fear, bumping and shuffling as they sensed the smoke and flames. The fire quickly found purchase.

Watching from the undergrowth outside the barn, the Celt and Pict brothers nodded in satisfaction of their work. The big Celt, seeing his task accomplished, was eager to be gone, and abruptly ran off in to the evening shadows, raising his fist in a farewell salute.

"You ready Little Brother?"

"Ready, the bridesto..."

The sound of splintering wood coming from the barn interrupted him. The Picts looked on in confusion. Kicking furiously, desperate to escape the growing flames, Kye was able to break the already damaged side of the barn without much trouble. The small gap he'd been using to view the track became large enough for him to push through and he scrambled away, coughing, gasping, and retching. With smoke induced tears blurring his vision, he crawled blindly, unaware he was heading towards the Picts.

"The runt Brigante stripling! How much did he overhear?" whispered the younger Pict.

"Too much," breathed the other, springing up.

Kye was an easy target and the hunting knife entered his stomach before he realised what was happening.

…....................

"I am growing tired of fighting fires," Marcus muttered to Lucius, seeing the smoking barn. "I need scalps for glory, not embers."

With a quick assessment of the situation, Legate Maxinius gave instructions for a rapid search of the area, detailing one group to release the livestock, whilst the others, including Marcus and Lucius, were ordered to fan out around the barn.

"Sounds like we will have mutton for supper, at least," replied Lucius. "And maybe we can source some glory yet. Whoever set this blaze cannot be far away."

"Not far at all. Look!" Marcus was first to reach the prone body and prodded it with his foot with a mixture of contempt and caution as he checked for signs of life. There was none. With his sword drawn, he rolled the body over to reveal the bleeding stomach wound and a face he knew but had never seen before. *He looks like me my Roman!* Jolinda's words echoed at him, freezing him inert momentarily before adrenalin pumped him into action.

"Kye!" Dropping to his knees, Marcus felt for a breath. "He is alive, his breath is shallow but he is alive. Lucius, find a medic." Tearing away clothing, Marcus tucked Kye's knees up to close the gaping wound, applying pressure to stem the blood flow and muttering a prayer of healing to Apollo that he had learnt as a child. "You must not walk with the spirits yet Kye Teviot."

Kye's eyelids flickered, possibly at the sound of his name, and he began to mumble. Marcus leaned closer to listen. The mumbling stopped as Lucius returned. Two medics plus the legate were with him. Grateful to hand over to the medically trained legionaries, Marcus roughly wiped the blood from his hands and picked up his sword. Dazed by the shock of his sudden emotions, with a swarm of thoughts and fragmenting images scrambling at him, Marcus was staring blindly at Legate Maxinius.

"Make your report, Guintoli."

Hearing the legate use his name snapped Marcus to attention.

"Sir! The native was found with a stab wound to his stomach. I gave medical attention to keep him alive for questioning. He was mumbling the words 'bridestone', Sir."

The legate's blue eyes once again held a piercing silent gaze on Marcus, as if he knew there was more unspoken. The conker brown eyes this time met the glare of his superior.

"Permission to search the area of the bridestone near the quarry, Sir," requested Marcus. The legate remained silent and Marcus felt forced to speak again. "It is my belief that whoever attacked the native is responsible for setting the fire, and the native is indicating they are hiding at the nearby bridestone."

"Big assumptions from incoherent mutterings, Guintoli. This native looks like a Pict rebel and could be responsible for setting the fire."

Marcus could feel his career opportunity hanging in the balance with this conversation. Lucius could feel it too, and stood without breathing, motionless, as a deer that fears danger. The prospects of promotion were palpable if he got this right, but his name was firmly marked if the moment went against him. Frustration was creeping in at the legate's uncanny perception. It seemed he knew when Marcus was holding back information. It was time to gamble and reveal his hand.

"This boy is Brigante, Sir. We searched his family's homestead earlier today and met with no resistance. There was no indication of rebel activity." With their eyes still locked, Marcus could see that more details were still required to satisfy the legate. "His name is Kye Teviot, Sir. He is not a Pict rebel. The boy's sister is known to me. She has been tutoring your daughter at the fort, Sir!" Marcus was the first to break eye contact, raising his chin a little and standing straighter to attention, as if by doing so, it underlined his words as the truth. In fact, the glacial stare was again too penetrating, and Marcus was not enjoying the scrutiny.

"Perhaps the Brigante craft tutor has been feeding information to her brother. Perhaps that is why she entered the fort."

"I do not believe this to be so, Sir."

"You would not be the first soldier to be duped by a pretty face, Legionary Guintoli."

"I do not believe I have been duped, Sir." Marcus remained resolute, bringing forth a slight nod from Legate Maxinius as he pursed his lips in thought. What he had heard of the Brigante tutor from his wife and daughter had also been favourable. He made his decision. Turning away from Marcus, he barked orders to the medics.

"Take the Brigante boy to the fort hospital. Keep him alive! I have questions that require answers." Pointing at Lucius, he requested his name. "Legionary Seniarus, are you willing to join Legionary Guintoli in a search of the bridestone area near the quarry? I cannot release further men from the campaign to accompany you on this sortie, which appears to be based as much on a hunch by your comrade, as on available facts, but I am sufficiently persuaded by your comrade's vision to allow the exploration."

"I am willing, Sir!"

"So be it. Report directly to me at the fort on completion of your mission." He strode away calling out orders as he went. Lucius exhaled through puffed cheeks, sagging slightly as the intensity in the air reduced as his commanding officer departed.

"Vulcan, god of fire!" exclaimed Lucius. "Our names are truly marked now. What happened to the anonymity you desired when we marched to *Arbeia*?"

"I need glory this day, Lucius. I would take anonymity if the gods would allow me Jolinda, but that route is not available. By helping Kye, I have part redeemed the slaughter of her father, but the crows still peck at my innards." Marcus thumped his fist to his chest. "I must find a way to leave this island, Lucius. Distance is the answer. Rebel blood will bring me recognition and I will request a transfer to another legion on the back of that." Lucius heard the steel edge return to his friend's voice.

"I am with you in this," he said, offering his forearm in a fisted salute. "Rebels for glory!" Clasping forearms, they held a hard stare, seeing the kindred depth of the other.

Chapter Thirteen

The fort was astir with activity following the return of the cohorts and Peterna was delighted with the results of the campaign. A positive thrum was circulating the barracks, an adumbration of good morale. He was pleased for his men, and relieved that his hunch had been accurate. Seventeen rebel warriors had been slain in total, all Picts, with another Pict captured, currently undergoing interrogation. No Roman losses, although one legionary had sustained a twisted ankle during the march. No settlements burned. The tally was not striking for a report, it was hardly a glorious battle victory he mused, but nevertheless Peterna was encouraged by the outcome. No doubt they had not flushed all the rebels from hiding, but enough to dampen this uprising. Sixteen of the seventeen killed had been cornered following information from some local Brigante farmers, thirty miles to the northeast, near *Alavna*. Their succour was particularly encouraging. It seemed they had their own reasons for disliking the Picts more than they disliked the Romans. Perhaps his concern of a united uprising such as Agricola had faced was not going to happen after all. Falco hadn't thought so. If the infiltration problem was contained to just the Picts, Peterna felt happy that the situation was containable. Yet, the senators in Rome may not understand this fierce tribal independence, he reflected. He would have to be careful with his report. His path was still unsure with no word from Hadrian.

The intelligence gained by the Sixth Cohort from the local inhabitants at the river settlement, had also led to results, albeit in a very individual way. Reaching the burning barn when they had, enabled them to turn a potentially damaging situation into a positive one. The local shepherds were indebted by the rescue of their livestock. Had they arrived any later, the sheep would have perished, as would the Brigante boy with the stomach wound and the blame, no doubt, heaped wrongly on the Romans. It was still not clear if the boy would survive, but his prospects were greater in the fort hospital than anywhere else. The latest dispatch from the hospital reported a fever, and, intrigued by this Teviot family, Peterna had requested immediate notice of consciousness, so he could question the boy personally.

The seventeenth Pict corpse had come from sending the two legionaries off to the quarry bridestone. An adequate result in itself, but the mission had proven extraordinarily useful by providing the only captured rebel for questioning. Peterna allowed himself a brief self-indulgent moment of congratulation. He'd acted on instincts that had not let him down.

"The matter is on a door hinge," he muttered, dragging his thoughts back to level reality. This small success would be easily lost amongst the affluent in the senate bureaucracy. An absence of reply from Hadrian was concerning him, it was long overdue. How should he interpret this silence? As ruin, as success, or was there a path betwixt the two? Perhaps he should contact Governor Falco, but reluctance made him hesitant. Unable to settle on any particular track of thought as an answer, and Jupiter knew he'd churned them all in to mire with his repetitive mental wanderings, Peterna tried to empty his mind.

Sitting with his left elbow resting on the desk, and head supported by splayed fingers across eyebrows, creating a soft light, he let his eyes close and welcomed the soothing effect of darkness as his right hand tapped a gentle beat on the oak desk. He experimented with different rhythms, soon settling on one and let the action, sounds and small vibrations absorb him. Two names echoed through the beat, *Marcus Guintoli* and *Lucius Seniarus.*

Ceasing his tapping and leaning back in his chair, Peterna considered the transfer request the two young legionaries had made during their report. His first reaction was to refuse. To send men, especially good men as these two were proving to be, to another legion when he was petitioning for more troops from Hadrian was illogical. This was reason enough to refuse their request, yet there was more. Guintoli in particular held his attention. There was potential lurking in him. Good leadership qualities perhaps, or simply a steely determination to succeed where others would succumb to failure. Peterna could see traits of himself in Guintoli and a wry smile flickered at his lips with memories of himself as a young man.

Yet, the transfer request had been put most decisively, stubbornly almost. Spoken with a firmness that suggested an underlying desperation to depart the Legion. Peterna pondered on this. Low morale was a problem he was working hard to eradicate, and improvements could be seen. Activity always helped, and the increase in training and recent campaign had lifted spirits in the camp, but he knew the situation was fragile. To ignore the intonation could be foolhardy. A rap at his door broke his thoughts.

"Enter!"

"Dispatch from Rome, Sir."

Peterna took the package eagerly, nodding his thanks and dismissal to the clerk, only to be immediately disappointed. He could see from the wrapping that it had not originated from the Imperial Senate. Thumping the desk in anger, he let slip a muttered curse.

"Abandoned, left to moulder!" Drumming a more choleric rhythm and breathing in heavy snorts, looking at the unopened package, indignant thoughts besieged him. How dare Hadrian and Rome do this - to him, to his family, to his men? Forsaken in cold and damp lands, forgotten at the edge of the Empire. What was the point of being here? Seething he opened the package and read the letter. It was addressed to his wife from her cousin in Rome, a positive reply for Julita and Cloelia to make an extended visit.

Glancing through the neatly penned scroll, he read with frustration that the word in Rome was that Hadrian was travelling to Africa. The Emperor had indeed returned briefly to Rome from Gaul, but was now continuing his tour in the Southern Provinces. Probably to win favour with the Jews by rebuilding Cyrenaica, thought Peterna. Lavishing Roman money on the Jewish city. The very city that the Jews had helped to destroy during their revolt. Where was the justice? Britannia, and the Twentieth Legion with it, was being overlooked.

Peterna knew that neither Julita nor Cloelia desired to go to Rome, but he hardened himself to this. They would be sent. He needed complete focus to end this campaign, moving things forward alone if necessary. Without supporting troops, it would be a slow and harrowing demise for Rome in Britannia. In his darkened mood, he envisaged his own quietus, preferring a murky ditch in battle to the slow ruin of disgrace. The prospects for the Twentieth Legion were cheerless and the reason for it abstruse. They were good soldiers and his now blackened spirit dowsed guilt upon himself for their ill fate.

Guintoli and Seniarus, he decided, could escort Julita and Cloelia to Rome as bodyguards. He brightened a little with this plan. Two men given respite, a seed in a forest, but it lifted a little guilt from his conscience. It resolved the problem of granting a transfer request at a time when he was petitioning for more troops, and he trusted their ability as bodyguards. Once in Rome, if astute, they may be able to adjure to a higher authority. He would give them the opportunity, the rest was up to them. Having made his decision, he personally scribed documents to allow passage to Rome for the party. Julita and Cloelia would be informed tonight and given one day to pack. Better his wife and daughter went swiftly now the decision was made. Guintoli and Seniarus would receive their orders tomorrow.

Turning his attention to the scrolls on his desk, he noticed a deportation advice from the surgeon. *Brutus Antonini – unfit for service – medical discharge advised.* The clerk had scribed a brief but telling report underneath indicating how the injury had been sustained. *Sword arm mangled following civilian brawl.* The last two words were condemning. Peterna remembered the incident but had no compassion. The Roman army did not tolerate such actions. The fortunes of Brutus Antonini had gone sour. Checking for further deportation advices, he found none. Rome's legislation did not allow a man to travel on deportation alone and, not wanting to spare further soldiers on escort duties, he added Legionary Antonini's name to the documentation for passage and moved on to the next scroll.

The day slipped furtively into evening and he barely noticed the clerk enter and light the oil lamps, immersed as he was in the necessary correspondence and record keeping the army demanded of him. Weariness broke into his work, and stretching to infuse energy, he noticed with surprise the demise of the daylight. It was time to impart his decision to Julita. Laying the stylus down with deliberation, he hardened his heart in preparation of the words he must say.

....

"Mama! No! I will not go! You cannot make me. Papa cannot be this cruel!"

From the next room, Peterna could hear Julita's level reply patiently explaining all the positive reasons for their departure to Rome. Her low murmurs were in sharp contrast to his daughter's hysterics. He knew Julita's heart was heavy at leaving and a shot of heat gushed through his chest as he admired her loyalty to him. Inwardly she may disagree, but outwardly she would show union to his decision and support his actions. His groin stirred with desire but there would be no lovemaking tonight, not with his daughter so distressed.

"But Mama, my love is in this Legion, my heart will bleed white if I am separated, I will marry only my love..." Cloelia's voice was rising ever higher. Peterna heard a sharp slap. A shocked silence began to fill with a whining weep and cross retorts from Julita.

"Your theatrics I do not need Child! There is much to be organised in scant time. Sleep will be unmanageable in this state, better we labour ourselves weary." Cloelia's weeping did not cease but came in more controlled snivels as her mother continued to witter as a distraction. "You must decide what to take and be harsh with your choices. We are confined to three pieces of baggage each. Three pieces only, Cloelia. That is the true crime here. How your father expects us to fit all we need in to such a small capacity I do not know."

Peterna smiled at this despite everything, shaking his head gently. His difficult task done, he left the house welcoming the frosty bite in the night air.

With her eyes swollen and head thick from the excess sobbing and lack of sleep, Cloelia could not have felt more wretched. With her tear ducts dry, weeping was no longer an option. Solace was not to be found through crying, and she lay wrapped in the velvet bedspread leaden with grief, a cold compress resting across her eyes to reduce their ache, listening to the servants muffled activities in the house and hearing the hoot of an owl outside.

The packing had gone on long into the dark hours before Mama had allowed her to retire. There still remained much to do and knowing she would be called upon again as dawn lightened the sky, she prayed for release into sleep, but her mind was racing like a chariot pulled by champion steeds. The pounding at her temples could have been their hooves.

Brutus was filling her thoughts. How could she leave him? Did he know she was going to Rome? Why had he not come to her when she cried? Reason argued that he did not yet know, but in her distress and tired confusion, loneliness crowded in with an invasion of uncertainty snaking through her, snagging in to knots of capricious fear that stabbed its victim with venomous doubts. Perhaps Brutus would not care she was leaving. This thought worried at her during a fitful rest and became firmly implanted as reality by the time she was roused by a gentle shake from her mother.

"Good morning Cloelia, it is late and we have much to do."

Blinking into wakefulness, Cloelia was surprised to see sunlight filling the room, as it seemed only a moment ago she had succumbed to sleep.

"What time is it?" she asked.

"Much later than I anticipated waking you." Giving a soft smile and in way of explanation, she added, "I was needy of your father." Julita was expecting an irascible retort at the mention of Peterna but Cloelia said nothing.

"Papa wishes to speak with you."

Silence again excepting a small sigh and a nod that caused a lock of hair to tumble across to her lips. The feist was gone from Cloelia, she was dead inside. Julita pushed the stray curl away.

"I will have a lavender infused rinse prepared for you to bathe with. It will soothe you. I know of a remedy to reduce puffiness too." Julita tenderly dabbed at the sides of Cloelia's sore eyes.

"Thank you, Mama." Cloelia's voice was a drear monotone. "I will bathe with the rinse but it is of no consequence how I look any more. Brutus will not see me and the old men of Rome will slaver over young breasts regardless of an ugly face."

"Where there is life, there is hope! Your grandmama on Papa's side taught me that. Later you may regret not making an effort with your appearance." Julita smiled at her daughter's melancholy. Julita had seen the documentation for their passage to Rome, including the name of Brutus Antonini.

It seemed the gods were keeping Peterna blind to the affection their daughter had for the legionary he was deporting, or she felt certain he would keep them apart. A ruined soldier was not in his plans for Cloelia and Julita was choosing not to enlighten him. What harm could it bring the young couple to share a little longer together? Besides, love was a strong protector and their journey would be hazardous. Once in Rome, society would doubtless divide them, although Julita was not against attempting to manipulate the course of fate should it be necessary. Had not Peterna's mother done the very same for her without the wrath of the gods befalling them all? And had she not been eternally grateful? The Roman way was not best in every sector. No, she would let events unfold and make a judgement later, calling on the gods in deep meditative prayer to guide her if necessary.

"I do not have the interest for them, Mama."

Julita continued as if Cloelia had not spoken.

"Use them lightly, and be ready to see Papa with me in a sundial sixth. Pay attention to his instructions and read the documentation of passage details carefully." Julita made her way to the door, adding, "read them carefully, but remain impassive."

Cloelia heard the words, but was too entangled in misery to unravel their message.

The fever had left Kye and he was propped on a bolster with his knees bent to remove the strain on his wound, concentrating on ignoring an itch beneath his dressings. His eyes were closed and his breathing shallow, anything deeper causing him pain. The legate's questioning had been direct and Kye was wondering if his reticence had been sensible. He was hardly holding the high ground over a pass, quite the opposite. Not only did his recovery remain at the mercy of the Roman physicians, his life it seems was indebted to the legion.

Yet brevity of answer had met every question, and within that brevity was protection for the Pict brothers who had left him to bleed and burn. Turning the conversation over in his mind, looking for justification of his mistrust of the legate, he could find none. The questions had been fair and logical in sequence, with no sudden change in direction to trick him. The legate had advised that seventeen Picts had been killed and one taken captive for questioning. Kye found himself hoping fervently that it was one of the brothers being held. Stories of the ruthlessness of Roman interrogation was sung by the bards amongst the tribes at gatherings and whispered from mothers to babes in cribs as lullabies, intended to soothe with their rhymes rather than make sense with their words. History remembered from previous Roman invasions.

Bitterness filled him and an involuntary sneer flickered his face, turning to a grimace of pain as his breathing deepened in response to the cruel recollections of his treatment by the Picts. Unwelcome memories cascaded and Kye, eyes wide and sweat suddenly beading his hairline, was reliving the intensity of the flames in the barn and the stabbing outside. Flashing images were linking at random, the cries of the sheep, searing heat and smoke, his throat constricting as if he were choking still. The relief at escaping the fire dissolving in to surprise and then resentment with the dawning realisation of cold steel in warm guts, his guts. The blade dragging through flesh, his life-blood slicking its silver sheen as the knife was removed, the dawning moment seeming to last an age, teasing him with confusion. Acrid bile and the taste of death burning his tonsils then, and a hint of the same now amidst this sudden panic.

Rigid in body, with fists gripping the bedroll, Kye forced himself to rationalise this crippling fear. Catching the movement of a tiny spider suspended on a single strand of cobweb fluttering softly, high on the wall opposite him, he channelled his thoughts to focus there. His horrors dissipated and Kye closed his eyes once more to deal with the pain emanating from his wound. His pulse settling, he regained a calm mind and body. Understanding a little better how sick he was, and thus, for the present at least, how dependent on the legate and his legion he was, Kye reflected that his answers to further Roman questions must be more forthcoming. His responsibility was to return and protect his family, how childish his earlier dreams of seeking adventure with the Picts seemed to him now. Kye was musing quietly over this revelation of his own maturity when Marcus entered his room.

Thinking Kye to be asleep, Marcus was silent, looking upon a face distinct in its masculinity, yet so familiar in features that it stirred him. Why had he come? Was it solely to check the medic's report, as he'd told Lucius and Brutus, so he could endorse his own records before he left? Or did he want more from Kye Teviot? The ten denarii bribe he used on the guard to gain entry alone indicated he wanted more, a lot more.

He wanted Kye to know the name of the legionary who had saved him, his name, Marcus Guintoli. To ensure Kye had this fact to remember and retell, linking his name to mercy in whispered thanks from the lips of the Teviot family. Whispered thanks that he hoped would outweigh the negative, should Jolinda learn of his other less noble deeds. To give the whole truth would have been kindest, but his mortal virtue struggled with that, preferring instead to impart the good and allow the gods to decide which of the bad to reveal.

Moving to settle in a chair, Marcus started when he noticed Kye was looking at him, jumping up, then feeling foolish.

"I thought you were sleeping," he said, resettling.

"Resting," Kye replied, noticing the dagger sheath strapped to the legionary's lower leg was empty. The atmosphere was awkward as Marcus cleared his throat to speak but said nothing. Kye wondered at his nervousness.

"You are over the fever," began Marcus, "that is good."

"I've a way to go yet before I'm useful."

Kye's accent jolted memories, shooting a bolt of heat through Marcus. This was more difficult than he'd anticipated.

"Who are ya?" asked Kye, tiring of the quiet.

"Marcus Guintoli." It was all he could say. Reaching in to his pocket, Marcus brought out his bone effigy of Jupiter. "Give this to Jolinda. Tell her..." his words tailed off. It startled Kye to hear his sister's name spoken by the Roman and he grimaced a little with pain. "Tell her..." Marcus, giving up and kicking the chair away in frustration, made towards the door. What did it matter, he was leaving for Rome in a few hours, with plans never to return to this misty island.

"Roman!" Kye had questions of his own. "The captive Pict, was he found at the burning barn?"

"Close by."

"There were two of them, brothers."

"I killed the other at the bridestone. You told me they would be there before the medics tended you."

Kye nodded his understanding. "Ya should've slaughtered them both."

"The captive is sick. If he is lucky, he will die before the legate has him nailed out. Either way he will be dead before you leave the infirmary."

"Has the legate the same in mind for me?"

"Not if you pledge alliance to Rome." Marcus detected a prickly resistance to this that brought forth a wry smirk despite the circumstances. "Not an easy thing for a Teviot, it seems. The legate's daughter has befriended Jolinda and that connection may save you if you co-operate at least. I advise you do not stretch the legate's patience though as his daughter leaves for Rome tonight, so will not be here to add further persuasion."

"I'm in ya debt Guintoli."

"We part as equals, Brigante." Incomprehension furrowed Kye's youthful brow. "Your Da died by my sword. I saved your life because I took his...I did it for Jolinda." Marcus had not expected to speak these words, but was glad they were said, the confession feeling strangely cleansing. For a short moment he was tempted to utter his *Geryon*, but he could not, it was too shameful. "I too am leaving for Rome, with plans to join a different legion. A drier climate will suit me, Syria perhaps."

"Syria," Kye played with the word on his tongue, vying for time to make sense of all he'd been told. "I ain't heard of it."

"Lands far from here."

Their conversation paused. Kye was holding the bone effigy. Raising it slightly he said, very deliberately, "I'll give her this. I hear ya message." He wasn't convinced he understood it all, but he'd grasped enough and maybe the rest would fall into place on reflection.

"Don't use ya gods to hide from ya own weaknesses, Roman." Marcus left without replying, leaving Kye to reflect again at his newly acquired maturity. "Where did those words come from Kye Teviot?" he muttered to himself, with only the spider as witness. "I don't even know what they mean. Them are words Ma would say." Pondering silently, he slipped into sleep, suddenly and deeply, as only those recuperating can do.

Chapter Fourteen

Darkness was shrouding the small group as they departed the fort along the Stanegate. It was four hours before sunrise, with a damp chill running through the air. The legate watched, standing alone outside the South Gate, re-checking the journey calculations to satisfy himself that such an early morning departure was necessary. It was, if they were to reach the fort at Vindomora before dusk. It was the cart that would hamper their speed, but Julita had insisted they travel with it. At least they were travelling without servants. The cart had been the compromise, and its covered top would at least afford them some respite from the elements. Not that the weather was always bad, but its unpredictability from one day to the next, indeed, from one sundial to the next, made it difficult to plan. It was no wonder the barbarians went to such lengths to worship their sun god.

The small port of Petuaria on the Abus Fluvius was their destination, which they should reach in ten days. A lack of tabernae this far north meant they would seek their first two night's accommodation at the forts of Vindomora, then Longovicium. Tabernae became more frequent from there and would serve them more conveniently along the roads. Enough coin was with the party to allow Julita and Cloelia to sleep and eat in comfort, the legionaries would have to negotiate their own accommodation, hunkering in stables or under hedges, but always close by.

It wouldn't be difficult to gain a passage to Gaul from Petuaria. Merchant supply vessels were arriving and departing weekly, and he'd ensured additional coin was available for a priority berth. Silver spoke more loudly than steel in such cases, but the extra security of a legionary sword gave him added assurance for their safety.

The south should give amicable travel to Romans, but bandits were rife in all areas and it was obvious the small party would be carrying a tempting cache. Road tolls, tabernae fees and sailing berths all added up to make travelling an expensive business.

Watching until they folded in to the shadows and he could no longer see the sway of the cart, nor the outline of the two legionaries walking either side of it, Peterna returned to the fort. They were gone and he immediately, and fully, focussed his mind to his task.

....

Three days into their journey and the transformation from sullen to vivacious was complete in Cloelia. She had succeeded in hiding her sudden willingness to travel from her father quite efficiently. Julita had put this down to prodigious in-observance by her husband, or was it exceptional performing from her daughter? Having seen Cloelia manipulate Peterna since a young filly, she should not be surprised. Yet how Peterna had failed to notice the disarming moment of registration, the moment Cloelia's own eyes read that Brutus was travelling with them, the gods only knew. Her eyes had grown to moons as she looked at the documentation of passage. She'd blustered for a moment, glanced up at Peterna, then across to Julita, then back down to the papyrus, before checking her emotions. The memory brought forth a gentle smile from Julita.

"You do not fool your mother so easily, my sly child," whispered Julita affectionately to the tumble of curls asleep on her lap. "If I am not mistaken, the names of the other legionaries travelling with us affected you also. Why was that, I wonder?" Julita continued whispering to her sleeping daughter, giving her thoughts substantiation. "I believe they were our musicians." The names had not registered with Julita, but she recognised Marcus and Lucius from that wet day of unorthodox celebrations. "And although it may be Brutus who makes you laugh, it is the brooding, square-jawed one that makes you flush. Something has passed between you that I have missed."

As the clouds grew darker with dusk, Julita surreptitiously observed Marcus from behind the cloth drapes of the cart that had parted slightly during the journey. He was certainly attractive. A little shorter than Brutus but solid in his stance, muscles honed through training. His smooth olive skin was in contrast to the pock-ravaged face of Brutus, and, although she knew he was from the people and not the nobility, his strong jaw line and straight nose hinted of aristocracy. He would not look wrong amongst them, yet his birth had placed him with the legions. Would he ascend the ranks? Did he have ambition? Few fully traversed the social classes but some unexpectedly ascended beyond their birth line. Would he be one of them?

Her eyebrows arched a little in surprise as she found herself wanting this for him. Why? There was something repining about him. A restlessness, an ache, something unfulfilled. It was a hard groove to hollow to reach the upper echelons from the lower caste, and seldom was worthiness triumphant over fortune. Only the few who could dance free of Mammon, the false god that thwarted the deserving, were in with a chance. And even then, some who could dance free did not seize their opportunity. The gods could tease.

Yet looking at Marcus in the gloaming, Julita felt he could dance free of Mammon. He had a quality about him, an aura of strength. Fortuna's aim would surely be true in his case. *Ah, the Roman and the romantic are colliding in you Julita.* A simper caught the edge of her lips as she acknowledged this thought. You want your daughter to have her wish and marry for love, but you want that love to be of a certain social standing. *Peterna would be proud of you!*

"Nevertheless," she muttered, "I think Marcus is the chariot to back, Cloelia, he has the advantage over the other two." Seeing a milestone beside the road, Julita parted the drapes further and peered to read the inscription:

> Loyal and Unconquered
> Imperator Publius Aeliues Hadrianus
> Vinovia
> A Thousand Paces

"Are we stopping at Vinovia?" Julita called to Marcus.

"Yes, Lady. The daylight is all but gone. We will find accommodation there for the night."

"That is good as I am growing weary of the day's travel. Cloelia however, will be bright and perky I fear, for she has slept these past miles heedless of the bumps and jolts." Julita was engaging in her chatter. "Did we pass through Vinovia when we first came to Britannia?" Julita pursed her lips in thought. "Vinovia...The Way of the Vintners...I do not recall the name."

"We marched through it. We did not stop here."

"Is it a large town? Will we have a choice of accommodation?"

"No, there is a single tavern." His wish not to converse was obvious in his brevity of answer. He was neither rude nor forthcoming. Julita continued in an attempt to make the conversation flow, giving up after a few more questions when it seemed an interrogation more than a conversation. There was time yet to build a rapport. Perhaps he would be more convivial on a full stomach. Peterna would not approve, but she couldn't see the harm in shedding the shackles of social status for the duration of the journey. After all, they were far from Rome and travelling was such a tedious business. It would help to pass the time.

....

The tavern was busy. A vibrant thrum of gruff laughter and constant chatter was pitted with playful squeals from the serving maidens, obvious in their encouragement. Sited on the main thoroughfare, it had been easy to locate and appeared to be the hub of the small town, taking the very name of the settlement. Off-duty auxiliary soldiers were high in numbers, with just a couple of local men sitting quietly at one end of the wooden serving bar.

The tavern owner had gone to great lengths to decorate the bar in the style of Rome and the menu was supplemented in Roman fare. Julita was surprised and quite delighted. Although still in Brigante lands, the Roman influence here was far more evident than on the northern frontier where *Britannia* remained untamed. It was but a day's march for a legion, yet the sense of acceptance was striking. There was no edge to the atmosphere. Clearly she had grown accustomed to the feel of this on the northern fort, for until now she had thought her husband's concern for an uprising exaggerated. The journey south was showing otherwise. No wonder Peterna wished her and Cloelia to leave. Chiding herself for doubting him, she silently praised his astuteness.

A shot of heat struck behind her ribs and she felt suddenly nervous for him. Why was Hadrian not heeding his warnings? Where were the troops to back him? An urgency to help flooded her and frustration curled her fingers, pressing lacquered nails into her palms. Perhaps she could advocate his argument to her cousin's husband when she reached Rome. His wealth would ensure high connections. But recalling Peterna's whispered warning as they embraced before parting, *"be wary in your choice of words with your cousin"*, she struggled to know what was right to do.

Peterna had shocked her by refuting Hadrian's orders and risking ruin. His loyalty to The Empire was wavering where it had always been so reliable, so solid that she had found it galling at times. But now it was questioned, she was fearful. Julita's roots were loosening and she'd never been parted from Peterna under such circumstances. Adrift, and wanting of his physical presence more than ever, she released her clenched fists and began gently rubbing at the marks left behind. The action was soothing and she transferred the massage to her temples, moving her fingertips in tiny circles up through her hair, remembering his touch. Her lips parted in a silent prayer.

Goddess Juno, let me draw strength from your breath.
I am tardy in my understanding, but I offer myself for his good now.
Great goddess, let it not be too late for him.
Give me health of spirit and guide my path.

Cloelia was calling from the adjoining chamber, irritation evident in her tone. Julita took a moment to complete her prayer before going to her daughter, welcoming the distraction from her dark thoughts. She must keep a healthy mind. Cloelia and the legionaries were a good diversion, and maybe she would learn something from her husband's men that would be of use in Rome. Yes, Juno was surely steering her to befriend these men.

"Can you help me with my hair, Mama? I cannot fix my braids." Cloelia was sitting on the edge of the simple bed still in her travelling clothes, braids in one hand, ivory hairpin in the other, and looking quite fed up. Her stola was draped over the chair beside the waist-high table, upon which was a large oval bowl, beautifully glazed in a mottled burnt orange design, with a matching chamber pot nestling beneath.

"All this trouble to eat up here alone. The stola, my hair, no-one other than you will see it," complained Cloelia.

"And I am not worthy of a little toil, I suppose."

"No, yes..." a sigh from Cloelia, "that is not what I meant..."

"It is what you meant, and I understand." Julita had raised Cloelia's arms and was trying to pull the tunic over her daughter's hair without disturbing the braids. It didn't work. "Let your hair down, I will comb and re-braid it when you are properly dressed."

"Oh, do not bother, Mama, really."

"No, I will bother, *really*," she mimicked Cloelia. "And you will bother, *really!*" Cloelia scowled. Julita smothered a smile. "I have decided we will dine downstairs."

It took a moment for the words to register. When they did, Cloelia let out a little squeal of delight, scattering the hairpins from her lap as she jumped up to hug her mother.

"Well, that is different then...*really* different!" Cloelia giggled. Julita rolled her eyes, then giggled too, brushed by the infectious excitement.

....

"Wine is on the menu, lads!" Lucius was stripped to the waist and scooping water from the wooden trough and vigorously rubbing his armpits. "A civilised tavern, wine instead of that foul tasting ale. And they have *garum*. Smell it! How I have missed that spicy fish aroma."

Brutus responded with his wide grin, rubbing his ribs as he stretched tall.

"Jericho dates and dried damsons too. If they serve them dribbled in honey, I may offer the chef a season's wage to travel with us."

Using his dagger with skill, Lucius turned his attention to removing the stubble from his chin.

"A clean tunic is called for," he said between strokes. "Fine food, wine and strumpet on hand. Do you hear those squeals? They say no, but they mean yes, yes, yes!" He pulled a lewd expression, squeezing his groin with his free hand. "I do not care that we are sleeping in with the horses, as long as I can share my straw with a woman on a full stomach."

Marcus jumped down from the cart.

"Let us pull stalks to see who eats in the tavern and who must add water to his wine. We cannot risk leaving the cart and horse alone, and one of us must stay sober." The legionaries had found it frustratingly slow going with the cart, walking at a tedious pace three times slower than marching rhythm, but they knew their orders. They'd checked the inn had only one set of stairs and were happy to see that the chambers each had a small window overlooking the courtyard and stables. Having escorted Julita and Cloelia safely to their rooms, it seemed reasonable to assume that they would remain there until daybreak. Julita had dismissed Brutus's offer of guarding their doors, saying she did not wish to feel like a prisoner.

Offering a choice of two stalks from his fist to Brutus first, he watched him pull out a long stalk. Brutus returned it to Marcus with a satisfied grin knowing he would soon be eating. Marcus replaced the piece of straw in his fist, keeping it out of sight of Lucius so as not to give him an advantage.

"Pull long, and your fill begins now, my friend. Pull short, and you will have to gird your loins until another day."

With an insouciant air, Lucius slowly drew a stalk, an ample smile furnishing his face as the stalk took an age to clear Marcus's hand, revealing it as the same lengthy one chosen by Brutus.

"Ye-es! I could say I am sorry, but I am not," said Lucius clapping Marcus on the shoulder.

"We will send a maid with a platter of food and watered wine for you to sup with the ponies. Do not detain her with your poetry!"

Marcus gave a display of regret, cursing blithely to Cupid. Once Brutus and Lucius were gone from the stables, his shoulders slumped. Looking down to the fist still grasping the straw, opening it revealed two stalks of the same length, both long. His heart was heavy and he needed some time alone, some quiet time where he need make no pretence. It was a relief to be in solitude with his anguish.

Sitting with his back to a cartwheel, he dropped his head on to his arms as they rested across his drawn-up knees and let the heartache sweep through him. Memories of Jolinda converged and rebounded at their will, jostling in flickers, whirring like slingshot. His limbs were leaden, as heavy as his father's anvil had felt to him as a child. He wanted to cry as he had in the tiny temple after Flavinus's death, but tears wouldn't form, his eyes remaining stubbornly dry and the pain a tight knot locked in his chest.

Moving his hands to cradle his head, he grunted as if a sword had slashed his flesh. It helped a little, so he let out a deep throaty growl, letting anger build and releasing it in a bestial roar, upsetting the horse as he did so. Snickering and stamping, the mare drew his attention, bringing him back to the moment.

Rising to settle the beast, a little sheepish in his manner that it had witnessed his display, he spoke calmingly.

"Hey, whoa...there is no danger. Shu-ush, all is well. I am but a fool." A mane was flicked at him and flaring nostrils snorted hot breath before the animal began to still. Aware of a soreness in his throat from the growl, Marcus managed a tiny self-conscious smile at the horse, a chestnut brown mare with a small white blaze off-centre by half an inch on her nose. "It will be better when I leave Britannia," he explained to himself as much as to the horse. Then, breaking into Jolinda's accented Latin, "I'm grateful to ya for listening me friend." Stroking the mare's nose, he leant against her flank, enjoying the comfort of the beast. "I'm grateful to ya," he repeated in a whisper.

....

Downing the first tankard of wine in one, Lucius wiped away the overflow trickling from the corner of his mouth with the back of his hand. He raised the empty tankard for an immediate refill, wanting to catch the maid who was passing. He'd been admiring her rear as she attended a nearby table. Now he was taking pleasure in her cleavage as she poured from the pitcher. Sensing his pleasure she smiled coyly in response, dipping a little closer and brushing a hip against him deliberately as she moved to the next table. With his eyes trained on her as she served the other patrons, Lucius felt a thrill charge him as he watched her flirt with the auxiliaries at the bar. Two other maids were circulating, but Lucius was fixed on this one.

"That wench knows her business," smiled Lucius, his eyes returning to the maid who had replenished his wine. "She is the best of the three, and I can pull rank over these auxiliaries. I will make her mine after we have eaten, Brutus. Fortuna is nursing me this day. The goddess leads us to a decent wench, in an area of lowly competition. The augurs are good." He puffed out his chest and rubbed his ribs with a smug smile.

"You do not consider me competition then, eh?"

Lucius chuckled.

"You, no. Marcus, yes, but he is with the horses. Be sure you do not send my maid to the stables with his platter."

"*Your* maid, is she?" Brutus cracked a smile and thumped Lucius's arm in merriment.

"I have no interest in your maid, fresh or spent!"

"Ah yes, I am forgetting the legate's daughter. Little opportunity there for a broken soldier my friend."

It was the wine that had freed the loose words. Brutus knew they were not meant as a barb but their truth sliced at his flesh. He dismissed the spike, refusing to let pessimism swallow him. '*A dose of Brigante spirit*', Jolinda's words echoed at him. Who knew what lay ahead for any of them?

"Perhaps you will have competition for your maid from those two in the corner." Brutus indicated the two native men with a flick of his eyebrows. They were the only non-Romans drinking at The Vinovia, and he could make out blue-dyed patterns behind the loose straggles of dirty blond hair, swirling marks that were as good as name labels. "Iceni Tribe, good of them to paint their necks like that. They are somewhat north of their boundary, odd. Perhaps, *your* maid has the burly one as her kin." Lucius dismissed them as competition with a disdainful snort. The arrival of a meat platter with a side dish of *garum* and a large hunk of warm bread diverted their attention.

....

Gruff but jocund singing reached through to the upstairs chambers as the evening progressed. Recognising the rhythm of it as an old marching tune from Italia, Julita smiled as she added the last pin to Cloelia's hair. The words were muffled but she knew the soldiers would be having fun with the lyrics, substituting the original, rather staid ones, with far less modest words of their own.

"I believe it is time for our entrance my daughter. Stand up and let me see you."

Cloelia obliged, adjusting her tunic so it lay flat beneath her lilac-hued stola. The upper section of the stola was tied around the ribcage, then fell with a flattering fluted edge across her hips where the hem was decorated with tiny, glass beads the colour of amethyst. The underskirt was made of the same quality linen and flared softly to her ankles, lightly weighted at the bottom by matching beads.

"A vision of beauty, Daughter. Papa would be speechless. Yet my amethyst choker would look finer than your chosen pendant, pretty though it is. I would be pleased if you would wear it."

"Oh no, Mama! I could not." Cloelia appeared a little alarmed, and reached instinctively to fondle her pendant as if she would be lost without it. "Your choker is far too expensive. It would be dangerous to wear such finery here. This cheap thing is more appropriate."

"But the stone does not quite match..."

"Mama, please!" I am comfortable with how I look. A vision of beauty you said."

Julita bit down the sharp admonishment that teetered on her lips at Cloelia's abrupt interruption. She did not want the evening to be marred by petty arguments. This night was important if she was to break through the crust of the legionaries and bridge a friendship.

"Yes, yes, you are right. Let us see if we can silence the rabble downstairs with a grand entrance. I think our guards will be surprised by our appearance. No doubt they will have started their meal by now, and sampled the wine too, I would imagine."

Cloelia touched her mother's arm, giggled and kissed her quickly on the cheek. "This is exciting, Mama. Thank you so much. I did not think you would allow it. To dine publicly with the legionaries I mean." Cloelia lowered her eyes, a little shy. "Papa would never allow it."

"And Papa will not be told, will he?" A mock-stern look brought forth another giggle, conspiratorial in nature. "*Should* the conversation ever arise with him, and I doubt it will, I will tell him we were with them for our personal safety. Now, let us descend. I am famished."

The singing became louder as they left the chamber. Julita paused at the top of the stairs. Smiling and wanting to be rid of any lingering residue of their earlier disagreement, she added, "It *is* a pretty pendant, where did you get it?"

"Oh, it was a gift...from Brutus." Cloelia didn't know why she lied to her mother, but the answer seemed to satisfy, even if not convincingly delivered.

"Gods above!" muttered Brutus, sobering rapidly with their appearance, grateful he had imbibed far less than Lucius, who had drunk enough to make focussing on the stairs an effort. "I thought they would keep to their chambers." He whistled softly between his teeth as he studied Cloelia's beauty, quite taken with the effect.

Reacting first, Brutus broke the hush by scraping the bench as he pushed it back to stand. He bowed with a theatrical flourish, all the while keeping his eyes locked to Cloelia's.

Lucius gave a loud belch, the wine already eluding him any decorum. The report resounded in the silence and all those present seemed to hold their breath collectively. Cloelia looked at Brutus, imploring him to do something, her excitement having turned to alarm. A public remonstration was surely due. Shooting Lucius a scowl, Brutus addressed Julita.

"Lady, my colleague is an ass, please excuse his poor manners."

Julita merely ignored everything, continuing to her seat as if nothing unusual had happened. Cloelia did the same, too nervous to speak. Lucius's maid acted swiftly, bringing wine sweetened with honey at Julita's request. Brutus slipped her an added coin, indicating she take Lucius to the kitchens. The other serving girls continued with their work, bringing food and refilling tankards, and before long, the thrum of low voices returned as the awkward atmosphere dispersed.

Cloelia was still throwing questioning looks at Brutus and flashing little daggers of accusation at him with her eyes. *Why did you let Lucius get drunk? Why isn't Marcus with you? Say something to put this right.*

"Where is Marcus?" Julita enquired.

"He is guarding the cart and horse in the stables, Lady."

"Has he eaten?"

"A maid will take him a platter shortly."

Their conversation remained uncomfortably stilted and Brutus began to fidget, rubbing his nose, then scratching above his ear. Conscious of his actions, he balled his fists and sitting on them, tried to ignore the developing itch on his nape. He failed, dealt with it, then folded his arms in an attempt to be still, only to have an itch occur below his ribs. He wriggled surreptitiously in an attempt to be rid of it. Judging he would fidget indefinitely unless the atmosphere altered, he drew a deep breath and plunged in to another apology. Anything, even a public dressing-down, was better than this acute and sudden attack of invisible lice.

"Lady, I must apologise again for Lucius. Your protection, and that of Lady Cloelia, is our main priority and uncompromised by the wine. We remain under oath to The Eagle."

To his surprise, Julita smiled warmly.

"The situation is quite refreshing to me Brutus. I assume Marcus drew the short straw and you can hold your drink better than Lucius."

"Mama!" Julita ignored Cloelia's surprise at her forthright manner.

"You are astute in our ways." Brutus was treading carefully, still waiting to be admonished.

"Brutus, I will be blunt with my thoughts. We are in this journey together, and I am aware that our safety is your future. You did not expect us to join you for dinner. Why would you? I wager you considered us safe in our rooms as long as you watched the stairs. I further wager you calculated the threat to be within your limits, withered arm included, with Marcus but a shout away." The mention of his plight stung, but Brutus remained silent. "Thus, I am in no doubt that the three of you concluded our safety was uncompromised by the inebriation of one. You have had little opportunity to celebrate of late."

Julita paused and smiled at Cloelia. Brutus shifted his gaze between the two of them, one eyebrow slightly arched, wondering if the seed of hope he felt sprouting was about to be ploughed aside or not. It wasn't. Julita ordered food and continued. "Let us dine together for a second time. This time you will be my companion as well as my entertainer. I would like to know the legionary who has captured my daughter's heart. Cloelia has told me you are a master raconteur!"

After a moment of indecision, a smile transformed Brutus's face, dimpling his pockmarked cheeks and sparkling in to his eyes with the mixture of mischief and fun Cloelia so adored. He liked the sound of that, *'the legionary who has captured my daughter's heart'*. Reasoning he had nothing to lose, Brutus began his first rambling story of the evening. By Jupiter, he was being offered a raft in the rapids and he was grasping it. This would be a tale to remember! Who, indeed, knew what lay ahead of them?

....

The wind had been rattling the barn door for some time now. It was coming in gusts, sweeping through the gap at floor level and bullying the dust and straw in to a rising eddy when it reached the far corner. Marcus was conscious of his growling stomach as he watched the dry whirlpool wane and stir with the flurries, depositing bits on the half eaten crab apple he'd discarded earlier, too sour for him to finish. Surely his platter would arrive soon. He was sorely tempted to seek it out regardless of leaving the cart, but he would wait awhile longer before making that gamble. He rubbed his face to rid the tiredness creeping over him, surprised at how cold his nose felt.

The mare gave a restless snicker, stamping her feet in agitation and he moved to soothe her, only then noticing his joints had stiffened with the chill air. It would be a long night if the weather didn't relent, spooking the horse as it was. The animal settled a little during a lull, then suddenly butted him as she swung her head fiercely, snorting in distress. Skittering sideways in panic, almost trampling Marcus under her hooves as he tried to regain his balance.

At that moment, the catch on the barn door lifted. Marcus sprung to his feet, grabbing his dagger from his greaves, all signs of hunger and weariness gone. *The horses were warning you. Fool!* As alert as prey that has scented danger, and inwardly berating himself for not being more heedful, he kicked the door fully open, and in a single motion grabbed the person silhouetted before him, swiftly twisting and dragging them off-balance, his dagger at their throat as he held them in a headlock.

The furore caused by the horse was increased when Cloelia screamed before raising her hand to her mouth as she tumbled in behind Brutus to see Marcus with a knife at her mother's throat. A gust of wind scuttled the platter as she dropped it, depositing its contents in the dirt. As recognition dawned on Marcus, he quickly released Julita, pushing her away slightly as if she were rotten, his pumping blood turning icy with fear of retribution, even before the situation was calm.

Bedlam continued. Cloelia huddled with Julita. Marcus rushed to secure the barn door, whilst Brutus fought to steady the horse. It would not be stilled. Marcus went to help.

"Cursed beast! What is her problem?"

"What is *her* problem? What is *your* problem? You just had the legate's wife at knifepoint." Brutus was incredulous.

"I did not know it was you." Marcus spat back, obvious beyond stating, but stated nonetheless. "What happened to the password?"

"I called it."

"Did you hear my reply? No, because I did not make one. And why did I not make one? Because I did not hear you!"

A further scream from Cloelia interrupted the argument. Looking to where she was pointing, the cause of the horse's upset could be seen. A mouse, contentedly nibbling at the remains of the crab apple, oblivious to the uproar.

"For all the dead in Acheron," cursed Marcus, letting go of the mare. One deft throw of his dagger and the mouse died with its meal spilling from its gut undigested. Without another word, he retrieved his knife, wiped it clean and tossed the dead creature outside.

With the rodent gone, the horse soon regained calm, but it was taking longer for the same to apply to the people. Nerves were fraught and the air smirched with tension. Julita was first to speak, smoothing the ruffles from her garments and attempting to regain composure. A strand of hair had fallen loose.

"Well, that was a new experience." She was annoyed to hear a tremble in her voice.

"Are you alright, Mama?" Cloelia said in a small voice. She looked every inch a fragile girl, standing frightened with her arms folded protectively across her stomach, each hand clenching an elbow. Brutus felt his heart dissolve at her vulnerability, but despite himself did not go to her, continuing instead to stroke the horse.

Marcus sensed he should make an apology, but was too wrought. Choking on the thought made him scowl and Brutus caught the full glower.

"I called the password," he said in defence.

"And what was my reply? Did you hear my reply?" The argument was rekindling, albeit shredded through gritted teeth, the restraining presence of the ladies telling. Marcus desperately wanted to thump something, both aggrieved that he should have to apologise, and aggrieved that he couldn't. "I thought you were bandits, the horse was telling me you were bandits..." he broke off from the explanation, his face beginning to heat in exasperation.

Brutus laughed, throwing his head back in a big guffaw.

"The horse told you we were bandits," he repeated slowly. "It seems you are no expert in the equine tongue, my friend?"

Marcus, still scowling, merely grunted. Brutus's sudden laughter had cut through the edgy atmosphere, lightening and releasing the dark mood. The anger in Marcus fell away so quickly he was unable to adjust immediately, and found he was trying to cling to it, feeling that a smile would be an admission of guilt somehow.

"She was agitated," he said, forcing his angry tone now.

"Agitated, yes..." Brutus crossed to the crab apple remains, "by a mouse!" He laughed again and threw the core at Marcus, who instinctively blocked it with his arm.

"Legionary Guintoli," the tremor in her voice was repaired and Marcus prepared for the worst, the formal tone causing Brutus to lose his smile too. Was his raft to be upended so soon? He locked eyes with Cloelia, pouring as much love in to his gaze as he could, chiding himself for not going to her earlier when she had looked so forlorn. He may now be forbidden. "There is a quote by Cicero, 'mice make formidable bandits'." Silence.

"Lady, ugh, sorry, I, um, I do not know that quote." Marcus was uncomfortable. It crossed his mind that the shock may have addled her mind. He'd heard stories of such things happening.

Julita broke into a smile.

"An apology, thank you. I accept." Ignoring Marcus's confused expression, she hitched her skirt and retrieved the discarded platter. "We will need another. Brutus, will you kindly escort my daughter to obtain a fresh meal for Marcus. I believe I am in safe hands." She looked pointedly at Marcus, adding, "you are adept with a knife and I can speak equine, we will do fine together."

Chapter Fifteen

The atmosphere within the small party as they left Vinovia was changed from when they arrived, as was the weather. The wind had stopped gusting at some point during the night and taken with it the damp, chill air. The morning had dawned still and clear, and long before the sun reached its high point, a candle of warmth trickled over the land. The day held the promise of Spring, and although several moons away, the potential of Summer. The whole countryside was sensing it, with leaf-buds unfurling, insects awakening and birds singing, seemingly at the glory of it all.

The mood of the party continued this carefree vein. Lucius was feeling the effects of his heavy drinking, but was jovial and boasting of his conquest in the kitchens, taking the jibes and taunts from his comrades in good humour. Julita and Cloelia found themselves giggling helplessly at the tales Brutus was relating. The more they laughed, the more he relaxed in to his storytelling, and so the cycle gained momentum until even Marcus shook his head with a genuine grin, the first for some time, more reluctant than the other two to drop his guard, Julita had noticed. Both with her and Cloelia, but progress was being made.

As the sun reached its midday vertex, Julita called out to Marcus,

"May we stop for a while? Our speed has been good along this better track." Marcus nodded and pointed to a copse of willow a hundred paces away to the right.

"I would wager a brook lies behind that copse. Wait here, I will look." He loped easily across to the group of slender-branched trees and was lost from sight for some minutes, before reappearing and waving for them to join him.

The brook was in fact a wide, shallow river, the size of it unexpected, hidden from view of those on the track by the contours of the ground as it angled upwards before a sudden drop of several feet in ground level. Once over the lip, large grey boulders, hewn smooth by wind and water, lay languidly, patient and solid in their inertia. Next to them, were smaller pebbles of varying colours, every one smooth, their size reducing until fine grains lined the water's edge and filled the river bed as it swept silently by with no business other than its own travels. The willow had hinted at water, but belied the grandeur beside it.

"An idyll," gasped Julita as she gazed over the scene. "My, this land is full of surprises."

....

The sun was soothing on his face, and Marcus kept his eyes shut longer than intended. Sleep had not come easily the night before in the stables and he was tired. He'd remained awake long after the ladies had retired to their chambers, sleep unable to claim him as the evening's events churned repeatedly in his head.

When Brutus and Cloelia had been collecting a second platter of food, Julita had wasted no time in speaking plainly to him. She'd offered a basis on which to build a friendship of equal caste while they travelled, nothing underhand and no promises of patronage once in Rome. Her desire for a level footing between them was, she said, propitious for a safer journey, and nothing more than that. She had said much the same to Brutus he discovered, and to Lucius too, although not until an opportunity arose when he appeared in the morning.

Marcus conceded it was certainly easier being able to speak evenly without concern for class, and he found himself liking the legate's wife, but he hung on to the wariness that prowled a small area of his gut, cautious of a sting in her tail. Cloelia was a scratch on his conscience too. Seeing his pendant around her neck had prickled. Why did she wear it? The flame was gone for him, he'd told her that, and even if it rekindled, he would douse it now he knew Brutus's intentions. Gods, Cloelia was his friend's only lifeline from ruin, and that was severely frayed. He wouldn't add to his woes.

At some point, there by the river with his back warm against the rocks and the land wrapping him with unruffled sounds, he must have slipped in to sleep as his thoughts faded without conclusions. He awoke with a start, his subconscious penetrated by a sound that didn't fit with the rest.

"A bit jumpy are we not?" smirked Lucius, who was sitting with his elbows on his thighs whittling a hazel stick with his dagger. "Were you chasing a deer or a woman in your dreams? My reckoning is, whichever you were after, they got away." Marcus grunted in answer to the teasing, an unease still spiking him.

Clearly, he had been dozing longer than he thought, as Brutus, Cloelia and Julita had made their way a hundred paces upstream, their footwear in hands and clothing tucked up out of reach of the shallows. They were examining the middle of the riverbed, Brutus with his sword in hand, no doubt hoping to spear a fish. Cloelia's giggle drifted over on the gentle breeze.

"A sestertia says it was a woman," continued Lucius.

"Quiet!" interrupted Marcus, cocking his head towards the horse, which was tethered to the willow on the upper ground alongside the cart. "There is something wrong." Seeing a doubtful expression from Lucius, Marcus added, rather testily, "Trust me, I speak fluent equine. A harsh lesson is a rapid teacher!" The mare had lifted her head from grazing and was stamping her hind legs and snickering nervously. It was enough warning. Both legionaries were on their feet in an instant, swords unsheathed and moving instinctively in opposite directions, running in a crouch to keep below the ridge. They would have to scale the ridge blind, not knowing who or what awaited them, but to delay was folly, speed of action was to their advantage.

Flattened against the dropped bank, his mouth dry and crazed moths filling his stomach, Marcus drew a breath and signalled to Lucius. Counting down from three with his fingers, they scrambled to the higher ground together, closing in on the copse from opposite sides. A moment of relief bathed Marcus at the absence of a horde before them, but he had little time to enjoy the feeling as he spotted two savages at the cart, one holding the mare steady, the second rifling through the goods, filling a sack. He despised the treachery of theft and could taste the bile of anger burn at his throat.

A yell caught his attention, and he saw that Lucius had unfortunately risen from the river very close to a third savage, a large brute Marcus noticed, and before Lucius could gather himself, a bestial flurry of flailing hair and limbs was launching at him, a Celtic hunting blade flashing in the sunlight. Lucius managed to parry the blade with his sword, the clash of steel discordant with the idyllic surroundings, but the surprise of the attack took him off balance and both men fell to the ground, losing their weapons on impact.

Marcus cursed as he began running to intercept the second native who was down from the cart and heading towards the fray. Lucius would have no chance of survival against two. The mare was stamping in fright at the sudden disturbances, throwing her head and Marcus was grateful she was keeping the third savage occupied, who clearly had no intention of letting go, the horse being a valuable asset. "Let us make it even numbers then," he muttered with a snarl curling his lips as he pumped his legs hard to close the gap, adrenalin fuelling his blood.

The second native caught sight of him and stopped racing to the fray, for a moment undecided. Marcus could almost read his thoughts. Was there time to lend his hand in finishing the Roman grappling with his brother before this second one arrived or should he turn to him now?

"B*rittunculi!*" Marcus found breath from the pit of his stomach to holler as he drove his legs on faster, a battle rage stoking his muscles so that the World became blurred at the edges, soft and obscure, everything slowing in motion, his focus solely on the quarry ahead. A guttural growl collided with his own shout as the native made his decision, and turned his attack to Marcus. Drawing closer Marcus could see the swirling designs of the Iceni tribe spiralling up his adversary's neck, and then his nostrils were filled with the man's thick odour, acrid as it scored through his senses. Marcus didn't slow his run at all, ramming his sword straight into the Iceni's guts, hitting him with such momentum that it carried the native two paces backwards until stopped by a willow, sliced right through and pinned to the tree by the sword. An expression of utter surprise was etched in his eyes at being taken so easily.

Marcus hefted his boot against the willow's trunk and pulled at his sword, freeing it with an explosive grunt. Dark, slick blood gushed from the wound, its pungent smell assailing his senses. Removed of the sword, the tribesman's body slid, almost gracefully, down the trunk to a sitting position, his eyes staring at Marcus. With precious little time to spare a thought, Marcus shoved the native's shoulder with his foot, sword ready if needed. The rictus of surprise remained as the torso slumped sideways and Marcus saw death again, a wanton vision of Flavinus flicking behind his eyes as if to sanction this deed as revenge.

Snapping back from the vision, Marcus looked to Lucius and then across to the mare, who was now prancing skittishly with the native astride her back. His eyebrows arched as he realised the rider was a woman, her hair having tumbled free during the tussle to mount the animal. He assumed she would run and cursed the loss of the horse. Lucius was still on the ground grappling with the big savage, wriggling and wrestling, but Marcus could see the greater size and weight of his opponent was beginning to tell.

The hold on Lucius's throat was suddenly released and he felt weightless. He rolled on to all fours, gasping in chunks of sweet air, gulping life back to his lungs. The dark fog clearing as he coughed and spluttered, the inside of his skull still banging in protest at the oxygen deprivation. Aware of a struggle nearby, he rose to his feet, hand to his pulsing throat, only to sink again in dizziness.

Steel versus flesh, even strong, brutish flesh, is no contest and Marcus wielded his sword with practised ease on Lucius's would-be killer quickly and decisively, giving him no chance to collect either weapon dropped in the first clash. The big Iceni warrior had been so immersed in the strangulation that he'd not registered Marcus's approach until too late, rising just at the last moment so Marcus once again looked into eyes showing surprise and not fear on a slain man. The killing-rush left Marcus, his muscles tremoring as he leaned over his sword, point in the dirt for support, bile stinging his throat as it always did when the killing action was over. He stood a moment, dazed.

The sound of hoof-beats dragged him upright, but the mare was still and tethered beside the cart as before. The girl hadn't scampered with the loot as expected, instead she had run to the first of the fallen Iceni, dropping to her knees beside the corpse. Her shoulders sagged but she uttered no sound, staring silently for a moment before reaching out with delicate fingers and gently lowering the eyelids. Death did not fit with the idyll, the soft breeze, the scenery, the sun's warmth breathing life into the ground. The dead bodies jarred in conflict.

Brutus appeared at the fringe of the copse, his sword looking awkward in his left hand. Julita and Cloelia stopped abruptly behind him, the three of them stilled by the vista. Cloelia's hands rose to her mouth, a gasp of horror escaping before she could extinguish it. The girl on her knees flinched with tension, but didn't rise or turn around.

Marcus flattened his lips, pressing them together and sheathed his sword. The girl didn't intend to flee it seemed, Brutus could deal with containing her. Relaxing imperceptibly, he went to Lucius. Resting on one knee with the other leg bent at a right angle with his forearm lying across it, Lucius's mind had stopped throwing sparks and steadiness was slowly returning. Red thumbprint indentations decorated his throat and swallowing was painful.

"You could pass as Iceni with those neck markings," said Marcus, his tone deliberately light hearted, his concern portrayed not by his voice, but by the arm resting on his friend's back as he crouched beside him. "A cheap method of gaining camouflage, I would say."

Lucius snorted in response and subconsciously rubbed his throat, wincing at the soreness.

"I had the big bastard under control," he croaked, giving thanks with his eyes and not his words, as was the way of the legions. He cocked a half smile adding, "It would have been quicker with a sword, but where is the challenge in that?"

Marcus grinned back and clapped him on the shoulder.

"Can you rise? We have a horse and maiden to rescue from the clutches of Brutus."

....

The Roman party resumed their journey in a more subdued manner, each lost in their own thoughts. Cloelia had fussed dreadfully over Lucius, until Julita injected some harsh words to end her gushing and send her in to a sullen silence. Despite his weak arm, Brutus had easily captured the Iceni girl who appeared completely vanquished, numb and acquiescent until Lucius stood before her. He'd raised his eyebrows on recognition, only for her to spit in his face and lunge at him with vicious fingers to his eyes. She inflicted few scratches before he slit her throat with little remorse for the woman he'd bedded in Vinovia. Flavinus was right, Roman women it will be, was all he had said after the event. The quiet comment stabbed a reminder at Marcus, who couldn't shake Jolinda from his mind. He wondered how Kye was faring. Was he still at the fort or returned home? Had he given his message to Jolinda? Did she know he was gone? So many unanswered questions cluttered his thoughts.

That night they took accommodation in a wooden *caupona* at Morbium, having passed several newly built stone villas, evidence of the nearby limestone quarries and the prosperity they were bringing to the area. The chosen hostel, with its basic bunkhouse sleeping accommodation, suited their desire to retreat from socialising, and Julita remained silent when she heard Cloelia creep over to join Brutus in the night.

Chapter Sixteen

The weather remained favourable for the next five days and they made good progress across the Brigante lands and down into the borders of the Parisi tribe. The ground was surprisingly dry, allowing them to keep away from the busy Via Dere, and take a much quieter route further to the east of the ridge that accompanied them south like a backbone of the land. Thus, they avoided the massive legionary fortress at Eburacum, home to the six thousand men of the IX Hispania Legion as well as Brigantum, the bustling administrative centre of the Brigante Kingdom, and arrived in Petuaria unchallenged. It seemed Brutus had been correct to think it odd to see the Iceni trio who had stalked them so far north. The Brigante and Parisi tribes were far less hostile to their presence.

High, pale grey clouds smudged the whole of the sky, but it was bright enough to cause Marcus to squint as he looked across the Fluvius from the jetty. The river was flat and wide with a smooth, velvety texture to the surface and he could just determine a single building on the opposite bank. Petuaria, in contrast, was quite large. The town had a wide variety of quality housing, several temples, and a theatre next to the stone municipal buildings. Most of the streets were paved, including the one that ran along the bank of the Fluvius in both directions from where he stood on the jetty.

Looking for the street's name, he smiled to himself when he read the elaborately inscripted stone, 'Via Abus', River Street – of course, what else would it have been called? And beneath the title, in the same finely carved lettering, was Londinium with an arrow indicating across the river, and Gaul beside an arrow pointing downstream to the sea.

Via Abus was astir with activity, even at this early hour. Marcus had left the others slumbering, having grown weary of his own inability to sleep. Jolinda was filling his thoughts, it seemed the nearer he drew to leaving Britannia, the greater the pull he was feeling to return to her. The walk was intended as a distraction. They would return as a party later to book a shipping passage.

Several traders were setting up stalls beside the jetty with souvenirs from the local potteries, so Marcus ambled amongst them. One stall in particular was exhibiting some handsome looking jugs and amphorae, and Marcus picked up a pottery strainer to examine its workmanship.

"This is well made," he nodded at the trader who ceased his unpacking and gave his attention to Marcus. The man had a hunch to his left shoulder and walked stiffly in an awkward gait, but it was with intelligent eyes and a clear, confident voice that he replied. Marcus estimated his age to be thirty or forty seasons.

"I can guarantee the workmanship of all these items. Made them with my own hands."

A flicker of surprise crossed Marcus's face at the fluent Latin of the trader, which held no hint of an accent. He'd expected broken Latin at best, with dull rounded vowel sounds to the words and accented enunciation, not this sharp well-spoken version. His puzzlement must have shown as the trader launched in to a friendly explanation without being asked, as if the scenario happened frequently.

"I was born to a slave girl of a wealthy Roman family who lived in the southern parts of this fair island. Luckily for me, the mistress lost her own babe soon after childbirth and adopted me as her surrogate son, freeing me first I must add." The perspicacious eyes held Marcus's for a moment before he continued. "My deformity," he shrugged his left shoulder slightly, "was not apparent until much time and expense had been lavished on my education. It is the fickle nature of Fortuna."

Marcus showed his agreement to that statement with a small nod and a wry smile. Few escaped the goddess's capricious ways.

"Do you scribe?" asked Marcus.

"Yes, I scribe. Latin and Greek."

"And yet you are a trader of pottery wares." Marcus raised his eyebrows and turned his palms upwards questioningly. Scribes were not normally short of well-paid business.

"I gain a greater pleasure from working my pots. My hands caress their curves. I have no family." He looked steadily at Marcus who quickly absorbed his point. "It allows me a greater focus to my work and that is why I am confident of guaranteeing the wares. Are you looking for a particular item?"

Replacing the strainer, Marcus shook his head.

"I have a long journey ahead, and I fear the pots would not travel well."

"It is not so far to the northern frontier, but perhaps you would like a clay doll as a gift for your special lady. They are small enough to protect inside a boot." The trader opened a piece of sack cloth revealing four clay dolls, that bore little resemblance to the shape of the human body. A circular base a thumb-length in diameter, tapered to a neck before widening out in to a head the size of a coin. There were no limbs, just two tiny protrusions imitating breasts but strangely hollowed out. Marcus found them quite ugly.

"Your destiny lies north Legionary, not in Gaul. You are chosen. Give this to Emperor Hadrian, he is in Britannia and also journeying north. The sweet perfume of the purple lavendula flower will be your salvation and cloak the stench you regret."

....

It was noon when Julita secured a berth of passage for them all on a Greek trading vessel named *Thekla*, moored a little upstream from the jetty where Marcus had been earlier. Although the sun had not penetrated the clouds completely, you could sense its whereabouts in the sky and the day was calm. They would sail with the tide that evening.

Marcus looked for the humpback trader as they passed the souvenir stalls on their way to the township for provisions, but the man was not to be seen. He wondered at what was in the second package that had been pushed on him, the thought passing quickly as Brutus caught his attention with the beginning of a rambling story.

With Brutus's fine entertainment, the packing and sailing preparations slipped the afternoon hours by quickly and the party ended up reaching the jetty with little time to spare. The captain was not happy and with a lot of exasperated arm gestures and exaggerated huff he claimed the luggage would have to stay.

"No time, we miss tide, luggage stay, we go now, persons only!"

Julita calmly gave the Greek some extra coins.

"His name, Barak, it means 'flash of lightning'," the captain explained to Julita, but loud enough to ensure they all heard. His tone and smile were genial but the glint to his eye purported a shrewder message, "it suits him well, yes…he is master with the whip, yes?"

Julita's only reply was a gracious nod of her head, as she and Cloelia retired to the captain's berth. It was the only private area on board the working vessel, and although small with just a crude bed of rush matting and a bolster pillow, the captain had negotiated a tidy sum for its use. Marcus, Brutus and Lucius would sleep with the crew amongst the amphorae of salt and crates of red tiles being shipped to Gaul.

Settling on the foredeck with Brutus and Lucius, Marcus pulled out his wrapped *tali* set. The distraction of playing dice would be welcome. With the soil of Britannia no longer beneath his boots, there was no running back to Jolinda now. The sever was final and his chest was leaden with the knowledge. The hunchback had been wrong about Hadrian and wrong about his destiny.

Thinking of the hunchback reminded him of the second package. He'd forgotten about it during their unexpected haste to make ready for departure. Feeling through his toga to check it was there, he shrugged imperceptibly. It was just more hocus from the fraud hunchback, he would open it later. Brutus was rubbing his hands in preparedness.

"Let us play *tali*. I may yet become a rich man before we reach Rome. Lucius, it seems our friend here will be easy pickings, his mind is distracted still by a special Brigante maiden." Marcus lifted his eyes to Brutus. "We hear what you do not speak, Marcus." The words were spoken gently. "The river offers a short swim, the sea will not. Lucius and I will see the legate's family safely to Rome, go back if you must."

The tension was shafted by the cry of a passing seagull. Marcus said nothing, but clasped the forearm of first, Brutus, then Lucius, in the legionary grip, before rolling the *tali* pieces with purpose. He acknowledged the gods with a determined, tight-lipped nod that his decision was correct, as the pieces fell in his favour.

Chapter Seventeen

The legate ordered the decaying body of the Pict brother to be cut down from the crucifix. The display of flayed and crow-pecked flesh had been good for the morale of his men, thus serving one purpose, but the interrogation had failed to provide him with any useful information. A Caledonian War Council had been mumbled once, but the fools meting out the punishment had been too brutal too early, on the sick-weakened boy and he'd withstood very little, dying soon after, muttering incoherently about elders and midges.

Six frustrating days had followed, waiting for the Brigante boy, Kye Teviot, to beat the fever, so he could be questioned further. Peterna had felt in a state of suspense the whole time and joined in with the gruelling drill regime that he was insisting the Cohorts continue with, just to keep himself sound of mind. His arms and shoulders ached from working the heavy wooden practise swords, but he preferred that to the restless nerves that tortured his sleep.

Teviot had co-operated with his questioning, confirming the existence of a War Council but denying knowledge of their location in Caledonia. Peterna had kept his expression level when he learned of the bribery at *Arbeia*, it was as he'd expected, but his jaw set rigid in the effort to remain impassive when Kye spoke of the Picts's intent to bribe some of his own legion to bring down his fort. His frustration at the lack of a war band to engage flooded his veins with hot blood that pulsed visibly at his temples.

Kye had admitted the Picts were looking to him for information on the Roman trumpet signals and he'd told of the meeting arranged for him at Swine Lake. The full moon was due in five days, and although both the brothers were dead, there was a possibility that others would gather there. It was the only lead Peterna had and he was debating the best approach to using it. Rubbing both eyes with a thumb and forefinger to relieve the tiredness that clung like dew, he strode to the hospital quarters. Speaking with the physician revealed Kye's wound was healing well now the fever was gone, and he was gaining strength and mobility daily. There would be no need to retain him for many more days. Peterna pursed his lips in thought with the rudiments of a plan as he reached Kye's room. How far should he trust the Brigante boy? Probably as far as an auxiliary from *Arbeia*, he concluded with bitterness.

Kye was standing beside his bed, arms leaning against the wall, gently raising alternate knees, when the legate entered his room. He acknowledged him with a nod but continued exercising, although his heartbeat grew quicker, not from exertion but with nervousness. An air of authority mixed with purpose swept in with the legate, and Kye sensed an ultimatum.

"The full moon is in five days," Peterna did not waste time with preamble. "You will keep your meeting at Swine Lake even though the Pict brothers cannot. It is most likely that others will fill their place. It is regrettable that our captive died before we were able to extract useful details of this War Council's plans. The task must be repeated." Kye understood immediately that the legate wanted him to lead the Romans to other captives who would be put to rigorous torture. His gut turned at the thought. Peterna continued, "the physician informs me that you are fit enough to be discharged, and so after the meeting you may return to your family."

"And if I don't agree to go to Swine Lake?"

"Then you will be held as an aggressor against Rome." The legate's tone and hard expression left no doubt as to the unpleasantness of this captivity. Kye determined it was an order, not a choice.

"What if no others turn up, can I still return to me family or will ya want more from me?"

"No more will be asked of you."

The two were silent as each stared deeply at the other, trying to read the truth. Kye broke the fog of mistrust with a puff that vibrated his lips.

"Swine Lake 'tis then."

The legate nodded curtly as he left. The boy was caught between a rock and a shield and Peterna would not falter in reneging on his words if it meant sacrificing one man for the benefit of many.

....

Even under the circumstances of his visit, Kye delighted in the spectacle before him. The night was not cloud free, but enough clear sky prevailed to allow the splendour of the full moon to shimmer over Swine Lake, as it crept above the horizon. The orb rose, sepia tinged, casting an eerie yellow pallor over the land and water. The daylight wind had ceased as if in awe of the rising moon that looked close enough to touch.

For a moment, Kye bathed in the magical hush, allowing the pageant to lure him to a place of great peace. Forgetting the legate and his men hiding in the scrub to his right, and the rest of the cohort concealed further away to his left, he was immersed in the embrace of the Spirit World that ascended with the full moon, feeling his ancestors like a warm blanket draping his back.

The path forward became clear with their presence. The Teviot family was named after these lands, or were the lands named after the Teviot people? It mattered little, the two were mingled and Kye soaked in the importance of his role, ambassador for his family, especially for their right to remain Brigante in Brigante lands. His loyalty need be with no other, not Roman, not Pict, not Celt. He would do right by his bloodline, and warm strength coursed through his body with this understanding of belonging.

A movement at the lake-shore caught his eye, a deer breaking from the trees to drink at the water's edge. Unhurried, it slaked its thirst, intermittently raising its head to sniff at the air for danger. Two more joined it and Kye watched as they grazed untroubled on the banks. The moon turned whiter as it rose in the sky with the passing minutes, and a breeze began ruffling the stillness once more, becoming braver, it seemed, as the moon gained in distance from the land.

The legate had a clear view of Kye from his hiding place, but could not see as far as the lake or surrounding shore. His sword was drawn as he watched the boy intently, reading his body movements for signs of tension indicating danger. Kye had sat a little straighter several times, cocking an ear to one side at the hoot of an owl or an increase in rustling leaves, only to relax in to a soft slump when the noise ceased and no person or persons appeared. Kye straightened again and Peterna drew in his brow as he concentrated, wondering what had caught his attention.

Something had startled the deer. All three had raised their heads simultaneously and were standing poised for flight, when as one they leapt gracefully away, their white rumps rising and falling like a warning beacon as they disappeared in to the trees.

Peterna forced to steady his breathing as his pulse rate increased with the unease. Every muscle was taut as he focussed on the sounds and visions of the evening land. *Come on...where are you?* He was clenching his teeth so tightly, a spasm flicked the corner of his eye. Seconds spread into minutes, a yawning chasm of time that extended like a cave in darkness, expectation clinging to the edges like smudging mist. Somebody was about, he could sense it, taste them almost. *Come on...whoever you are...you hold the information I need.*

Yet no person or persons appeared. For how long he and his men lay waiting, Peterna was unsure. It seemed only moments, but his cramped muscles were an indication that the gods had played tricks with mortal time. The cold was seeping in and checking the arc of the moon, he realised the evening had slipped furtively into night.

The legate grimaced as he shifted position, the undergrowth crackling beneath him.

"Centurion, take a score of men and sweep the area down to the lake." His mouth was set in a firm line and he spoke with a muted tone. Somebody had been near earlier, but he couldn't sense them any more. "Acheron!" he cursed quietly to himself. *Why had they not broken cover to speak with the Brigante? When had he lost whoever it had been?*

....

The tracks of a lone man were found in the area during the sweep, but that was all, and the Romans and Kye returned to the fort as they had departed, aware of nothing more than the existence of a Caledonian War Council that was plotting something, somewhere, sometime.

Rubbing the tiredness from his eyes with a thumb and forefinger, Peterna tried to focus on the plan that had been forming during the long wait by the lake. He felt so weary. Rising from his desk, he moved to the window and could see a hint of dawn light creeping in from the right as he stared towards the North Gate. Chewing on the inside of his lip, he mulled over his options. He had such little information...it always came back to that. He watched as the first drops of rain peppered the courtyard, and thanked Jupiter for at least holding back until their return from the vigil. The gods had not deserted him entirely then, he mused. Deciding there was nothing to be gained from tired introspection, he called for the guard to bring Kye in. He had time for a few hours of sleep, and the new day may bring word from Hadrian, but first he must speak to the Brigante.

The legate remained pensive, watching the raindrops merge their pattern as they grounded with more frequency, leaving Kye to look at his back in the gloaming silence. Maintaining the stillness, Kye stood barely breathing, his mouth set straight and firm, his wits alert. All his tiredness was gone, sliced away like unpalatable pig fat. Was he going home at last? Or would the legate go back on his word?

After an age, Peterna spoke without turning.

"Somebody was at the lake. Do you know who?"

"No," replied Kye, although the face of the one-eared Celt leaped to the fore.

"Do you agree that somebody was there?"

"I..." Kye cleared his throat... "the deer were spooked by something."

"Something or someone?"

"I didn't see anyone, but..."

The legate left the sentence hanging and Kye continued in a beaten tone,

"...but I reckon someone were there."

Pursing his lips and folding his arms, Peterna turned slowly to face Kye, his blue eyes piercing even in the half-light. The boy had given the answer he wanted to hear. A small lead was still trailing and Kye was aware of it too.

"A guard will escort you from the fort via the North Gate an hour after sunrise. It is my belief that the War Council will make contact with you. Rome rewards her allies favourably."

"Are ya asking me to be ya informer? I did what ya wanted me to...ya said that would be it."

"Your family is known to me, as is the location of your homestead. I have no quarrel with the Teviots, but let there be no doubt that Rome will prevail, and be reminded that Rome gives protection to her allies but will quash her foe. Let there be no misunderstanding between us now. It will be in your family's best interest that you find out what you can about the intentions of the War Council and report the knowledge directly to me." The legate did not invite a reply as he turned to the window once more. "You may go." Tapping a finger gently to his lips, Peterna knew he was once more playing a frustrating waiting game. He couldn't have a battle without a war band, he'd played fire against fire with some success, now he would play deceit against deceit. If the War Council wanted information on the Roman trumpet signals, they would get it, he would feed it to them on his terms, but he must wait for the link to be made.

Chapter Eighteen

Indignation had burnt at Kye as he was marched from the fort, yet try as he might to keep the anger sharp, it dissipated as he made his way across the familiar wild landscape towards his homestead. Had it really been less than two full moons since he'd stormed out? It felt much longer, and scorning his earlier immaturity, Kye acknowledged the change he could see in himself with a wry smile. The goddess Bridget knew what he'd lived through to reach this point, but he hailed himself a man because of it.

Reaching the top of the rise, he stopped momentarily as his heart flipped slightly on seeing his homestead palisade atop the next knoll. The wooden stakes obscured the dwellings, but a rush of warmth pressed behind his ribs as he noticed curls of smoke rising from the central hut, its roof of rush matting just visible. He could visualise Ma stoking the embers with fresh logs and hanging gutted fish to smoke them. No doubt she would have a vegetable broth simmering, its earthy aromas floating above the smells of freshly burning hazel wood and the staler odour of ashes. Jolinda might be scraping a fur or salting a hare. Whatever the job, she would be humming softly, injecting insouciant optimism.

The Roman Fort was now out of view behind him and he thought about his eldest sister as he resumed along the last track to home. How would she take the message from Marcus Guintoli? Subconsciously, he put his hand to the small, leather pouch slung about his neck, feeling the bone effigy of Jupiter inside. What relationship had Jolinda had with this Roman warrior? A prick of hatred rose at the loss of his father to this man, yet was balanced by the debt of his own life to the same sword. How much did Jolinda know of the events and how much should he tell her? Guintoli was gone from their lives now. Kye struggled to recall the lands he was travelling to…Syntia…no, Syria, that was it. The name hardly mattered, it was far from Britannia.

It was strange how life unfurled. Up until the day he'd followed Jolinda to the fort, he'd thought it was Tamsin who was softening to the Roman ways. Apart from wanting to trade with the Romans, Jolinda had appeared to value the Brigante independence as imperative. So what had changed in her to become involved with a legionary and befriend the legate's daughter too? By the Sun, he felt the Teviot's were being ruptured apart, his self included. Should he, would he, pass information to the legate as ordered? The face of the one-eared Celt came to the fore again. Kye had not disclosed the man's involvement with the Pict meeting to the legate, but maybe he should. His gut said this was the person skulking at Swine Lake, but he couldn't be sure. He sighed at finding his own loyalties dividing. One thing he could see clearly, was the necessity of trading with the Romans, and he acknowledged Jolinda's vision in that.

"Sweet henbit!" Ma dropped her skillet in shock. The hut fell silent. "Well, ya never know what the chill wind will bring, does ya? Have ya stories of honour to tell us Kye Teviot?"

"Aye Ma, some."

Eyeing her son for a moment, Ma took in the steady confidence that had been absent a moon before.

"Then ya worthy of a seat at this table, son. Aaron fetch the mead, we celebrate a Teviot reunion this day." Kye grinned with relief and solid happiness at being home and welcome.

....

The chilly dawn light was freckled with drizzle, but Kye enjoyed the refreshing droplets on his face as he crossed the yard to the goat shed. It was a good feeling to be back tending the animals, and an even better feeling to be back in the fold of the family. The recounting of his time away had gone on late in to the night and resumed again throughout the next day as he tried to answer the questions launched at him with as much honesty as possible, even sharing with them the pressures put upon him by the legate to become an informer. Ma had been distraught, not understanding how he could even contemplate the idea, until Kye quietly explained that although the Romans took Da's life, they had saved *his* life from the dirty blades of the Picts. *He*, at least, owed them a debt of honour. Ma bristled about her chores after that, bemoaning she didn't know what to offer the spirits as prayers any more. Kye had met Jolinda's eyes at this reaction and saw her query. Although he'd carefully made no mention of Marcus Guintoli, he sensed she knew they had met. He would hold his tongue until they were alone.

He didn't have to wait long, as Jolinda sought him out in the goat shed that morning, bringing with her a shaft of damp air as she entered. Drawing up a stool, Kye leaned his shoulder to the goat's flank and began milking, steam rising from the spurts as they landed with a rhythmic tune in the wooden pail. Without being asked, and without looking up, Kye recounted his conversation with Marcus, recalling the details easily.

"Are ya sure of ya facts?"

"Aye, Jolinda, I am. It were Guintoli who killed Da and it were Guintoli who saved me." He stopped milking and retrieved the leather pouch from around his neck, passing it to Jolinda. "There's a message that goes with this. If I could scribe I'd let ya read it in private."

Jolinda's heart felt a skewer.

"He's gone ain't he?"

Kye nodded. "Far away."

"And the message?"

Breathing deeply, Kye stood before his sister. He was taking no pleasure in this.

"He said to tell ya he made a vow before he met ya. A vow his gods won't relinquish him of."

"Did he say what the vow was?"

Kye shook his head and moved to hug his sister, but Jolinda stiffened as he tried, pushing him away.

"Don't be nice to me now, I ain't ready. I can't make sense of it all. Does he think we couldn't be together 'cause he killed Da? Is that it?" Her mind was spinning and she was flushed with fear. An altogether different fear to that of a warrior facing death, but the fear of grief, the price you pay for loving. "But he saved you so…" she shrugged, not understanding, not having the words to express herself, looking from Kye to the bone effigy in her hand, and back to Kye again.

"I don't know if this will help, Jolinda, but I'll tell ya it all. Guintoli offered the information about killing Da, I wouldn't have known otherwise. He said we part as equals 'n' that seemed important to him. I think he took a risk coming to see me in the hospital."

Closing her eyes and squeezing the bone piece tightly in her fist, holding it firmly against her lips, Jolinda whispered a prayer to her goddess Bridget and to his god Jupiter uncaring that the two might clash.

"For all it's worth, Kye, thanks for keeping his name from your tales. He's g…" she stumbled over the word, "gone, so will ya continue to keep it to ya'self? I couldn't bear to hear Ma use his name in her lamenting."

"The Romans have no names to me. Now, we'd better be about our chores or Ma'll be lamenting over that!"

Jolinda gave a weak smile appreciating the attempt at humour but not being able to let it reach her, not yet. In time she knew she would laugh again, but the ravine was deep and lonely for the present.

"Kye, I need to ask ya…" chewing on her lip with the worry of the Afterworld weighing on her, Jolinda couldn't have felt more wretched, "…do ya spit upon me shadow for laying with a Roman? Especially the one I chose."

Kye returned to milking the goat, measuring his words before answering.

"Two moon cycles ago I hated the Romans 'n' all they stood for. When I tracked ya to their fort, I felt ya were betraying me. I would've given me life with the Picts to destroy that place, taking as many legionaries with it as possible. But that were two moons ago 'n' I've spoken with the spirits more closely than I care to remember since then. I don't much care for the Romans, the Picts or the Celts, but I'm proud of the Teviot blood that runs in me. That's what I've learnt, I'm proud of who I am, but I dirtied me face getting there …no, I don't spit on ya shadow."

……………………

There was no sobbing, just a silent rivulet of sorrow soaking the pillow as Jolinda lay hoping for sleep. Turned on her side, looking away from Tamsin sharing the bed beside her, the tears from one eye leaked across the bridge of her nose to merge with the flow from the other. She had succeeded in containing the sadness during the daylight hours, but in the still of the dark night the grief spilled out. The release of sleep was mocking in its absence as Jolinda's thoughts played over, swirling with empty answers. *What vow Marcus? Why did you have to go?*

Unexpectedly, she felt the warmth of Tamsin's embrace as her sister pressed herself to Jolinda's back, nestling in the curves. Unexpected but welcome. They lay moulded as one and Jolinda accepted the comfort like a lamb accepting protection from a ewe. Tamsin ran her fingers lightly along her sister's bare arm, soothing in its tenderness. With a practised measure she continued stroking until she could feel Jolinda give herself over to the caress, drifting in to relaxation without repose, a most welcome state of rest more beneficial in many ways than sleep. Tamsin whispered in Jolinda's ear.

"Marcus was mine. *My* touch aroused him to wildness." Stunned by the words of venom breathed so softly, they struck at Jolinda with discord. Tamsin continued, "you and he were the gossip of the tavern, but I had him first, *him* and Lucius together, but the sweetest were the second time in the open wildness of the hills with the Standard Bearer too embarrassed to watch. Marcus were beyond control with desire. I *worked* him."

The shock mangled Jolinda and she rushed from the bed retching. By the time she ceased vomiting, beads of sweat were prickling across her forehead. Crumpled beside the toilet pit outside the hut, her hair clinging in straggles to her face, shivering in reaction to the violent heaving as much as the chill morning air, still no respite came from the unexpected torment. Tamsin was beside her again, remorseless in her cruel mocking, enjoying her sister's humiliation as she recounted explicit stories of her debauchery.

"May ya father forgive ya Tamsin Teviot."

"Ma!"

"Ya have his blood on ya hands, don't ya Child?" Ma spoke with a solid calmness, her voice strong with clarity gained from understanding and insight. "Ya let us believe ya were raped. It's why he went for revenge, to protect ya name, and he died for it. 'Tis clear to me now that ya ain't the innocent. Ya planned it all, but it went wrong when ya miscarried, didn't it? Ya grief were genuine enough, them were unforced tears, but they weren't for the degradation were they? No, them were for the loss of the Roman child ya carried."

Jolinda choked back a sob.

"A legionary's pay is good and they look after the women who carry their seed." Tamsin stood tall in defiance. "He would've taken me to a better life than this! Marcus or Lucius or another, it matters not to me." Tamsin looked at the pathetic state of Jolinda. "Ha! 'Tis sweet it turned out to be the one you've given ya heart to that thinks he wronged me. I thought the Spirits had turned against me when I miscarried, but it seems they had a greater picture to draw. Shall I tell ya the vow Marcus made? The vow that his gods won't relinquish him of?"

Puzzlement shadowed Jolinda's eyes.

"The tavern is a *huge* source of information. Ya should try it, far more reliable than trusting one man." In contrast, Tamsin's eyes were sparkling, overflowing with bright bitterness. *"Roman women only,* that's his vow, my legacy to ya!"

Fragments of conversations between Jolinda and Marcus jostled to the fore, darting in short bursts like racing minnows. *Your name, it sounds Roman.* Her vision danced and blackness smudged the edges. *Pledge your alliance to Rome.* All noise ceased as she collapsed letting the dark world claim her.

....

The air in the hut was pungent with earthy odours, thick and cloying, as the herbalist wafted smouldering leaves over Jolinda.

"The murmurings are a good sign. The Spirits are sending her back to us." Humming a soft melody, the herbalist purveyed calm, contentment and wisdom evident in the threaded wrinkles of her aged complexion. Kye had fetched her at Ma's request when they'd been unable to rouse Jolinda from her slump. By the time he returned, Tamsin was gone. Jolinda lay quiet again and Ma's troubled eyes sought the herbalist's. "A little longer is needed. The Spirits know best. They will release her when they're ready. I've seen this before, she is coming back to us, and we must be patient." The herbalist resumed her humming swaying with the tune, causing a thick tumble of grey locks to fall free from the clips attempting to tame the wild mane.

Ma continued her bedside vigil, not knowing when she fell into slumber, but awaking with a start at Jolinda's gentle voice.

"What did I do to make Tamsin hate me?" The herbalist was gone and the air in the hut was clearer although the earthy odours remained. Tears welled in Ma with relief and anguish and she wiped them quickly away, wanting to be strong for her first born looking so fragile in the box bed.

"She is gone. May the Spirits forgive me weaknesses in raising such bane. On me life, I never thought I'd favour a le…legionary over one of me own flesh." Jolinda heard the tremor in Ma's voice and noticed her chin lift slightly. These were difficult words for her. "It may've been a Roman sword that bled the life blood from ya Da, but it were his own pup that truly slayed him. Ya Marcus is…welcome at this hearth."

Jolinda felt as if a hot poker was slicing her chest and branding her heart with grief. It was too late, he was gone. Her eyes beseeched her mother who was weeping openly now, the tears falling unbidden and unchecked, and Jolinda saw the troubled scratch of fear slanting deeply through them. "We must appease *Bridget* for the debauchery wreaked by our own, *my* own flesh. The lore demands we share sacred rites with the duped across our threshold, or ya Da…" Ma swallowed hard, half catching her breath, unable to complete the sentence. There was no need, Jolinda knew the Brigante lore, the teachings were instilled by the druids to the clans, and although the Teviots kept their own counsel as much as possible, their roots were still fixed by the ancient whispers. Unless they put right this wrongdoing, the Teviot Ancestors would wander in restless despair in the Afterworld, unable to find peace and eventually driven mad by the turbulent roving, their disquieted spirits would haunt and taunt the living to castigation. Against the grain, a tiny speck of hope seeded in Jolinda's heart. Kye came to crouch beside the bed.

"If it takes me to Syria, I will find him and bring him back." Jolinda's chest heaved with love at the earnestness of her brother's words, at the same time collapsing with the enormity of his search. She tenderly cupped a hand to his cheek, and Kye covered it with his own.

"Ya a man now and the uniform fits." Kye understood her meaning, recalling the day he sneaked up on her returning from the fort. Jolinda had been right to scoff at him then, he had been immature. "Da would be proud." Kye's nostrils flared as he tried to control his emotions.

Chapter Nineteen

The pine mast splintered with an agonising groan and the broken section shattered several amphorae as it landed, spilling salt over the deck. A huge wave crashed over the Thekla, its power breaking the latticed guardrail along the vessel's side and sweeping the salt and pottery pieces away with a sucking sound. The cries of fear from the slaves could be heard by the five Romans huddled in the crude cabin, no more than a box on the deck, but an area that afforded some protection as long as the timbers held firm. Greek curses from Barak and shouts from the captain punctuated the sounds of the stormy sea.

"I wish Papa was here," Cloelia's lower lip trembled as she whispered the words to her mother.

"Yes, my petal, pray with me to Neptune that we see him again." Julita breathed words of an orison into her daughter's hair, looking over her head at Brutus trying to determine his features in the dark.

The cabin was square in shape with sides just long enough to accommodate a prone man for sleeping. There were no windows and the lamp that normally hung from the ceiling hook was thankfully safely stowed, leaving the hook to rattle alone as the boat listed and rolled to the mercy of the sea. Marcus and Lucius were both sitting with their backs braced to the sides, legs spread wide but bent for purchase. Brutus was in a similar position but wedged in to a corner with Cloelia nestling between him and Julita. Marcus muttered along with the orison to Neptune as the vessel listed perilously before up-righting itself and rolling over in the opposite direction with the momentum. Further terrified cries came from the slaves.

"Poor bastards," muttered Lucius.

"At least they are chained to the oar stations," replied Marcus. "If these timbers give out, we will wish we were chained too."

"But if the boat goes down, we can at least swim freely," added Lucius, who felt the force of Brutus's boot for his comment, for Cloelia could hardly breathe with dread.

Another wave of water doused the Thekla with a booming crash followed by a scream of pain that was washed away. The Romans heard the captain shouting Barak's name, followed by a wail of anger to Poseidon.

As quickly as the squall arrived, it left. There was no partial easing of the violence, the sea simply went from fury to calm, and the Thekla was left bobbing idly, as battered and bruised as its survivors. Marcus eased open the hatch.

"Roman! Your legions are renowned for their swordsmanship. Now would be an effective time to show your skills, I think. Barak is gone, my leg is broken and I need you to unchain these slaves." The Captain's leg was not only broken but mangled below the knee which had been crushed by the falling mast, pinning him to the deck. This had saved his life or he too would have been swept away with Barak.

"Unchain them?" Marcus was incredulous.

"Unless you know how to raise the bow sail…aagh!" The Captain's face blanched a grey hue with the pain. The slaves were sitting mute at their oar stations, but Marcus could feel a dangerous hatred emanating from them that prickled the hairs on his nape and he didn't like the idea of unchaining them. The rest of the Roman party joined him on deck from the cabin. Cloelia gasped at the sight of the Captain's leg.

"If it's that bad Missy, then we'll saw it off and get me a wooden one eh? But let's get to shore first. Now stop pandering around Legionary and unchain them slaves, but mind you keep their shackles on for now. The oars are smashed and we need that sloping sail up. There's three of you with swords and only six of them, but don't underestimate the desperate strength the smallest channel of freedom can give to a crushed soul. Let's get this vessel moving before we're swamped by pirates. Get the sail aloft, then perhaps you could shift this bugger that's pinning me leg!"

....

The Thekla was at the mercy of the winds and the tides and it seemed to Marcus that they drifted for an eternity. In truth it was not longer than two days and Fortuna had been beside them for they did not encounter any pirate vessels during their drift, and gentle rain had been sent by Jupiter to slake their thirst, but the sea remained calm. The presence of the legionary swords had kept the slaves subdued. Cloelia and Julita had kept busy tending the Captain.

"We are heading back to Britannia it seems," Lucius informed Marcus. "Brutus has been learning from the Captain how to read the stars," he nodded upwards at the clearing sky. "Fancies he could find himself a new career as a sailor now," he added with another glance upwards, more rueful this time. Marcus chuckled but it was half-hearted.

"Do you believe we can control our own destiny, Lucius, or is it charted for us already?"

Lucius thought for a moment before replying, he could see the hard set of Marcus's jaw and knew he was struggling with returning to the island frontier.

"The gods play *tali* with us my friend, but there are choices within the game."

Marcus absorbed that with a slight raise of his eyebrows. The pair remained silent, staring out towards the distant land beyond the gay-coloured bow sail. Brutus joined them and the trio held their own thoughts until Marcus broke the hush. Reaching in to his toga, he pulled out the secret package given to him by the hunchback trader in Petuaria. He opened his hand to reveal a small block of polished wood with carvings on four sides depicting victory scenes. A seated figure of Mars in full military regalia, with victory trophies to the left and right featuring Dacian shields was clear. The detail was exquisite. Brutus exhaled a breathy whistle.

"Where did you get that?"

"From the trader who sold me the *tali* pieces." Marcus passed it to Brutus and Lucius for a closer inspection. "It was the strangest conversation. He said I was chosen and that my destiny lies in the north, not in Gaul, then gave me this..."

"*Gave* you it," interrupted Brutus who was unusually brief with his words.

"Yes, said I was to give it to Emperor Hadrian."

"*What?*"

"This is from the Dacian Wars, is it not?" Lucius was squinting at the detail on the wooden block. "We need a lamp." He made off towards the cabin.

"And quite how are you supposed to give it to the Emperor, and why anyway?" Brutus was bemused and becoming sceptical. "Did this hunchback have a full set of quern stones in his mill?" He tapped his finger to his temple to indicate his meaning, shaking his head and scowling.

Marcus sighed thoughtfully and sucked on the inside of his cheek.

"According to the hunchback, Hadrian is in Britannia and journeying north."

"Well, that settles it for me then," said Brutus. "Everyone knows that the Emperor is touring the Southern Provinces and having a graciously Greek time of it, with all his wondrous spendings on the arts he so adores." Brutus was finding his speech again. "Cannot say I blame him," he added with a philosophical expression. "Why risk confrontation, or indeed, fraternisation, with the harsh B*rittunculi* when you can bask in glorious, commodious southern hospitality and warmth...mmm...olive groves. The block must be a modern working, the hunchback a jester and we the fools for even a momentary belief in it."

"You are most probably right, Brutus. I gave his words and the package no heed until a few hours ago, but in all the Known World I thought I had escaped the clutches of this island, and that decision was hard, only for the gods to bring me back. Why?"

"Must there be a reason other than a storm and a westward wind?"

"*For-tun-a!*" exclaimed Lucius, returning swiftly to the others. He'd been studying the carvings under the lamp in the cabin with Julita. "It *is* from the Dacian Wars. Not only that, but the Lady Julita was astonished to see it. The legate has a silver brooch with the same design, presented to him by Emperor Trajan for outstanding service in the Dacian Wars." Lucius could hardly contain his excitement. "There's a tiny imprint of the seal of Trajan's house burnt in to the wood, look, just here..." he showed them both, "...that matches the markings on the legate's brooch apparently. This is genuine Marcus. What are you going to do with it?"

"Apparently I am to give it to Hadrian, who is in Britannia, and heading north, which is where my destiny lies." Lucius frowned at him in confusion.

Marcus shook his head as if to unscramble his mind. "Pah! Brutus is right, it is an absurd notion." Marcus decisively replaced the carved block in his toga. "We are going to land wherever this broken vessel takes us, then set sail in another as quickly as possible. The Greek can take his chances with his slaves, we owe him nothing. It is doubtful he will survive anyway, gangrene will most likely set in and poison him. We have a duty to the legate who has entrusted his family to us and we *must* get them safely to Rome."

"We no longer have the documentation of passage," added Lucius whose excitement had dissipated. "We will have problems getting a berth without it. That and the baggage went with the storm. We should make for the nearest fort when we land." Marcus cursed, they really were in the mire without the documents, but he was desperate to leave the island as soon as possible. It was as if its tendrils were slowly wrapping around him again, ensnaring him. It would take an age for their story to be verified and new documents issued. Worse, the episode would be logged on their records and their careers didn't need further complications.

"No, we should leave as quickly as possible."

"Marcus, it is not practical to…"

"We leave!" Marcus cut him off sharply and Lucius, knowing more words were useless, strutted away cursing with frustration. Brutus held his own counsel for a few minutes, letting the spike go from Marcus's anger.

"Let us see where the winds and tides take us, Marcus my friend, we may yet have the decision taken from us."

....

Brutus was right. A party of warriors, a score strong, were awaiting the arrival of the Thekla as she beached on to the shingle, landing with a shuddering groan. It began to rain.

"By the gods," muttered Marcus. "These lands know how to welcome a soul! Foul weather *and* Iceni Warriors." His disposition was still decidedly sour.

"Let us hope they have not learned of a small Roman party killing two of their warriors and their woman," muttered Brutus, immediately regretting his words at seeing the colour drain from Cloelia's face. There was no time to add comfort to his words as the Iceni warriors aggressively herded them from the boat, stripping the men of their weapons and immediately separating Julita and Cloelia from the group.

One of the warriors was standing aloof several paces up the beach from the activity, clearly the leader of the local warband. A gold torc adorned each upper arm and Marcus was keeping a steady gaze on him, his pique at being back in Britannia so great, it was overriding all fear and judgement. He looked ready to rush at the man, and Lucius, seeing the danger in Marcus, warned Brutus with a discreet flick of his eyes. Brutus knew he must act quickly, so raising his hands in a gesture of submission and friendship, he opened the conversation, addressing the leader with a biddable tact.

"Our ship, as you can see, is damaged and in need of repair. We were heading for Gaul, away from these shores, when a storm hit us. With all oars broken, we were at the mercy of the gods and the drift has brought us to your lands. We would ask for your help, with the vessel and with the injured man." Brutus indicated towards the Captain. The Iceni did not break his silence and Brutus felt his heart quicken and sweat form in his armpits. Although allianced to Rome with a client king, their safety of passage was not guaranteed. If they displeased these people, there were no witnesses to prevent their murder.

The Iceni tugged at his bearded chin thoughtfully, and Brutus noted the intelligent eyes. This was clearly not a hot-headed axe wielder, more likely the son of a noble. A gasp of fear from Cloelia punctured the hush, and prompted the Iceni leader to speak harshly in his native tongue. A younger warrior was displaying his lust at her, and a heated exchange flared between the two tribesmen before the younger backed down, sloping a short distance away to skulk. Although maintaining a silent composure, Brutus was unable to control the angry flush that reddened his cheeks, and the Iceni leader noticed the flare of colour. He cocked an eyebrow and a knowing smirk creased the corner of his eyes.

"So, the pock-marked Roman cares for the golden haired one." He spoke in fluent Latin, the shingle shifting noisily beneath his feet as he loped casually closer. "Ship wrecked on your way to Gaul, eh?" The Iceni leader reached within three paces of Brutus who was standing a little ahead of Marcus and Lucius. Folding one arm across his body and supporting the other by the elbow, he again tugged at his beard in thought. The beach was silent except for the waves breaking on the shore, hissing as they sucked at the shards of shells and pebbles on their retreat. "You present me with somewhat of a problem. I have seen enough of the Roman Army to know you are from the Legions, and my men are baying for your blood." He held both hands up in a gesture of arrogant calm, still with an air of mischievous fun about him. Lucius shot sharp warning glances at Marcus in an attempt to keep him still, for an attack was futile with the numbers against them. "I am aware we should not be spilling Roman blood, we are alianced are we not?" The torcs flashed in the rainlight as he brought his hands to bear on his hips, enjoying the tension he was creating with the silence punctuated speech. "Yet revenge is burning in the heart of my men for the loss of their heritage and who would be witness?" Turning away from Brutus, the warrior moved across to Julita and Cloelia. Julita pulled her daughter close to her protectively, flaring her nostrils with fear and pride under the steady gaze of the native. "Why would three legionaries be travelling to Gaul on a Greek merchant vessel, and with two women in tow? Not slave women either, your demeanour belies your bedraggled appearance Lady." Julita's pulse was racing but she would not avert her eyes from his in defeat. "Yes, you intrigue me. Who are you?"

"You are astute in your deductions, and to whom do I have the pleasure of conversing?" Julita's throat was tight with fear and her voice did not match the strength of her words, but she drew on an image of Peterna for courage. The Iceni threw back his head and laughed with a richness of ease. With a click of his fingers he pointed at the Captain, and in an instant the closest warrior slit the injured man's gullet and the Captain quickly bled out staining the shingle. Julita flinched but stifled the scream that rose within her.

"Lady...I ask the questions." All humour had vanished. "Who are you?"

....

"What will happen to us Mama? Where have they taken the others? Oh, I feel nauseous." Cloelia rushed to the large earthenware bowl, beautifully finished with a deep blue glaze that was standing beside a delicately decorated dressing table inlaid with oyster shell. Grabbing the edge of the bowl and feeling sweat beads pepper her brow, the sickness swelled to her chest but would not surface, thus she hung her head on her hands and moaned for wretched relief. Her breathing was ragged and Julita crossed to give comfort.

Feeling afraid herself, calming words were difficult to find. Instead she rested one hand on her daughter's back and gently pulled the blonde ringlets back with the other, tucking them behind Cloelia's ears to keep them from tumbling forward again.

After the Captain had been killed, Julita had answered all the Iceni's questions openly, giving all their names, their intended destination and, under the warrior's probing inquiry, had revealed more than she'd wanted to about the legate's concerns at the northern frontier. This was pressing at her temples now. Why had the Iceni been so interested in the movements of the Picts? Had she somehow betrayed Peterna with her answers and endangered him further? Shaking the thoughts away, she sighed and moved towards the bed.

"Come and lay on the bed beside me Cloelia. Try to rest. It will do no good to worry ourselves to sickness. Papa would not want it, nor Brutus, and we must be strong for our men."

"Where do you think they have taken Brutus, Mama? And what of Marcus and Lucius?"

"They are most likely in guest accommodation in the other wing."

The villa was vast and styled on a country residence from Italia, not dissimilar to her cousin's home near Rome. The well-furnished cubiculum they were in looked out on to a colonnaded garden with its central fountain of stone fishes spewing plumes of silvery water in different directions across the shallow tiled area. Such tiled areas doubled up as foot baths in warm weather in Italia, yet the absence of seating indicated that did not happen here. Leading outward from the fountain was a fine mosaic path, depicting scenes of the forest as it curved its way round the garden. It was all very tasteful and obviously the home of a prominent Briton.

"Hospitality has been shown to us Cloelia, and what reason is there to think the same is not being given to the others?"

"Then why are we separated?"

"Child…" Julita sighed, "…it would be unseemly for legionaries to be guested with us. Do not forget the difficulties society poses for you and Brutus, even in these lands. I fear our days travelling have cocooned you of this." Julita was not prepared for the angry lash of her daughter's tongue in reply.

"Mama, you are a fool! We are not guests, we are not free to leave! They play with us and I am afraid for Brutus. I cannot rid myself of the darkness in the Iceni's eyes as he lusted for me and they know Brutus cares, they saw his reaction and I fear he is disadvantaged because of it. And I am helpless away from him."

Julita's cheeks burned crimson. She was shocked at being called a fool by her daughter, but that was not the worst. She felt the truth in Cloelia's perceptive words, but having shielded her child from harsh realities for so many years, she found herself unable to voice her agreement. This sudden demand to relinquish the role of protector was confusing, so to keep her own world in balance, Julita found herself making light of Cleolia's fears. It was the wrong thing to do and brought forth a further torrid outburst. The air in the cubiculum was at once stifling. Sweat beads returned to Cloelia's forehead and she rushed for the earthenware bowl moaning again for the rising sickness to quell. Julita made no move to comfort her this time, instead she cupped her hands to cover her own face and wept silently.

....

The plight of the legionaries was serious and Marcus was responsible for their predicament. When they arrived at the villa and the ladies had been removed to their cubiculum, unable to contain his distress at the foul luck of returning to the soil of Britannia any longer, his temper had split. Rushing at one of the warriors, he was quick enough to wrestle him down, and so piqued was his wrath, that a second, and third, struggled to constrain him. But constrain him they did, and his life was spared only by the timely arrival of a large and formidable woman with wild auburn hair hanging to her waist, whose bark not to shed blood on the villa floors was enough to cower the warriors. Marcus, Lucius and Brutus were now strung up in the stables awaiting their fate.

With their arms raised as if on a crucifix, their shoulders were aching and despite the damp weather, all three legionaries were sweating borne from a mixture of physical discomfort and fear. Blindfolded, every noise was highlighted, the rain dripping from the roof, a branch slapping intermittently against the outside of the stable, the horses within snorting, and swishing their tails. Brutus had guessed at three horses. The breath of one that came close had caught him unawares raising the hairs on his nape and shooting his heart into his stomach. A persistent fly pestered at Lucius, crawling across his lips causing him to spit it away, then worrying at his nostrils producing a snort, then teasing at his ear when all Lucius could do was shake and flick his head in an attempt to rid the irritant.

"*Acheron!*" he growled out the curse. "I would prefer a tribe of Iceni warriors to this wretched creature. Why do they keep us waiting for our fate? It will be a flogging at best, but *Mithras* let them get on with it."

"If Fortuna smiles tonight, we will be dead by sunrise," Marcus answered in a grim tone. Brutus grunted his agreement.

"I see the spirit of the Eagle flies high in the pair of you!" chided Lucius. "Remind me not to come to either of you when I am down on fortune in the future. Ill omen can turn on the wing with a change of wind. How many times have we seen it happen? We are Legionaries of Rome, of the Twentieth, we can outwit their minds." Lucius was trying to infuse optimism in to his comrades, but Marcus was resolute in his pessimism.

"What reason is there for them to keep us alive? We have nothing to bargain with and I fear we are fodder for their resentment at being under Roman rule. The Iceni pretend to bow to Rome but for their own gain only, their loyalty burns for themselves and they can use us to sate their bloodlust without reprisal. I say again, if we are lucky, they will grow bored of the torture before dawn and end our misery. I will make amends to you both in the shadow world for getting us in this situation."

His speech was made with conviction and met with a hollow silence, his two comrades being unable to find a reply. The fly continued its exploration of Lucius's face, causing him to curse again but say nothing else. A hush befell the stables, heavy with unknown, pitted only with snickers from the horses that sensed the pervading anxiety.

Their waiting ended as the rain ceased. The door scraped open and their drowsiness disappeared immediately, tension pouring fresh energy in to sagging limbs and each stood taut in their crucifix shapes. Behind the blindfolds, eyes were round and searching, darting towards the sounds but blighted in seeing by the folds of the coarse sacking. Single footsteps thudded over the earth. No words were uttered, just clicks of the mouth to encourage the horses to move. Brutus had guessed correctly at three, as each was led separately from the stables.

Within a few moments, the door scraped again and the three legionaries waited for the next move. Nothing happened. Marcus was first to find his voice.

"Who is there?" No reply came. Marcus's heart was thumping hard in his chest, he repeated the question hoping his voice would remain steady and not betray his fear. Again, no reply. Marcus wished he'd taken more heed of the native tongue, as he tried haltingly in Bryothonic. This at least brought movement from the mute visitor, who crept close enough for Marcus to smell him, the stench involuntarily wrinkling his nostrils in repulsion. A prod to his ribs made him flinch.

The door scraped and Marcus's tormentor greeted two newcomers with a growl of pleasure.

"Seems their fun will now begin," muttered Brutus.

For what seemed an age, but in reality was little more than half an hour, Marcus, Lucius and Brutus endured great mental torment, but little physical abuse from their captors. Keeping them blindfolded, shouted taunts with sudden lunges to within finger-width of touching them were interspersed with silent spells of cold metal knives being stroked across their throats or along their crotches. Each legionary was soaked in anguished sweat and exhausted by the time a fourth captor joined the throng. His arrival altered the atmosphere immediately.

"Remove their blindfolds!" He waited for this to be done then greeted them as old friends. "Romans, it is good to see you. And looking finely entertained by my men. A formal introduction is overdue I feel. I am Trewak, High Prince of the Iceni. First born to my father, the client king of our tribe." He gave an endearingly crooked smirk at this last remark. "Client king, an interesting phrase dreamed up in Rome." The legionaries remained silent, bar a grunt from Marcus. Amusement twinkled in Trewak's eyes as he sauntered closer to Marcus, staring at him hard for a moment before moving across to Lucius and Brutus. "Your comrade appears to have a disgruntled disposition about him still. His attitude towards us is the reason for your extended discomfort, but I assume you have already determined that for yourselves. I detected a severe dislike of our lands and people in him earlier." Trewak stopped in front of Brutus, pursing his lips in thought. "Hmm, the pock-marked one." Folding his arms, the prince continued to think. "You have an interest of the heart with the pretty, young maiden I believe. That could prove useful to me. Tell me…if you were made to choose between your irascible comrade here or the maiden, which would it be? No, do not answer…" Trewak held up his hand dramatically, "…it is the question of a fool. And I am no fool," his eyes flashed with excitement.

Turning on his heel, he swaggered across to Lucius. The other Iceni tribesmen were enjoying the display of their High Prince, whose presence filled the stables. Their deference to him was obvious. Lucius was still being plagued by a fly. It landed on his chin and with the High Prince standing before him, he resisted the urge to shake it away, tightening his lips as it crawled across his mouth towards his nose. The atmosphere became thick with silence as the intensity of the moment grew. Trewak watched as the insect probed at his captive's nostril. The desire to be rid of the creature burned at Lucius, his nostrils twitching involuntarily at the invasion, and tear ducts filling in auto response, but he narrowed his eyes and stared defiantly at the Iceni prince, using hatred to endure the fervent irritation. Mercifully, the fly completed its exploration before breaking the will of Lucius, who felt the test was a score to the Romans. Trewak threw back his head giving a hearty laugh.

"I like you. In our language, we call them 'fia'," he tapped his finger to his lips and nose, tracing the path the fly had taken on Lucius. "I will call you 'Fia'. It is a pity…Fia…that you and your pock-marked comrade are in this predicament. It is simply that you are with one who cannot contain his anger." Trewak clasped his fingers together beneath his chin in a dramatic thinking pose. "I too have borne punishment in the past for no other sin than being in bad company, it rankles with me." A chink of light flashed off his arm torque as he rubbed his chin in a show of deliberation, ending with a shake of his head in false compassion. "Yet I am unable to think of any reason to spare your currish lives. You serve me better as game for my revenge embittered warriors. So be it!" Nodding at the waiting natives he ordered the Romans be stripped of their clothing. "The night is long, make sure they see one more sunrise. I will not stay to watch as there is beguile awaiting me elsewhere. I have a legate's family to entertain." A crooked grin teased on to his face, and he said almost to himself, "and a trip to the northern frontier to plan."

Marcus heard the aside and felt a fresh twinge of anger stab at him. Loyalty to his officer and colleagues of the Twentieth surged to the fore providing renewed mettle.

"What is your plan for the northern frontier High Prince?" Marcus shouted over the shoulder of the Iceni who was about to strip him of his robes. The native growled as Marcus struggled as much as his bound body would allow, so hampering the Iceni in his task. Trewak looked mildly amused.

"A revolt, High Prince? The Picts have failed and you will fail!" The breath was taken from Marcus by a heavy thump to his ribs. Grasping the opportunity whilst Marcus was still, the Iceni ripped his toga from his shoulder. The wooden block that had been hidden in the garment was flung free, landing in the dirt close to Trewak.

"What have we here?" he muttered bending to collect it. Marcus sensed an opening and seized it, a small chink of hope forming.

"It is nothing of consequence."

Trewak examined the block, frowning at the carvings in the fading light. A nauseous groan of pain came from Lucius as his tormentor rammed his knee in to his bollocks. Brutus winced and tensed himself in preparation of the same. He too was alert to the narrow opportunity opened by the sudden emergence of the polished block of wood, but wasn't yet sure how Marcus was going to play it, so remained silent.

"So, you think me a fool do you Roman?" Trewak narrowed his eyes in concentration as he deciphered the carvings. "Why would you keep this hidden close to you if it was not important? Hmm? It has significance, of course it does." Still studying the carvings, he added almost distractedly, "come Warriors, I know you seek revenge, but the agenda has changed. Let them hang naked a while. I think our king and the priestess should see this.

It was the longest of nights as Marcus, Brutus and Lucius shivered in and out of exhausted sleep. Conversation had ceased long before dawn as each retreated into his own thoughts as thirst and hunger took their toll. With daybreak came a breeze that swirled the dust in the stable. The horses had not returned. The breeze strengthened as the day progressed, and the stables moved and moaned, but it wasn't until dusk fell for the second time that an Iceni warrior reappeared.

Brutus gave a parched grunt but could manage nothing more, his eyes rolling with fatigue and dehydration. Marcus and Lucius were in a similarly distressed state. Focussing briefly, Marcus noted a hunting knife strapped to the Iceni's thigh, and watched helplessly, unable to rally any strength, as the warrior pulled it from its leather sheath. Fighting against his drooping eyelids caused them to flutter creating a flickering vision and a blurring of movement towards him was all he could decipher. The expectation of death tightened his throat, so it was a shock to hit the ground as his bonds were cut and it took a moment to comprehend what had happened. Brutus and Lucius were also released and each of them tried to rally from their slumped positions.

A girl appeared with platters bearing bread and ale which she left beside them before scurrying away. The warrior toe-poked the three legionaries and gestured they should eat, before leaning languidly next to the entrance, using his hunting knife to clean dirt from beneath his fingernails. The girl reappeared carrying fresh clothes, Roman togas and leggings, which she placed over a horse tethering rail and again left quickly, giggling as the warrior playfully slapped her bottom as she passed.

"Ill omen turns on a block of wood as well as a wing, it seems," murmured Lucius after emptying his platter of food and drink. "I would never have thought this bitter brew could taste so good. There is always hope whilst the Eagle soars!" The Iceni threw the clothes at them and they duly dressed.

....

The strong wind continued in to the evening, pushing the rain clouds swiftly across the darkened sky, but the air remained dry. The small party maintained a steady loping pace across the flat land. Trewak was leading the way, followed by Brutus, Marcus, Lucius and five Iceni warriors. They trotted in silence, the spike gone from Marcus, his anger blunted by the welcomed physical activity. Brutus, now accepting that time would reveal their destination after his enquiring conversation with the prince, although tersely shortened, had at least revealed that Cloelia and Julita were safe, and Lucius, content simply to be released from the confines of the barn.

Deviating from the grassy track, Trewak guided the group in to a coppice of hazel, the ground rising slightly before he motioned them to stop. Ordering his warriors to watch the legionaries, Trewak went on alone.

"Waiting again," grumbled Marcus.

"The most part of a soldier's life involves waiting," replied Brutus, "master that and a great career is yours."

"What are we waiting *for*?" asked Lucius.

"Not what, but *who* I would say" muttered Brutus. The answer, when it came some while later, was quite a surprise.

Lucius let out a low whistle, "phew, the ass rubs the ass, what have we here? Quintus Pompeius Falco, Governor of Britain meeting furtively under cover of darkness with an Iceni Prince, in the middle of nowhere without a single bodyguard. The stain has a stench I dislike, be wary."

"And what is our involvement? Seems it has something to do with that hunchback's block of yours Marcus," added Brutus. They witnessed a handshake then saw Trewak leave and watched as Falco climbed the rise towards them. Marcus looked round to discover their own escorts were gone.

"Jupiter! Those natives have the stealth of a stalking fox. It appears we are alone with the Governor, is Fortuna with us or against us this night?"

Falco reached them. "She is with you Legionary Guintoli." Marcus's gut flipped over at hearing Falco speak his name. "And you will learn that I have the hearing of a bat!" His voice hinted at amusement, but his stony expression belied this. "Let us make haste, in silence, to the fort. We will talk in depth when I am sure the land is not listening. The legate's family is safe, that is all I will impart for now. Come, we follow the course of the aqueduct."

Chapter Twenty

The fort looked as imposing as ever to Kye as he left the crags behind to approach the North Gate, its timber palisade rising to the height of three fully grown men, bold and stark, unnatural in the barren hills. A shiver tingled at his nape as he drew near to the ditch and he exhaled with a loud puff, chivvying himself for the task ahead. He didn't want to do this but needed the legate's help to begin his search for Marcus. The challenge came from the gate tower.

"Kye Teviot, I've business with Legate Maxinius." He raised his arms in a passive stance and waited, swallowing nervously. One edgy guard, one single arrow, and it could all end here.

"State your business."

"I've information for the legate, stuff he asked me to find out."

"What information?"

"It's for the legate." Kye sent a quick prayer of thanks to Bridget that his voice was holding steady, the goddess only knew how for the rest of him was trembling. He heard hobnails clicking on the wooden steps.

"Wait in the ditch, and keep your hands in sight at all times," was the order from the tower. Kye did as instructed, slipping backwards as he descended but keeping his dignity by landing on his feet at the ditch bottom. Ten minutes elapsed before another shout ordered him to approach the gate. Kye obeyed, hands instinctively aloft, entering the fort as the gate rattled open.

"The legate will see you, but all weapons stay with me." The guard was intimidating in full armoured uniform, typically stocky and muscular. Keeping his hard stare on Kye, a flick of his brow brought a second guard forward who searched Kye, deftly removing the hunting knife and checking thoroughly for further weapons before grunting satisfaction, then handing over a temporary gate pass to Kye. "You will be escorted to the *Principia*."

Being inside the fort was invoking bad memories for Kye, the barn fire, his stabbing and subsequent rehabilitation. Sweat was clamming his hands as he passed the hospital, and a bead of panic was beginning to swell in his stomach, as he recalled the Pict brother slumped on the crucifix. Snippets of conversations sprinted through his mind, colliding, but mercifully jolting to an end with Jolinda's words 'Da would be proud'. Exhaling to calm himself, Kye repeated these words and, regaining control reminded himself why he was here. *If it takes me to Syria, I will find him and bring him back.*

They turned in to the court yard of the *Principia* and made their way under the portico. Kye had forgotten the grandeur of the stone columns, contrasting so beautifully with the terracotta tiles. The size of the building alone was intimidating and he again found it necessary to plump his courage. The guards on duty at the arched gateway saluted his escorts with a thump of fists to breastplates as they entered the building, hobnails clicking against the stone flooring of the corridor. He was ushered towards a waiting room, more like a holding cell thought Kye, as the door was closed firmly behind him. Feeling for the amulet at his throat, he rubbed it for comfort. Jolinda had tied the soft strip of deerskin hung with a single piece of polished flint tenderly about his neck on his departure, whispering a charm for protection. Its smooth coldness was soothing.

After an age, a clerk appeared announcing the legate would see him. Kye quickly followed, only too pleased to leave the dingy room behind, eager to begin his quest.

Peterna Maxinius was also athirst at Kye's visit, but was concealing the fervidity behind a calm mask. Despite the attempts of his officers to unearth gossip in the taverns, a task they were throwing themselves in to with relish he'd noticed, no news, not even a honey dribble had come to the surface regarding the Pict War Council. The frustration was grinding. It seemed the Teviot boy was his only lead, yet negotiations could prove costly if he revealed such a poor cluster of *tali* pieces.

His glacial blue eyes studied Kye for a moment, one hand cupping his chin with the index finger resting across pursed lips in a pose of thought. Tapping lightly against his lips, he let the silence draw out. There were not many who withstood his penetrating gaze without fidgeting and Kye was no exception, although the legate noticed a growing maturity in the Brigante since their previous meeting.

"It is agreeable you are here," began the legate. "What information do you have to impart?"

"I found out who were at Swine Lake." In truth Kye was only guessing it was the one-eared Celt at the lake, but his quest would falter at its start if he didn't give a solid account. The Celt had been at the War Council meeting as well as the burning barn and that was compelling enough evidence of his involvement. The man had done him no intended harm, but no favours either, and under the circumstances Kye had wrested his conscience to accept he must betray this fellow for the needs of his family.

"Rome will be pleased."

"I ain't doing it for Rome," retorted Kye, his pique rising despite his best efforts to match the legate's calmness. Peterna was playing his hand well.

"Of course not, you are a Brigante and everything you do is therefore for the good of your family." Kye shifted in his chair, unsure if he was being mocked or not. "As I said before, Rome will prevail and She *will* give protection to her allies, thus you are doing right by your family in giving your information." A frown tangled Kye's eyebrows as he wrestled with what to say. It was time to be measured.

"I ain't here for Rome's protection, I need information in return for mine," he blurted. Surprise wrinkled across the legate's brow changing quickly to a prickle at this young native's audacity. Producing the effigy of Jupiter given to him by Marcus, Kye burrowed on, his cheeks flushing with a mixture of nerves and determination. "I was given this in the 'ospital by one of ya legionaries. Said he was going to Syria. I need to find him." Peterna's eyes narrowed a fraction, knowing instinctively Kye was after Marcus Guintoli. *What was it about that legionary?* Recalling Guintoli's involvement with the Brigante girl, his swift mind was working ahead, a pregnancy most likely. Kye confirmed Guintoli's name in answer to the legate's questioning, but would only state it was a personal matter.

Pursing his lips, Peterna gave Kye the fullness of his piercing gaze, frosting the air as he thought. He needed whatever details Kye had for him, scant or otherwise, it was the only lead available. Torture was an option which he quickly dismissed. *Acheron*, he had no bile for torturing this boy, and further delay was futile. Guintoli would be half way across Gaul by now and he need not divulge the party's destination as Rome. Indeed, Guintoli may find passage on to the Syrian deserts from there, it was not Peterna's concern. Once Julita and Cloelia were safely delivered to her cousin, the legionaries were released from his command. It would be up to them to battle their way through the bureaucracy. No, it would not endanger his family to give Guintoli's departure port.

"The trail starts at Petuaria, across to Gaul." Kye felt ice-shards spitting out at him and quickly fired out a prayer to Bridget, sweeping the same up to Jupiter, needy of all the gods under the legate's scrutiny.

"The one-eared Celt. He collects rent at the warehouses in the settlement."

....

"Bring more ale wench!" Gius Autemius banged his tankard on the bench table. The decurion was slurring his words. Putting his arm round his subaltern's shoulder he pulled him close to whisper conspiratorially, then threw his head back with a raucous laugh at his deputy's response. "Yeah, but the fool bummed the last note! Did you hear that trumpet split out a squeak? In front of the legate 'n' all. Wench, more ale dammit!" The pair drew glances from the other customers. There was still a pale lightness to the evening sky and the inn was yet to become busy. "Fill it up," he held out his tankard, "and my buddy's here." The wench did as instructed and made to leave. "Wait wench," Gius restrained her with a strong arm around her waist and drank the contents of the tankard in one effort. "Re-fill," he demanded loudly, "better still, leave the jug." Gius let the girl go with a hefty slap to her bottom. He was enjoying himself.

The subaltern took a long draught straight from the large earthenware jug only to be reprimanded by Gius. "Use your tankard slob! We ain't buglers!" Both men threw back their heads in further raucous laughter. The small cluster of locals didn't share the joke. Noticing their lack of jocularity fuelled the two drunken Romans in to explaining. "Friends, friends, you would think it funny if you had seen our bugler," slurred the decurion. "Bugler-the-incompetent, ha! Give him a simple three-tone tune to master and he blows it. Ha, blows it, pun, pun, pun…" Gius gave a hearty rendition of one short, one long and another short trumpet blast of differing notes. "Simple!"

"Didn't sound like that though did it?" The subaltern gave his rendition producing a sharp high-pitched squawk in place of the last note. "Thought the legate was gonna crucify him right then. Three bloody times in a row he bummed that last note. Sounded like he was bugling to muster an army of bleedin' cockerels."

"Join us friends, join us," Gius waved the two closest men to their table, offering them ale and repeating his three-tone rendition as he poured, sending a great glug splashing to the floor as he missed filling their vessels. The subaltern echoed the tune adding his squeak.

"Muster the cockerel cohort! Ha, ha, ha!" A lot of back-slapping accompanied the ale-fuelled nonsense and before long the pair of Britons were mimicking the Romans and all four were blasting on imaginary trumpets held in fists put to their lips.

"That's it my friends, you have it! The cohorts are mustering on your command," declared Gius. Another jug of ale appeared and the four men continued to josh until the subaltern suddenly stood, producing a soft salute before losing his balance and falling noisily against the bench. Gius hailed the centurion with a hearty welcome to join them, ignoring the man's stony expression. His arrival with his optio had gone unnoticed during their revelry. "Centurion Pollux, Optio Senaca," he slurred, "we're building bridges…"

Without word, the centurion tossed a denarii at the bartender and grabbing Gius firmly by the arm, marched him from the inn, followed by his optio more or less carrying the still-trumpeting subaltern, whose legs seemed not to obey him. A smile flickered the corners of the bartender's mouth as he bit on the coin, reaching with his other hand to rub at the scarred stump that had once been his ear.

....

"By all reports Gentlemen, I am told you play the trumpet as foolishly as my bugler." The legate ceased pacing, halting to observe the decurion and subaltern standing to attention in his office, the flickering orange light from the brazier softening their outlines in the otherwise dark room. "Centurion Pollux and Optio Senaca from the Seventh Cohort have reported finding you in the tavern, drunkenly divulging information crucial to army intelligence to civilians. Is this correct?"

"Yes Sir!" Autemius answered as clearly as he could through his bruised and cut lips.

"Their report states that you quite clearly divulged the new three tone series of trumpet blasts for mustering the cohorts. Is this correct?"

"Yes Sir!"

"And a brawl ensued between you after they removed you from the tavern which is how you sustained your injuries. Is this also correct?"

"Yes Sir!"

The legate resumed his pacing, hands clasped behind his back, thinking, stopping again to address his men further. "Your injuries are regrettable, but always a risk of such behaviour somewhere so public. It would appear my senior legionaries still have the edge over my senior horsemen in hand combat, although you gave a good account of yourselves for drunken oafs! As I say, regrettable." A pause as he studied their swelling faces, broken and scuffed raw. "Divulgence of army information to civilians is a serious offence… and I must thank you Gentlemen for making such a fine job of it!" The legate broke in to an uncharacteristic boyish grin, thumping a fist in to an open palm. "Yes! Fortuna has embraced us at last. The unexpected arrival of Pollux and Senaca has added an eloquent authenticity to the ruse. From what I have been told, their timing could not have been better, and your performance must have been believable to fool them, and if they were fooled, so too was the one-eared Celt. Excellent subterfuge Gentlemen, excellent. Finding the Celt tending the bar was indeed luck from the gods. I have made Centurion Pollux and his optio aware that you were acting under orders, and they have withdrawn the allegations made against you. Another pause. "However, Pollux wishes me to tell you that the theatre should be your chosen career as you act the sop far better than you fight, ahem…" Peterna arched an eyebrow at Gius, certain he must be scowling at the remark, but unable to tell beneath his battered features. The decurion was of Germanic descent, and nearing the end of his service career when citizenship to Rome would be awarded. Trust and friendship had grown strong during Peterna's command and choosing Gius to confide his plan to had been easy. The subaltern knew little of the full plan, and feared his senior officer's threat to personally remove his tongue should he utter a word of what he did know, enough to keep silent on his part in the ruse. "Let me be clear that neither he nor Optio Senaca will be punished for the brawl, their reactions were understandable given the circumstances, and there is to be no ill feeling between you because of it. Your orders are to lie low and rest for a few days. A commendation will be added to your records and I will personally ensure the treasury stretches to a bonus in your next pay packet. Subaltern, you are dismissed. Decurion, stand easy but I require a moment more of your time."

The legate strode with purpose to his house. The place was quiet without Julita and Cloelia and a stab of longing dug behind his ribs, but he wouldn't let it undermine his mood. At last he could move on with his plan of flushing out the elusive Pict War Council. Uncovering their members could be enough to win him favour in Rome without a massed battle, and then he could be reunited with his family and enjoy a contented retirement.

A servant appeared with a bowl of steaming parsnip soup and a hunk of fresh bread that Peterna heartily devoured, he'd not noticed his hunger until the food was before him. Using the warm water from the finger-bowl, he rinsed his face and shifted to the couch beside the hearth. Watching the jumping flames dance over the burning logs reminded him of the attack on *Arbeia* and he stewed over the bribery that must have been involved. Chewing on his top lip and staring deep into the fire, he reflected on his plan. *A chain is only as strong as its weakest link.* Where was the weakness?

At dawn the false three-tone signal would be sounded eight times to rally eight cohorts and they would march for the day. The next sunrise would see five cohorts mustered by the same signal sounding five times and they would march again. The route would vary but it would encompass as many homesteads as possible. His army was to be visible. The land would resound to eight three-tone signals again on the third morning leaving the fort very quiet once more, then revert to mustering four the next day using four of the false signal. It was imperative the one-eared Celt was fully convinced of the mustering signal. Peterna nodded, gently satisfied that the man would be. This part of the plan was sound.

The next stage lay in giving the barbarians an opportunity too tempting to ignore. He would rest his men for two days, and then begin a series of marches again, following the same pattern, leaving the fort almost unmanned every other day. Two days off, then marches again. The War Council would be baited, yet getting them to take the bait had always been a weak spot in the plan, until Fortuna had handed him a golden dice, a double throw of luck. Yes, finding the Celt serving in the tavern meant Gius could present himself once more without arousing suspicion, and spin a yarn of personal growing hatred for Rome, his beaten features adding weight to his story. The decurion's obvious Germanic looks would help. The Twentieth Legion had a smaller than average number of auxiliaries, and it was well known throughout the lands that auxiliary soldiers widely sold their secrets for silver, less so a legionary born to Rome. The Celt was not the brightest spark from the campfire, but smart enough to spot a man open to bribery. This should prove too tasty a morsel for the War Council to discard and Peterna could feed further false details to the barbarians to set the trap and net the perpetrators. He trusted Gius to the hilt. Satisfied he could strengthen the links no more, Peterna retired to a welcome sleep.

Chapter Twenty-One

Falco answered the guard's challenge with the day's password and the East Gate at Durobriuae Fort was quickly opened. The group of four entered still keeping their silence. There was an edge to the atmosphere inside the fort, immediately discernible to the legionaries, but not easily fathomed. They exchanged nervous glances as Falco led them to the Principia. A heavy presence of guards was noticeable. A snap of fingers brought a cleric running to greet them and Falco accepted the papers from him without breaking stride. The cleric imparted a few swift messages on the move and bowed slightly as he held the door open allowing the four of them to enter a spacious, but dimly lit room, before closing the door with a soft click and leaving them alone.

"Serve yourselves wine and biscuits." With his back to the legionaries, Falco warmed his hands beside the glowing brazier, turning to re-face them after a few moments. "Be seated," he nodded at three stools before taking his own place in a large, leather chair opposite them, separated by a small marble-topped table, the arrangement of the furniture indicating they'd been expected.

Falco placed the polished wooden block on the table. "Marcus Guintoli of the Twentieth Legion, you have been seen by Consus Didinius the hunchback as a 'chosen one', favoured by the gods." A chill rippled Marcus's spine and his veins swelled with pumping blood, he didn't like the boding. "I am not a man given easily to portent, but the Emperor places great stock on the visions of Consus, and as the Governor of Britannia, it is my duty not only to obey the Emperor, but to consider the impact of ignoring a 'chosen one' whose destiny I am informed, lies at the northern frontier." Falco's upper lip lifted in a slight sneer as he mentioned the north. "The hunchback, you may recall, was born to a slave girl of a wealthy Roman family living in southern Britannia. His birth name was Calbraith, meaning British Warrior, but he became Consus Didinius on adoption by the mistress of that house who lost her own child to a fever. The slave girl was given freedom in exchange for her baby, whose deformity did not show until a decade had lapsed, long enough for the mistress to love him as her own."

Falco paused in his dialogue to fill his goblet with wine. Lucius shifted his sitting position, knocking the table slightly as he did so causing the wine to slop. Falco ignored the spillage but the tension was tight in the room. "Consus, a well chosen name. It means 'good counsel'. The mistress just happens to be second cousin to Trajan, making her second cousin removed by a generation to Emperor Hadrian. A distant relative but blood ties nonetheless. Emperor Hadrian is tolerant of a disability as much as he is tolerant of race and religion, believing a man with a disability is given a talent to compensate. I and many others may not wholly agree with the Emperor, but we are all servants to the gods and I do not believe in continued coincidences." Brutus rubbed at his nose, all three of them were fidgety. Politicians! Why did they not reach the crux by the straightest route? They would make excellent raconteurs except their ramblings nearly always preceded a scorpion sting rather than a hearty laugh. Where was this tale leading?

Leaning back in his chair, with his right ankle resting on his left knee, Falco continued. "Consus was only in Petuaria for one day, and you Guintoli, only visited the trade stalls the single time. A freak storm damages your vessel, I have heard of no other wreck reports. At the mercy of the tides and winds, you could have been washed up anywhere along the coast of Gaul or Britannia, and Neptune served you to the hands of a certain bodacious Iceni Priestess. You are familiar with the writings of Cassius Dio? He records the uprising of Boudicca and the burning of Londinium by a fire so hot that the remains of the settlement melted in to a layer of red clay ten inches thick in places. Suetonius Paullinus, the military governor at the time, subdued this formidable Iceni Queen but her memory is legendary. Dio says of Boudicca: 'she was huge of frame, terrifying of aspect, and with a harsh voice. A great mass of bright red hair fell to her knees, she wore a twisted torc and a tunic of many colours, over which was a thick mantle, fastened by a brooch. Now she grasped a spear, to strike fear into all who watched her'." Falco lowered his resting leg and moved his torso forward bearing his hands to his knees. His eyes burned as pin-pricks reflecting the low torch light as he stared intently at Marcus. "Does this remind you of anyone? Yes, Priestess to the High Prince Trewak. She is bodacious, as spirited and lively as this previous Iceni maiden, how fortunate then that she is the mother of Consus Calbraith Didinius! Following her freedom at the time of his adoption, she practised within the druidhood, rising quickly in status due to her uncanny likeness to Boudicca, in both stature and manner. It is indeed useful for Rome to have the son of such an influential Iceni Priestess in the pay of Hadrian's personal household. My position as Governor in these lands is made easier for it by keeping the Iceni Tribe contained." A rap on the door brought the cleric shuffling in.

"You are to be received in thirty minutes Sir."

"Thank you, we will be ready."

Brutus shot an inquiring glance at Marcus and Lucius. Who would *'receive'* Quintus Pompeius Falco on the fort? The exchange was not missed by the Governor who collected the polished wooden block from the marble topped table and tossed it across to Marcus.

"Yours I believe. It has saved your life once already, you may require it again. We are to attend the commandant's house. My cleric will escort you to the bathhouse where you will find fresh tunics. You have time to shave. Report to the main entrance of the commandant's house in precisely twenty-five minutes."

....

Julita was wishing the wine had been watered. It had been quite some time since she'd tasted such an exquisite vintage and her head was floating from drinking a little too much. *Foolish woman,* she chided herself silently. Now more than ever her husband was relying on her having a clear head. Her heart fluttered unnervingly at the thought of jeopardising his safety by uttering the wrong words, yet as much damage could be wreaked by remaining silent. The direct ear of the Emperor would unlikely be hers again. It was an opportunity she must grasp.

Tall, trim and strong with soft, wavy hair, her eyes were drawn to his beard. Some said he grew it to hide natural blemishes in his skin, but there was no evidence of imperfection elsewhere, so perhaps it was grown for his love affair with all things Greek. It was widely known he'd received a lavish education in Greek culture. The people called him *Graeculus*, 'the little Greek' because of it. When Peterna had served under Trajan in Dacia, Hadrian had held the public official post of Quaester, supervising financial affairs. Julita recalled Peterna remarking how unusual it was for a Roman of such high status to understand the tax system as Hadrian did. The man was passionately interested in detail and desperate to master things he didn't already know, and possessed an extraordinarily good memory. Julita sipped at some water knowing that she must decide which path to walk along. *Goddess Juno, mother of Mars, let me draw strength from your breath.*

Hadrian wiped at his beard with a cloth and called for a toothpick. Julita waited with decorous patience for him to speak first, feeling the silence magnify as Hadrian fastidiously cleaned the dregs of the meal from his teeth.

"You have been through a regretful ordeal, your daughter must be weary." Hadrian did not speak unkindly, but there was no denying the veiled instruction that Cloelia retire immediately. In truth, she was thankful to escape, feeling awed in Hadrian's presence and finding the expected etiquette cloying. She was desperate to see Brutus. The freedom of travelling had lulled her to believe they had a future together, but the restrictions of Roman status were pressing down from every corner of the fort, intensified by the propinquity of the Emperor. Julita waited for the door to click shut behind Cloelia before speaking.

"Your Imperial Majesty, it is indeed the greatest honour for you to receive us, and with such kindness." Julita was sincere, dipping her head in respect as she addressed Hadrian and continuing with her eyes looking down at the couch in deference, her nostrils flaring as the emotion threatened to spill. She would not allow tears before the Emperor. "It has been a difficult return to this island and the comfort of the fort and your protection is truly, truly welcome. We had heard you were travelling the Southern Provinces Sir. It is a mercy you were not or I fear my daughter and I would not be alive now. My family is in your service, Imperator."

"Your husband has served Rome well during his career, decorated by my uncle during the Dacian Wars. I remember the ceremony Lady Maxinius." Julita's pulse smartened, sensing a ripple in his tone. "Is he still the loyal imperialist I knew him to be?" Julita raised her chin to meet the Emperor's gaze, she would not cow where Peterna was concerned. This was her chance to fight for him.

"Sir, my husband holds Rome and his troops in his heart. He is concerned of a barbarian uprising on the northern frontier and feels strongly that the only way to have peace in Britannia is to sweep through the lands to the north of the border, thus claiming Caledonia to end this campaign." Julita had shown her hand, the path was laid. "Extra troops were denied to him…" Julita swallowed nervously knowing this order had come from Hadrian, looking away briefly before gathering herself once more, "…he fervently believes this decision will begin the decline of Rome. He remains your loyal servant, Imperator."

"So loyal that he questions my orders not to advance the frontier." Julita was shaken by Hadrian's directness and her breathing came in quick, shallow gasps as she waited for the Emperor to continue. "I am receiving reports that Legate Maxinius is increasing the level of activity in the area, inciting a rebellion even, rather than consolidating and controlling the region. That is treason, do you speak in his defence for it?"

"Sir, yes I do! Sir, I implore you! My husband is a loyal soldier, a talented officer," words began to fall in a flurry from Julita as her panic mounted. "I beg you will not judge his actions without experiencing the frontier for yourself. It is forsaken, and bleeds strain and weeps spurious quiet, so different to this Romanised south." Julita swept her arm round to encompass the country in demonstration, knocking over a goblet but ignoring the spilling red stain on the pristine white cloth covering the table. "I was guilty of being blind to the dangers until I travelled south. The fort was my home, I rarely ventured from it. Peterna possesses the tactician's skill to see beyond the current mood. Sir, I beseech you visit before condemning."

"Amid arms the laws are silent."

"Sir?" Julita was baffled by such a short and level response following her disclaim. *Goddess Juno, have I said right?*

"It is a quote by Cicero." Hadrian would not be drawn for the moment. "Have you heard that the dome is being prepared to top the Pantheon in Rome?"

"I…yes," Julita was too choked to add more, not able to make conversation with her husband's fate, and therefore her own, hanging perilously.

"It is impressive, one hundred and thirty-eight feet in diameter. Two techniques, key to Roman construction, make it possible. Techniques that no other civilisation has mastered, the shape of an arch and the production of concrete. The stone for the Pantheon columns comes from quarries in Egypt, laboriously transported by carts to the Nile, up to Alexandria and on to Rome." Hadrian's eyes were alive with pride and passion that Julita was finding difficult to share. "It will be the greatest of Roman achievements in construction, a beacon of our power." Julita managed a weak reply.

"It is Peterna's wish that I take our daughter to see the Pantheon." It seemed the correct reply, as Hadrian broke in to a broad smile.

"And so it shall be. You will continue your journey to Rome, I will release two of my Imperial Guards to escort you. I have a mission for your previous escorts, and a journey to make of my own…to the northern frontier." Julita bit hard on her lower lip to keep from trembling with relief. Peterna would at least be heard directly.

"Thank you Imperator."

"Amid arms the laws are silent – we sometimes need to bend the rules made in the senate to fit the world of combat. An arch and concrete, your husband has much to learn."

"You speak in riddles to me Sir, but I can speak with confidence when I say that your presence in the north will boost morale a thousand-fold."

Chapter Twenty-Two

"Quintus, be seated. My plans are to change. After speaking with Lady Julita, I intend to travel directly to the northern frontier. I fear Maxinius is closer to inciting a rebellion than quashing one and it is time I made him aware of our new strategy. Perhaps we should have outlined it to him last year during your visit." Hadrian drummed his fingers against the desk as he considered the situation. "Are you quite sure he did not know of your survey during that visit?"

"The survey was undertaken in complete secrecy, the legate suspected nothing," replied Falco. Hadrian nodded.

"Then I believe he is loyal, but misguided and that may in part be my own fault for excluding him from our plans so entirely. Yet his methods are Dacian. He was trained by Trajan and sees expansion to the Empire as the only way forward and this frustrates me. No doubt he sees your own success in beating the local rebellion a few years ago as a beacon, but Rome must change if it is not to fall. We do not have enough troops to deploy to all corners of the Empire. I must delay no further in sharing my vision of the new politics with him, or we will lose the whole of Britannia and its many riches. And neither can I leave his questioning of my orders unaddressed, the senate will be in anarchy if they find out."

"I concur. Yet the danger to Ocella is real. The rumour of an assassin grows stronger. To lose his specialist skills would be a great setback to your project at this stage."

"Has your network of spies anything further than rumour to gird their loins for?"

"Nothing firm, but Cepheus has been mentioned and we cannot take the risk of ignoring what we have heard."

Hadrian stroked at his bearded chin, a habit he was fond of whilst thinking. Cepheus was a cult renowned throughout Rome for its many successful assassinations, hired by the wealthy to deal with their dirt. Its members were harboured by the nobility of Greece and were named after the Greek King in mythology The shape of the Cepheus constellation had been adopted as the cult's symbol.

"Yes, we cannot afford to lose his skills at this time. He will take some persuading to leave his grand project at the hot springs. It is a shame I cannot go there to surprise him in person, his expression would be worth the Treasury's gold, but I am needed in the north immediately. You must go to Aquae Sulis for Ocella in place of me. Consus's 'chosen one' will accompany you with his two comrades, plus two of my guards. To travel with more will slow your journey and draw attention, which must be avoided."

"Am I to use force to bring him to you if necessary?"

Hadrian smiled at an untold thought.

"Even with Ocella's inimical nature, force will not be necessary with a 'chosen one' in your party. Ocella is personally familiar with Consus Didinius and his visions, the sight of the wooden block will awe him to obeisance, you have my assurance on that. Enough discussion Quintus, send in the three from the Twentieth, I will brief them. Our journeys begin at dawn and the gods will see us together again at the northern frontier in swift time." Hadrian clapped a strong hand on Falco's shoulder as the two embraced. "It is an exciting project Quintus, and the planning now makes way for the implementation."

The edge to the fort's atmosphere was explained when Marcus, Brutus and Lucius entered the living quarters of the commandant's house. They recognised The Emperor before Falco announced him. The coin images in circulation were a good likeness and a bust of Hadrian was displayed in an alcove as you entered the Principia of every fort. Standing to rigid attention, it was military discipline that kept their jaws from dropping open at his presence.

Hadrian took a moment to study Marcus, satisfying himself that he was the hunchback's 'chosen one' by referring to the sketch received from Consus by courier to the fort a few days after the transfer of the wooden block in Petuaria. The package, as instructed, had been kept unopened in the security of the sunken strong room in the Principia, which housed the pay chest and men's savings vault. Hadrian had not known about the sketch until reaching the fort. Letting his gaze sweep across the others and back to Marcus, he marvelled at the powers Consus must channel to see beyond the flesh. He truly believed the gods had given Consus deliverance for his disability. The start of a poem he'd scribed came to mind, but he tucked it away, returning to the task in hand.

The meeting was short and formal. Hadrian briefed the three legionaries with their orders, giving no heed to any questions, or any explanation for his choosing them for the mission. They were made to repeat their oath to the Eagle Standard, which each did unerringly, kneeling in turn before the black and gold silk-threaded banner.

"The armoury will equip you, be ready to depart at first light. Speed is essential on this most important mission. A mission not without peril, but one which offers you all rich rewards in opportunity when you succeed, w*hen* you succeed, failure is not an option." Hadrian paused to underline the fact. "I relinquish you of your duty to Legate Maxinius's family. They are now under my direct protection and will continue to Rome with my guards as escorts." Hadrian concluded his brief with a salute to the Eagle Standard. Marcus, Lucius and Brutus, as was expected, responded with their battle cry:

"*Twentieth Legion of the Eagles, proud to fight for Rome and comrade!*"

....

The dawn slinked in and Marcus watched as the streaks of dark grey cloud turned vivid pink, striking against the powder blue clearness between. The promise of the beauty was soon lost as the sun inched higher and disappeared behind a greater mass of cumulus that seemed to build with the warming sky until a uniform grey prevailed. Patting the neck of his horse as he waited for his comrades to finish their preparations, Marcus tried to make sense of the confusion he was feeling.

After receiving their orders from Hadrian the evening before, the three of them had been sent directly to the armoury and supplied with new equipment. The weight of a sword against his leg again felt good, reassuring. He noticed Brutus had his strapped to his right side and made a mental note to renew their practise of combat drills at every opportunity. His skills were improving but would never match his ability prior to the damaging fight with the Celt. The events of that day still scoured deeply.

From the armoury they'd paid a short visit to the washhouse before turning in to the barracks. Brutus had disappeared for a while following a message hurried in by a servant. Lucius had fallen asleep within minutes, snoring with a puff and Marcus envied his ease of mind. To Lucius, this mission was auspicious. Marcus recalled the shine in his friend's eyes at the prospect of favour with the top laurels, his excitement as he chuckled at the thought of a red horsehair crest. *What other chance do we have?* His words echoed at Marcus. *Do you remember the days you wanted anonymity, then rebels for glory? Now look, an incredible opportunity to make our names and fortunes. By Jupiter, Flavinus is watching our backs still!*

Thinking of Flavinus had brought a flood of feeling. An ache of a smile at the childhood memories, innocence exploded by his death, strength plucked from recollections, shared experiences, sometimes fading in detail but vivid in their having happened. Then 'the vow' expunging everything, *Roman women only*, Jolinda, Jolinda…

This island held the temptation of something so beautiful, Marcus feared it. The thought of returning to the northern frontier, returning to within a few miles of Jolinda's homestead without seeing her was clawing, riving at his heart. He would not go to her, she would not want him, but having torn himself away once, to do it again was cruel punishment. Desertion had fared as a lesser torment in that dark moment, but Brutus had returned at this juncture. One look at the sincerity in Brutus's eyes, and Marcus knew his fate was not to run to escape his rising panic.

"Cloelia has explained about the 'Chosen One', the block." Brutus had spoken in soft low tones to keep from waking Lucius and the other legionaries asleep in the barrack block. "This Ocella fellow we are to rescue will only be persuaded to leave Aquae Sulis by the tongue of Hadrian himself or by one nominated by the hunchback. Marcus, our mission will not begin without you. Cloelia has not been told details of Hadrian's project for the north, but it must be vital to bring The Emperor here. The legate is unintentionally ruining Hadrian's plans apparently, hence his noble's desire to rush straight up there." Marcus had listened without adding comment. Brutus had seen strain lour the honest gaze being returned to him. Lucius had continued to puff out an airy snore. "It is the opportunity I have prayed for since my deportation Marcus, only ruin awaited me in Rome. Cloelia knows it. The status-strangled city will not let us be easily. To have any chance at all, I must be able to provide for her. This mission is my lifeline. We all know this is the truth." The moment to run was passed and Marcus buried it. "Cloelia asked me to give you this." Brutus had gently placed a pendant in Marcus's palm. "She said it belongs to Jolinda and you must return it."

Marcus had stared mute at the pendant he'd bought for fifteen denarii and wondered if Brutus knew its significance. He didn't, Cloelia had said nothing more and Brutus had not questioned her on the matter. These were all people he loved and trusted.

"I am not special Brutus. It is a curse to be 'chosen', but let us begin and finish this mission, so we may move on." There was nothing more to be said, so the pair had clasped forearms in the legionary salute and parted, each wrestling with their private thoughts as they had tried to sleep.

Marcus was jolted from his reverie by his horse jerking its head at the arrival of Brutus who walked his mare alongside.

"The Governor is saying his farewells." Brutus rolled his eyes with impatience.

"And you?" enquired Marcus. "I thought Cloelia would be here to wave you off?"

"Her mother would not allow it for fear of a public disgrace. She knows her daughter well and tears before Rome's Emperor for a departing lowly legionary would be wholly frowned upon. Nay, more…it would be a social caste disaster, wholly!" Brutus shrugged resignedly. "She is probably right and it is something I must accept. This mission should help drag me to respectable social heights, and if all that fails, it should at the very least provide me with some suitable tales to recite." Brutus gently slapped Marcus on the shoulder. "I am feeling good my friend and can feel the raconteur returning." His melon-slice grin broke free. It was infectious and Marcus returned it with a smirk of his own.

"I have missed that raconteur!"

Falco shouted orders for his group to form up beside him, and the six saluted as they walked their mounts passed Hadrian and his guards. Even before the gates were rolled open, Brutus was beginning his first rambling story recounting the message from Cloelia that Lady Julita had given on their last evening.

"Knowing how fluent you are in the equine language, the Lady Julita wishes to say, in her inimitably tactful way, with a beautiful twinkle in her eyes and a smile of warmth teasing those sparkling eyes, that she has no doubt we will succeed in our mission, no doubt, not a scrap nor a corn grain of doubt, just as long as you listen to the horses when they speak."

Chapter Twenty-Three

Pulling the blanket up around his ears, Kye hunkered into the wooden shelter, a passenger waiting shack on the Via Abus, and stared despondently at the wind-whipped Fluvius. A big tide was being ruffled by the gale blowing in from the east, and the normally smooth surface of the big river was dissected in to choppy, incongruous swell that argued and battered itself as it surged angrily in land. There were no traders on the banks and there would be no boats leaving Petuaria this day.

The first splatter of rain hit his shelter horizontally, and Kye shuffled a little further from the open side to avoid the raindrops that spilt in. His view across the Fluvius gradually disappeared as the rain became constant, river and sky merging in to a blurry mess. Still with the blanket draping him for warmth, Kye chewed on a gristle stick and an unleavened grist loaf, swilling the meal down with the last of the mead from home.

Petuaria held no trace of Guintoli. Kye hadn't known what he'd expected to find, but silently admitted to himself that he had expected to find something. This seemed a naïve notion now, credulous in believing that a town of this size would reveal a clue to show the man's trail. Paved streets left no footprints. For two days, sunrise to sundown and beyond, Kye had roved Petuaria giving a detailed description of Guintoli over and over, asking after him in the taverns, whore-houses, at the jetty, with traders of the town, quietly with priests in temples, even stopping passers-by as he walked the streets. Nothing, it was as if those people who drifted within the towns of stone buildings adopted the same lifeless trait. Yet a cave has an echo Kye reasoned, grasping at hope. The legate had said the trail started at Petuaria, and crossed to Gaul, perhaps there would be a thread on the far shore.

Leaving Britannia and travelling to foreign lands was not something Kye had thought he would do. He had trekked to the east shores of the Votadini one season, when Da had dabbled unsuccessfully at trading with the spice boats, but he'd not been drawn to return. He was comfortable in the rugged inlands, and his childhood dreams had always been to explore the northern lochs and mountains that were described in the songs of the bards. In truth, he was unable to comprehend the distance across the sea, and it irritated him. Yet, when he had looked out to the horizon earlier and channelled his concentration by imagining the number of shields laid flat, nose to tail, that would fill the vast stretch before him, fear had prickled at his spine. The legendary army of Boudicca, sung by the bards as the largest ever formed in Britannia, would not reach the skyline, and Gaul was distant still. Perhaps it was a blessing not to comprehend, he didn't want to try any more, but the fear was rooted and no matter how much he buried it, spores would surface unwillingly like magma through a fault line. "Damn you Guintoli," he muttered. But Kye would not go home without the legionary, his family were depending on him, his oath binding and a longing to succeed searing his soul.

"You will not need to leave this isle to find the one you seek." A strong voice came with a shadow.

Kye was on his feet in an instant, the blanket discarded.

"Who are you?" he demanded, crouching ready to spring forward, his hunting knife drawn and threatening. Kye's heart was hammering and he cursed his lack of vigilance, and foolishness at sitting away from the open side of the shack. There had been no sound of approach. Alarm was ringing like the blacksmith's anvil at the strange silhouette that blocked his escape, and Kye held back from attacking, his mouth suddenly dry, unsure at that moment if the apparition before him was mortal or not. He realised it was as the initial shock dispersed and his vision adjusted, picking up features of the caped shape that was shining with dampness. "A hunchback," Kye gasped, taking an involuntary step away. His palms were sweaty but he kept a tight grasp on his weapon.

"Yes, and this weather causes my hump to ache. I do not care to be out in it. I am Consus Didinius." Consus continued to speak in a light manner as he entered further in to the shelter, loping in his strange gait. "I am alone, armed with a steel blade of my own but it is not drawn and you have far greater agility than I." Kye remained cautious. "I heard a stranger was in town looking for a legionary. You describe him well, yet I was pleased to hear you mutter his name in confirmation."

"How long have ya been eavesdropping on me?"

"Long enough for my hump to ache! I needed to be sure our interest was in the same man. Give your description again." Kye did as instructed. "Yes, yes, you have his chiselled features accurately."

"Marcus Guintoli of the Twentieth."

"He has passed this way. Why do you track him?"

"I've something of his to return." Kye was careful with his words, reluctant to reveal much but aware this lead was important. The hunchback rubbed at the top of his hump and neck, grimacing a little.

"I am in too much pain to dance in conversation with you. I will be direct. Why do you track Guintoli? If your answer satisfies me I will help. If it does not, I will leave and Guintoli will remain as a ghost to you." Kye exhaled with a puff through loose lips. Why did he always seem to hold the lowest score in knuckleball when he negotiated with the Romans?

"Are ya Roman Consus Didinius?" The gods must have been guiding him to utter this question, for the words tumbled out without thought or reason and appeared to catch the hunchback off guard. Not something that happened to Consus Didinius, born Calbraith, a warrior of Britannia by birth turned Roman advisor, very often. He didn't reply but Kye sensed the sway. "Would ya understand the lore spoken by my people, the teachings by the druids to the clans?" The wind and rain filled in the brief silence, buffeting and clattering the shelter with its continued assault. "These ancient whispers are why I'm chasing Guintoli, my sister duped him and me family wants appeasement. We mean him no harm." Kye had spoken the truth and was gambling on the hunchback having depth beyond his Roman front.

"The lore demands you share sacred rites." Didinius's reply came in a distracted undertone, a long ago memory brought to the fore with potent clarity. Snapping his focus back to Kye, the hunchback came to his decision. "You have a choice." Kye's speculation had paid off. "Guintoli is travelling on Imperial business to the southern plains of Britannia before returning to the northern frontier." Consus made no mention of the dangers of the mission. "You may return to your homestead to await his arrival, or make speed southwards, I have knowledge of where you will find him." Didinius was throwing his own round of stones now, but with an open palm. They both knew Kye would not, could not, go home without his quarry. There was no choice. "Come to the stables near the milestone on *Via Mansio* at dawn. I will meet you." Not waiting for an answer, the hunchback lurched out of the shelter, leaving Kye with renewed hope and energy as he sent quiet thanks to the goddess Bridget.

....

The snare had only wrapped round one of the hare's hind legs instead of both, leaving the frightened doe with more mobility than intended. It hadn't helped her and Aaron felt badly when he saw she'd scrabbled so hard to get free that the snare had worked through the hide cutting the flesh raw to the bone. He puzzled at where he'd gone wrong in setting the trap as he deftly cracked a rock across the tired animal's skull to end her misery. Ma would be pleased with the meat but he could feel Da's reproach at his error. At times he could feel his father's presence so strongly, so suddenly, that he'd turn with a heart-skip nervous of what he would see. At other times, he would struggle to recall his face.

Aaron was grateful the days were lengthening, allowing him more freedom from the homestead. It had been a gloomy place of late, heavy with sadness he couldn't fathom. He'd stopped asking about Kye and Tamsin. It seemed Ma didn't know when Kye would return, although she fervently believed he would. He must, he will, was all Ma would say. As for Tamsin, she was just gone, neither Ma nor Jolinda would say more. Aaron shrugged it off, it was nice not having Tamsin irritating him and he was quite enjoying trapping alone, and no doubt Kye would be back before the salmon headed upstream to spawn. They always went together to watch them jumping, filling their nets with easy pickings. Aaron loved that outing.

He also loved going to the Leaf-bud celebrations at the bridestones, to give thanks for the rebirth of the lands. It was a two day festival of songs, dance and merriment and the quarry area would fill with families from the hills and forest close by. He'd been told that some gatherings numbered as many as five or six score, but theirs was usually much less, yet still a throng in his eyes. A great fire would burn between the bridestones with food, ale and stories in abundance. He hoped the rituals to celebrate the promise and fertility of the coming leaf-bud season would also lift the gloom from the homestead.

Throwing the dead hare over his shoulder, Aaron made his way home. With luck he would have time later to go to the bridestones to check on the size of the fire pile, adding his own sticks as was customary.

Entering his homestead palisade, Aaron arrived as Jolinda was embracing a man in farewell. Recognising the lanky build, but also the floppy cowhide hat of Yhurgen the Trader, Aaron shouted a greeting. Yhurgen was several seasons older than Jolinda and had been a regular visitor over the years. Aaron liked him, and his travelling tales.

"Ya caught yons a good meal there young Aaron."

"Will ya come back tomorrow 'n' join us for the stew Yhurgen?"

"Thine offer is kind lad, but the trade routes is open 'n' I must be away soonest." Yhurgen came from the coast due west of the Teviot's steading, not a long trek but his words and accent differed quite noticeably.

"But ya'll miss the Leaf-bud celebrations, Yhurgen."

Yhurgen tousled Aaron's hair. "The early trader catches the treasures. Can't afford t' dally at this year's festival, lad." Aaron frowned thinking it odd as Yhurgen usually set off after Leaf-bud and came back with plenty of treasures, but Yhurgen didn't give him time to respond. "Offered me services t' ya ma and sister as a work-hand, heard Kye was travellin' a while, would stay this season if they'd a said aye, but them proud women folk ya have there. Sent me a packing, so's I'll be straight on me way." He tipped his hat and Aaron watched him lope away. He was thinking it would be good to have Yhurgen helping on the land.

The hare stew tasted good. Aaron bolted it down, wiping the dish clean with meal patties.

"Hungry were ya Aaron?" Jolinda wrinkled a smile but it didn't reach her eyes. She was cross with herself for still having a heavy heart. Try as she may to lighten it, her core was leaden.

"Ma, why didn't ya accept Yhurgen's offer of help? He said he'd stay." Aaron had been mulling over their conversation of the day before, it had unsettled him, and his question was blurted clumsily and with a hint of accusation. Ma and Jolinda exchanged a fleeting glance before Jolinda dipped her head and busied herself clearing the dishes.

"A trader must travel," was Ma's curt answer.

"But he sounded like he wanted to stay and he would've been useful," Aaron persisted. "And now he's not even staying for Leaf-bud." His words tumbled in to a disappointed sulk.

"Well that ain't no bad thing," replied Ma, "The man can talk the bark off a tree!"

"But I love his tales." Aaron's elbows were on the bench and he dropped his head on to his cupped hands, resting his knuckles against his temples and squashing up his cheeks to meet the deepening frown of his forehead. "It ain't too late to catch up with him, Ma. He won't be far away yet. I could fetch him back, I know he'd come."

"No, Aaron. That's me final word, the day is too young for an argument. Now please go 'n' check on the chickens." Aaron knew his mother's tone and it wasn't for arguing with. He wasn't pacified by her answers, yet neither could he form his own concerns in to a logical order, so he settled for a stroppy retort.

"Leaf-bud is ruined," he mumbled.

"Oh, stop ya sulking child, go 'n' fetch the eggs." Ma ushered him away and went to help Jolinda with the dishes. "One minute I think he's a man, next he's a babe again. I ain't so sorry me youngest is not yet fully grown though." Ma put a gentle arm round Jolinda's shoulders.

"Aaron has a point," Jolinda sighed. "Leaf-bud won't be any fun without Da and Kye, and Yhurgen does have a way of telling his tales, he spins the yarn smoothly for sure." Jolinda gave a flat smile, "I know a Roman raconteur too…" She re-busied herself with the dishes. "I couldn't have him here this season, Ma, my heart ain't free. Maybe next year…"

"Ya could do worse than he, Daughter. Yhurgen is solid. He'll be back, that's a certainty, so maybe next year…" Jolinda's chest heaved with a crushing feeling, not pain, more a contraction of fear that she would not see Marcus again. It wasn't helped when she heard the trumpets sounding from the fort, their strident notes carried on the crisp dawn air. Her stomach churned as she counted the signal as Cloelia had taught her to. Eight blasts, yet the signal was different. Were they rallying eight cohorts? Was there unrest at the fort?

Chapter Twenty-Four

The tavern was surprisingly busy for late afternoon, with a good number of Romans filling the ale-stenched room downstairs and a steady parade filtering upstairs too. Jolinda could see the one-eared Celt directing business from behind the bar near the stairwell. Taking a deep breath of resolve, she nudged her way to the quieter end of the bar. If Tamsin was here, she would at least be kept busy in the upper chambers, she mused, feeling wretched to be reminded of her sister's pleasures. This was Jolinda's first visit to the tavern since Ma had banished Tamsin from their homestead, indeed her first visit to the settlement. She'd not wanted to see anyone and it was necessity that brought her to the tavern now, to negotiate a trading stall for the coming season with the Celt. She didn't wish to see Tamsin.

Jolinda made her way towards the one vacant stool beside the bar, tucked in the far corner, arriving at the same time as Gius Autemius. Despite the split skin and grazes still decorating the decurion's face, Jolinda recognised him from her time on the fort with Cloelia, as someone who frequented the commandant's house more often than most. Some swelling remained around his eyes, with bruises deepening in colour as they matured before fading in repair, but the anger was gone from the beating he'd sustained. Gius, in turn, recognised Jolinda and courteously indicated she take the seat. Jolinda thanked him with a small nod and thin smile, nerves stealing her voice. Ordering an ale for himself, he offered Jolinda a honey mead to drink.

"Thank ya, but no, I'm just waiting to see the man," Jolinda nodded towards the Celt and covered her ear with her hand indicating who she meant, adding quickly why she wanted to see him, slightly flustered that her intentions may be misunderstood.

"I am waiting for the Celt too, and not for *those* reasons either," Gius chuckled at Jolinda. We will doubtless be last on his list of priorities. Legionaries on a day off with coin to squander will always come first."

"The fort's been active these past few days." Her eyes made the statement a question.

"Practise drills. It is the legate's answer to avoiding trouble. He fears idleness in his troops leads to restlessness, which in turn leads to recalcitrance." Jolinda showed surprise, which interested Gius. "I detect you distrust my answer."

"No...well yes...maybe. It's just, well...ya usually only rally that many cohorts together when ya campaigning. Unless I've got that wrong, the trumpet signal's different to before." Gius said nothing and Jolinda felt the need to explain, a flutter creeping up her spine. "I...I spent some time on the fort tutoring the legate's daughter. We became close friends and she taught me to count the trumpet signals." Gius was giving Jolinda a direct gaze but its meaning was not easy to interpret beneath his bruises.

"Ah, here comes our man." Gius said in a loud hail, raising his tankard in salute as the Celt headed towards them. In a quieter growl to Jolinda, he added "say nothing further on the subject of the trumpet signals. We will talk more of it later in private." The Celt acknowledged them both with a grunt and Jolinda, recoiling slightly from his rank breath, tried to steady her rapid heartbeat. The Celt spoke first, his manner brusque.

"Come to pay ya sister's dues have ya? The whore disappeared with coin of mine. Ya Teviots owe me." He was a brutish, burly man and Jolinda was intimidated, grateful that the tavern was busy. Even more grateful when Gius interjected as once again nerves stole her voice. It was a difficult thing to have your confidence shattered.

"Finagled by a lass, eh?" a friendly tease rippled through the decurion's words, "trade appears to be handsome enough to cope with the loss, but here, take this as settlement for the girl's dues and leave her sister alone, we're just becoming nicely acquainted." Gius threw several denarii at the Celt who grunted in response, his lip curling a little but the sting gone from his ire. He didn't want to lose the custom of the decurion. Gius had been frequenting the tavern daily since his drunken trumpeting display, spilling out his thoughts to the Celt. It was clear the man was struggling to remain loyal to his legion and revenge against the legate was throbbing in the Celt's ear stump. The Pict War Council was bestir with the fresh information he'd passed to them. The stalled plan to infiltrate the Roman fort and bring about its demise was regaining impetus, but more detail was needed and Gius was the linchpin. A decurion open to corruption was a valuable asset and not one the Celt wished to lose because of the Teviot family. He would spit on their graves later. Jolinda found her voice.

"Me sister is gone then?"

"She's gone 'n' good riddance to ya filthy trollop kin." He swept up the coin. "Ain't any need for me to track her now," he growled. Jolinda winced with humiliation, but was relieved Tamsin was gone. "I heard ya brother Kye has run off too. Ain't much loss either." Gius guffawed at this comment which was baffling to Jolinda, causing her pique to outshine her embarrassment.

"I came here to negotiate a trading stall with ya, not defend me brother," she said crossly, her neck and face reddening with the flush of the outburst. "If ya don't want me coin this season, ya'd better say so and I'll be on my way." The Celt snorted with derision. He was tempted to double the rent out of spite but thought again of the consequences of upsetting the decurion.

"Same rent as last season…in advance of each moon." He couldn't help but add the latter stipulation.

"I didn't pay in advance before."

"I didn't scorn the Teviots before. That's ya deal, take it or leave it." With that, the Celt walked away to organise a fresh group of legionaries congregating at the bottom of the stairs.

"Evil man, to be cursed!" Jolinda fought the welling tears. "What does 'e know of loss?" she said to Gius. "Kye has good reason to be travelling." A tear escaped as she blinked. "Sorry, this ain't your fault and I shouldn't be bending ya ear."

"An interesting phrase given the circumstances." Gius chuckled gently at her choice of words, covering his ear with his hand as Jolinda had done earlier to indicate the Celt's missing feature.

"Oh…" it brought forth an unexpected smile from Jolinda when she realised what he meant, melting away the anger. "I didn't mean that, but he *is* an evil man." She wiped away the tear. It was the first genuine smile to brighten her face since Tamsin's revelation.

"I agree, yet he serves Rome well."

"He does? Is he a spy?" Jolinda was incredulous.

"No, he is a bad judge of character! And I am not. Let me escort you from here Miss Jolinda Teviot. I wish to talk in private with you."

....

It was strange to be back inside the fort, both comforting and distressing to Jolinda. Memories of her happiest time with Marcus were more tangible here, welcome for the love that was wrapping her, painful for its loss. Cloelia, Brutus and Lucius, they had all shown her such friendship in this place and their absence weighed like an oak bough. She missed them but was once again surprised at the safety she felt within the Roman walls, despite its unusual emptiness.

Legate Maxinius greeted her respectfully with professional warmth, calling immediately for refreshment. On leaving the tavern, Gius had asked Jolinda to keep her silence in what she knew about the trumpet signals. He'd given honest answers to her questions, but she remained, not surprisingly, unsure of the truth. Gius had, after all, been putting on a display for the Celt, how could he expect Jolinda to be readily convinced? The ruse he had put in place could quickly be undone by what she knew, thus he had readily brought her to meet with the legate when she'd asked. Jolinda was hoping the legate may have news from Cloelia.

"My decurion," Peterna acknowledged Gius with a small nod as he spoke, "has asked me to explain our situation in a little more detail to ensure you understand why he has asked you to keep the knowledge you have about our trumpet signals to yourself." Legate Maxinius gave his customary penetrating gaze but Jolinda did not feel discomforted by it. "He has explained that the Celt at the tavern believes him to be open to bribery against Rome." The statement was made in to a question by a rise of intonation at the end. Jolinda acknowledged it with a nod. "He is not. You were witnessing his fine acting skills to keep up the façade with the Celt." Jolinda looked to Gius, then back to Peterna.

"So when he laughed with that filthy Celt 'bout me brother being no loss, he didn't mean it?"

"He did not mean it. It was only to keep up the façade of being open to bribery. Did your brother tell you of our long vigil at Swine Lake?" Jolinda nodded. "Are you aware of the Pict War Council?"

"I know it exists. Me Da always said it caused trouble."

"He said…?" Peterna had noted the past tense. "Your father is no longer alive?" Jolinda looked across to Gius, then, frowning, shifted her gaze to the flag-stoned floor. In the presence of these two military men who treated her with kind respect, whom she liked, and within the solid walls of the fort where great friendship and love had wrapped her, Jolinda unexpectedly found herself telling the story that linked her family so intrinsically with Marcus. It didn't feel like a betrayal to kith or kin, it was simply the right time for her to speak of the sadness. She related the tale honestly and simply, withholding the names of Marcus and Lucius, referring to them only as legionaries and when she was finished gave a small, bewildered shrug at how she had condensed so many moons of heartache in to a few moments of words.

The legate leaned back in his chair, hands clasped in his lap, slowly rolling his thumbs as he recollected events which had first brought Legionary Guintoli to his attention. Jolinda had given him more pieces to the mosaic and his swift mind was shuffling them in to place. The resulting picture explained the attack by a single Brigante, that had always troubled Peterna who didn't like uncharacteristic events. It also explained Guintoli's excessive unease about the slaughter that day and his subsequent desire to leave Britannia. And the reason the Teviots wanted to find him, the personal matter Kye had adhered to, was some complicated local folk lore, although his deduction of a pregnancy had not been completely wrong. It was a tangle that, unravelled by his perfunctory mind, left him annoyed. He could ill afford to lose troops, especially promising men, and especially due to a misunderstanding over foolish urges, which, in essence, is what this scenario played out as. Pah! Why does Jupiter allow Cupid to tease men and women to confusion? Stilling his thumbs and leaning forward, Legate Maxinius was driven with intensity to conclude the meeting and convince Jolinda to aid their plan.

"Your brother helped lead us to the one-eared Celt in exchange for information on the whereabouts of Guintoli. His information has enabled us to put a plan in place which we hope will bring us the ringleaders of the Pict War Council, thus end their push from the north before it escalates into something more bloody. We aim to quash this rebellion in its infancy to maintain order and stability in the area, your area. Time is pressing as we cannot, *must* not, allow the Picts any opportunity to gather more numbers. We are asking you not to discuss what you know, what my daughter has taught you, regarding how we muster our cohorts." The reference to Cloelia was poignant. "False intelligence has been passed, by Gius here, to the Celt regarding our trumpet signals and if doubt is cast, it could prove costly to stability in these lands."

"I ain't interested in all the politics." Her innate Brigante spirit shone back at Peterna's Roman passion, "I don't want to live under Roman rule, but I ain't against living alongside ya. I love me family and I love *your* family, so if ya swear on ya daughter's life that ya telling me the truth then I'll keep me silence, 'cause I don't want to live with the threat of war." Jolinda knew he would not swear on Cloelia's life lightly.

"I swear on my daughter's life that my words are true." The room appeared to lift of tension.

"Is there news from Cloelia?"

"One letter. The party reached Petuaria safely and secured a berth on a Greek merchant vessel. I can only assume they are now travelling through Gaul." Sadness spiralled Jolinda at the news. She had hoped they were still in Britannia. How would Kye ever track Marcus now?

"Thank you for your understanding on this important matter. With good fortune, we will net the perpetrators soon and restore peace. That is my ardent wish." Jolinda wasn't sure she *did* understand, not fully. It crossed her mind that the legate was inciting local trouble rather than quelling it, but she would hold her silence for those who had treated her with kindness. If the Romans pulled out entirely, the feudal tribes of the north, especially the Picts and the Votadini would no doubt create their own skirmishes, so perhaps it was better to hope the Romans could police the area without battle "I bid you farewell. Gius will escort you from the fort."

Walking along the Via Principia, the echo from the decurion's hobnails highlighted the absence of troops in the fort which was usually a bustle of noise and activity. The stark sound was penetrating. The pair were almost at the North Gate before Jolinda spoke to break its rhythm.

"Is Gaul an enormous land?"

"It is many times greater than Britannia, but all roads lead to Rome." Jolinda grabbed this simple statement and kept it with her as hope.

Chapter Twenty-Five

For the third time that day, the six horsemen were taking a soaking as they cantered over the chalk downlands. The weather was swinging from sunny spells to heavy showers, the sky changing from a welcoming powder blue to an unfriendly hue of pewter. Fortunately, the strong breeze controlling the changes was warm and was drying the riders in between the deluges. As they crested the rolling hill, the wide river valley opened up beneath them, undulating in smoothly sculpted ripples of green velvet heavily peppered with swathes of yellow and white flowers.

The lengthening daylight had allowed Falco and his group to ride for long hours, thus reaching their destination on the fourth day without beasting the horses or the men. He was keenly aware that legionaries were always happier on foot, and although saddle sore, they would at least arrive in the city reasonably fit. This was imperative to Falco who had a high stake in keeping Ocella alive. A new Governor would be succeeding Falco in the next season and it was extremely important that the project he'd seeded and nurtured for Britannia flourished before his departure to Rome. It would be a beacon of his rule under Hadrian and critical to his political status in the forum. Ocella, with his specialist skills, was pivotal to the project's success.

Small-eyed as his name suggested, beady in their stare down his pinched nose, the engineering architect was arrogant and Falco disliked him as most did, with Hadrian being an exception, seeing qualities that amused him. The rumour of a death contract was no surprise. It did not originate with the State, Falco knew that. No, the assassins would come from the private sector, hired by a wealthy patron Ocella had crossed somehow, a personal dislike, and these were always the hardest to monitor.

Seeing the start of the city buildings hugging the valley contour below, Falco urged his mount a little faster, hunching his shoulders against the rain as he marshalled his thoughts. He knew these hills well and spearheaded the group towards a wooded area, joining a track which led them down to a stream. Following the stream west, the running water sparkling as the sun, again master of the sky, flickered its rays through the canopy of young leaves, Falco led the group in through the open gates of a deserted courtyard villa.

"There is water and meal for the horses in the stables, and we should find a hamper to douse our appetites." Falco dismounted and guided his horse across the cobbles, the others following. "We will be here only as long as it takes to feed the horses. It is imperative we press on to Aquae Sulis. Ah good, there it is." Falco pointed at a large basket covered with a cotton cloth, the aroma of fresh bread wafting from it. "Our arrival has been expected," Falco explained as he saw an exchange of surprise pass between Marcus and Brutus, "the reason recondite. I will now expand the brief you were given by Emperor Hadrian." He allowed his gaze to sweep across them all. "We will find Ocella at the temple of Sulis Minerva, the ever growing complex at the hot springs of which he is overseeing the building. We are to escort him to the northern frontier with haste, where the Emperor awaits his expertise for another project, details of which need not concern you now." Falco swept his eyes over the group again, this time settling on Marcus. "Trouble clings to Ocella like a limpet latches to rock, and danger cloaks him like seaweed. We believe hired assassins are closing in. It is not a surprise as he leaves many upset in his wake. The man is opinionated, vocal and publicly known to over indulge in food with an active interest in young boys. He has twice survived an assassination attack, but we cannot risk his luck ending just yet." If Falco was meaning to disguise his personal dislike of the engineering architect, he was failing. His top lip curled with contempt whenever he spoke his name. "That is the background to this mission, so keep alert at all times. One other point before we leave, Hadrian assures me Ocella will come quietly as we have a 'chosen one' amongst us," this time Falco purposefully kept his gaze away from Marcus, "scepticism batters me here, so be clear that we bring him by force if necessary."

"It seems the Governor is not as convinced by your chosen status powers as the Emperor," Brutus muttered to Marcus as they readied their horses.

"Me neither," replied Marcus. "Falco is certainly edgy."

"Assassins make us all edgy." Assassins were held as animus fighters within the legions, their tactics dirty and devious.

"Stinks of politics," interjected Lucius, "but bring it on, eh? The messier it gets, the better it will be for the red horsehair crest." He mounted his horse with enthusiasm, eager to get going. Brutus followed his lead.

"You are right Lucius, glory for distinction. Come on Chosen...*Twentieth Legion of the Eagles, proud to fight for Rome and comrade!*" Marcus felt a pulse of adrenalin lift his spirits. He was a trained fighter and comfortable with these men beside him.

"To glory," he echoed the response.

....

The pavements surrounding the steaming pool were bustling with bathers arriving and leaving, whilst others took their time relaxing in the green waters. The place was noisy with activity and the sounds of workmen nearby was adding to the hustle. Newly erected stone pillars of a golden hue, smooth and as yet bare of graffiti, had been added to supplement the oak piles driven in to the mud by engineers fifty years ago. The oak had provided a stable foundation strong enough to support the irregular stone chamber that had first surrounded the spring, but Ocella's grand plans required something more.

The original chamber had been dismantled, the lead lining the stone carefully removed and currently stacked in a locked vault for safe-keeping. It would be re-used within the new building which was to include a caldarium, tepidarium and frigidarium as well as further temples to various deities. It was to be the grandest bathing complex in Britannia. At present, the pool was open to the sky and the water shimmered with steamy reflections of the rising pillars. It was the only calm area to be found. Falco came striding through the throng from the engineering area.

"Ocella is in the Temple of Minerva. Follow me and keep alert." His unease was palpable. The temple was marked by a handsome stone carving of the head of Jupiter. Under less stressful circumstances, Falco's enquiring mind would have found this interesting and questioned the link with Minerva and the great thunderous god, but today he was focussed solely on his mission.

Two sentries were guarding the door to the small temple, hardly large enough to accommodate three men, and barred Falco from entering. Marcus was just able to see beyond them, the inside of the temple illuminated by a score of tapers arranged along the edge of a low plinth-stone altar. A bellow of fear gave a clue to the shapes Marcus couldn't quite decipher. Falco heard the commotion from within, and with his head full of visions of assassins, his nerves split their husks and he murdered his way past the two guards, to arrive just as Ocella pulled his ceremonial dagger across the jugular of the bullock, its head held back and high by a guiding rope through a ring in its nose. A wail of relish rushed from the throat of the priest holding the tether, his eyes vivid in fervent shine, followed by a stream of monotonic chanting.

The priest let the beast slump to the floor. Ocella raised his arms in prayer and offering, a puddle of slick dark red, almost black blood, pooling at his bare feet. Falco recoiled at the sight and smell of the sacrifice. He was furious, the veins in his neck bulging with angry power. The ritual complete, Ocella turned nonplussed towards the intrusion.

"Welcome Quintus. The death and rebirth of Attis is celebrated." Sacrifices to celebrate the god of vegetation at the vernal equinox was a custom of ancient Rome that few continued to adopt. "Your guards are dead," spat Falco. Ocella raised an eyebrow in response.

"By your sword?" Falco glared an agreement, anger filling his chest and strangling his speech. "Then they were useless at their position and deserve to be dead. The great god Jove has acted as my sentry in their place." Ocella was unmoved by the event. Falco's voice exploded.

"Pleb! It is you who will be dead! Any assassin could make a sacrifice of you whilst your head is ranting to the gods! Attis? No-one sacrifices to Attis any more and the wheat still grows." Falco was exasperated and his words could be clearly heard by those within a wide radius outside the temple, and a small crowd was forming, drawn by the commotion and the dead guards. Flies were already crawling across the most bloodied areas of the bodies. Marcus was becoming uneasy, sensing the growing curiosity in the crowd, knowing that a mob can suddenly gain in spirit and turn nasty without having a cause, momentum encouraged simply by its numbers. He shifted his hand to his gladius in readiness, comforted by its feel. Brutus and Lucius repositioned themselves slightly so the three of them were a barrier to the temple's entrance. The two Imperial guards did the same.

Yes, the wheat grows." Ocella was irritatingly calm and refusing to be ruffled by Falco's anger. "I have seen swathes of it, vast areas of the high chalk plain less than a day's gallop to the east of here, covered in verdant young shafts, cultured by Roman hands using new technology. These lands have never seen such intense crop farming. Virgin methods, unfamiliar methods, let the old ways, secure in their successes, embrace the new for safety. I will sacrifice one bullock and Attis will turn the verdant sea to golden sands for us to reap in leaf-fall. Enough to feed all the legions under the eagle from one area no larger than the city walls of my beautiful Turino. Now, if you will excuse me, I have a concrete arch to nurture with Bonus Eventus beside me." The priest took his cue, raising his arms once more and beginning a prayer to the god of successful enterprises, slowly tilting his head backwards until the whole of his eyes rolled white.

"What are they doing in there?" muttered Marcus. A movement at the back of the growing crowd caught his attention. What stood out about it he couldn't say, but a shaft of alarm cleaved him. His fingers tightened around his sword hilt as he searched the faces for a clue as to what had startled him. He could pick nothing in particular out. Another stirring to his left brought forth a silent curse. His palms were sweating.

"A serpent is slithering amongst this mob, Brutus. We cannot wait here for it to strike." With that Marcus ducked into the temple. Falco started at his entrance.

"Report!" he snapped.

"Sir, an unfriendly mob is gathering, we should leave now."

"How unfriendly?" he hissed.

"I sense unseen danger at its flanks, Sir." Falco studied Marcus intensely before reaching a decision. He'd read Guintoli's military records, the lad had a certain perception that Falco couldn't afford to ignore. An assassin could hide easily in a crowd. Moving quickly across to the altar, Falco interrupted the priest's fervent praying by displaying the Trajan wooden block in front of Ocella.

"You are familiar with Consus Didinius, I believe?" The priest was immediately silent. Ocella stumbled back a pace, reaching for the temple wall to steady himself. He paled, gasped and Marcus thought he would collapse. Falco indicated to Marcus to bring Ocella. "This way Chosen One," he deliberately addressed Marcus with this title. Hadrian had known plenty when he'd said Ocella would co-operate in such presence. Pulling the dead bullock off the plinth, he pushed the stone slab to the side, grunting at its weight. Beneath were steps leading to a passage. "The passage splits in twenty paces, take the left fork. You will surface in back streets, go left again until you reach the fountain of the boar. There is a hidden chamber under the fountain. We will find you there. Priest! Come with me."

Marcus grabbed a burning taper, handed it to Ocella and followed the engineer down the uneven stone steps in to the musty passage. The air was dank.

…........................

Falco emerged from the temple with the priest to find Brutus, Lucius and his two Imperial Guards, swords unsheathed and shields up, forming a protective crescent around the entrance, the sight of them enough to keep the horde five paces away. Jostling from the middle of the throng was causing a constant rippling of the front line as the ever thickening mass of people, attracted by curiosity, seethed in movement. Brutus felt the ache in his right arm, now his shield arm which still felt unnatural.

"Form up on me and let us get through this mob. The target is temporarily removed, and we must reassemble with haste. Priest, stick to my heels like a burr to sheep's wool. Antonini, watch him. Seniarus, Praetorians, we are looking for shadows on the flanks, report anything that seems odd, keep sharp. We go." Falco led the formation boldly through the crowd, his keen hearing focussing on sounds above the massed murmur, his eyes narrowed and flaming. A pathway opened as they forged on, people parting as stalks of barley do as a fox passes through.

The mob was less dense at the southern end of the baths and Falco spotted a group of auxiliaries, dust covering their uniforms where they'd been cleaving stone blocks. He shouted orders to them to remove the bodies of the dead guards to the city fort. He would see they had a proper cremation later and made a mental note to mark their records as 'death on service'. Their families would receive some recompense from Rome's treasury at least and it would serve to ease his conscience.

"Keep moving, stay close to the Governor." Brutus bundled the priest along, his flowing robe hampering his footsteps. Brutus just wanted to get out of the baths and reunite with Marcus as quickly as possible, the ache in his arm was distracting and maybe this contributed to his lack of vigilance. A sudden shout and splash made the group look to the pool, but the threat was from the other direction. A lithe figure, smooth in movement, in contrast to the ragged crowd, hooded, bold, floating at the edge of the thinning horde. The priest raised his hands to point from his jowls - the sign of the boar.

Outside the hot springs, in the open streets, Falco hurried his group on, cursing as the priest was slowing their progress. The man stumbled and Falco ordered Brutus to carry him, at the protest of the religious man.

"What is the hurry?" he gasped.

"Your patron is in danger priest, do not complain!"

"In danger from who? In peril from what?"

"Assassins!" snapped Falco, his temper bulging with impatience once more.

"But we saw no assassin, you saw no such serpent. I will run at my own speed."

"And you would know the serpent if you saw it, would you?" snapped Falco. "Carry him! If he complains further, silence him."

Puffing with an audible spit, Ocella oscillated along, the exertion of moving his bulbous gut at least bringing some colour back to his face. Marcus was encouraging him to hurry, wanting to be out of the tunnel as soon as possible. Cold mud splashed up his leg as they ran through an unseen puddle, but soon the ground began to slope upwards and an air stream sputtered the taper before the darkness was thinned by seeping daylight. Ocella ditched the torch as the end of the passage grew visible, slowing to a walk and waving Marcus to pass him, flinching with tension as Marcus brushed by in the narrow confines, whispering 'Chosen' with the little breath he had. Marcus ignored him, uncomfortable with the awe in the man's voice.

Kneeling in the shadows of the passage, its entrance cleverly disguised by tumbling ivy, Marcus peered through the tendrils along the narrow street. It reminded him of Petuaria, paved and guttered although the stone of the houses was a soft sand colour rather than grey. The houses to the right were not terraced, each enclosed by its own wall topped with fancy ironwork both decorative and functional, with solid oak gates completing the security. There was clearly wealth in this area. Soft music, a harpist playing in one of the detached dwellings, drifted along the deserted street. Beyond the last house, which Marcus estimated to be seventy paces away, the paved roadway dwindled in to a rough path that meandered over unkempt scrub and disappeared in to woodland. Looking left the street curved, taking the terraces round with it.

"What lies between us and the boar?" Marcus spoke softly to Ocella.

"We go left." The engineer's reply came as a dazed squeak. Marcus frowned at him wondering if the man had lost his senses before footsteps took his attention back to the empty street. He listened to the hurrying echoes, his pulse quickening with anticipation, then settling again as a young mother came in to view carrying a basket, an infant bound to her bosom by a sling with another older child of three, maybe four seasons, clinging to her free hand. The child stumbled on the paving and Marcus watched from his vantage point in the shadows as the mother took her time to comfort the tot before moving on, passing their hiding space without a glance.

"What is round the corner and how far is it to the boar?" Marcus asked again. Ocella was mute so Marcus shoved his rump with his boot. "How far is the fountain?" The shove did the trick and Ocella seemed to judder from a stupor.

"Huh? The boar, yes...it is just a few houses beyond the corner. It is a multi-faceted structure that nestles neatly between the end of one terrace and the start of the next. The door to the chamber is hidden behind the two boars rising on their hind legs and is activated by pulling the bronze tusk, an engineering masterpiece, the joy of which I have only been able to share with a few. An annoyance I have grieved over until now, when its obscurity is my salvation."

Gruff laughter from the street ceased his flow. Marcus flexed his fingers around his sword hilt, narrowing his eyes on the small group of dust covered auxiliaries approaching.

"Who is it?" puffed Ocella.

"Auxiliaries, from the work site. What are they doing round here?"

"Madam Ninaretta..." Ocella gave a distasteful shudder, "...she is not of my choosing but her brothel thrives." They drew quiet as the group passed and Marcus watched them turn down a passage between two of the walled buildings.

"Madam Ninaretta has a rule," explained Ocella, "visitors to the main gates, clients to the side passage. It is a farce, but the misguided influentials of this city feel it protects their reputations. As if entering via the gates for all to see fools anyone, dolts! They will lust to her doors in a steady stream as the shadows lengthen." There was no mistaking his disdain and Marcus surmised Ocella's desire for young boys was not in agreement with the rules of the establishment. Not willing to be drawn into the engineer's prejudices, Marcus ignored his rant. His mission was to deliver Ocella alive to Hadrian in the north, he didn't have to like him or agree with him, just deliver him and the sooner they met up with Falco, the sooner they could get away from Aquae Sulis and the assassins he had felt were lurking at the edge of the mob outside the temple.

Marcus was conscious of the passing minutes and his eye twitched as he pondered what to do. The lack of others to mingle with would make them conspicuous in the street, but a coin is double-sided, no people meant no assassin. There was no choice but to break cover. "Right, we go. Keep pace and keep silent." Grabbing Ocella by the arm, Marcus lurched him up and through the cascading ivy, allowing him no opportunity to argue. A dark cloud splattered its first rain in large spots as the pair hurried in the opposite direction of Madam Ninaretta's. Unseen, a lone figure came running from the woodland.

…....................

Brutus dumped the priest unceremoniously from his shoulder, relieved to be free of his burden. He was blowing hard from the exertion of carrying the man and keeping up with the pace Falco had set. The priest glared in protest but said nothing, turning instead to surreptitiously sweep the square with his eyes. A grand mosaic surrounded a raised set of stepped seating in the centre of the square, with other resting areas and decorative rowan trees dotting the edges. Several groups of people were enjoying the forum. The priest couldn't see who he was looking for amongst them, but he was confident the assassin was nearby.

Five streets fed in to the square, two broad, the others narrow. The broad roads entered from the south and west bringing carts, horses and oxen, as well as pedestrians, directly from the baths and the city's administration centre. The narrow streets were much less used, servicing pedestrians and single horse riders only, leading to different living areas of Aquae Sulis. The smallest of these ways curved quickly out of sight and it was this street that led to the fountain of the boar.

"Imperials, form rear and take charge of the priest. Seniarus, Antonini, form front with me." As a huddle they jogged to the narrow street, the noise from their hobnails on the paving causing some in the square to look up, but the sound was commonplace in the city and interest in them was lost as they disappeared round the corner. Falco slowed the pace as they neared the fountain, the sound of the gently spewing water filling the deserted street. Stopping suddenly, his heart fluttering, Falco whispered a curse. Drawing his sword he gave orders for the Imperial guards to wait with the priest and for Brutus and Lucius to proceed with him. Blood was staining the gutter beside the fountain.

Fearing the worst, Falco hurried to the side where the two full size stone boars were standing on their hind legs, fore trotters touching in an arch, heads raised in twisted anger at the gargoyle mocking them from above. Each boar had two short tusks protruding from its snout, only one was cast in bronze. Falco leaned his weight against it, the tusk acting as a lever, thus opening the secret door. Brutus raised his eyebrows in surprise at Lucius.

"Wait here, the chamber is small." Falco didn't hesitate in entering, now was not a time to ponder what may greet him. Taking the six steps in two strides, he plunged in to the semi-darkness throwing himself to the right as he landed, knowing that the floor sloped upwards on this side and would afford him a small advantage if he survived an assailant's initial thrust of death. No attack came and as his eyes quickly adjusted to the half-light, he shouted for Brutus to join him. "What do you make of this?" Brutus took in the scuff marks in the sandy floor.

"One person, little movement."

"Hobnails?" Brutus crouched to inspect the prints more closely.

"No, no hobnails Sir, just a lop-sided square," his respect for the Governor was growing the more he worked with him.

"Any signs of blood on the steps?" Brutus tracked back up.

"No Sir, whatever happened occurred in the street."

"And what did happen?" snarled Falco as he resurfaced. "Did Guintoli reach the fountain? The evidence indicates he did not. Was Ocella left in the chamber alone? Where are they now? Alive or dead? Either way, it is not looking good for your comrade. Find me answers, and find them now!"

"Acheron!" cursed Brutus quietly under his breath to Lucius, as Falco returned to the guards and priest. "Marcus would not have left Ocella, I do not care what Falco thinks, I know that to be true. Perhaps another was waiting in the chamber for them."

"And I have the hearing of a bat do not forget, Antonini!" Falco roared. "Start caring what I think, your career, your life, teeters on it!" Falco stopped in mid-stride as if struck by a thunderbolt directly from Jupiter. "By the gods, Cepheus!" The priest tried to run but Falco was quicker. In a blur he had his hand about the priest's throat, his eyes ablaze. "Show me your sandal Priest." The sole confirmed what Falco had seen imprinted in the patch of mud beside them, the constellation of Cepheus, a triangle above a lop-sided square, the same square scored in the sand of the chamber, the mud revealing the complete picture that the dry sand had withheld. The truth dawned on Falco and he drew his words in a low, tight voice. "That fool Ocella could not keep his mouth shut could he? Had to brag to someone of his engineering feat." The priest's eyes were bulging under Falco's grip, but they shone with a defiant pleasure and he raised his fingers to his jowls in a truculent gesture that became his last act. "You were right Antonini, another was waiting in the chamber. I ignorantly thought only I and Ocella knew of the boar's secret." The priest slumped, his face puce, and Falco maintained his death grip, driven by the bile taste of treachery.

"Sir, there is a trail of blood," Lucius reported.

"Show me." Leaving the priest where he fell for the flies and crows to share, Falco and the four soldiers resumed their search for Marcus and the engineer.

Chapter Twenty-Six

Events for Marcus had taken a bad turn as he and Ocella had reached the fountain a score of minutes before Falco. The engineer would have been killed had it not been for a casual remark that pricked at the instincts of Marcus enough to sharpen his wits. Seeing the seal of the bronze boar tusk was broken, the engineer had assumed Falco was inside the chamber. "How did he reach here first? Even for a hare against a slug, the distance defies my physics." Leaning on the tusk as he spoke, Marcus had yanked him away from the fountain, interrupting the smooth opening of the door, thus hampering the assassin's attack. Ocella stumbled to the ground, and Marcus faced their assailant with his gladius drawn.

There was little time to think but any advantage the assassin may have gained from surprise, was levelled by his momentum being reduced as he snagged his robe on the half-open door. Off-balance, he sliced at Marcus, the tip of his long, curved blade just reaching, scoring a bloody arc across Marcus's upper arm. Battle rage gripped the legionary and he stabbed at his attacker's gut, his shorter blade proving more agile at close quarters, but the assassin was nimble and twisted, falling forwards and Marcus could smell garlic on his rank breath. Acting quickly, Marcus smashed the hilt of his sword in to the assassin's face, splintering bone and teeth, the force of the hit crumpling the assassin unconscious. Raising his arm for the killing stab, a scream of pain from Ocella stopped him.

Spinning round, he saw a dagger protruding from the engineer's thigh. A movement on the roof of the terrace opposite the fountain revealing a second assailant. The dagger had penetrated deeply an inch above Ocella's knee. The engineer was white with shock, his rolls of stomach fat wobbling in ripples as he spasmed in fear. Cursing, Marcus knew they must move quickly. Closing his mind to Ocella's moans, he uncermoniously lifted the engineer on to his shoulder and started running in the direction of the tunnel.

Unable to look behind or up, Marcus could only focus ahead, gritting his teeth at the weight of Ocella. His plan was to find cover in the woodlands, a weak plan, but all that seemed available. Passing the tunnel they'd used to escape from the temple, Ocella's groans had subsided in to a delirious mumble. Marcus could hear running footsteps behind him. Digging deep on reserves of energy, he pumped his legs harder, the notes from the harpist who was still playing only floating on the edge of his awareness, his concentration taken by the cadence of the footsteps from behind which he sensed were gaining on him.

Death is certain, the day uncertain. A favourite proverb amongst the legions which coursed across his thoughts. Marcus kept running, passing Madam Ninaretta's brothel, expecting the assassin to strike from behind at any moment as the footsteps were sounding so close. Yet he reached the end of the houses, the path across the scrub softer underfoot. Dragging for breath, he carried his charge forward, a clear track swathing through the broad-leafed trees, a mixture of beech and oak, with shrubs of hazel and brambles filling the gaps, growing denser further inside the copse.

Without breaking stride, Marcus veered away from the track, dancing between the undergrowth and hastily slipping Ocella, now unconscious, on to the ground beside a thicket, drawing his sword and turning in a single fluid motion, eyes fierce, expecting an immediate confrontation. It was a surprise not to find one and his mind raced to reconcile the oddity, the adrenalin keeping him taut with tension. Checking Ocella, he found a weak pulse, but before he could give further medical attention, a cracking twig snapped his attention back to the direction of the track. Nothing came in to view, but listening intensely, almost stalling his breathing so every sound could be detected, Marcus was convinced someone was there. The downy hair on his nape prickling as he crouched behind the thicket, alert and ready to strike, a spider waiting for the fly, an asp marking the shrew, yet his prey was also stalking him.

Staying hidden and praying to Apollo to keep an arrow of quiet sedation on Ocella, Marcus focussed on the closing footfalls. He could see his trail wasn't difficult to follow but running further was futile, his best chance now was to fight, and his palms grew clammy at the devious tactics he expected to face. Marcus sensed his tracker stop, and knowing it was only seconds to his discovery, seized the opportunity to charge from his concealment, crashing and yelling with as much vigour as he could muster, hoping to startle a momentary advantage. It may have worked but for the face that stared back at him.

"What the..." shock etched an explosive expression of incredulity on Marcus and he pulled out of his sword charge clumsily so that the pair bundled heavily together falling in a clinch. *He looks like me my Roman!*

……................…

The trail of blood had led Falco and his group to the terraced dwellings, but despite a thorough search of the premises and threats to the old couple inside, no bodies or information had been uncovered.

"We search every building in this street. Question every occupant. Someone must know something!" Falco blustered. Moving systematically through the terraces revealed nothing. "They cannot just disappear!" Falco was rigid with irritation as they reached the first of the detached dwellings.

"Sir, look!" Brutus had found another blood trail, a much bigger pool this time, and drag marks scraping from it were pointing towards Madam Ninaretta's side alley. Brutus and Lucius began to follow the trail, but were halted by Falco.

"Wait, watch the alley, I'll go to the front gates." Within a minute, Falco was admitted via the heavy oak door, leaving the Imperial Guards guarding the entrance.

"The Governor is clearly a 'front gate' client," winked Lucius, and Brutus appreciated the light-hearted comment, knowing the flippancy was only to cover his concern for Marcus. It was not long before the pair were hailed from the side door by Falco and ushered to an upstairs room, where the strong smell of camphor greeted them.

Madam Ninaretta was humming as she swabbed and bandaged Ocella's stab wound, the gentle tune giving calm to the scene. Marcus immediately welcomed Brutus and Lucius with the legionary's forearm clasp and a back slap each, smiles of relief all round. Falco addressed his men keeping his voice soft in the darkened room.

"Well done Guintoli. The prognosis is that Ocella will live."

"He must rest Quintus," interrupted Madam Ninaretta, her voice an accented golden tone. "A lot of blood was lost. For seven sunrises at least, he must rest."

"We leave in two." A series of rich tutting sounds scolded this remark, Falco ignored them. "Guintoli has told me there were two assassins, one is dead, the other injured but living on last sighting. I want a moon and sun vigil on Ocella, two of you at any one time, two hour shifts, Imperials first. Send for me as soon as our fat friend here regains consciousness. Madam Ninaretta has kindly provided a room for you to use, food will be brought up. Do not abuse her generosity and do not leave this building. Guintoli, you know which room. Dismissed but keep your wits about you and your tales between each other."

"What happened?" hissed Lucius as Marcus led them down the corridor. "How by Mars did you get away from two assassins? I am beginning to believe you are 'chosen' and it is unnerving me." Putting his finger to his lips, Marcus took the uneven stairs three at a time, pausing as he reached the closed door.

"This is what happened..." quietly opening the door, he stood aside to let Brutus and Lucius in. Kye was sitting on the narrow bed cleaning his hunting knife. Brutus was the first to recover from the surprise, and breaking in to his melon-slice grin, he showed Kye the legionary forearm salute, an honour the legions reserved for their own or adopted allies, and began a typical rambling welcome. When he'd finished, they settled down to listen to the fates that had brought Kye to Madam Ninaretta's at the right time to save Marcus from the assassin.

"So the hunchback sent you to this dwelling?" asked Lucius. Kye nodded. "Why here? It was only chance that Marcus was passing. He really must have visions straight from the gods." Lucius shifted his eyes nervously to Marcus, who frowned uncomfortably at his suggestive logic.

"I was told to seek refuge with Madam Ninaretta. 'Go to the front gates' was my instruction, but there weren't time for that. Puppets of the gods we were." Lucius nudged Brutus with his elbow, winking at Kye.

"Seems we have another 'front gate' customer here." Kye knew enough to blush as they laughed.

"Ocella is not keen on the Madam," interjected Marcus, he'd been quiet whilst Kye had related his struggle with the assassin, studying him as he spoke. He looked so much like Jolinda and Marcus could feel the tendril of destiny delving, tightening and it was quickening his pulse as he fought the feelings. He wanted to ask Kye about Jolinda, but the words stayed buried. "And I am guessing the lack of friendship is reciprocated. Madam Ninaretta tends him only as a favour to Falco. There is a light shining there. That is why Consus sent Kye here. The hunchback knows this is a safe-house for Falco in trouble." Marcus wanted to dispel the myth of being chosen. "His deformity does not give him visions Lucius, he is just well informed. Stop looking at me like that."

"Like what?"

"Like *that!* Brutus club him if he does it again...hard!" A light rap on the door interrupted the argument, and two maids entered with freshly laundered tunics, muslin drying cloths and steaming water. Grinning, Brutus draped an arm round the shoulders of Marcus and Lucius, seizing the opportunity to lighten the broiling mood in the room.

"Comrades, it is good to be together again and as there is to be no distraction from any fine fillies, I fear you will be in the line of trajectory as grand as the mighty Roman ballistae to receive my most extravagant, most expansive and most popular of stories, legendary beyond the walls of our fair city to which my dearest wends her way as we speak, celebrated also at the edge of the Known World by our Brigantian companion, fellow and now blood brother..." Brutus steered Marcus and Lucius to the wash bowl, talking all the time. Throwing a cloth to Kye, he used his skills as master raconteur to bring the group together in chortling entertainment, weaving his topic cleverly towards the northern frontier and introducing Jolinda naturally in to the laughter.

"It is time for our first stint with Ocella." Brutus hauled the guffawing Lucius to his feet and launched him through the door before anyone could debate whose turn to guard it was, leaving Marcus and Kye alone to talk.

…......................

Despite Brutus's best efforts, the atmosphere plunged to stiffness between Marcus and Kye, the double noted song of the great tit outside competing with the music from the harp, drifting in to fill the silence within the room. Both made an effort at light-heartedness, in a stubborn attempt to avoid a conversation that itself was intractable. The stiffness remained.

"I had not expected to see you again," Marcus began awkwardly.

"I hadn't expected to come looking for ya."

"Why did you?"

"In short, for me family. Brigante lore." Marcus threw Kye a puzzled look. "It's complicated Roman, but important enough for me to track ya to Syria had I needed to."

"You would have followed me there?" he said incredulously. The conversation was becoming easier as it progressed. Kye untied the deerskin pouch from around his neck and handed it to Marcus.

"Yes, I would have followed ya to Syria. I'm glad ya ain't got that far," he added with a small shrug and a rueful grin. "Missing me goats!" Marcus pulled the effigy of Jupiter from the pouch. "She ain't returning it, ya got to give it back to her in person." Since parting from Julita and Cloelia, Marcus had succeeded in blocking Jolinda from his thoughts, the all-male company and quick-paced mission healing in its enclosure. Being with Kye was re-opening emotions, and a shaft of hope that Jolinda still wanted him slanted in before his *Geryon* jumped forward to shroud it.

"I cannot be with her, it is as I told you, I made a vow." Pain was adding an edge to his tone. Frustration was adding urgency to Kye's.

"Ya vow was misguided Roman and ya wrong to live by it." Kye's bold statement drew a fierce scowl from Marcus whose inherent pride didn't take kindly to such criticism. "Hear me out, Marcus." It felt odd to utter his name but Kye was acutely aware that his persuasion would have to be brutal in its directness. "We know..." he stopped and started again, "Jolinda knows, about you and Tamsin, but it weren't your fault. Tamsin duped ya. Her act was one of profligacy to escape the homestead, the blame is not with ya. And Da...Tamsin lied to him...his blood is on her hands, not on yours." Kye was quite breathless as the words tumbled out passionately, "Tamsin is gone, Ma ousted her 'n' I ain't sorry." He tailed off, dropping his eyes to the floor and frowning, the lore whispering shame on him.

Drawing his fingers through his hair, Marcus tried to make sense of it all. Kye spoke again in a more measured tone. "Ya see Roman, I had to come for ya to reset the balance. Tis important to me that we remain as equals." Marcus's expression showed he remembered their conversation at the fort's hospital. "Saving ya from the assassin atones for ya saving me from the Picts. Da ain't part of that equation now."

"Is that all your Brigante lore states? One favour of life for another? That is surely every warriors ethos."

"The ancient whispers root more deeply than that."

"Thought they might," muttered Marcus, who was beginning to feel the grip of *Geryon* lifting, the monster turning its three heads in search of Tamsin instead, as his harboured guilt was shifting to her.

"We need to share sacred rites across our threshold with ya for being duped or Da cannot rest in the spirit world." Jolinda had explained enough of the lore for Marcus to understand the implications of this restlessness to those family members still living. Rubbing the stubble on his jaw, abrasive as sandstone from lack of attention, the words of the hunchback came to him, *your destiny is in the north.* Marcus could feel the strength of Jupiter guiding him and a wave of blithesome hope lifted him briefly before the weight of his vow to Flavinus pulled his heart to the depths of the darkest river.

"We are all puppets of the gods Kye," he said earnestly, "your lore, my vow. My orders are to escort Ocella to the northern frontier, beyond that I have not been told. I will share rites with your family if I am able, but my vow, misguided or not, was made and binds me to Roman women only." Relief swept through Kye, it was a compromise, and enough to bring peace to the Teviots at least. Jolinda would recover from a broken dream given time, and anyway, he mused, maybe seeing her again would lend mortal reality to this stubborn Roman's armoury. Joyfully, he slapped Marcus on the shoulder and cheekily showed the legionary forearm salute to him whilst uttering praise to Bridget, uniting the two realms. His delight was infectious and Marcus grinned too. He would see Jolinda, she would welcome him, that was enough for now.

Chapter Twenty-Seven

A freshening wind was scudding the rain clouds keeping the eastern tribelands of Britannia dry but bleak. Hadrian was grateful for the lack of rain, but the relentless chill to his bones was tiring and he rode without speaking. Travelling in secrecy had forced his small group to take a route through the lands of the Corialtavi tribe that followed the Car Dyke north of Durobriuae, before veering northwest along the Fosse Dyke, thus avoiding the forts and towns in the region. Pottery and tile manufacturing sites pitted the area and Hadrian would liked to have learned more of the industry, his relentless zeal to understand the new driving his interest, but time was pressing him to ride hard. His priority was to consolidate the northern frontier and it was imperative he reach Legate Maxinius as soon as possible. His mood was dour.

Consus Didinius was waiting for him at Drax, a small settlement at the head of the Abus Fluvius, and the news the hunchback gave added to his silent gloom, and increased Hadrian's urgency, seeing him back in the saddle before dawn of the next day. On the advice of Consus, he took a direct line through the heart of Brigante territory, keeping to the valley rather than tackling the more inhospitable terrain of the peaks to each side. Safety was being weighed against speed. Fresh intelligence was unravelling in the north causing stirrings amongst the Picts. The information was already several sunrises old.

…....................

The legate didn't bother to assuage the young legionary's nervousness at having to wake him. His thoughts were on who was arriving at the East Gate in the dark hours creating enough of a stir for the centurion on guard duty to deem it necessary to send for him. Rather than irritation at being roused, Peterna was eager and he sent for Gius to meet him at the gate, thinking the visitor most likely to be from his decurion's network of local informers, bribed handsomely from Rome's coffers. Gius had already learned that the Pict War Council had taken the bait fed to the one-eared Celt, and was now hoping for news on how the Council was reacting. The sharp wind swiped away the dregs of tiredness as Peterna hurried to the East Gate.

The legate returned the centurion's salute.

"Six men at the gate Sir, gave me this." The centurion held out a scroll for the legate. "Demanded I give it to you immediately. Direct orders from the emperor they say. It has Hadrian's seal Sir, but I kept them waiting outside the gate, cannot be too careful Sir. They are armed with Roman equipment but not in uniform and we have no orders to expect anyone. Seems odd." A dart of disquiet punctured Peterna's enthusiasm. Quickly prising open the scroll, his expression furrowed as he read the message.

"Saturnalia..." he muttered, his puzzlement increasing. "Here to improve troop morale." Gius arrived as Peterna's confusion was clearing. "Great Jupiter and Mars be united! Centurion, send a runner to the kitchens with orders to prepare a platter. The best wine! Gius, with me." A blister of tension filled the guardroom, each man standing immediately straighter. Looking earnestly at Gius with determination brightening the sharp blue of his eyes, he added quietly, "If the dice I have played leads to ruin..." Gius held up a hand to stop him, the words unnecessary.

"Rome may turn against you, but my friendship never will." Gius lay a strong hand on Peterna's shoulders. "Our agreement will be honoured and I will take good care of Julita and Cloelia. Your memory will not be tarnished with us my friend." Standing to attention, Gius saluted his officer. The legate returned the gesture.

"Open the gate Centurion, we have Imperial guests!"

…....................

Despite the early morning hour where darkness still caped the sleeping fort, news of Hadrian's arrival spread through the barracks as swiftly as the surging surf sweeps over the sands of a flat beach. Soldiers pricked awake, some disbelieving, others curious and immediately placing wagers on the fate of their legate. What had he done to warrant an Imperial visit? The fort stayed dark but a murmur of apprehensive excitement clung to the night air like an autumn fog that hugs the ground.

Within the hour, the Imperial party was dined and refreshed and Hadrian dismissed his guards to the sleeping quarters of the house offered for their stay. He asked Gius to leave them too and although grammatically a request, Gius, understanding the order behind it, saluted and smartly marched from the room leaving the emperor and the legate alone.

"I can see I must raise my profile within Britannia," began Hadrian referring to the lack of recognition by the men at the gate. "I will commission a bust for the fort, and perhaps another for Londinium, in bronze if my plans go well." He was sitting casually, one long leg bent up across the other so the foot was resting on the opposite knee, goblet in hand gently swilling the wine to an eddy, watching the swirling patterns with light-some intrigue.

"It is an honour you are here Imperator, yet a prodigious shock. You cannot blame the men for not recognizing you. They do their jobs well under difficult circumstances. Had you sent word of your arrival, the welcome would have been different." Peterna was defensive, probing, nervous, curious, all at the same time, eager for the opportunity to explain his view, cautious of erring his reasoning with an ill-timed remonstrance. For all his readiness, he was completely disarmed by Hadrian's next words.

"Lady Julita and your daughter send their personal greetings." Hadrian held up his free hand in a placating gesture at the alarm in Peterna's expression. "They are quite well and two of my best Imperial Guards are ensuring their safety to Rome. Their first berth met with a freak storm which turned them back to these shores. A chance series of events led them to me which can only be interpreted as the guiding hands of the gods. It is right that Cloelia should see the Pantheon, though I fear I may have bored Lady Julita with my stories of its build. I have an appetite for the detail of a project meaning I sometimes labour a conversation to death." Again, he held out a placating hand. "They are both well despite the ordeal of the storm and in safe passage now." Peterna's chest thumped alarmingly wondering what of his plans Julita may have revealed to the emperor. She had left the fort without fully understanding the difficulties of the area, and begrudgingly too. He forced his thoughts to be rational.

"And what of my men who were travelling with them? Did they perish?"

"They are with Falco on my orders." Peterna flinched with surprise.

"With Falco? Doing what?" There was a silent pause before Peterna regathered his wits, adding 'Sir' almost with reluctance, his eyes narrowing a little in distrust. Peterna found himself concurring with his fears that Hadrian was not a worthy successor to Trajan. The heat of disappointment flushed his temples. Hadrian drew his slender fingers in slow strokes pensively across his bearded chin.

"You are a loyal Imperialist Maxinius, with many years of exemplary conduct to the Empire, not least during service in Dacia." Peterna's guts fluttered at the mention of Dacia recalling his talk with Julita. Had his wife misguidedly told of his faltering loyalty to Hadrian? "I sent orders to consolidate and control."

"Yes, Imperator but I stand by my statement that advancement is imperative or Rome will begin its fall and implore you to reconsider for the good of the Empire. Sir, I am your eyes here on the northern frontier and would not be serving you justly by following blind orders. Give me troops so I can quash these Brittunculi once and for all and claim these northern lands for the Empire." His dice were played. Hadrian stood suddenly and turned away from Peterna. The silence tapered long.

"You are not my only eyes in the north, Legate." The rebuke was stinging. "I have heard that you are inciting a rebellion, and I am sure you do not need reminding of the uprising faced here by Agricola. These tribes will draw you in to battle in the mountains where the terrain is more savage than its people."

"Sir, we can quash an uprising from the Picts and claim a glorious victory if you give me more troops." Peterna refrained from saying 'Africa is favoured over Britannia' but the sentence hung in the air without being uttered. "Agricola failed because the uprising was united, the northern tribes merged to rise against him. It is exactly this that I am acting to avert by luring the Picts in now." Peterna struggled with the fury that was rising in him. Words, once spoken, could not be retracted and loose words uttered in anger could see a man crucified. He measured his anger. "At present, there is no sign of an amassed army of Picts, yet the northern frontier is volatile and numbers could be gathered in time. We must not rest on Caesar's laurels. The War Council is working to strike and hide, demoralise, stab again, withdraw and hide. Arbeia was razed by fire from *within*, Sir. *Within!* The rebels are using bribery and infiltration as weapons, *with success!* Yet, the weakness is their clannish disputes. The Brigantes do not like the Picts, the Carvetii dislike the Votadini, the Creones squabble continually with the Epidii who in turn detest the Taexali, whilst the Picts exasperate them all with their mindless aggression! If we exploit these tribal feuds, the Pict War Council will never gain united support. I have plans in place to capture the Pict infiltrators which should result in reducing their sword fodder a little at least, more importantly it will keep the tribes squabbling amongst themselves and divide their strength."

"So you choose to use tactics as devious as those you despise from the rebels, enticing them to your doorstep using whispers of treachery and false trumpet signals…how loyal is your decurion Gius Autemius?" Peterna was startled by Hadrian's knowledge and burned with indignation at his disparaging tone, the burning shot through with cold fear. Who was gathering such guarded information and reporting to the emperor, and did they know more than he did? Had he perhaps overlooked some important detail? His mind wheeled with unbidden thoughts that Gius and Julita had brought him down. "Do you truly believe slaughtering this trickle of the Pict War Council's sword fodder will bring the elders, scattered in their fortresses, Dunnadd on the west, Beinn Dearuigg to the east…" Hadrian was throwing his arms in the directions of the compass, remonstrating as he spoke, his powerful voice resonating "…Klibreck high in the north, in to the obeisance of Rome?"

Peterna looked Hadrian squarely in the eyes, his own a cold icy blue, challenging the judgement of the leader of the Known World. "Rome must have supreme domination of these northern lands. The Empire, *your* Empire Imperator, must conquer and claim them or Rome's power is lost. Trajan knew the importance of expansion, we fought long and hard for it in Dacia and you are a hare's breath from seizing all here in Britannia. The safety of the structure of the Valiant Empire relies on it." Hadrian's expression was black, the legate's fate sealed within it, but Peterna forged on as a man does when he has nothing further to lose. "The Picts have taken the bait dangled by Gius, believing they know when the fort is at its most vulnerable," the legate viciously stamped back invading thoughts that Gius had somehow crossed him, angry at himself for allowing them any conviction. "Contact of crucial impact is expected imminently."

"Bribery is a lowly weapon of war." Peterna's guts writhed at the edge of scorn in Hadrian's voice. "It is best left to the use of the Senators in the Forum. It does not suit you Maxinius, neither are you adept at using its power. Do not be ashamed at that." Hadrian's tone became more measured and Peterna felt a flutter of unexpected hope. "With the guidance of Fortuna, my arrival may be in time to salvage the stirrings you have caused, not just in the north, but the south too." Peterna's brow rumpled, inviting further explanation. "Yes, the south! You have grossly underestimated the distance your plot has wend." Hadrian used thumb and forefinger to pinch the bridge of his nose, eyes momentarily closed as he expunged the tiredness. "The Votadini are especially interested in this new intelligence and look keen on assisting the Picts. You will be faced with insurgents from two boundaries simultaneously, and I doubt it would stop at just the Votadini." The news Consus had given him at Drax jumped to mind. The client king of the Iceni tribe had died suddenly of a seizure. Was it natural causes or poison induced? Either way, the headstrong son, Trewak, was the new king, and a change like this always caused ripples as the new tribal leader made his mark. And what better way than to join in with a concerted strike at the Romans? The priestess would be earning her treasury funding for a while he suspected. "Quarrelling Caledonian tribes or not Maxinius, Roman control is faltering in what was stable areas due to your ill judgement and indiscretion." Hadrian did not wish to discuss the Iceni with the legate at present.

"I acted with Rome's best..." Hadrian raised a hand to silence Peterna's defence.

"You are a loyal Imperialist Maxinius, but times are changing and Rome must change too. I wish to keep intact the Empire which has been imposed upon me by divine instruction. That is why I am in Britannia, secretly reviewing the Empire's defences. Expansion is no longer ideal, we must consolidate and control the frontiers. It is the same in Africa, deployment there is essential to keep the frontiers from collapsing. Consolidate and control, that is key, *control!* Rome has the best of this island, let us allow the northern peasants their harsh wilderness."

"The Brittunculi will never cease their harrying." The legate sagged, arms to knees, head bowed in mawkish defeat. His fears of Hadrian's unworthiness were borne to be true and feelings of betrayal for his great mentor Trajan, and for Rome, sickened him. His own ruin was sealed and his heart lurched with mortal fear, concerns for his family central to his dread. Hadrian continued to speak but only odd words broke through to Peterna...defence before expansion, Egypt, Judea, rebellion in Mauretania, limes, Ocella, new techniques...

Ocella, that small-eyed weasel! That was a name the legate had not heard in a while, it brought his focus back, the moment was not missed by Hadrian.

"Ah, so you remember Ocella from your younger days? An obnoxious man on many fronts but a specialist engineer who has proven his worth, and my chief architect on the Sulis Minerva complex. Have you heard of the project Maxinius? A fine example of compromise within Roman rule. We have peace, content citizens that are easy to police, all under the rule and domination of Rome and its laws, and adding nicely to her treasury. I would have you hear me out on my plans for Britannia's northern frontier including the Twentieth Legion." Despair was lodged in the legate's throat as a tightening lump, disabling him from speaking, but Hadrian could see a seed of attention re-enter the glacial pools that once again held his own stare. "My plan of defence before expansion has been proven to work elsewhere in the Empire. Notably, the rebellion of Mauretania was quelled by the construction of a lime. Its network of forts and ditches function as a filter, protecting the areas under our direct control by funnelling contacts with the interior through the major settlements – consolidation and *control*, Maxinius."

"We have a lime already, it does not work here." Peterna's voice was a flat monotone in contrast to Hadrian's enthusiasm.

"But this will be the Limes Britannicus, a fabulous expression of Roman power! It will be a wall built like no other, ten foot thick, a score high and eighty miles wide traversing the entire island from the mouth of the Tineas Fluvius to Ituna Aest. A grandoise concept, a statement of our superiority in construction and engineering, in politics and riches. The north cannot survive without trade with the south and we will control this trade and movements between. We conquer through political control. It is beautiful Maxinius and the Twentieth Legion will be pivotal in its construction." Despite himself, Peterna was slowly drawing from Hadrian's excitement, but his disposition was still pessimistic.

"It would serve as a lime to control passage but I cannot foresee its political statement of power, the turf will blend as a pimple against the Caledonian mountains. The Picts would scoff at such a structure."

Hadrian's eyes were sparkling, his demeanour pure exorbitance. "Limes Britannicus will be built of stone!"

"*Stone?*"

"A stone wall! It will start at the undulating Tynea valley, ascend the granite outcrop of the Whin Sill, gradually descend along the softer sandstone ridges, and down to the flatter land of the Ituna Aest crossing three rivers on its way. Nothing will perturb its route."

"Thorough surveying has been undertaken already…" Peterna was thinking aloud as he tried to catch up with the detail being passed to him, his mind picturing the route described. Hadrian was standing tall and proud, hands on hips and a broad smile widening his beard, allowing his legate time to absorb his plan.

"And it will be finished in plaster and white-washed, letting its shining surface reflect the sunlight and be visible for miles around, the power of Rome gleaming with it."

"Falco, it was Falco when he visited last year who did the survey, was it not?" The first signs of a smile crept to Peterna. "You have been planning this a while, Sir," his respect returning as he realised that he and his legion had not been forgotten at all, not left to moulder but influential in the emperor's most grandest of plans.

"Ocella has developed new arch and concrete techniques, still in their infancy, but proven techniques. We will build this wall as no other using his specialist skills, along with the Twentieth's expert stonemasons and engineers. The Twentieth Valeria Victrix Legion, Valiant and Victorious, will lead the work under Ocella's direction, starting with the construction of controlled crossing points, fortlets if you like, which are to be positioned at one mile intervals along the entire route. As the construction progresses, I plan to employ thousands of native labourers to do the digging and hewing, fetching and carrying. Further stonemasons, clerks, engineers, whoever, whatever is needed to support your legion, will be sent up from the Second Augusta and Sixth Victrix Legions. In but a few years we will have a majestic barrier across the width of Britannia, keeping the south safely within our rule, and a statement to the barren north that we will live alongside them. That is the beauty of the scheme, we may concede land to the Picts and their sparring northern tribes, but it will be in exchange for peace, and yet it will be Rome who will control their trade with the south, and Rome who will become rich on the revenue charged for passage through Limes Britannicus!" Hadrian was animated with enthusiasm, the effect passing to Peterna. "With peace, we can police the Empire effectively, without peace, the Glorious Empire will collapse. Although it is impossible for Rome to continue to expand her frontiers, she can dominate such out-regions by trade control. Ocella will be the chief architect and Platorius Nepos has been appointed to oversee the project. His term in Germania is ending in two moons and he is to replace Falco as Governor of Britannia." Hadrian ceased his animated speech, and raising his goblet, drank a toast to this magnificent plan.

Peterna studied the man before him, seeing his emperor with new respect. 'Greekling' the men called him for his intense love of the arts, yet he also possessed acuity of mind that out-stripped Peterna's own in forward visionary. Who would have thought it…a massive wall of stone rising along the Whin Sill ridge, gleaming in white, to rival the very mountains of the north? *Grandioso!*

"I see you approve of my vision Maxinius."

"Yes, Sir, I do."

"So I become a worthy successor to my uncle?" The smile had faded from Hadrian, replaced by an unblinking stare of stone that only Medusa could beat. "Lady Julita spoke of your wavering loyalty." Shards splintered into Peterna's chest and a cold heat swept to his face. So his wife had shared his confidences with her loose tongue. Hadrian's excited tone over the grand plan had lured the legate into thinking that no reprisals were coming regarding his obeisant written response to orders. But had Julita sealed his ruin instead?

An urgent knocking at the door interrupted them. The same young legionary who had woken the legate earlier that night, entered on command. Stamping to attention with an elaborate salute, the lad's eyes flicked nervously from his legate to his emperor. Peterna had no time for his nerves.

"Report!" he snapped.

"Decurion Gius Autemius requests your immediate presence in the courtyard, Sir!"

Chapter Twenty-Eight

Falco was forced to concede to Madam Ninaretta regarding travel plans for Ocella. The engineer was burning with a fever, his skin hot and dry, deep rose in colour. Madam Ninaretta was placing cooling swabs to his brow and watching with distaste as the blubber round his ample jowls trembled with the sickness.

"There must have been poison on the assassin's blade, Quintus. It is the only fathomable answer. His wound is clean. There must have been poison."

"It is feasible," growled Falco, whose mood had plunged to a grim depth.

"What other explanation can there be? It has to be poison."

"Poison, yes. But did it come from the assassin's dagger?" Ninaretta gave Falco a sharp look.

"I have personally monitored his food and drink, Quintus. Be careful with your accusations, your tongue is always barbed when you are cornered." She knew his moods well and was respectful of his sharp mind and a match for it. "Emperor Hadrian must wait as the gods decide. Ocella's fate lies with Apollo and the goddess Angitia. Do not flatter yourself to be their equals." Falco sneered at the rebuke but bit on the truth of the words. Ninaretta continued swabbing her patient, giving Falco time to reflect, hoping for an apology but not receiving one as Falco's anger strangled such a pleasantry. She let it go. "Please open the shutters Quintus. The fresh air may help Ocella. Until the next sunrise will be the critical period for him. If he is to pull through, he must break the fever by then. I will stay with him until he sweats or demises."

Falco stood beside the open shutters for a moment looking down on the alley, before ordering Brutus in from guarding the door in the corridor with Lucius, to guard the open window in the room.

"Kill anyone who attempts to enter this room other than those in our party. That includes maids, servants and slaves, as well as assassins! No indecision will be tolerated." The orders were terse and supported by a demeanour of granite. "Are my orders clear, Antonini?"

"Yes, Sir!" Brutus saluted to attention as he bellowed his response.

"Demise is not an option!" Falco stalked from the room without allowing an answer and Ninaretta's nostrils flared with repressed anger, which she released via a stream of colourful Celtic retorts, causing Brutus to stifle a smirk.

Falco burst in to Guintoli's room with no easier manner, to find him gritting the blade of his gladius to clean the steel to a shine. Wet and dry rags of soft hide lay ready to remove the fine layer of silt he was rubbing in. Kye was resting fully clothed on his bed and bolted upright at the intrusion, reaching automatically for his hunting knife in a single motion.

"Guintoli, you will ride to the northern frontier as quickly as possible." Falco did not waste time with preamble. It was not the day for it. His tension was obvious, revealed in part by the rapid tapping of his right index finger against the side of his thigh and further given away by the twitch in his lower jaw caused by the constant grinding of teeth between speaking, a habit in times of anxiety that he was not aware of. "You will report directly to Emperor Hadrian of the reason for our delay."

"Yes, Sir!"

"Teviot, are you willing to ride with Guintoli?"

"Yes, Sir!" Kye's maturity shone through again with this response. He was not sworn to the legions, so strictly speaking did not have to acknowledge Falco in this manner, but it would have been a foolish man who displayed a lack of respect under the circumstances, and getting Marcus to the north as quickly as possible suited him entirely.

"Make your preparations and report to me in fifteen minutes. Fresh horses will be ready for you. Guintoli, a word in private."

…......................

Marcus didn't care for the pull of destiny he was feeling as he and Kye travelled northwards. Both were immersed in their own thoughts with something gnawing at Marcus that wouldn't reveal itself. Silently repeating the message he was to deliver to Emperor Hadrian on arrival, he tossed its implications round in his head. *Priestess advises of recent Brigante informant in Iceni camp, Gius Autemius jeopardised.* The decurion was respected within the legion and known to be a close friend of the legate. Marcus pondered on why he in particular could be in danger and why was a Brigante informing to the Iceni? The tribes were quite a distance apart and not reported as bosom cousins. Kye had shrugged dismissively when Marcus had asked of any historic partnership between the two tribes, then looked questioningly in return, the response reminding Marcus of his oath of secrecy. The message was for Hadrian only, so he receded to the taciturnity of thought.

Several miles of riding and no conclusions later, he shook his head to clear his mind of the politics. Let the senior officers decipher the problems, he was not paid to do so. Yet a rodent continued to gnaw at the seed as if Marcus was responsible in some way for endangering the decurion.

Chapter Twenty-Nine

Hadrian kept hidden in the shadows of the courtyard as Peterna strode purposefully across to where Gius was listening intently to a woman who was holding the hand of a young lad, both natives and both looking frightened. What did this visit signify? The emperor had learned from his travels that it was often the small incidents that were the most portentous in consequence, and, unable to hear from his position, he watched keenly as decurion, legate and natives conversed. The woman was clearly distressed and he gleaned an urgency from the body stance and swift exchanges between his officers.   Peterna returned to Hadrian.

"What is the trouble?" enquired Hadrian.

"The woman's daughter is missing, Sir," replied Peterna. Hadrian raised an eyebrow inviting further explanation. "The family is known to us and it is out of character." The legate rubbed at his eyes and exhaled a puff of frustration, knowing he must expound the situation, and with time pressing there was nothing for it but to share only the bones. This was not going to assist his cause with the emperor. "The daughter's name is Jolinda Teviot and there is a high chance she is being held for interrogation by the Pict War Council. The girl has knowledge regarding our trumpet signals and it puts my plan in jeopardy. And at the eleventh hour!" Peterna slapped his thigh in annoyance, his temper splitting with the exasperation of it. "I will not allow the treachery of Arbeia to destroy the Twentieth Legion. The Pict infiltrators must be lured in and their threat expunged. We must find the Teviot girl before she comes to harm."

Hadrian was thinking of the effect this development may have on the wider picture. How would the tribes react to discovering that Rome was reduced to such acts of deceit in warfare? It was not the Roman way, honest superiority in battle tactics was Rome's fighting strength. If the legate's foolish plan was revealed, it would show weakness to the barbarians, and with interest from the Iceni and Votadini already sparking, it could prove to be the catalyst of an inferno.

"Maxinius, your plan has stirred a bigger nest of filthy asps than you know. An unsavoury business indeed! Do you know where the Teviot girl may be?"

"Gius has a lead, Sir! The local tavern keeper."

"Bring him in for questioning, I concur that the girl must be rescued." Hadrian turned away, his annoyance evident by his posture.

"Yes, Sir!" Peterna gave orders to the clerk who swiftly departed leaving the emperor and the legate alone. Squaring his shoulders to attention and breathing deeply, Peterna gave the forearm salute to Hadrian's back. "Sir, I was wrong to question your orders," he barked. "My actions were fed by ignorance which was not of my own doing, but borne of loyalty, nonetheless, I was wrong not to follow orders. May I know what fate you have decreed for me, Imperator?" Maintaining his salute, Peterna fixed his eyes on the Eagle Standard displayed on the wall above Hadrian's head and waited, his pulse fluttering alarmingly in his chest, but he must know his fate.

"'Life shrinks or expands in proportion to one's courage'. An interesting quote by Plautius, another being 'the ass rubs the ass'." Hadrian turned slowly to face his legate. Despite his self-discipline, Peterna's eyes flickered down to meet the emperor's, before quickly returning to the Eagle, silently imploring Hadrian to get to the point of the message. The uncertainty was abhorrent. He would meet his doom with strength once he knew what it was. "My lawyer Julianius Salvius has been appointed the task of listing all the current laws. A laborious assignment that will not be complete before Ludi Florales next year at the earliest, but an essential task that must be accurate if I am to reform the system which is at present dominated by laws made by the Senate and Assemblies during the Republic. Many in the Forum are opposed to any form of reconstitution to the Republican Laws, for the old ways die slowly, but as emperor I have the power to implement amendments and I intend to do so for the good of all Roman citizens. What are your thoughts on this subject Maxinius?"

Peterna was in no mood for a political discussion, but forcing his mind to focus, tried to grasp the relevance of the topic to his situation.

"Sir, it is your duty as emperor to ameliorate for the good of all citizens."

"So, your opinion is that I should reform the laws? Any in particular?"

Peterna was beginning to see the relevance, and the power bestowed upon this one man rocked him a little. Was Imperialism an improvement on the Republic? Should Rome be ruled so wholly by one mortal? Hadrian could save or bury him. Were the gods guiding the emperor or had Imperial Rome accorded such ascendancy to raise him beyond their touch? The hairs on his neck prickled uncomfortably as he wrestled with his conscience, his heart sinking horribly as he realised his reply would be curbed by self-preservation. Hadrian saw the realisation and nodded.

"Stand at ease, Legate," his tone was softer. "You know that under current law you are to be stripped of rank and honour for disobeying direct orders. Your family name will be disgraced in Rome and ruin awaits you, a bleak retirement indeed. I can see you are wresting with righteous honour or survival and feel aggrieved by your own weakness in hoping I will amend that particular law first." Peterna closed his eyes with the shame of the truth. "That you are not denying it, lends weight to your honesty and integrity Maxinius. We are all of us, puppets to the gods." Peterna met Hadrian's gaze. "Yes, Legate, I am too. For if I were not, I would pass legislation immediately to save you from ruin. You proved your loyalty to The Empire in Dacia and I trust in it still. I am willing to overlook your mistake of judgement. However, it takes far longer to instigate reform than it does to grind grain to flour, and the senate will enforce the law as it stands." Nausea clutched at Peterna's guts but he found his voice.

"Sir, I do not envy you the task of gaining support from the senate in reforming the legal system, nor comprehension from the people to whom change in the law is frightening. The gods indeed play their games with us by offering a hint of salvation just distant enough to be out of reach."

"Yet, the gods may let us dance with this. A slim chance prevails if we can keep your hearing out of the Forum until after Ludi Florales. I will work with Salvius to speed the process of the Reform." Peterna dropped to one knee in reverence, dipping his head, relief sweeping through him.

"I am honoured to have your support Imperator, and indebted to you beyond my life." Hadrian grunted.

"Your life is not yet secure, pray to your favourite god Maxinius. If we are successful, your debt is to your wife, for it was the earnest words of Lady Julita that weighted the scales in your favour." Solace wrapped Peterna at hearing Julita had not undone him, engulfing him so suddenly that tears threatened with the relief of it. He was grateful that his head was lowered as he mastered his emotions, a hot breeze seeming to gush noisily through his ears. All was not lost, there was hope.

………………………

A clatter of hooves on cobblestones announced their arrival and Peterna slapped his thigh with anticipation of action at last. Gius had taken longer to return than expected allowing doubt and worry to multiply its seeds. Abiding foul time is a known favourite worm hole of despair. Now the legate could influence the completion of the task, the doubts slipped away and his focus turned to the Celt. The Celt had been trickling trouble his way for far too long, he should have drawn his sword across the barbarian's throat instead of removing just his ear that day in the civilian township. No courtesy would be afforded him this time. The legate paced the corridor to the portico with purpose, his mind filling with black tortures that would make any mortal speak. His own guts were churning with revulsion, presentiment and eagerness, all driven by fear. He could not fail with this task, there was no margin to weaken. He and Gius would do this personally, the Celt must be broken quickly and the Teviot girl found forthwith.

With his thoughts preoccupied, he missed the clue that the horses in the courtyard were steaming with sweat from a long ride, much further than that of the civilian settlement. Nor did he register that neither man had his hands bound, as both were freely tending their mounts. Thus it came as a shock directly from Jupiter's thunderbolt to be looking in to the conker brown eyes of Marcus Guintoli.

Chapter Thirty

Hadrian was in the bathhouse, thus it was a segment third of the sundial more before Marcus updated him on Falco's delay due to Ocella's ill health and delivered his message from Falco to the emperor in private consultation. It was a mere minute or two after that when he was ordered to repeat the message in the presence of Peterna.

"Priestess advises of recent Brigante informant in Iceni camp, Gius Autemius jeopardised." Hadrian watched as Peterna absorbed this latest information, jostling it in with the brief outline of events Marcus and Kye had been able to give him before seeing Hadrian. Standing astride with arms folded in front of his body, Hadrian spoke decisively.

"The old client king of the Iceni is dead. His first born son, Trewak now heads this tribe. Legionary Guintoli is aware of his impetuosity." The legate's eyes darted to Marcus wondering what experience he had endured with the Iceni. "The combined intelligence provided to me from my eyes in the south and the north, leads me to believe the Iceni, led by Trewak, have travelled north on a mission which involves your decurion. Should he have returned from his sortie to rescue the girl yet Legate?" It was Marcus's eyes that darted to the legate's this time. *What girl?* The legate did not have to tell him, the gods shouted Jolinda and his pulse raced as his heart tried to hammer its way out of his chest. He again felt the gnawing rodent scuttle responsibility around him for Decurion Autemius's predicament, but he held his own counsel for lack of a coherent connection. A breathy gasp of ire rasped from Peterna.

"Acheron!" and he thumped his palm with his fist.

"That is answer enough," stated Hadrian.

"Decurion Autemius is true to Rome, Sir." Peterna was immediately defensive, thinking that Hadrian was seeing Gius as double-crossing and untrustworthy. "This news completes the frieze and explains his tardiness in returning. Gius is being held too. We must mount a search for him and the girl. It is my guess they are being held together and the Celt is still our link." Hadrian pursed his full lips in thought. "Sir, I would state my life on the decurion's loyalty." Hadrian raised his eyebrows at Peterna.

"That is not a high stake for knuckleball or tali at present Legate!" Marcus now wondered what fortune was against Legate Maxinius. Had the goddess of good luck deserted them all in the north?

"Then I state the life of Lady Julita on Gius's loyalty," Peterna added tenaciously, his gaze fixed on the emperor. Hadrian arched his left eyebrow in silent response. Playing with the life of a loved one in such a manner would not be spoken lightly.

"Who is your travelling companion Guintoli?" Hadrian enquired, the sudden question startling Marcus.

"Kye Teviot, Sir. He..."

"Teviot? Is he kin to the girl?" Hadrian interrupted sharply.

"Yes, Sir, brother and sister," confirmed Peterna.

"Then this is a divine sign and I will not ignore the augurs. Bring him in and send a runner to prepare horses and alert my Imperial Guards." Hadrian's decision was made, in truth, influenced more by Peterna's oath on his wife's life than on the augurs, but using the omens as key was easier on his conscience should the decision be wrong. "I will join you in the search for Autemius and the Teviot girl. Guintoli, the Chosen One, and the boy Teviot will assist. I cannot allow the muscle of the Iceni to be added to what you have started Maxinius or the rebellion will gain impetus beyond our resources. I *will* construct the Limes Britannicus and it *will* be built in stone! *No* savage will thwart my plan!"

....

A flurry of orders and preparation only afforded the legate a moment alone with Marcus before the rescue party was due to leave.

"Chosen One?" enquired Peterna. "Is that good fortune?"

"A curse by a hunchback, Sir, but not all ill-fortuned as the hunchback was the adopted son of a relative to the emperor, and the birth son of the Iceni Priestess who is kept in the secret pay of Rome." Marcus quickly showed Peterna the Dacian wooden block. "Trewak found it on me, and his intrigue led him to confer with his priestess, who recognised it as her son's marker, which in turn saved our lives and secured our release to Falco." Peterna wanted to hear the whole tale concerning the party's journey, to know what his beautiful wife and daughter had encountered and endured, but he pushed these thoughts away. For now, he must focus on the immediate challenge. "Sir..." Marcus hesitated.

"This is no time to be coy, Legionary. Speak what is on your mind."

"Sir, after departing this fort on our way to Petuaria, we engaged with three Iceni." Something unknown was still nettling at Marcus regarding Trewak's interest in the decurion. "We first saw them in the tavern at Vinovia. They tailed us from there and tried to rob us. Two warriors, one was wearing a gold arm torc, and a woman died in the skirmish. I cannot make a connection with Decurion Autemius's plight, but it is unusual to see Iceni this far north." The gold torc was a significant indication of high status within the tribe.

"Were there witnesses to the killings that may have reported to Trewak?"

"No Sir," although Marcus faltered as he answered, suddenly remembering the sound of hoof beats leaving the scene. *It wasn't the mare.* "There could have been a fourth member," Marcus corrected, "we only saw three in the tavern, and a fourth was not noticed at the scene, but I did hear fading hoof beats. Acheron! I heard a rider! It did not register with me until this moment, Sir." Why did the legate always succeed in finding more detail in Marcus's mind than he knew was there himself? It was as if the man's glacial blue eyes could pierce through the flesh and skull to the pulp behind and decode the secrets.

The question of 'who' rattled unanswered as the rescue party, headed by five Imperial Guards, followed by Emperor Hadrian, Legate Maxinius, Legionary Guintoli and Kye Teviot departed the fort turning east along the Stanegate.

Chapter Thirty-One

The bustle in the warehouse from the bartering of the hawkers and market goers, was loud and busy enough to conceal the short scuffle at Jolinda's stall to all except those in the immediate vicinity and they chose to ignore the plight of one woman being hefted away by two odious men, ugly in appearance and character. The men were known to be employed by the one-eared Celt who acted as a go-between for the landlord, so it was assumed this was a rent evading issue, although the trader in the neighbouring pen did notice that the following sweep of the evader's stock, normally taken swiftly as compensation for the unpaid rent, did not occur. He decided to close his trading for the day, surreptitiously pilfering some of the unguarded goods as he left.

Jolinda had worse to worry about. Gagged, blindfolded and bound at her wrists, with a heavy rope looped twice around her upper arms and torso, the assailants either side were forcing her along. It was terrifying running unsighted. Dry twigs were cracking underfoot and the panic of careering full in to a solid tree was difficult to control. Stumbling on the uneven ground, she would have fallen but for the rope around her pulled taut between the assailants to keep her from going down, yet bruising her arms as surely as the hard earth would. She wanted to fall, to stop the blind running, the terror of the unsighted flight was choking and she mewled in fear, the whimpers muffled by the chaffing gag.

The snapping of twigs underfoot ceased, their footfalls becoming hushed. A cross-wind caught at Jolinda's face, its sharp bluster indicating they were no longer running through a copse but on open land. The panic dropped a notch, the mewling reducing to gasps. The ground began to incline, steadily at first, then more steeply slowing their pace. Jolinda felt the familiar springiness of heather beneath her tread and knew they were ascending the purple-clad moorland that she had climbed so often as a child with Da in search of grouse. His presence on the moor was a comfort giving her small courage. She concentrated her efforts on listening and feeling to picture where she was.

The trio climbed in silence. A buzzard cried above them. The blind terror of the run through the trees was now replaced with reasoned fear. Where was she being hauled and why? She knew her captors worked for the one-eared Celt but nothing more. The terms of the rent for the warehouse had been met, so what explanation was there for this treatment? No answer was forthcoming, just a tenebrous foreboding that hammered at her heart. *Marcus, where are you when I need you my Roman?*

The walking got harder as the heather thickened, narrowing the path and Jolinda couldn't see to place her steps, thus the wiry network of stems were frequently snagging on her skirt and tripping her footing. It started to rain.

"Come here!" One of the men growled and Jolinda felt rough fingers pulling at the blindfold. The broken sacking was ripped away, flooding daylight causing her to blink in pain at the sudden exposure, although the discomfort would have been much worse on a brighter day. "Now let's move faster before the weather closes in."

Wending round to the leeward side of the tor, they descended and rose and descended again before stopping in an area of loose boulders, split away from the rocky outcrop above by frost action over the decades. The junction of a cross-path lay ahead, and the brook that busied its way down the valley beside them, was teasing with its clear waters. The gag had drawn all moisture from Jolinda's mouth and she longed for a drink to ease her parched throat. It continued to rain but the clouds didn't drop in to the valley, clinging instead to the peaks.

"Put her blindfold back on." Jolinda's stomach lurched, but bound she was helpless to defend against the burly men and so was plunged back to darkness.

Horsemen arrived, sounding like a whole army in number in Jolinda's sightless world. She could hear the animals snorting and stamping the ground and some hawking and coughing of men, but no person spoke in the exchange she could sense was happening. Her heart beat quickened as a rider came to stop in front of her, silent but omnipresent, bringing spirits from the Afterworld to shiver along her spine. An intense moment passed before a second rider joined the first, dismounting fluidly, with something in his deportment announcing leadership.

Trewak immediately removed the gag from Jolinda's mouth and gently offered his water skin to her dry lips, speaking quietly as he did so. "They would not bind a beast as thus. I am sorry for their poor manners and your discomfort. Come, we must ride." Guiding her by the elbow, he led her to his horse, lifted her on and swiftly mounted behind her. "Hold on to the mane. I will not let you fall." His accent was southern.

"The blindfold..." Jolinda hoped.

"It must stay for now." Trewak spoke softly in to her hair, providing no explanation and Jolinda didn't ask further, the unease ebbing with this stranger's calm authority, the small kindness of the drink a seed that swelled rapidly in such arcane circumstances. With strong arms encircling her as Trewak took up the reins, Jolinda leant in to his body, soaking up the security it proffered, riding as one on the horse. If she could have seen the body, contused and beaten, tied across the rump of a horse to the rear, she would undoubtedly feel differently.

The pass between the peaks became rockier with altitude, but the incline was steady and the horses made good progress, slowing a little when Trewak led them along a spur away from the main track. This less defined path veered round to the west and soon the group was hidden from view by a small ridge within the main valley. A series of caves presented themselves, giving rise to a satisfied grunt from the Iceni king, acknowledging the accuracy of his priestess's vision. Lifting Jolinda from the horse he carried her to the second cave, explaining in his soft lilt that her blindfold would soon be removed.

"Why am I here?" she asked. "Will ya untie me?" The questions went unanswered as Trewak stooped to enter the cave, the air colder inside from dampness seeping down the stone. The cave was tunnel-like, reasonably wide and elongated so that its end wall was not immediately evident to eyes unaccustomed to the dark, but low ceilinged so that a man must remain bent. Placing Jolinda to the floor he gave orders for his goatskin to be brought from his pack and a fire to be made.

"Do not try to stand, the shelter is low. The blindfold will be removed soon." A pause was interrupted by a deep cry of pain from outside, followed by a guttural curse, silenced by a thud. Jolinda held her breath, listening, trying to make sense of the sounds, her fear rising once more. Had the curse been uttered in Latin? She wasn't certain.

"The blindfold...please..."she implored, struggling in vain to free her wrists. Hearing him leave she cried after him, panic turning to heaving sobs. Someone knelt in silence before her and she experienced the Afterworld spirit-shiver once more. Shards of hatred bore through the blackness that muted her crying by stealing her breath. Recoiling from the enmity, she hunched as if in a shell and shivered. The person left and others entered, men grunted and wood scraped over stone. A fire was lit, the dry moss flaring, kindling crackling, a man hawked phlegm, thus it was a surprise when a woman spoke.

"It may be a kindness not to see."

"No, no...please," her voice was a shaky whisper, she tried more forcefully, "...please, I must see! Please!"

"A friend of yours is here who did not co-operate with my Lord."

"You are a priestess?" The term 'Lord' was interpretive.

"Yes, priestess to Trewak, client king of the Iceni with whom you were upon the horse, and Priestess to his father before him, a gentler man than his son."

"Please, the blindfold Priestess. I would see my friend." A poignant stillness was punctuated with a groan from within the cave.

"Turn from the flames." The priestess first untied the binding around Jolinda's wrists, "you will not fight when you see," and then removed the sacking from her face. The freedom from restraint was exalting, a short-lived elation that disintegrated as her eyes adjusted to the flickering light from the fire. The wood being dragged over stone was a cage, barely large enough to hold the Roman soldier cramped and bloodied inside. The priestess positioned herself between the fire and the cave opening, Jolinda crawled over to the cage.

"Sweet Bridestone! Gius?" The decurion's great frame was curled with knees bent up to his chin, his arms tucked underneath, head forced down against the sapling cross-slats. Clearly beaten senseless, he rallied a little on hearing his name. Jolinda spoke to him urgently, aghast, "Gius? Can ya hear me? It's Jolinda Teviot." She was rewarded by a grunt, but Gius had obviously been drugged and was incapable of conversation. Looking swiftly over the cage, she could see it was built solidly and secured fast, the type they used to trap wolves. Gius twisted his face towards Jolinda who winced at the battered features, his head rolling away again, propped from falling only because the cage was so small. "Ya've always been in a fight when I see ya, Gius," she reprimanded softly, reaching her fingers gently to the cage side, wanting to comfort him with her touch through the gaps but fearful of causing more pain. A shadow came over the entrance as two Iceni warriors stooped to inspect the captives. The priestess began a meditation chant. "Why have they done this to ya, why?" cried Jolinda, unbidden tears welling and spilling over as she blinked. "How can I help ya?"

"Tell my Lord what he needs to know and your Roman friend will be spared further punishment." Jolinda jumped. The priestess had ceased chanting and slipped further in to the cave closer to Jolinda and the cage. Gius grunted unintelligibly once more. "He is brave to his cause and would die mute, but you will tell my Lord what you know, just as soon as you hear the decurion scream, you will talk."

"Is that why I'm here?" The priestess nodded. "What could I possibly know that is so important to bring the Iceni king to our borders?"

"The trumpet signals for the Roman fort. My Lord has learned that your decurion friend is feeding false information to the Pict War Council. He would have the Council believe he is open to bribery, but my Lord has been told otherwise by a vehement source." Gius mumbled incoherently. "The effect of the herbs will lessen with time. Be grateful for him whilst they are strong in his blood." Jolinda was acutely aware that the priestess was right, she would not be able to listen to Gius being tortured, Trewak would be told everything she knew, and although she didn't fully understand the intricacies of the implications, it was clearly vital to bring this new client king so far north. It could not be good for the fort and reprisals for the local Brigantes was inevitable. Would there never be peace in her land? Her life was inextricably entwined with Britannia and Rome, nobody would win unless everybody could win, and, disloyal as it made her feel for the old lore was deeply instilled, she felt the Romans came closest to really wanting a peaceful existence. Men such as the legate and Gius Autemius, and Marcus and Brutus too, were searching within the framework of campaigns to bring an end to fighting albeit through subjugation, but as a Brigante she knew well enough that her people would be content with letting the Romans think they had total control, the old ways would permeate quietly through and never be lost, even under the rule of Rome.

Trewak however, and here she fluttered with confusion for he had been kind to her and she'd felt his softness and wanted to believe in him, was, it seemed, dangerous like the Picts and Votadini. Bloodshed and skirmish charged the veins of these tribal leaders and without invaders to repel, they would surely continue the ancestral feuding. Animosity was their standard, peace their enemy. It therefore weighed heavily upon her that Trewak would gain an advantage over the Romans through her evidence. Dropping her head to clasped hands, kneeling, she rocked gently, humbly citing prayers, searching for divine influence from both Roman and Brigante gods, prepared in her bleakest moment to put faith in them all, for what else could she do?

" I have met those you pray for, Marcus Guintoli and Brutus Antonini," interrupted the priestess, a secret urgency in her tone. Jolinda looked at her in astonishment. Jolinda's attachment to Marcus added a different slant on matters as far as the priestess was concerned. Links to her son's 'Chosen One' were not to be ignored. The girl could be more precious than first realised.

"Oh, is he well? Where is..."

"Keep your voice low," hissed the priestess, "the warriors outside must not hear us speak of this. He was sent to Aquae Sulis in the south with Governor Falco, but my son believes the destiny of Guintoli lies here at the northern frontier. He will return to fulfil this destiny." The shadow from the guarding warriors passed over the cave again. One knelt at the entrance and shouted in.

"Captives givin' you any trouble Priestess?"

"No trouble, but bring a little water, I wish to wilt a further mix of herbs." To Jolinda she whispered, "would you trust a priestess of the Iceni?" The eyes of the bodacious priestess locked unblinking with Jolinda's, reflecting the tiny flames from the camp-fire. Jolinda felt this formidable woman's force. "My loyalties may not lie where you first think." The connection between the two women was broken by the return of the warrior who crouched at the cave access, once more cutting out the light. The priestess moved to collect the skin of water he offered, ending the conversation with Jolinda by re-starting the earlier chanting as she prepared some herbs.

Jolinda closed her eyes to think, resting her arms and forehead against the cage. *Marcus was still in Britannia. What of Kye? Was he travelling to Gaul and beyond in vain? The priestess, which side of the battle did her banner fall on?* It was to be a long day and night waiting for answers.

Chapter Thirty-Two

The circle of hewn oak stumps positioned on the gentle south-facing slope high above Swine Lake was of special significance to all the tribes north of the Tinea Fluvius. Following the united uprising against the northern campaign surge by Agricola led by Calgacus, Chieftain of the then Caledonian Confederacy, each tribe had carved their insignia in to an oak bough and ceremoniously added it to the heather-free clearing, knocking the sturdy stumps well in to the ground to provide longevity to the structure. The hard oak wood had stood up to the harsh weather well over the four decades, albeit lichen was covering the carvings on the northern side of each post.

The meeting within the wooden circle consisted of two Elders from the Pict War Council, two from the Votadini tribe, plus Trewak and his cousin representing the Iceni. Several warriors from each clan, including Trewak's nine, were congregated a distance away outside the ring, sharing stories amicably as their horses grazed. One girl, sulking that she was excluded from the inner circle, was sitting alone from the group.

The ground was damp from the morning's rain, but the clouds had broken and the late afternoon sun was casting long shadows across the slope as it fell upon the circle.

"I bring you news that my father has died," Trewak addressed the meeting. Formal introductions had been made in traditional manner and courtesy dictated that he now explain his visit and reason for requesting the meeting. "And with his death goes the subservience that we, the proud Iceni, have displayed to Rome. I cannot be the client king he was." The statement was bold and direct and Trewak looked for reactions from the Elders around him, but the old men had played these games before and their creased faces remained passive, concealing their thoughts. A smoking pipe was passed around the circle. "I've heard you're planning a raid on the forts following a successful..." he paused, looking for the right word "...infiltration of the Roman supply base at Arbeia."

"What have you heard?" enquired an Elder.

"That you've intelligence of the Roman trumpet signals from a bribed link inside the Twentieth Legion, a decurion." The Elders neither confirmed nor refuted this allegation and Trewak continued, eager to strip the flesh from the bone. "Thus, you know when the fort is most vulnerable and have the bonus of a high ranking Roman on the inside. It's the largest jewel-stone in the torc to have such a Roman from a legionary fort under your pay." Smiling wickedly, he tapped the torc on his arm before accepting the pipe and inhaling lightly. Trewak wanted to keep a clear head.

"You have travelled far to meet us, High Chief Trewak of the Iceni," replied an Elder of the Votadini, using the formal archaic title afforded to a tribal leader of the isles. "Are you looking to join with us in our venture? It is one of stealth, not of loud glory, and I wonder if this rubs against your grain?"

"It does, Lord of the Votadini. I prefer a battle triumph and in that I would lead you." A subtle frostiness fell over the group and Trewak allowed a silence to draw out.

"Your manner is direct," growled the Pict Elder, "and your tone suggests you consider our method a lowly one?" It rubbed at the grist to have a young, upstart bluntly goading them, knowing also that many of the younger Picts, his own grandsons included, would agree with this sentiment. The Pict War Council had encountered much protest at their plans, only properly gaining support on the successful razing of Arbeia. Walking over to the oak trunk carved with the Pict emblem, he stood with his back to the others in the circle for a moment, contemplating the uprising of his youth, a battle he had fought in and survived, whilst his father, cousins and kith had died. "A wise man learns from history," he spoke quietly, his resolve strengthening as he moved around the stumps looking at all the tribes involved in maintaining their independence, remembering the bloodshed, bloody imprints on his memory. "The result will be our glory in time. We sting and retreat, irritate and undermine, harass and the Roman resolve will crumble from within. To find a corrupt decurion is indeed a treasure and can only be a sign of the degeneration that is beginning. And all this achieved without massed battle, without losing another generation of fine, strong warriors. The glory may not be recognised during our remaining life, but the generations to come will acknowledge the cunning that swelled their families by avoiding conflict and they will be ardent to our spirits. The bards will sing of how the Pict War Council, allied with the Votadini, kept their lands free and their people alive." The old man proudly removed his woollen drape and goat-skin tunic to stand bare-chested, revealing both tribal tattoos and scars across his whole torso. "Will you join with us, High Chief Trewak of the Iceni, in becoming a greater man than a jejune leader of warriors?"

"You speak persuasively venerable Lord of the Picts, but your wisdom is not absolute. Is knowledge of the Roman trumpet signals vital to your plan?"

"It is key, if we don't wish to sacrifice our warriors."

"And the decurion is essential too?" Concern flickered across the hoary Pict's eyes, which although old in years, displayed a youthful clarity and held Trewak's steadily awaiting the blow he could feel was coming. "As I thought...then you need to be told that the decurion is a loyal puppet of the legate and has played you all for fools!"

It took some time for Trewak to persuade the Pict War Council and the Votadini that he was speaking the truth, and the weakening sun just dipped below the ridge across the valley from Swine Hill, bringing dusk to the circle as Trewak's cousin led the girl back to the mixture of tribal warriors. Her flowing, silver tinted black hair caught in the breeze, blowing across her face that was no longer sulking, but shining with intrigue and self-importance at being heard in the circle. It had been her oratory, piecing so much together that it could not be a ruse, that had finally convinced the Elders that Gius Autemius was not open to bribery. The old men had questioned her evidence, cross-examined her with shrewd knowledge of their own and debated her answers both logically and heatedly, sometimes intimidating, other times almost with gentleness, using all their guile to bore through to the truth.

"I have a personal reason to inflict pain on the Twentieth Legion," began Trewak, "following the incident at Vinovia that my girl spoke of..."

"Where the Legionary from the Twentieth let slip loose words to the serving wench?" interrupted the Votadini chief?

"Yes, a casual remark of the decurion's great debt of patronage to the legate, meaningless without the later verses to the song. The serving wench belonged to my younger brother, both were slaughtered as they slept along with a cousin," Trewak acknowledged the cousin beside him whose brother had also died in the skirmish at the idyll, although the story was being told differently. "Murdered for the treasure they carried, by a small group of Romans, too cowardly away from their legion to allow their quarry to face them. The girl heard and saw it all, the murders at Vinovia as well as the ruse played out by the decurion before your man, the one-eared Celt. The girl had been treated with kindness by my brother when she was at a low ebb, knowing him to be Iceni, she sought out his tribe to tell us of his story. The spirits of justice surely guided her to me, for it was a perilous journey for a lone maiden." Trewak paused, staring away from his listeners as if reflecting on an inner pain, quickly resuming in a brusque manner giving his full attention again. "It grows dark and we have much to do. We, the Iceni, propose to lead you in destroying the fort the Roman's call Vercovicium."

"Alas, you're eluded if you think it can be done without help from within and without knowing when the fort is at its emptiest."

"My priestess will have that knowledge before the sun rises."

"Your priestess has travelled to the north with you?" There was surprise in the Votadini's voice. "Then courtesy dictates we offer you accommodation at our dun." Trewak declined, the prickliness between the tribes evident.

"Lords, we will celebrate with you in your duns before we return south, but for now we would prefer privacy with our captives."

"Captives, who is it you hold, King Trewak?"

"Your key and my own."

"You hold the decurion?" The Pict Elder hawked spittle to the grass, losing patience with the young, blue-tattooed warrior. "You've proved his word is not worthy, what use is he?"

"As bait, my Lord. There is a woman, a Brigante who has spent time at the fort, befriended by the family of the legate and Gius Autemius. She has knowledge of the trumpet signals you so desire and my priestess will get the truth from her for she will not be able to watch the decurion suffer." There was a rumble of murmuring from the Elders and Trewak felt the smug warmth of knowing he was sitting on the highest pillar. He excused himself and his cousin from the circle, diplomatically allowing the Elders an opportunity to talk. The Pict War Council and the Votadini quickly reached a decision, for this fresh intelligence resurrected their plans, and they were prepared to accede to Trewak rather than allow this chance to slip away.

"We are excited by your news, High Chief of the Iceni and invite you to lead with us. The omens are favourable for success." Trewak smiled broadly, shaking the hand of each Elder.

"What omens do you purport, my Lords?"

"The highest, a chance spotting of a hunchback meeting with a small party of Romans, passing northwards through the Votadini lands." This was the finest omen, for the bards in every tribe in Britannia sing of the ill luck which follows those who meet with hunchbacks. "This same party was seen entering the Vercovicium fort." An icy prickle threaded suddenly through Trewak's blood, the feverish words of his dying father shadowing the ice. *Priestess...hunchback son...Hadrian.* Did his priestess have a dark secret? It was a barb that stabbed at him which he tried to ignore. The bodacious Iceni Priestess, formidable in appearance and spirit, had been influential in his upbringing and he desperately wanted to believe in her, yet the barb was festering deeper and the next words of the Votadini Lord buried the thorn fully in his flesh. "There was a high-ranking Roman officer amongst this strange little party who spoke to the hunchback. Not in uniform, but obvious by his deportment. Perhaps your captives can tell us who he is and why he visits?" The suspicions Trewak wanted to ignore slammed at him like a fist of iron clad knuckles, and suddenly he was eager to return to the caves.

Chapter Thirty-Three

Searching out the one-eared Celt had been a simple task. The fool had been drinking heavily in the tavern, fuddled both by ale and the joy of the treasure received from the Iceni as reward for his work. He disliked the Teviot girl anyway, and hatred for the decurion was flowing like lava from an active volcano now he knew of the ruse against him.

Marcus and two of the Imperial Guards had no difficulty in extracting the drunken Celt from the tavern. He came noisily but willingly, not properly aware in his inebriation and those around him were unprepared to intervene with the steely soldiers. Had the two hoodlums working for him held their nerve and remained at their bench, the Roman party would not yet be riding hard towards the cross-paths near Swine Hill. Instead, the two who abducted Jolinda from her trading stall, had bolted for the back alley straight in to the sword point of Roman royalty and it had not taken much to wring the information of her whereabouts from them.

Kye jumped from his horse to inspect the tracks at the cross-paths. The trails were muddied in the damp ground, traffic having passed recently thus obscuring some detail from a couple of days ago, but it remained clear that a sizeable group had taken the northern path towards the temple on Swine Hill. He led the Romans on, anxious that time was not on their side, driven by angry fear for his sister's safety. The path became rockier and Kye dismounted again when they reached a spur veering round to the west. The trail was less obvious but still visible.

"This path leads round to caves," Kye told the legate.

"Habitable?"

"Yes, Sir."

"How far are they from here?"

"Twenty minutes, we can only walk the horses on this path."

"Can they be accessed from any other route?" demanded Hadrian.

"Not easily, Sir. The caves can be approached from the north but only on foot as the crag needs to be scaled and it is a fair distance to detour round from here."

"What do you suggest Legate?" asked Hadrian.

"There is not time to detour. Our approach must be direct. How many do you estimate in their party, Teviot?"

"A score, no more Sir." Maxinius nodded his agreement. The odds of nine against twenty were reasonable, although the legate flinched at including the emperor in such a rash situation.

"Maxinius, you are an open tablet," muttered Hadrian, "and you insult me with your indecision to engage because I am present. We will move better on foot from here."

"Sir, let me lead," said Kye. "I know this path well. It twists 'n' turns with barely any shrubs for company 'til ya reach a clutch of blackthorn. The caves are just a hop from then. If we ain't been seen by that point, I could recce alone. Ya'll be close enough to pounce if needed and they may just parley with me as I ain't a Roman." It was a hatched plan, yet the best they had. The legate nodded, decision made.

"Guintoli will recce with you. Humph!..out of uniform, he too looks barbaric!" Marcus took the snub as it was intended, a morsel of humour injected to diffuse the tension, albeit slight.

Marcus and Kye made their way round the corner, leaving the rest of the Roman party hiding beside the cluster of blackthorn shrubs. He felt vulnerable, naked, without the familiar bump of his gladius against his leg. The short sword was the trademark of a Roman Legionary no matter how native they otherwise looked, and Marcus had reluctantly left it with the legate, strapping one of Kye's hunting knives to his thigh instead. His hand dropped to touch the blade's handle as the caves came in to view, adrenalin sharpening every sense. His heart was hammering at his ribs. *Jolinda, are you here?*

The area seemed empty and sharing an exchange, Marcus gave a small nod of acknowledgement to Kye knowing instinctively his plan. A stealthy approach was futile, better to announce their arrival and attempt to explain their presence as innocent.

"Anyone at 'ome?" Kye called out, his Brigante accent deliberately heavy. Silence. "We're lookin' fa shelter." A ptarmigan squawked making them both jump.

"Acheron!" hissed Marcus unsheathing his knife. The bird took flight in its cumbersome manner. "The place is deserted, it's unnaturally quiet somehow." He kept his voice low, frowning as he tried to pinpoint his unease. In truth, it was no more peaceful than would be expected in the absence of people, it simply appeared that way as Marcus had been hoping, far more than he realised, that they would find Gius and Jolinda here with the Iceni. He was ready for the confrontation, only able to begin dealing with the situation when they knew properly what it was!

"Someone's been here recently," said Kye, "and they haven't tried to hide the fact." He pointed at the ash of a deadened camp fire which had been diligently kicked out but not dispersed or covered. Marcus indicated they should check the first cave with a nod of his head in that direction. Satisfied nobody was inside, they moved swiftly to the next. With their initial search confirming the area was empty as they'd sensed, Marcus whistled for the others to join them, before returning to inspect the caves in more detail.

It was Kye who found dried blood on the floor of the second cave and Marcus who spotted the charcoaled sketches on the wall nearby, but it was Hadrian who understood their message. Etched on to the wall were three schematic drawings. Hadrian studied them for a moment.

"Gius and the Brigante girl have escaped with the Iceni Priestess. Where would they go?" Hadrian demanded, re-studying the drawings. The legate hurried over to look. "See here, Maxinius, your decurion's insignia and the symbol of the Brigante goddess, Bridget."

"And what is this one, Sir?" asked Peterna, pointing at a third sketch, runic and indecipherable to him on first glance. Hadrian tapped his finger below the third sketch.

"That is the picture that tells me the message is from the Iceni Priestess and that she is aiding their escape." The legate looked again.

"The hunchback son," he muttered as he made sense of the scrawls.

"Where would they go?" repeated Hadrian. "The priestess does not know these northern lands and she would not risk the Teviot homestead nor be fool enough to head directly to the fort. Guintoli, do you know of somewhere that is special to the girl?" Marcus could think only of the bridestones but they were for worship and would not provide hiding cover. Hadrian ducked out of the cave to find Kye. "Teviot, where would your sister hide?" snapped Hadrian, his patience as thin as spider's silk knowing time was short. "A family known area perhaps?"

"There is a place," said Kye slowly, thinking as he spoke. "Yes, 'tis the most likely place Jolinda would go. A shepherd's hut, our Da used to take us there, it's kinda special to the Teviots."

"Do many know of the whereabouts of this shepherd's hut?" enquired Hadrian.

"Some locals know of it, but 'tis tucked away from any trading routes. Yes..." Kye repeated emphatically, slapping his thigh with confidence, "...'tis where she would go, a three hour walk from here, it won't take us long on horseback."

"Any better ideas Legate? Guintoli?" Both men shook their head. "Then we gamble on this hut. Let us make haste. It would seem likely that the Brigante informant the priestess warned me of in her original message travels with Trewak, thus it worries me that they too will guess of this hut as a hiding place." Kye looked sharply at Marcus and everything fell in to place for both at the same time and Marcus heard the roar of the *Geryon*.

"The hoof beats at the idle," said Marcus.

"Tamsin..." whispered Kye. "She will remember the hut for certain. Sir, the only way to it is via a coombe. Strategically it's a terrible place to hide."

Chapter Thirty-Four

As soon as Trewak reached the spur that led round to the caves, he knew his fears were grounded. No horses, no out-guard. The scene awaiting him at the caves was similar to the aftermath of a drunken victory celebration and his eyes looked upon his sleeping warriors with steel.

"Drugged by the priestess," he rasped, his voice as bitter as the herbs used to outwit him. Seeing the cage, its door open, he dismounted and bent to study it, dropping silently to one knee as he processed the possible scenarios of the escape. Kicking the cage angrily, he stamped it in to pieces. "Burn that and brew some tansy from my pack, make it strong and force it down these men! We have a fort to infiltrate! Cousin, with me," and moving away from the group, Trewak squatted on his haunches and silently brooded. His cousin hunkered down with him and was sensible enough to wait for Trewak to speak first.

"We can't do it without the decurion and the girl." Trewak was in the blackest mood and the veins at his temples stood out throbbing viciously. A raven-black beetle had the misfortune of scuttling across the ground in front of where he was squatting. Trewak watched the creature's valiant effort to scale a fallen twig, letting it struggle before picking it up and calculatedly pulling the hard casing slowly away from the fleshy pulp below. If the creature could scream, the noise would have been ear-splitting. The act did nothing to alleviate Trewak's ire. Aware that he should probably explain his priestess's betrayal to his cousin, the words wouldn't form, stuck fast by the perfidy. The effect was as sharp as the physical pain from a score of hammered nails to his chest, yet the betrayal could not be removed as easily to give relief. He was angry with himself for failing to acknowledge the suspicions he'd harboured earlier, he just hadn't wanted to believe them of his beloved priestess. *Fool!* Yet hindsight gave the waters clarity. "Bring the Brigante informant to me," demanded Trewak, "I will speak with her."

Tamsin was nervous of Trewak's seething anger. Although not responsible for her sister's escape, she was shouldering the blame for the blood ties.

"Where would your sister go to hide?" demanded Trewak.

"I...I don't know," faltered Tamsin, shrugging and frowning. She was afraid.

"Surely the priestess would take them directly to the fort to seek Roman protection and warn them of the imminent attack," remarked the cousin.

"No," the reply from Trewak was terse and definite. "She would not do the obvious." A shout came from the caves, the charcoal etchings had been found and Trewak left Tamsin thinking whilst he inspected the drawings.

"Where would she hide?" he hissed when he returned. The hunchback meeting with an important Roman champing at his thoughts. Who was his priestess connected to?

"I know of a place, a shepherd's hut," Tamsin said shakily. She was remembering happy summer visits just as Kye had, but the family loyalty was buried, masked by memories of the baby she had miscarried, and the soured sequence of events that had destroyed her plans. She would see her sister dead and weep tears of joy at the sight. Her own future lay now in aiding the Iceni king to success. "I can guide ya to it, my Lord," she said more boldly.

"How far is this hut?" Trewak glowered.

"Three hours on foot, my Lord."

"In which direction? Towards the fort?"

"Away, to the north, Lord Trewak. We pass through the forest that lies west of Swine Lake, there are many paths through the forest, but they all lead to a confluence of two rivers." Tamsin was gaining in confidence as she recalled the way to the hut. "From here, there is only one route to the hut. It follows the River Teviot," she said proudly, "and it passes through a long, narrow coombe." Trewak's eyes flashed with understanding.

"How far to where these rivers meet?" he demanded.

"Two hours plus a half more to reach the rivers, Lord."

"We'll do it in two," he growled. "Rally those men able to yomp," he ordered to his cousin. "Leave any still incapable, we cannot afford to move slowly. Our priestess has slipped up, she possesses many skills but the tactics of warfare are not among them, and not a strength of the Brigante girl either it seems. If we can reach the river crossing before they leave the coombe, we have them trapped." His raw anger was converting to an excited revenge, fuelled further by his deductions that the cave etchings were a message to the priestess's Roman connection. "And I believe, Cousin, that our quarry will be of the greatest bounty. The usefulness of the decurion and Brigante girl may be supplanted, either way, sabotage of the fort will continue."

Chapter Thirty-Five

It was a relief to reach the hut and a bonus to find it lightly stocked with grain, some dried meat strips and firewood. For the second time that day, Jolinda thanked the goddess Bridget for the formidable size, and strength, of the priestess. Gius was a big man and hefting him from cage to horse, then horse to hut would not have been possible with a slighter woman helping her.

Still sedated with herbs, moving Gius was like heaving two dead goats together. They laid him on the rush matting on the far side of the central hearth.

"How long before he wakens?" asked Jolinda.

"It is hard to predict. The herbs vary, but he mends as he sleeps."

"I'll fetch water 'n' tether the horses."

"Tie them close, they will warn us when we have company." Jolinda frowned at the comment.

"Ya say it as if ya expecting someone." The priestess didn't look up from the stones she was arranging in a small circle on the dirt floor before her, but began to explain her connection to Rome. "Hadrian? The emperor of Rome? " interrupted Jolinda. "I've seen his face on the Roman coins. He's here in Britannia?"

"Yes, and he will find us."

"How? How does he even know ya in the north to be found, let alone that we're in this hut?"

"I left etchings. He will know, and your brother will guide him to us here."

"Kye is with Hadrian?" Incredulity was creating a pipe to Jolinda's voice.

"And Marcus Guintoli, if my hunchback son has done his job well." Jolinda's pulse skipped, faltering her thoughts and she stared dumbly at the priestess. "I have good news for him when he arrives." Jolinda could only shrug her shoulders in puzzlement. A kind smile teased at the corners of the priestess's mouth. "His vow to the Roman gods can be revoked. I have studied the lore, Breton and Roman, and a hunchback has a powerful connection between mortal and immortal." Gius groaned in his slumber, breaking Jolinda from her inertia. A little breath of surprised happiness escaped from Jolinda.

"Oh, Priestess…there is hope." The priestess gave a small nod before waving Jolinda to the door.

"Tether the horses close." Now was not the time to cloud the hope by revealing the news that Tamsin travelled with Trewak, and with hate and revenge as partners too. It was a concern that the Iceni party could reach them at the hut first, for the priestess felt sure the Brigante sister would guess their hideout as well. It was a race she could not influence the outcome of, so she turned her attention to her herb pouch instead.

Every time one of the horses whickered, Jolinda jumped. As the evening shadows lengthened, so the wind picked up, and Jolinda clenched her fist each time in reaction to the dull scraping noise the leather drape made across the dirt floor as the breeze sneaked in beneath it. Waiting and listening, waiting, jumping, listening. It was a strain on her nerves. Thus it was a welcome distraction when Gius mumbled his first words on release from the priestess's herbal potion. Speaking to him softly, gently bathing his battered face, she explained where they were, filling in the detail following his confinement as best she knew.

"The legate will come for us. The priestess says Hadrian is with him. Can ya believe it?" Jolinda was talking for talking's sake, crooning to soothe her patient. "Tis a pity ya ain't looking ya best for ya emperor, Gius Autemius," she chided in mock rebuke, wiping the spittle that leaked from the edge of his mouth. It was a worrying sign and Jolinda fretted that his mind was no longer sound. Gius drifted back in to sleep and with the dregs of the daylight gone, there was nothing for Jolinda and the priestess to do other than listen and wait. Inevitably, Jolinda too succumbed to sleep, exhausted by events. It was the priestess who heard the horses' warning.

Stamping agitated hooves to the turf, they whinnied once before being quieted. The disturbance was short and neither Jolinda nor Gius stirred. Sitting cross-legged with her back rod straight, the priestess's ample stature held poise in the soft light. If Trewak came through the drape, she would swallow the paste made from the smooth black fruits of the wolfberry plant that had been prepared within the circle of stones. The poison would act quickly in this pulp form. Having watched the writhing agonies in others, she knew the muscle cramps and pains would be excruciating, but it would be a short and merciful death and far superior to the life Trewak would now give her. The cowards way out she mused, and selfish, for there was enough only for herself.

For all her meditation techniques practised as an Iceni Priestess, the wait to discover who had arrived was testing, whoever was outside was taking longer to enter than expected. Her palms sweated around the small glass vial of liquid death held close to her lips. For all her strengths, she feared the unknown journey to the Afterworld. Ignoring a rodent scratching in the low thatch that roofed the hut to the ground, loneliness swept through her as she stared intently towards the drape.

Jolinda woke shouting a scream, not a piercing scream, a low yell of alarm followed by fearful gasps as she scrambled backwards on hands, feet and bottom away from the shapes of men appearing at the hole in the side of the hut. All was noise and confusion. The priestess too lost her composure by the unexpected direction of the attack, the surprise jerking her shaking hands causing the contents of the vial to splash against her lips and spill down her chin. She paled on recognising Hadrian. Jolinda whimpered with relief as Kye stood tall and proud at the hole in the thatch, a grin cracking light to the dark.

"Sorry to surprise ya like that Sis! I remembered Da had to fix a section of the roof one year, 'nd he made a panel of thatch 'cause it were easier than patching the damage with separate stalks, then added a handle 'cause it were easier to move that way. Took me a minute to find it, but I didn't want to come in via the door in case ya mistook me for an unfriendly." Kye was across the hut and hugging Jolinda who buried her face in his shoulder.

"Never have I been happier to see ya Kye Teviot," she breathed. "Marcus?" she whispered.

"Outside, talking to the horses," Kye whispered back with a chuckle, knowing Jolinda would not yet understand the joke of the equine language story. "Ya have a lot to catch up on Sis, but right now we've got to get away from here. It's not safe." Jolinda pulled away a little to look questioningly at Kye. Hurt flickered through his eyes. "Tamsin travels with Trewak."

"Tamsin..." recollection of the hatred Jolinda had recoiled from when blindfold in the cave and on the horse with Trewak came forth. "Tamsin...of course. But why is she with the Iceni warriors?"

"Revenge?" Kye shrugged. "She is rotten and I care not."

"Said like a Roman," Jolinda commented. Kye shrugged again.

"Brigante and Roman, blood brothers with both. Marcus is waiting."

They observed each other for a moment, absorbing the other's presence with a beautiful intensity that was interrupted by the legate rushing from the hut with the distressing news that the priestess was showing the first signs of poisoning from the wolfberry mixture that splashed over her lips. There wasn't time for the niceties of a welcome.

"She imbibed such a small amount, but the toxins are lethal. Her pupils are dilating. Guintoli, fetch fresh water from the river." Addressing Jolinda, he asked if she knew of an antidote as he ushered her back inside.

"There ain't no antidote to wolfberry." The legate slapped his thigh in frustration. The guards and Hadrian stood aside for Jolinda who knelt helpless beside the priestess.

"The Spinners have thread my fate, Child. There is nothing to be done. It's not as I wished but there is nothing to be done." There was acceptance in the priestess's voice.

"But it was just a splash," implored Jolinda.

"A splash the gods intended. They are pulling me to the Afterworld, they have their reasons." A stomach cramp drained the colour from the priestess, beads of sweat bubbling up on her forehead. Leaning forward to manage the pain, her wild, red hair fell about her like a cape. When the spasm passed, she called to Hadrian. "You will ensure the safety of Consus, my Calbraith?"

"You have my word, Priestess." Hadrian spoke firmly but with tenderness too. "Rome has a debt to you for your service in keeping the old Iceni client king in obeisance so skilfully. You have helped many from Britannia to a better Roman life without their thanks, for they did not know.

Consus, Calbraith, Rome's own Counsel and your British Warrior, will reap the rewards for your work as well as his own service to me."

"Find him quickly, and I..." a more violent cramp gripped her and Hadrian side-stepped to avoid the sudden projectile vomit, "...bring Guintoli to me now," she whispered, spitting out the dregs of bile. "I have news to impart before you end my suffering." Her eyes held steady with Hadrian, who nodded grimly. Jolinda cuffed away unbidden tears.

The hallucinations were beginning more rapidly than the priestess had hoped they would from the single splashed drop of poison wolfberry. Fighting to control the fear that came with the distortions presenting themselves, she held tightly to Jolinda's hands. Jolinda had never seen the effects of poison before, it was frightening, the priestess's rapid pulse rate visible by the swollen veins raised in her hands and throbbing at her neck, the terror palpable. Hadrian ordered Peterna and Kye to wait outside and speed Marcus inside.

"No, no..." The priestess tried to pull away from Jolinda, recoiling in horror at the worm crawling from Jolinda's nostril, its tiny mouth opening to the size of an asp's revealing gaping fangs as it writhed free, beady eyes that burned bright as amber, sucking her in as the ever widening jaw drew close to swallow her.

"Whatever you are seeing, Priestess, *is not real*," urged Jolinda. "It is the poison, only you are seeing evil, everything in this hut is as it was a few moments ago, everyone here is your friend." Gius cursed as a man but with the fear of a child that senses another's pain but doesn't understand it. The priestess heard his curse as an Iceni war cry, loud and threatening and the asp's fangs became axe heads patterned in blue swirls, each one dripping in blood and gore. Hadrian drew his sword, he would end the priestess's misery which would only get worse. "Lord, please..." Jolinda beseeched the Roman Emperor, "a few more minutes, let Marcus hear her." Hadrian neither sheathed his sword nor moved forward and Jolinda returned her attention to the priestess continuing to talk softly, forcing her voice to steady and maintaining a firm grip on the sick woman's hands. "Marcus will be here very soon and he...we...need you Priestess. Focus on what you wish to tell him." The priestess squeezed Jolinda's hand in response and summoning her strong will, succeeded in controlling the fear a little, shoulders sagging as she breathed slightly easier. The leather drape was pushed aside and Marcus hesitated at the doorway. Hadrian indicated he should enter.

Jolinda stretched an arm out to Marcus without looking at him, keeping her focus on the priestess. Catching a corner of his sleeve, she tugged him to kneel beside them. A surge of wonder filled her just to feel him near, it was a comfort but there wasn't time to revel in it.

"Marcus is here Priestess...his vow," she prompted. The priestess shrank back pulling away from Jolinda, terror once more burning in her dilating pupils, which grew so large they obliterated the colour giving an unearthly appearance of a full black moon against a white night sky. The cramps came again, viciously seizing her guts, and the priestess cried out in pain and fear. Hadrian moved closer. "Priestess! Please..." beseeched Jolinda, "the vow, how can Marcus overturn the vow he made?" Jolinda choked back a sob as she released the priestess, knowing the woman was lost to them, the delirium in full control now. Marcus guided Jolinda from the hut, leaving Hadrian to carry out his promise. The priestess's scream ceased in mid-shriek and Marcus, feeling Jolinda flinch, held her a little tighter. The scuffing wind dropped suddenly as if Jupiter were holding his breath in response. The night air was silent and still.

Chapter Thirty-Six

The body of the priestess was strapped cumbersomely across a horse, the emperor refusing to leave her behind. Gius was sober enough to sit astride the legate's mount in front of him, albeit drooping forward against the animal's neck, with leather tethers looping round his waist and under the horse's girth to keep him from falling. Spittle still leaked from the corner of his mouth.

Thus the group left the shepherd's hut following the River Teviot as it flowed in a tumble of white water bouncing over rocks in a steady descent to the valley bottom, the last of the snow-melts giving extra vitality to its journey. The path beside the river was narrow, forcing them to travel in single file, the riders letting the horses find their own footing in the dark. The wind picked up again, this time bringing rain. The legate was leading the line, Kye second, then Jolinda, followed by Marcus, with Hadrian at the rear. The Imperial Guards had been ordered to wait at the start of the coombe where the two rivers met and Peterna was anxious to reunite with them. There was no way of knowing the whereabouts of the Iceni and the legate was uncomfortable. Skulking around without intelligence was akin to fighting on the battlefield with blind scouts, a very bad strategy.

The valley became wooded and the River Teviot led them through alder and hazel, giving the riders need to raise their arms at times against the supple branches bending and dipping as the storm grew in strength. Peterna protected Gius from the dancing branches and chilling rain as best he could, his heart aching for his once strong friend, reduced to such a state. The legate was tense and his horse sensed his concern, tossing its head nervously causing Peterna extra consternation. It was a night to be beside a roaring hearth in a hall, not roving unknown countryside pitted with hostile natives.

Not a sound was spoken until Kye gave an owl's hoot warning. The legate had failed to recognise Ravenrock in the dark. Ravenrock, so named for its loosely crow-shaped appearance, was the pre-agreed dismount point and marked a route up the coombe's side. Marcus and Kye would climb to the top from here and report back. The vista should allow sight of the Imperial Guards at the rivers-meet in the valley below. Peterna drew his horse up sharply, inwardly reprimanding his loss of concentration. Jupiter knew he should be more alert, darkness...no, his mind had drifted!

"Be right back," Marcus mouthed to Jolinda, winking boyishly. She was cold, tired, thirsty and discomfited, yet her heart swelled with warmth at his casual wink. *My Roman,* so legionary yet shot through with Brigante in native cloth, unshaven and dishevelled, as he scrambled off with Kye, quickly out of view.

The wait was like listening for the death rattle in the breath-struggling sick. The horses sensed the tension, stamping and flicking their heads, eyes rolling, confused between fleeing and obeying their riders' restraining signals. In truth, the wait was not as long as it seemed, Marcus and Kye soon returning with the news that the Imperial Guards had answered the pre-arranged signal. The way ahead was clear and no Iceni warriors had been sighted.

"Let us get out of this coombe before we lose the favour of Fortuna," muttered Peterna, hardly daring to breathe, having been convinced the Iceni would be snapping at their heels and trap them in the coombe.

"Yes," agreed Hadrian. "She is showing the face of *Bona* on this at least." Jolinda could hear the grimness in the emperor's voice and wondered at the fondness he must have had for the priestess. She had learnt from Marcus that the Roman's believed their goddess of luck had two faces, good luck and bad luck, and would turn her head on a whim. Jolinda tried to recall the Latin word for 'bad' as the group urged their horses past Ravenrock and on to the end of the narrow valley to reunite with the Imperials, who eagerly joined the party, leading them south as they left the River Teviot and its coombe behind.

Their chosen track through the forest was wide, flat and turfed, allowing them to move at a slow canter, riding two abreast. The speed was checked by Hadrian and Peterna whose horses were carrying the weight of two. Away from the coombe, the storm seemed less violent, the raindrops softer in the unchannelled wind and the spirits of the military men was buoyed at leaving the prime ambush ground behind. With so many tracks through the forest, the chances of running in to the Iceni was greatly reduced. It was highly possible they could reach the safety of the fort without confrontation, and then Peterna would have more troops at his disposal and be free of the added pressure of protecting the emperor. He silently prayed that Fortuna didn't turn her face, but his prayers were ignored as soon as they were formed.

Jolinda fell from her horse, tumbling to the grassy ground, hunger and tiredness affecting her judgement. She was in the middle of the group and those riding behind swerved to miss trampling her, pulling their horses up and raising shouts to alert those ahead. They didn't hear the shouts and Peterna looked on in anguish as Hadrian and two of the Imperial Guards continued to ride on, Jolinda's mount running with them.

"Guintoli! Chase them! We cannot afford to split. Go!" ordered the legate. Marcus spurred his horse hard and galloped after the three men. Kye was dismounted and beside his sister, shaken and cradling a sprained wrist, but without serious damage thanks to the forgivingness of the damp turf. The legate wheeled his horse round to confront the Teviots, but remembering his own lapse of concentration at Ravenrock a short while ago, he checked his anger.

"Get her on your horse with you," he said gruffly to Kye. "We must catch up with the others." It was then they heard the battle cry. A curdling howl to twist any gut. The legate visibly paled as his blood turned cold, his ice-blue eyes reflecting the turned face of Fortuna at the realisation of their double misfortune. Of all the tracks, Trewak had chosen correctly, and to come upon them at their weakest moment. "*Mala*," he breathed, supplying the Latin word Jolinda had forgotten.

"Twentieth Legion of the Eagles, proud to fight for Rome and comrade!" bellowed Marcus as he charged towards the fight. "No! Poena...not the Imperator! Punish me another way!" Marcus could see that Hadrian was still on his horse, the war-trained stallion was rearing and kicking with its iron shod hooves at the attacking warriors. The Imperials' horses were down and Marcus could see one of the Guards sprawled lifeless where he'd fallen in the initial attack. The second had the time and elite sword skills to slay one Iceni before the numbers overwhelmed him. Nine Iceni, could he and Hadrian hold them off until the legate arrived? "Poena!" he pleaded the name again, "I will keep my vow. For you, Flavinus!" His sword swung with the harnessed power of Mars, as he sliced the head clean off the shoulders of one warrior, blood spurting in an arc across the rump of his horse as he careered in to two more swirl-tattooed men, knocking them flat, but sending himself crashing against the neck of his horse, who bucked in response, unseating him. The impact of his arrival was profound. He wasn't adept at cavalry combat, but the battle rage was on him and he rolled instinctively, avoiding the wielded axe which thumped in to the ground, harmlessly burying itself to the shaft.

There wasn't time to think, only to react. He grabbed the axe free and was on his feet, using the weapon in his left hand as a shield, thrusting it at the form in front, then stabbing with his short sword. *Three inches of point beats six inches of side.* The hours of practise drills taking over, but the axe didn't protect like a large, oval shield and Marcus cried in pain as a sword slashed across his forearm. Angered, he thrust and stabbed forward again, turned and stabbed, frenzied amongst a muddle of bodies in the dark and wet, unaware of anything other than his immediate peril.

Marcus fell, his leg buckling beneath him as the strength was taken from it by a sword cutting through the muscles just above the back of the knee. Collapsing sideways, he heard an angry roar from Hadrian that stopped abruptly. Marcus twisted to look towards the roar, but could only see a cluster of legs before something hard thumped into his back and he sprawled fully on to the turf, arms splayed ahead. The impact knocked the axe from his wounded arm, but he tightened his grip on the more familiar hilt of his sword and succeeded in hanging on to the weapon, but as he made to rise, a triumphant Iceni warrior dropped over him, pinning him down, and Marcus's ears filled with the crazed victory death cry. Feeling the weight lift a little as the warrior straightened to swing his axe, reaching high above his head to give the weapon momentum to deliver the fatal blow, he struggled again in a last attempt to get free, but the Iceni's bulk was too great.

Marcus grunted with pain as the iron axe head landed bluntly against his shoulder, its wielder following swiftly in a slump of unkempt hair. It took a brief moment to register that he was still alive, a surprise, then fresh sounds filtered through the battle fog that had wrapped him, and Marcus heard a fresh clash of steel and Kye yelling angrily in his native bryothonic tongue. Relief and weakness washed through Marcus. He tried to wriggle from beneath the dead Iceni warrior, but his energy was bleeding from his leg wound, and so he was grateful when the body was pulled away. The solace was short-lived, expecting to see Kye, he instead saw Tamsin, brooding with hate standing over him clasping a dagger with both hands, poised to plunge.

    She hesitated, whether through fear, remorse or regret for a love that she'd wanted, Marcus would never know, for the hesitation was her undoing. Tamsin died by a Roman sword, collapsing in slow motion to land in a heap beside Marcus, his Geryon reduced to a crumple of limbs and dark hair. Marcus closed his eyes, weary beyond his control.

Chapter Thirty-Seven

The surgeon gave a nod of assent to Hadrian and the legate, giving approval for them to enter the hospital room. Washing his hands and forearms vigorously in a bowl of hot water, he reported on Marcus' injuries.

"The wound is closed. It is clean and the sutures have taken well. I doubt I need to tell you he lost a lot of blood, but he will recover with rest and good food. Two inches lower and he would have lost his knee, so his luck could have been much worse. How is your shoulder, Sir?"

"Sore, but in tact." Hadrian winced as he lifted his arm to test the joint, bruised by a sword hit, but unpunctured thanks to the finest metal segmented armour.

"A short visit only Gentlemen, please." The surgeon strode from the room. Marcus heard him leave and was aware of his visitors, but chose to keep his eyes closed. He still felt indeterminately weary.

"The new segmented armour worked well for you," said Peterna to Hadrian. "Rome must look at mass producing it at an affordable price for the legions."

"My armour did its job, Maxinius, but it is not the only reason I am alive," replied Hadrian. "Guintoli is another reason," he inclined his head towards the bed, "Trewak's greed is the third. He had an opportunity to kill me but stopped. I could see the gold ransom fill his eyes. It was enough time to allow you to arrive, and on such hinges, history swings." Hadrian was pensive, tugging gently at his beard as he often did when reflecting. Marcus sensed the emperor come nearer. "Legionary Guintoli, I believe you are awake?" Marcus dragged an eyelid open.

"Sir?"

"My orders from the surgeon are to be brief, so I will be direct. Your bravery was exemplary and your sword skills as good as any Imperial Guard. I am unable to reward you formally as my visit to Britannia is unofficial and you must swear an oath of silence to the events. Your legate is here to witness the oath, so I ask you now, Legionary Marcus Guintoli, are you in a fit state to make an oath?"

"Yes, Sir!" replied Marcus, his tired state not allowing sharp thinking. He made his oath of silence, repeating the words of Hadrian in the presence of his legate.

"Although I cannot reward you formally, I can offer you my patronage in Rome as personal thanks for what you have done. We will not talk of this now, and as I must depart immediately, details will be left with Legate Maxinius for when you are stronger. A swift recovery Legionary, your destiny was indeed in the north."

Marcus slept.

"The danger of an immediate attack is over with the death of the Iceni king and his warriors, Maxinius, but the death of Trewak will have repercussions and I am eager to quell these through political methods. It will be harder without the priestess in their camp, but it is possible I can utilise Consus in this area. It is imperative I return immediately to Rome to implement my plans. Control is clearly needed here in the north, your concerns have been proven right, but more policing is required in the south and I do not have enough troops available for both. The Limus Britannicus is the answer. As soon as Ocella arrives, the project must commence. The Twentieth will head the skilled jobs and I will release the Augustus Vitrix to labour for you in a few moons. You will oversee the beginning phase and remain on this project until the reforms are passed as we discussed, then I will counsel the senate to replace you. If we succeed in keeping your hearing away from the Forum as we hope, by the second Saturnalia latest, you will join Julita and Cloelia in Rome for a handsome retirement."

Peterna nodded gravely, unable to raise a smile. It was a lifeline, he knew that, but the rope was long and would take an age to pull in. He was facing at least one, possibly two further winters in Britannia, and without Julita, for Hadrian had spelled it out that she and Cloelia must remain in Rome now they were there, to subtly champion his cause with discreet comments at social gatherings. Such events were a platform to distract the senate from delving questions. He would miss his wife's comfort. Gius too, would be greatly missed, his ruined condition forever a source of guilty pain to Peterna. The emperor was arranging for Gius to receive treatment from his own physician in Rome, but Peterna held out little hope of his friend regaining his wits, the violent beating had left him simple. Gius's family would take his burden and Peterna swore an oath in the temple to lend support, if his own fate allowed.

"I'll give humble prayers to Bridget every day for the care of ya surgeon. He has skills far beyond any healer I know." Jolinda watched the sunlight dancing down through the slatted high window adding silver streaks to the lime-washed wall of the hospital. The air smelt fresh and earthy as the sun bathed the damp ground, a welcome change from the storm which had blown on for a full forty-eight hours after the fight in the forest. "Ya wouldn't be here without his skill Marcus," she reminded. "Ya look better shaven," she added gently, reaching to squeeze his hand, the burn blisters still evident as scars. Marcus relished her lingering touch, warm and comforting...reprehensible.

The sounds of the fort filled their silence, a centurion shouting orders as he drilled his men, hobnails clicking over cobblestones, a horse whinnying from the stables and the general background hubbub an active fort produces.

"Ma is lookin' forward to ya coming to the homestead," Jolinda said softly. She knew it was a difficult subject to voice, but needed to speak it. "The sacred rites will be spoken, we'll share a meal and Da's spirit will rest." Marcus said nothing, his jaw setting involuntarily at the mention of it. "Both Kye and Aaron will speak the rites. Aaron has grown up such a lot this past season, he asked if he could deliver one of the middle passages."

"How many passages are there?" Marcus found his voice.

"Six for this lore."

Silence befell again. Marcus had agreed to share the rites but the vow was still menacing between them, more so since the Iceni attack. To Jolinda's dismay, Marcus had stubbornly refused to seek out the hunchback, dismissing the priestess's claim that his vow could be revoked. He had also dismissed her offer to Romanize as a half-hearted appeasement to his gods. She had propounded to pledge alliance to Rome and forsake her Brigante customs as he'd asked her to those moons ago, but they both knew she could never renounce her family and Marcus would no longer ask her to. Kye was a blood-brother to him now.

"Who is Poena?" asked Jolinda quietly, half holding her breath.

"The goddess of punishment," replied Marcus, moving his hand away from hers.

"Why were ya calling to her?" she probed. "The legate told me ya were screaming the name when ya rushed in to save Hadrian." Jolinda was awkward with guilt that she'd been talking to the legate about it. Marcus matched Jolinda's frown with one of his own, but said nothing. Jolinda pressed on mulishly determined to fathom his mind. "So ya thought the gods would take the life of Hadrian as a punishment to you because ya wanted to be with me?" Marcus was uncomfortable with the frankness of the conversation. "I need to understand, Marcus. 'Tis important."

"Yes!" he snapped, "Poena was playing with the emperor's life to punish *me! The emperor's life!*" Marcus felt sick at voicing his fears and was straining to keep his temper in check. Jolinda was forcing him to think about an impossible situation. "I must live by my vow or the gods will hector incessantly! Can you not understand that?" Exasperated, he sat up turning his back to her, wincing as he shifted position.

"I believe, as the priestess believed, that ya vow can be revoked."

"It cannot!"

"Marcus, please..."

"You tell me your father will wander the Afterworld in restlessness unless we share your sacred rites. That is your Brigante lore, it cannot be changed. Kye would have travelled the Known World to find me, to Syria to find me rather than repudiate the lore! My Roman vow is as inviolable." He raked his fingers angrily through his hair. Hot tears filled Jolinda's eyes and she was grateful Marcus was turned away from her. She understood, but did not want to accede. To accede would be to accept this truth, and with acceptance, their separation would follow. Despite that, Jolinda could find no line of argument against this logic. "Let us speak of it no more." Marcus's tone was softer. "We will do right for your Da tomorrow."

"And then?"

"And then I have a hearing with the legate to learn of the details of my patronage from Emperor Hadrian and my next posting."

Chapter Thirty-Eight

Nine sunrises following the departure of Hadrian, the fort greeted the arrival of Falco, a belligerent Ocella complaining loudly about the lack of a metalled road, Brutus, Lucius and a small travelling protection group.

Marcus's leg wound was much improved, but his dour disposition was not. Since sharing rites in the Teviot homestead, he'd been assigned to armoury duties and the rote of sharpening a stock of spare *pila* was growing tiresome. Non-absorbing, it meant his thoughts would trudge a beaten circle from Hadrian's patronage to Jolinda, then on to his vow's intransigence, then back to the patronage that was taking him to Rome. He was weary of the circle that just would not blend.

Unable to repress his desires, he'd shared Jolinda's bed after the Teviot's sacred rites. She'd made love to him with such tenderness that it had left him trembling. A mistake, again he had been weak of flesh, the stirring just made it all the more difficult to leave. The armoury duties had kept them apart since and the arrival of Falco's group meant he would begin his journey to Rome in a few days. This departure from Britannia would be final!

Hadrian's patronage was an undisclosed financial sum, to be collected from a private address on the Palantine Hill overlooking the Forum in Rome, the pulsating business heart of the city. Marcus pressed the palm of his right hand against his ribs feeling for the ring securely hidden inside his tunic, a habit he mustn't get in to as any observant thief would read the sign it flagged. The ring displayed the Dacian War markings, the same markings as the wooden block from the hunchback, and was valuable in its own right, but also gave access to claiming Hadrian's patronage on personal presentation in Rome.

A visitor outside the armoury brought Marcus from his thoughts, a welcome distraction. He heard the guards checking the security pass. It was Brutus. He rolled in like a wave of wind through a barley field, greeting Marcus with the forearm salute and several back slaps.

"Ocella pulled through then?" asked Marcus.

"The old weasel has tough flab, my friend. Combine that with the tenacious nursing skills of Falco's temptress the forcible Madam Ninaretta and the poison was never going to win." A half sliced grin crinkled Brutus's eyes. Marcus smiled despite his despondency. It was good to see his friend again.

"Why speak one word when you can speak ten, eh Brutus? What are your plans from here?"

"Ah, now that is not a subject to dwell on, so perhaps I should be concise with my words for a change. Deportation on medical grounds still covers it."

"What? Have you not been rewarded for the mission?"

"You were the hero Marcus. There is no room in the Legions for dead wood. My arm is buggered, deportation it is."

"But you had hopes of...Cloelia..."

"Deportation," interrupted Brutus firmly, a twitch catching the corner of his eye as he fought to keep a light-hearted composure.

"And what of Lucius?"

"Lucius is Lucius, still chasing the laurels, still chasing the strumpet. The latter is in easier reach but he has put in a request to be Ocella's personal guard during the Limus project which could be the start of a lucrative career if he can pull it off."

"He is staying in Britannia then?" Brutus gave a nod. The pair fell silent, both a little morose and Marcus examined a *pilum*, twisting the iron arm-length shank to check the edges of its pyramidal head. "Are you leaving the fort with Falco, Brutus?"

"Yes, as soon as Falco sorts the administration of the project, we will be on our way to Rome. Did you know Falco's term as Governor in Britannia is over? Aulus Nepos is succeeding him." Brutus sat on the bench opposite Marcus, picking up another *pilum* head to inspect.

"Nepos...is he a kinsman of Hadrian?" Marcus didn't mention he would be travelling with the same party to Rome. He would have to tell Brutus soon, but guilt at his good fortune compared to his comrade's ill fortune, trapped the words in his throat. How much money was his reward, he wondered. Would it be enough to buy some land to farm or just enough to bump up his military salary? Soldiering was all Marcus knew, leaving the Legions was a daunting thought. Brutus must be feeling the uncertainty a full cohort-times worse.

"If not a kinsman, then a very close friend. He is bringing the VI Victrix Legion with him. Hadrian is investing heavily in this Limus, his vision is grand. It is typical of my fortune to be leaving the area as it becomes an interesting focus. The senate will be watching its progress. You and Lucius will do well to stick with the Twentieth now."

"I thought you would be keen to reach Rome." Marcus was implying a future with Cloelia.

"Only ruin will greet me in Rome. I must face reality. I cannot provide for her." Brutus couldn't remain looking at Marcus, instead he turned his attention to inspect the *pilum* more closely and began rubbing an edge with a moulded lump of grinding stone. Marcus watched his friend, silent in his understanding, letting the sound of the long, smooth strokes of heavy stone against metal fill the void of conversation. He returned to sharpening the *pilum* he held, his own heart tight at the prospects that lay ahead. Brutus was about to ask after Kye and Jolinda when the armoury guard entered the store with a file of legionaries to equip for a training session behind him. Marcus and Brutus were detailed to help allocate the heavy, wooden practise swords and shields. The room became full of noise and bustle.

"Remind me later, I have a message for you from Consus Didinius," Brutus shouted to Marcus above the cacophony. Marcus looked up sharply.

"The hunchback?"

"Yes, remind me..."

………………………

Every muscle in Jolinda's back and arms was aching. She and Kye were clearing an area of scrub hoping to create an arable patch large enough on which to grow a worthwhile crop of barley. Marcus had put the idea in Kye's head over breakfast the day after sharing Sacred Rites, that selling barley to the Romans could give the Teviots a sustainable source of income if they could produce a decent crop yield.

Kye had excitedly set about the task, seeing its possibilities and wielding sickle and fork with demulcent purpose. Nine sunrises on, Jolinda was exhausted, the task seeming too great. Seeing Jolinda standing with hands against the small of her back, arching a stretch, Kye called across telling her to take a break.

"I'll fetch refreshment," she called back, drawing the back of her hand across her forehead and tucking an escaped tress back into the wide hair band knotted at her nape. Rain clouds were building and Jolinda aimlessly watched their drifting shapes as she walked the half-mile back to the homestead. To her right she could see the turrets of the Roman fort imposing on the landscape. The wind was taking the shouts and sounds of the training drills away from her, so the lark on the wing was serenading her walk, giving the fort a tranquil mien, wrong in keeping with her memory of the industrious hustle inside.

Marcus had warned her he would be on duty and unable to leave the fort for a while. He would know his posting by now, was it to stay at the northern frontier or was he soon to leave Britannia? Jolinda had given her soul over when they last made love, it was a beautiful thing and a terrible thing, for a petiole of resignation was growing as each day passed without a message, no matter how hard she tried to remain positive. From within the silence, she could hear his vow clamouring in mocking victory.

"Ya just tired, Jolinda Teviot," she mumbled aloud, then prayed to Bridget. If Marcus left, at least she would know to accept Yhurgen when he returned from his trading. It seemed as if the dense brambles scratching at her life since Da died were being cleared by a greater force than her. There was much to be done whoever she slept beside.

Ma was humming at her chores as Jolinda entered the homestead, at peace with herself now the family spirits were restful, although lines of strain from the period of grief had aged her appearance.

"Ya look exhausted Child, sit down for a moment." Ma fussed over her daughter and Jolinda smiled at her kindness accepting the steaming heather-infused brew. "How ya getting on with the clearing?"

"Slowly," replied Jolinda ruefully, giving a little snort of exasperation.

"Aaron should be nearly done milking the goats, he could help ya for a while. I can manage the rest here today."

"No disrespect to Aaron, Ma, but we'll need more than just he to help. If we turned the fort out on our land, we'd still struggle. No...I take that statement back, the Romans work like bull ants as a unit. If we could borrow the Legion for a moon, we'd have enough prepared ground for barley to feed *two* armies!"

"Perhaps ya should put it to ya Marcus."

"Perhaps I should." Ma saw straight through her daughter's poorly disguised bravado.

"He ain't left yet, my girl. Ya'll see him soon." Jolinda breathed a positive sigh.

"Yes, and tomorrow I am going to make enquiries at the warehouse about the new blade ya can get that drags through the soil behind an ox. We've nothing to trade, but maybe we can borrow one this season and pay for it a bit each leaf-bud." Ma frowned, uncomfortable with the suggestion but had no ideas of her own to offer. "I'll get back to Kye," added Jolinda, rising from the bench. "He'll be famished 'n' I promised refreshments." Ma nodded.

"I'll send Aaron along when he's ready. Mind ya stop at sunset, the rain'll see it dark earlier tonight. I'll have dry clothes 'n' hot food awaiting ya."

....

It was late in the afternoon before Marcus and Brutus were alone again. They had been detailed to join the training cohort on the practise ground. Neither was fit enough to undergo full drills, but both relished their participation and emerged sweat-grimed, rain-soaked and muddy from the three hour session. The bathhouse was humming like an active beehive afterwards and it wasn't until the pair left, tingling from the rigorous cleansing, that they found any privacy. Heading down the grassy slope away from the bathhouse and the East Gate, shoulders rounded and leaning forward a little against the strengthening rain, Marcus opened the conversation about the hunchback, broaching the subject with curious apprehension.

"The hunchback is an unsettling character."

"Ah yes, your message," Brutus cut in. "Consus Didinius, hmm, an odd character indeed." Brutus mimicked the hunchback's loping gait, his cloak emphasizing the movement with its sway. "His message is odd too, obscure in meaning, enigmatic in its secrecy, equivocal even or maybe oracular?"

"Brutus...the message?" interrupted Marcus, sensing a rambling speech brewing and in no mood to be patient. Brutus reached to the pocket inside his toga, pulling out a tied silk sachet which he juggled lightly in his left palm.

"Grow these for Sancus. Grow a whole field." He offered the sachet to Marcus. "That was the message." Brutus slid a quizzical sideways look at Marcus. "Mean anything to you?"

"Sancus..." mumbled Marcus confused. A thunderclap surprised them. "Jupiter!" exclaimed Marcus, the hunchback's message suddenly becoming clear. The king of gods, sky god, god of rain who uses the thunderbolt as his weapon was speaking to him, again on this grassy slope, the very same place he had uttered his vow to Flavinus. "Sancus is god of oaths and good faith." The dawning brought a fervid excitement, the first in a long time, making his heart thump wild blood in a burst of pleasure, his thoughts darting like minnows in clear water on a sunny day. He tried to net them into a sensible order for Brutus. Waving his fist, bunched protectively round the silk sachet, towards his friend and then high up towards the sky. "These must be lavendula seeds. Brutus, I remember the words of Consus, *your destiny lies north, the sweet perfume of the purple lavendula flower will be your salvation and cloak the stench you regret.* I dismissed him as witless. "

"Yet he also told you Emperor Hadrian was in Britannia when all the Known World had us believe he was visiting the Southern Provinces," interjected Brutus, catching up with Marcus's rush of explanation. "The hunchback has vision."

"Yes! *Grow a whole field.* A lavendula farm. Kye and Jolinda could grow this alongside barley on their land."

"Did not Flavinus have an uncle who marketed lavendula perfume in the fields east of Rome?" A second thunderclap cracked from the clouds and the rain increased its intensity. Marcus turned his face to the rain and laughed as a child without care, the most joyous gift an adult can receive. The two accepted the soaking as a sign from Jupiter.

"My path is now clear, Brutus. I will stay with the Twentieth on this limus project and help the Teviots out of ruin. I will build a temple to Sancus beside the lavendula fields." Marcus rummaged beneath his cloak, fumbling for a moment with wet fingers, garments tangling before he was able to produce the Dacian ring. "Take this, Brutus. My destiny is here, yours is to claim the reward from Hadrian. I hope it will be enough to give you hope with Cloelia." Brutus hesitated. "Take the ring." Marcus nodded his sincerity. "XVII Palantine Hill." Brutus accepted the ring.

"I will collect the patronage," he said solemnly. "Then I will head east to find Flavinus's uncle and return to your fields of purple loaded with the knowledge of producing perfume from the lavendula plant. Together we will smother the stench you regret. That is my vow to you." They clasped the forearm salute. Still holding on, Marcus again tipped his face to the sky, and smiling, shouted into the storm.

"Twentieth Legion of the Eagles..." and Brutus joined him to finish the cry *"...proud to fight for Rome and comrade!"*

Riding across the downland, uncaring of the storm still lashing, Marcus was eager to share his plans with Kye and Jolinda. The silk sachet was with him. Establishing the farm would be hard work but he felt exhilarated at the prospect. They had a future together, the farm was their future and he would make it succeed or die trying. He may have to leave the Twentieth Legion at some point, but not yet, they would be stationed here for several seasons under Ocella's project, and that was also a comfort. He wasn't ready to tear away from the only vein he knew. A stone wall, here at the northern edge of the World, who would have thought it? And he would be a part of its creation. Marcus was smitten with delight as he passed the barn with a goat skin stashed in a haymow from a day that seemed an eternity ago, that may yet find use in pleasure. It was good to feel alive.

Made in the USA
Charleston, SC
02 September 2014